ANGEL OF THE ALLIANCE

LADY HELLGATE • BOOK FOUR

GREG DRAGON

ANGEL OF THE ALLIANCE

This is a work of fiction. Names, characters, organizations, places, events, and incidents are either products of the author's imagination or are used fictitiously.

Copyright © 2020

Thirsty Bird Productions
All rights reserved

Cover Art by Tom Edwards

For more books by the author
GREGDRAGON.COM

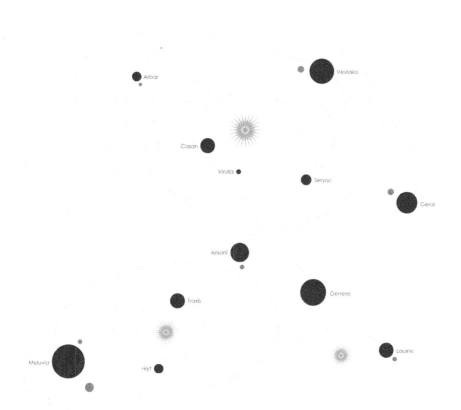

Arbar

Vestaiia

Casan

Virulia

Seryac

Gerai

Arisani

Traxls

Genese

Meluvia

Hiyt

Lauine

The Galaxy of Anstractor

PROLOGUE

On a luxury skiff named *Lucia*, slowly making its way to the station, *A'wfa Terracydes*, fifty-five citizens of the planet Arisani were dancing and drinking to a talented Meluvian band. They were guests of Jorus Kane, the eldest son of Jorus Yog, the same Jorus Yog who was king of Moss-Ekanoe, one of the wealthiest nations on the planet.

Prince Kane was to meet Ry'ot Lomark, president of Lomark Enterprises, on the planet Genese. Their goal was to marry the resources found on the prince's land to the starship-building empire of Lomark. To the guests at the party, the prince was simply on his way to another business meeting, but what they didn't know was how much it would change the face of the galactic war.

Lomark Enterprises' biggest customer was the Alliance Navy, who needed vessels of war for space, as well as replacement parts and satellites to compete with the Geralos world conquerors. War was good business for both men, and so Kane was celebrating with his best friends, their significant others, and the band.

Everyone was indulging, except for the men and women on the bridge. They were distracted, too busy puzzling over an incoming ship, who despite their hails would not respond.

Arisani space was filled with civilian ships; lots were luxury, like *Lucia*, but most were merchants trading wares. Yet this ship did not look like any of the models they knew, and the three crewmembers were arguing over its nature.

"Does it matter what species is at the helm?" the pilot, a Vestalian by the name of Mobius Rath, said. "I need to get us moving or a collision is going to happen."

"Are you mad? We must not break course or disturb the guests," said a server, who had come to the bridge to give the captain her tea.

"Do as I ordered and hail the ship, Mr. Rath," said the captain, an Arisani matriarch named Gortalier.

Mobius Rath, turned on the woman and gestured wildly at a flashing icon which warned of an impending collision. The captain didn't seem to care about Mobius's attitude or the warning, she just wanted him to hail that ship.

"Brace for impact," he shouted into the intercom, just before they were thrown into the air.

The incoming ship had broken past their shields to breach the hull. For three seconds of silence, they all experienced a weightless blackness as the artificial gravity gave out. When it returned, Mobius was slammed into the deck, but not before clipping the edge of a chair with his forehead.

Lights flickered on, but the *Lucia* was no longer moving, and all around the ship was screaming, along with the sound of something violating the hull. Gortalier and Mobius exchanged worried glances, putting aside their power play to be unified in fright.

"Pirates?" Mobius mouthed, and the tall, flaxen-skinned captain nodded slowly in response. Then suddenly they were both moving, reacting on instinct to try and save the ship.

The captain made for the adjoining passageway that held a locker filled with weapons, but she tripped over the body of the server, who had passed out from her fall. She stood up quickly and took the time to see what else she'd missed. Her eyes stopped and widened in terror when they found a window and saw the broadside of the alien ship.

Gortalier fumbled for her communicator, "Th-this is your captain speaking," she managed, climbing back up to her feet to find the door. "I must request that all passengers make their way to the mess ... and, uh, lock and seal those doors. All crew, attention, this is a code black. We're about to be boarded. Take emergency precautions. Seal all hatches and power down the airlocks."

Hoping, perhaps a bit too optimistically, that the prince and his entourage would comply with her orders, Gortalier shook the server back to life and brought her with her into the passageway.

"You're Vestalian. Do you have any training with weapons?" she said to the woman, who was a raven-haired waif in her early twenties.

"No, I do not have any training with weapons," she said.

"Doesn't matter. Here," Gortalier said, tossing her a pistol, which she clumsily caught and examined quickly before looking to her captain for instructions on what to do with it. "These invaders are likely pirates, and you know what they do to young women. The safety's right here," She quickly showed her how to arm and disarm the pistol's trigger. "For now, we'll keep it off. Follow me closely. We're going to the galley. Mr. Rath?"

"Yes, Skipper," Mobius Rath said quickly, and Gortalier saw that he had been waiting for her command.

"Contact the *A'wfa Terracydes* and tell them what is happening, then come to the galley and join us. We're going to need all the help we can get."

"*Lucia* is a civilian ship, ma'am, we have no way of defending," he began.

"What would you have us do then, Mr. Rath?" The Arisani captain turned on him, her chalky visage now a mask of rage, and her neck expanding like the hood of a cobra. Large, golden eyes, once thought to be beautiful, now had the appearance of smoldering coals. The captain was livid, so Mobius Rath quickly found his wits and got to working on the communication.

While Mobius wanted more than anything to get on the controls and urge the *Lucia* back to life, he knew what had happened, and that they couldn't escape. That incoming ship had rammed them, crippling their engines and leaving them exposed. The invaders were already coming aboard, confirmed by the increase in the shrieks from their passengers.

Inside of the mess, thirty-five frightened men and women huddled together, waiting for their captain to act. Prince Kane was unconscious, having struck his head on a table during the crash, and was being tended to by his wives and bodyguards.

Five of his personal guard stood at the door, pistols raised, two kneeling, two standing, and a single lookout braving the passageway. But they assumed wrongly that the invaders would be coming through that door.

Two shots punched holes in the glass separating the galley from the dining area. It was from there that the enemy came, shattering the glass and killing one of the men at the door. As the guards made to retaliate, several more shots dropped another man, and the three remaining quickly gave themselves up.

A uniformed ruffian climbed through the open portal that once was the window and stood before it, brandishing a pulse-rifle. Behind him stood four more men, wearing a motley of colorful fabrics interlaced with armor plates. They were unshaven, gruff, miserable-looking sadists, and it only took one meeting of the eyes for any spacer to know who they were. These weren't ex-Navy deserters playing at pirate. These were the real thing.

The leader, dressed in Alliance dress blues, had an ugly scar across a dead eye, which looked to have come from a las-sword. He smiled cruelly at the occupants, then raised his rifle and threatened them with it. Looking behind him, he gestured to his men, and they knelt down and started working on something bulky lying on the deck.

After several long seconds, they stood back up and hoisted a severed head into the mess. When it finished rolling, everyone saw that it belonged to the captain, Grotalier.

Screams resumed and more invaders rushed in, punching and kicking the inhabitants until they started to beg for mercy. The invaders didn't say what they wanted, and they didn't seem to care that they were attacking a prince. Kane was lined up in a row along with the rest of the prisoners as the dangerous man in uniform went down the line, taking inventory of them.

Several men and women were asked if they were pure Vestalian or mixed species. Then they were separated by planet of origin after being placed in stasis cuffs. Four more people were killed for either fighting back or trying to make an escape, and once that happened there was no more dissent.

In the cockpit, Mobius had gotten hold of *A'wfa Terracydes* and was relaying their situation to the controller. When the hot muzzle of a recently used pistol touched his exposed neck, however, he ended the call and lifted his hands in surrender.

"Please don't kill me," he said. "What do you want from us?"

"Vestalian dog," the invader said before striking him over the head. "We want your brains."

1

As far back as Helga Ate could remember, the simulation room had been a place of refuge. Not only did it allow her a chance to escape the routine life of the Navy, but simply playing around inside of it could strengthen skills that were necessary to succeed. For this reason, an Extraplanetary Spatial Operator (ESO) made it a crucial part of their weekly training.

It was the simulation room that first introduced Helga to the joy of flight. As a cadet, bullied and ostracized, the simulation room gave her access to the cockpit of a Vestalian Classic. In this vessel built for combat, there was no one to stop her from flying. No check-in with the CAG, no waiting her turn; she could simply grab the controls and escape for several hours.

Now as a seasoned operator, tested in both spatial and planetary combat, Helga still felt butterflies when she sat inside the booth and strapped on the nodes, gloves, and helmet. Sometimes she wished that it was real inside of that world, where the Alliance was truly allied, and there were no saboteurs or xenophobes forcing her to keep her guard up.

In simulations the enemy was defined, allies were reliable, and all of her efforts made a difference in the war. Here, things made sense to her as an officer. Here, she felt empowered. Here, she felt home.

Admittedly with everything she had experienced as a Nighthawk, the thought of simulating combat no longer excited her. She had learned quickly that some things were best left in memory, and trying to reclaim that joy only managed to taint that special place inside your mind. Now she found herself stuck on what to do: simulate a lukewarm version of combat or pick something else, like raiding a base on one of the planets.

Helga stepped inside the simulation booth. It was a cozy space, with red carpeting and a holographic menu displaying all the categories available. There were official training simulations, like defending a crippled starship in enemy space, and ground war scenarios to help acclimate the spacers with planetary gravity.

For the first time she turned towards the latter, looking at what they had to offer. It was all new to Helga, who had only ever done the spatial experiences. With her hands on her hips, she observed the selection, fascinated, like a wine lover's first time attending a tasting. There were invasion scenarios on Traxis, a few choices on Meluvia—but she had already experienced the planet firsthand—and Genese had a civil war simulation, but even that didn't grab her as a worthwhile exercise.

She scanned for Casan, knowing it would be futile, and was surprised to find a defense scenario on the mountains of Al'haad. As she moved her hand forward to select this experience, she felt a gentle tugging on her arm. Helga removed the mask to see who was disturbing her, and was surprised to find Dr. Cleia Rai'to, one of the new crew members assigned to the *Ursula*.

"I'm really sorry to bother you on your off day, Lieutenant, but Commander Mec is requesting your appearance on the bridge."

"He couldn't hit my comms?" Helga said, confused.

"Yes, but I wanted to speak to you, briefly, so I volunteered myself," she said, proudly.

Her smile was so radiant it was off-putting, making it difficult for Helga to think clearly. The doctor was a good-looking Traxian, a species rarely found outside of their planet. They were amphibious and reclusive, though their hardy physiology made them the ultimate survivors. Being open and peaceful had caused them to be preyed on by the Geralos, so they joined the Alliance to support the war.

Cleia's history was still a mystery, but she had been born on Sanctuary away from the actual war. Like many of the citizens of that station, she had expressed a want for adventure outside its walls, and since the Nighthawks were in need of a physician, she had practically begged Cilas to join the Nighthawks.

"Speak to me? What about?" Helga said, taking the lead. She had really been looking forward to the cerebral escape but Cilas was commander, so she had to obey.

"Well, I have been working on a calendar of sorts, for my check-ins with the crew, and I've figured it out and I'm ready to begin. For my first patient, however, I thought that a woman would be nice, and it would give us a chance to get to know one another better."

"Oh, Dr. Rai'to, that's sweet, but to be perfectly honest, I don't think I'm going to be chatty if you're probing my body for defects."

"That isn't what I'm going to do. Just ask some questions and get your vitals uploaded to the system. Everyone needs to be scanned and placed into the database, so that the *Ursula* can help me keep you in shape. Lieutenant, you concern me with that 'probing' comment. It makes me think that you don't take me seriously. Is my station to be a nuisance on this ship?"

"Maker, Doc, it's called a joke. You're going to need to lighten up if you're going to survive with this team. Look, I'll be your experiment or whatever. Just know that this body belongs to the Alliance, and if you break it you're getting the airlock." Helga stopped and gave her a glare, but Cleia merely blinked her large blue eyes. "That was a joke. *Thype*, you know what? Let's go. Put me on your calendar."

"Oh, that's wonderful!" Cleia exclaimed, and her timing was so off that Helga wondered if she meant it sarcastically.

She found the passageway leading to the bridge and stopped when she reached the mess hall. Inside, at the biggest table, was the big man, Quentin Tutt, playing a game of cards with Sun So-jung, who everybody knew as "Sundown."

"Who's winning?" she said, flashing a wicked grin, and the two men exchanged glances before returning to their game.

"The grease-head's winning, but not for long," Quentin said before laying down his cards, which caused Sundown to wince in terror.

"Holding those the whole time, eh?"

"Yeah, don't you Jumpers have x-ray vision, mind-reading capabilities, something like that?" Quentin said, reaching for the triad of candy bars in the center of the table and dropping them on the small hill that was growing in front of him. "Want to join us, Lieutenant? I know that sweet tooth of yours wants in on my collection here."

"While it is indeed tempting, Quentin, I am going to have to pass since I'm wanted on the bridge immediately."

"Sounds serious. What have you done?" he said, his face becoming a grave mask.

"Nothing, except give us a smooth launch from the station. Enough with the jokes. Do you have any idea why there's all this urgency?"

"Why don't you go ask the commander?" he said, and she had to stop and really think about whether or not he was still joking.

"Are you—"

"I'm not being serious." He laughed. "I don't know, Helga, you're going to just have to go in cold."

Helga rolled her eyes out of frustration, and was surprised to find Cleia still standing there, smiling like a Cel-toc. *Thype me if she isn't as frightening as she is cute*, she thought, as she nudged past the doctor to make her way towards the bridge.

Cilas was in his captain's chair hunched over, and upon seeing them enter he stood up and smiled at her warmly.

"Commander," she said, trying to keep a straight face.

It felt odd to be so formal even though he was her superior. Nighthawks were close, having gone through so much together as a team on even footing. Before Cleia it had been just the four of them, and most of the time rank was merely a formality. Cilas especially was a complex situation; he was her superior and lover, and it was barely a secret on the *Ursula*. Yet here she was calling him commander, and for what? Cleia, the Sanctuary recruit?

"Lieutenant Ate," he replied, applying his own brand of dry sarcasm. "Thank you for bringing her, Dr. Rai'to," he said, touching his chin. It was a Traxian greeting, and the doctor returned it, beaming so bright that Helga swore that she was flirting.

When Cleia exited the bridge, she turned on Cilas, one eyebrow raised with suspicion, wondering if there was anything behind the exchange.

"No," he said immediately, as if he could read her mind. "It's just a respect thing. Traxians are big on authority, you know that. Anyway, how are you? I didn't take you away from anything important, did I?"

"I was starting my simulation training. Nothing official, just wanted to sharpen up on a few things. Is everything alright, Rend? Doctor said it was urgent."

"Dr. Rai'to may have exaggerated a tad. Not her fault—when she saw me earlier I was in a frenzy trying to locate the earpiece to my comms. Next time we're home on *Rendron*, or at one of the stations, we should pick up some extras. It was my last one, and we're in the middle of nowhere."

Helga walked forward and leaned on the railing that separated the captain's perch from the cockpit. Below her she saw the Cel-toc, Zan, another Sanctuary addition to their motley crew. Zan's database was an extension of the *Ursula*'s mainframe, though she operated as her own entity and was considered a part of the crew. For now, she was the ship's primary pilot until they could recruit another qualified spacer.

Though Helga was one of the best pilots of her age, she couldn't assume the role, since the Nighthawks needed her on missions. She grew up with Cel-tocs, so she didn't feel any emotion towards Zan, though the android had proven to be just as social as she was technical and had tried to engage Helga in small talk.

"Before we get to it, how are you, Nighthawk?" Cilas said, sipping slowly from a steaming mug.

"I've been doing well actually. No more fatigue, and I've gotten back a bit of my appetite. You know you're not well when you actually crave the taste of a protein ration." She laughed. "I scarfed down a whole half of one earlier. Hate being sick, it doesn't happen often, but when it does, ooh maker take me. Why, were you worried?"

"Just a little, but Ray took it personally since he made you that drink."

"Uh, that was coincidence; it's not his fault. Is he really blaming himself for me getting sick?"

"He's been in the range for an entire shift, firing off his guns. I've only seen him on his duty rounds, and when he comes up to get food and drink. Something's on his mind and he isn't talking. The only change around here has been your illness, so this is my attempt at logic."

"Ray can be sensitive. It could be anything; in a lot of ways he reminds me of Brise Sol."

"Come on, Hel, he is nothing like Brise, not one bit. He's loyal to a fault, braver than most spacers I know, and he respects the chain of command. When I give Ray an order, I walk away knowing it's done."

"Alright, let's not go down that dark path," Helga said. "What I meant is that they share similar passions. They love hard and hate harder, which makes disappointment devastating. Ray is a sniper, yes, and one of the best graduates from BLAST that any team could hope to have, but Brise was an engineer playing poorly at ESO to make his family proud. I'm not arguing, Commander, just clarifying my statement."

Cilas seemed to think for a time as he held the mug to his lips, then brought it down slowly with a sigh.

"That was a tough time for everyone. We lost our team and got captured, then found ourselves trapped inside a pod, stranded, hoping for rescue. Emotions were high, as they should have been, and much of mine clashed with his. We were lucky to have you," he said, smiling. "Your diplomacy showed me that you had what it takes to be a leader in this Navy. Anyway, enough about old Nighthawks, let's focus on the now."

"Actually, Rend," Helga said, turning about to face him, "I was thinking, now with the *Ursula* as our ship, we could reactivate Brise. You're the commander, you have the power now to put in a request. We can bring him back onto the team to be our chief engineer. Cilas, he would make the *Ursula* sing. You remember how he modified our pod out of nothing."

"I do remember. He was one of the best, but I also recall him defying me whenever and wherever he could. We need an engineer, Hel, but not that one. He was your friend, and I know you think you could keep him in line, but you cannot quit the Navy, then come back to a post as chief engineer."

"Of course you can't, Commander, but I feel it necessary to remind you that Brise was showing signs of trauma. He was shaken after Dyn and needed a psych and time, but Commander Lang wouldn't afford us that, and he felt cornered and alone. It was either he left us or maker knows what he would have done."

Cilas seemed to consider this as he grew quiet and went back to staring at his mug. "Brise is out, Hel. Even if I wanted to risk it, the Alliance would never allow him to work on this ship. There'll be other engineers, possibly as talented as Brise."

"Not the point," Helga mumbled, but decided against pushing, since Brise was a sore subject for Cilas. Anyone else and he would have considered it, and with his reputation, sway the Alliance to give that person a second shot. But Brise was as emotional as they came, and would speak out of turn to the point where he had shouting matches with Cilas, his then lieutenant.

Brise would bring out the worst in their normally stoic leader, and she had been forced to play mediator on more than one occasion. He had been a disappointment to Cilas, both in the field and off, but where he shone was on vessels like the *Ursula*. What she wanted was to bring him aboard, not as a Nighthawk, but someone loyal and committed to her and the ship.

Cilas, however, was a closed book on the subject of Brise Sol, and she missed him. Their banter was always a treat, even on the cycles when they thought that they would die inside that escape pod.

"Helga, listen to me. You see our team and how we mesh? It keeps us alive in the field. You and I are close, but if we're on a mission, you respect the chain of command. I asked you to do some hard *schtill* on Meluvia, and you didn't hesitate. Not you, Quentin, or Ray; you did as you were ordered. That goes a long way with me, a long way. You just don't know, and you see Brise, for all his genius, when I needed him to act, he did not budge."

"Oh, he knows he failed you, Cilas, it's what broke him in the end. He didn't feel like a Nighthawk. You're right, of course, he was insubordinate, and we cannot have that in the heat, but hear me out. I was thinking about the *Ursula*. He could be the ship's engineer, not one of the Nighthawks. He would be crew, like the doctor, and he would have to answer to you."

"I'm sorry, Helga, I can't do it. I can't imagine being stuck long cycles out here with that man defying me at every turn. Do you even know where he is, if I considered it? You two keeping up somehow on comms?"

"No, but Loray Qu knows how to find him. She contacted him to attend our ceremony, when we got the medals for surviving Dyn."

"Dyn," he whispered. "Feels like it was fifty years ago for me. It's clear in my mind, but it feels unreal, as if I just dreamed it, or someone knocked me out and planted it inside my head."

"It's still real for me," Helga said, "and even on the days when I forget it, as soon as I close my eyes and fall asleep, I'm in that camp all over again. At least I have you to discuss it with, as a fellow survivor of that hell. Can you imagine what Brise is going through, all alone? No one to hear him on that deeper level of understanding?"

"Yeah, of course I feel sorry for the guy," Cilas said. "We just can't work together, though you're right, he'd serve as a great engineer on someone's ship. Begs to question his ambition, though, and choices in life. Why take BLAST if you're not ready to come out here in the middle of the *schtill* and spill the enemy's blood for your captain? He could have been a junior engineer on the *Rendron*, work his way up and become chief."

"Cilas, he was a Nighthawk, and he was ready to kill the way we were all ready to kill, but when Lamia turned and slaughtered everybody, it doused the fire in him. He was like a frightened little boy sometimes, and he couldn't sleep, which kept him cranky. Those things matter, but you ignored them, being so upset with him, and he began to feel boxed in. You know what he told me once, back when the three of us were stuck inside that escape pod? He said that the maker spared him to become something great, but he wasn't strong enough to go through with it."

"Sad as that is, Hel, Brise Sol is out," Cilas said. "And as long as I am team leader, he will never be a Nighthawk again. You forget that he left his post and retired, which is not only unheard of but a slap in the face of the Alliance. Commander Lang approved his discharge, but another commander would have air-locked him instead. Wherever he is, he's doing much better than dead, and I wish I could say the same of the Nighthawks who came before him."

Helga shrugged. "I know, but I had to at least try," she said.

"For you, I would do just about anything, Hel, and you know that," he whispered. "But not this, not him. We need Nighthawks, and growth is our number one priority, but forget Brise for anything Alliance-related. He made his choice and he is out."

2

The briefing room on the *Ursula* was one of the upgrades gifted by the engineers in Sanctuary. They converted a section of storage and a portion of berthing into its own sizable space for the Nighthawks to use. Anyone new to the crew would have thought that the corvette had come with this compartment already built-in, and though the terminals were much newer than those on the bridge, nothing really stood out enough from the rest of the sizable warship.

It was an octagonal shape, with chairs wrapped about a central table with a starmap floating above it. There was a coffee machine for sleepy spacers, and the bulkhead was fitted with a flexible display. This allowed for the facilitator to expand the starmap to every corner of the room, placing them inside of a scenario, or showcasing images on all eight surfaces.

There was room enough about the space to accommodate twenty-four spacers, so the six people in attendance could move about quite easily. Yet, they all sat next to one another, waiting for Cilas to start. Helga was in the front, bordered by Raileo Lei and Quentin Tutt, while Sundown sat directly behind her with Cleia on his left. The chairs themselves were hard but comfortable; it was almost as if they adjusted to your weight.

Helga rubbed at her knees. They had been summoned to do something but they didn't know what, and she knew that earlier, Cilas had been in his cabin speaking to the captain for hours.

He walked in looking sharp as he always did. It was as if being commander of the *Ursula* had somehow transformed him into a proper officer. The mud-craving, take-charge Marine had been replaced by a commander who looked ready to host guests of the Alliance council. He was in dress blacks with golden buttons, which made him seem older. They all stood up and saluted, including the doctor, and when he waved his hand passively they sat down.

"I have lots to cover, so I'm going to do my best to be clear," he said, powering on the screens to show a large red planet. "Approximately 32 hours ago in Arisani space, a luxury-class sloop headed to the moon of *A'wfa Terracydes* was stalled and boarded by what we believe to be pirates. This intel came from one of the pilots, who managed to send out a distress call. Demands were made of the Arisani Union to provide several space ships or the hostages would be killed.

"One woman was murdered to show that they meant what they were saying, but the Union sent their Space Force instead. Now, these weren't Alliance-trained Marines or operators, these were volunteer soldiers and armed civilians. This so-called Space Force was used to dealing with smugglers, not a hardened group of murderous thugs. They attempted negotiations but the pirates cut them down, then they murdered five more civilians to make a point.

"They then separated out a group of Vestalians and took them to a satellite where they've been left to await maker knows what. As for the pirate cruiser, it jumped to Genese, where the demands have now switched to them wanting a ship no smaller than a corvette. Our mission is on that satellite. We are to approach it in stealth, rescue the Vestalians, and take one of the pirates into our custody. Now, my gut is telling me that this pirate nonsense has everything to do with the Geralos," Cilas said.

He looked directly at Helga, who knew exactly what he meant. The two of them had dealt with pirates after their disastrous mission on the moon of Dyn, when they learned about a slavery-ring that involved the capture of Alliance Navy personnel. Using implants and torture, the pirates were breaking in pilots and engineers to use them on their vessels as highly-skilled slaves. The spacers that didn't break, or weren't needed, however, were sold to the brain-eating Geralos.

"This satellite, is it over Arisani?" Helga said.

"Hiyt, actually, but Arisani could be close depending on the time of the year."

"I bet there's a Geralos camp somewhere on the planet," she said.

"It's on the moon of Argan-10, which orbits Arisani. There is supposedly a Geralos ship flying to the satellite from there. Our mission is the rescue; we are to avoid engagement as much as possible. The Alliance wants to break the ring, but they want to inflict as much damage to the Geralos as they can. For now, we get them and squeeze the traitors for information. If we can get the location of the camp, we are to evaluate the opposition and report back to *Rendron*."

"How *thyped* up is this?" Raileo said hoarsely. "Our people are selling their own to the very enemy that massacred our planet. Rescue operations, Commander? I want to kill every last one of them. Can't the Marines pull the taxi routine? We should be sent to Genese to take those *thypes* out."

Cilas stopped and stared at him, his flat features a grave mask of disappointment.

"Sorry for the outburst, Commander. Please finish your brief," Raileo said.

"As I was saying, this is a rescue operation. We are to pull out those civilians and take them back home to Arisani. Now, we are required to capture one of these pirates, but the rest can be yours to do as you will, Mr. Lei. Lieutenant Ate, we need to set a course and be at that satellite as fast as we can muster. Nighthawks, get prepared. We're donning PAS suits and rifles for this expedition."

They made to get up but the commander stopped them with a wave of his hand. "Let me remind you that this is what we signed up for. Helping the people of Anstractor. You're going to get your chance at punishment, Ray, maybe not this mission but when we're given clearance to root these pirates out. So get locked and loaded, we've got action, and stow the comments when it's time to listen. Are we clear?"

"Yes sir," he said with no sign of offense, but Helga noticed that he kept his eyes forward.

"Alright, let's get moving," Cilas said, and walked to the doorway as they stood up.

Sundown was quiet, and Raileo still seemed distracted, but she saw Quentin stop before the commander and give him a stiff salute. Cilas returned it, and joined him in exiting the compartment. Helga made to follow them out but a squeaking sound made her stop and look over at Cleia.

"We have barely been on board and now everyone is off to go get themselves killed," she muttered. "What are we to do with no commander, and I haven't even started my examinations."

"Chin up, doc," Helga said, urging her up and out of her seat. "We're hard to kill, so don't you worry, we'll be back in time for you to run your checks and put us on your calendar or whatever." She pulled up short when she saw the waiting Cel-toc, and motioned her over with a summoning gesture. "Zan, I want you to plot a course to Arisani space, bringing us in near the satellite, *Maahes*. When you have it ready, alert me on my comms, then wait for my command."

"Yes, Lieutenant," the Cel-toc said in an effeminate, synthesized voice. It always reminded Helga of the breeze that blew through the trees back when they were on Meluvia in the jungle. It was a pleasant voice, smooth but for its tinny quality, and she loved giving orders to the android just to hear her talk.

"You will want to dress in a 3B-XO, Doctor Rai'to. There should be a suit in your office, next to your berthing inside of the storage locker. Have you worn one before?"

"I have but I don't see the need for one now. You don't intend for me to join you out there with the Geralos, do you?" she said, her mottled blue skin visibly lightening a shade as her eyes grew large.

"No, you won't be leaving the ship this time, but you will still need to be prepared in case we manage to get boarded. The 3B suit will protect you, so wear it beneath your uniform and strap on a sidearm. You're on a Nighthawk ship, Dr. Rai'to. This is going to be your life from now on. Are you sure you're ready for this?"

"I have been through disasters before," the woman stated proudly, raising her chin up at Helga. "I was one of the first to volunteer for the starport disaster on Sanctuary, and I assisted in administering care to the wounded, all while there was still an imminent threat. I am just shocked at the timing. I thought for sure we'd have more time before anything major."

"Yeah, well, you better get used to this. The Alliance is one needy *cruta*, and she doesn't understand the word no."

With that Helga left her and took the lift down to the dock, where she made her way to the passageway that held the compartments where she, Quentin, and Raileo berthed. At the door to her compartment she stood, taking it all in. This was a ritual that she had started doing before their trip to Sanctuary.

A Nighthawk's life was unpredictable, dangerous, and short, so she never knew when she'd be captured again, or end up in a recovery room fighting for her life. With her career being so eventful, she had begun collecting souvenirs from the happier moments. One was an old PAS helmet that had saved her life from a bullet, and the other was a Revenant pilot's helmet that had come from her friend, Joy Valance.

She should have been hurrying, but the thought of Joy stopped her in her tracks. Like the commander, her relationship with the lieutenant was a complicated mix of personal and professional. The woman was her best friend, her big sister, mentor in certain aspects, and possibly a rival, now that she had crossed the line with Cilas.

This was all in her head. Guilt had a way of creating forks on paths that were straight and narrow, but she would never know until they returned to the *Rendron*, and the three of them could face-off in all that awkwardness.

"There's no time for this," she reminded herself and stepped over to the mannequin that held her PAS. Next to it was a terminal with a diagram of her shape, along with a readout on maintenance that the armor required to be at its optimum state. She scanned these items quickly, noting that they were all superficial or cosmetic. It didn't matter either way. Time was not on their side, and there were civilian lives at stake, all dependent on their egress and the timing of the Geralos invaders.

Helga removed her clothes and moisturized her skin before sliding into her 3B XO-suit. The alien leotard slid on easily, already acclimated to her shape, and once she was fully dressed it adjusted, becoming tighter like a second skin. First it felt suffocating but before long she didn't notice and had to glance in the mirror to make sure that she was clothed.

She walked around the mannequin, letting her fingers caress its smooth black surface. "Here we go," she whispered. "Back into the *schtill*." She forced a smile and for some reason it worked, lightening her mood.

By the time she was dressed and ready to go, her mind was free of distractions and she was ready for what was to come. She slipped the helmet into the crook of her arm and stopped to take one more glance in the mirror. Would this be the last time she would get a chance to scrutinize herself? This thought came and went as it always did before a dangerous mission.

"Let's go," she heard Quentin shout from outside, and though it wasn't a command, she took it as a sign for her to get on with it. Bypassing the lift, she used her rocket boots to fly up to the railing that ran around the dock and pulled open a door leading to the main passageway that would take her to the bridge. Her wrist-comms buzzed and she saw that it was Zan, alerting her to the course being set.

She found the cockpit and sat next to the Cel-toc, who looked almost human reclined in the co-pilot's seat. "Ready on your order, Commander," she said, turning to look back at Cilas as he sat perched upon his captain's chair. Strapped into stations on the starboard side of CIC were Raileo and Quentin, fully dressed in their PAS including the helmets.

The doctor was nowhere in sight, but she had enough training to know to get into a station before a jump, so Helga didn't worry for her; she just assumed that she would have wanted to be around other spacers during a risky jump. She noticed that Sundown was not in place either, and for a brief moment she wondered about the two of them.

"Take us to Arisani, Lieutenant," Cilas said over the intercom, which was code for, "Get your rears strapped in or risk being sucked out into space if we have a breach."

Sundown finally emerged, dressed in the armored skin suit that was the battle uniform of the Jumpers, with his las-sword secured to the back of it and a gun-belt hanging loosely below his ratty duster.

On his feet were some specialized Sanctuary security boots that would allow him to jump and hover when activated, similar to that of the PAS. He stood out from them, which was dangerous since being unique could denote rank to the enemy. Suspected leaders were the sniper's favorite marks to drop, but this wasn't a big concern for the Jumper. He stepped into the nook of a station and activated the magnetic locks before tipping an invisible hat at her.

"Doctor Rai'to, are you strapped in?" Helga said, affording her the courtesy, just in case she wasn't thinking clearly.

"I am, inside of my office," Cleia said, and Helga looked over at Zan and gave her the nod. The Cel-toc strapped in and removed her hands from the console and Helga took over, checking on the status of the *Ursula*. With Zan hooked into the system of the ship, she could have simply asked for a report, but she preferred to read them over hearing them from the android. Soothing voice or not, there were some things she preferred to do the old-fashioned way.

"*Ursula*, we are cleared to jump," she finally said, and just like that they were off.

3

One minute the holo displays and terminals were showing nothing but blackness and the next there was a large red planet against the inky backdrop, with a neat ring of debris wrapped around it. The *Ursula* was back in Alliance space, having jumped from the mysterious quadrant of Sanctuary, now wiped from the ship's navigation to preserve its secrecy.

The ship's AI spoke, informing them that the jump had been a success and all systems were a go. Helga looked over at Zan and winked, and the Cel-toc responded with a slight bow and smile. She hadn't been taught to do this; it was just something she would do whenever any of the organics treated her as something other than a machine.

It was Helga's way of telling her that the controls were hers, and this was reinforced by the young lieutenant pulling her restraints and standing up to look back at the crew. "We're back in Anstractor," she said, throwing her hands up in a celebratory gesture.

"Planets, to think that I survived to see this day," Sundown murmured, forgetting that his comms were live.

"Back in the *schtill*." Quentin stepped out from his station to join Cilas at the back of the bridge. The corvette's layout was different from conventional space ships, with the bridge and CIC occupying the same space, separated by a raised platform upon which sat the captain's chair.

There was a railing to allow Cilas to stand and look down on the cockpit and its segmented stations, but for all intents and purposes, it was a wide-open deck, allowing the crew to move about without any obstruction. On the overhead were handles, and more stations recessed into the bulkhead so that in the event the artificial gravity failed, they could always find a place to take control of the ship.

Helga and the Nighthawks joined them back there, as they stood at attention about the starmap.

"Welcome home, Rover," Cilas said, causing the Jumper to regard him curiously.

"Rover, Commander?" he said and then seemed to think on it for a second. "I've been called everything in the book since arriving on Sanctuary, but this one is a first. What does it mean?"

"It means that you're our wild card, brother," Quentin said matter-of-factly.

"Plus it works better than, 'Jumper who dresses like a pirate,'" Helga teased before averting her eyes to where Raileo Lei had returned from retrieving Cleia Rai'to from her office. "Welcome to Anstractor, Doc," Helga said, and the woman bowed deeply before rushing over to the cockpit to stare out at the planet in front of them.

"Thank you, Lieutenant Ate," she said. "I never thought I would ever get the privilege."

Cleia had been born and raised on Sanctuary station, which was an isolated refuge that served as the Alliance's headquarters. No one knew the location of Sanctuary, and its access was carefully monitored and controlled by an advanced A.I. To gain access to the station took having the money or position to get the council's attention, and then there was normally a vote, followed by rigorous process to confirm that you weren't a threat.

Getting in was impossible, and getting out was nearly as hard. The Nighthawks, having been given access and then clearance to depart, were only allowed this privilege due to their last mission, which was to deliver a cadet whose mind had been taken over by the Geralos.

The trip—both arriving and departing—was only possible through the Ursula's A.I. communicating with that of Sanctuary's. The route was unknown, and the station itself was always on the move, so even if the course was tracked, it would be difficult to return once you left. Even still, ships that approached without Alliance credentials were destroyed, and Sanctuary was armed with enough tracers to mince up a Geralos fleet.

Sanctuary's citizens were meant to stay on the station, living out their lives peacefully until the war with the Geralos was won. Cleia and Sundown were exceptions, having been given clearance by the Alliance council to aid the Nighthawks efforts. So, for the Traxian physician, being here and seeing Arisani was a dream come true, and

Helga saw the tears in her eyes when she walked up to grip the back of her chair.

"Alright, so now that we're here," Cilas said, bringing their attention back to him. "First order of business, we need to appraise the state of that station, the proximity of any non-Alliance warships, and a point of entry. I am open to ideas, but remember that we must remain dark to the enemy. If we're exposed they could start killing the hostages or call in a fleet to take on *Ursula*. Any thoughts?"

"I can deploy a drone to scan their perimeter and give us a visual," Raileo said.

"Any objections to the drone?" Cilas looked at them one by one. "Looks like it's unanimous, we're using a drone. Chief, get started right away, and report if you see anything remotely suspicious."

"Aye aye, sir," Raileo said, seeming happy to feel helpful once again.

"Second, *Ursula* is too much ship to be in the vicinity of that satellite. She will stay here, cloaked, while we use the dropship to make our approach. Lieutenant Ate, set a timer on the *Ursula*'s system. If we haven't communicated our status and are not back on board within five cycles, I want an SOS primed for the *Rendron* to send some help. If there is no answer when that SOS is sent, I would like for one to be sent to *Aqnaqak*. In the event that one isn't answered, then *Ursula* is to jump to Meluvian space, where she is to orbit while sending out a beacon, requesting Alliance help. In our absence, once the five cycles have expired, Dr. Rai'to is to be given communication clearance. Did you get all that?"

"Got it ... automate rescue protocols with the closest starships, starting with mother, cycle through the rest, and then automate a jump to friendly Meluvian space. Once there, set a beacon, but give the doc freedom to the ship's console. You don't have any phobias related to automatons do you, Doc? Mechanophobia, technophobia—"

"No, Lieutenant, I do not," Cleia said. "I grew up inside of a house run by Cel-tocs, and as a doctor, I am quite familiar with interfaces, readouts, and advanced machine intelligence. You can rely on me, Nighthawks. I may be a—how did I hear it—'pampered Sanctuary elite, with no idea of the war,' but my family are proud of our history. I grew up appreciating the Alliance, and it is why I am here, aiding the effort."

"You being here is our privilege, Dr. Rai'to," Cilas assured her. "One of the truly great things with us visiting Sanctuary."

Though Cleia Rai'to kept a look of defiance, Helga saw her skin change from an aggressive shade of lavender to the light powder blue that they were accustomed to.

"Sergeant Tutt, please see to our loadout. We don't know what's coming, so let's pretend that we're about to drop in on a nest of Craqtii. We'll be bringing the refugees back, as well as one hostage, so we're going to want to pack some stasis cuffs, as well as some medical equipment. Sunny, just get ready for action. I am going to update Captain Sho, and then we need to get moving."

"I'm already set, so I'll assist with loading the Thundercat," Sundown said, then the Nighthawks saluted in unison before breaking off to carry out their orders.

When Cleia made to leave the bridge, Helga touched her on the arm. "Hey Doc, a moment. After hearing the commander's orders it made me think. Are we set up for taking in the wounded? None of us paid attention to that medbay before you came on board," she said.

"We have eight beds currently," Cleia replied. "Twelve if we convert the tables—which can easily be done. Why, Lieutenant? Are you expecting a lot of injuries?"

"Yes and no," Helga said, "but you heard the commander. None of us knows what is waiting for us on that satellite, and the pirates have already killed several innocents. We are the reconnaissance for the Alliance, so our job is to spy and pull out as many hostages as we can. I'd imagine there will be some wounded already, but once the bullets start to fly, we're only going to add to it."

Cleia reached out and awkwardly touched Helga's shoulder, an attempt at the Vestalian sign for friendship. "Whatever comes, we will figure it out, together," the Traxian said. "And thank you for caring enough to ask."

"I am also trained as a field medic," Quentin said. He was already on the lift, ready to ride it down to the dock, but had heard enough of their conversation to chime in. "Dr. Rai'to, I'd be able to assist with anything you ask of me."

Helga watched the doctor to see if she would accept, since it was Quentin who had inferred that she was one of Sanctuary's elites.

"I would appreciate that, Sergeant," Cleia said, which shocked Helga speechless as she stood there watching the exchange. "We are very different, the two of us, and working together I hope to harmonize our similarities."

Harmonize our similarities, Helga mouthed the words, wondering if it was a Traxian idiom.

"If I don't get to see the two of you before you depart," Cleia continued, "I pray that Cyris grants you good fortune beneath her watchful eye."

They thanked her and separated to take care of their particulars, and Helga grabbed Zan to program her to do as Cilas had instructed. Once that was finished, she went back to her berth and tidied up everything, as if she expected to be gone for a long time. It was the Navy way, but beyond that, doing manual work allowed her to mentally prepare for what was to come. When she was finished, she walked to the dock, and took one final look at her surroundings.

"Deploying drones," *Ursula* announced, startling her, and Helga hurried to the R60 Thundercat, where she walked below a wing to its swollen belly and ramp leading up into the cargo hold.

She could hear laughter as she made her way up, and found Quentin and Sundown handling ordnance. They greeted her, but she didn't stop to chat. Instead she found the cockpit, where she started a sequence of preliminary checks. She had only touched the Thundercat on her first tour of the *Ursula* but hadn't bothered till now to sit and play with the controls. Now she realized that she had been mistaken when she wrote it off as a standard dropship.

The R60 Thundercat had a torpedo launcher, installed below her stern, and the wings, which she thought were an unnecessary cosmetic addition, held four energy cannons that were enough to eliminate the shields on any fighter. Dramatically, Helga leaned forward and placed her chest on the console, spreading out her hands as if to embrace it.

"I'm sorry I underestimated you," she whispered, before sitting back to resume her preparation, starting down a long checklist permanently embedded inside her head.

"Commander," said Raileo Lei, over the comms. "Commander, our drones, Chiron and Arae, just arrived at the Satellite, Maahes, and there are no ships visible near her dock."

"Maahes, huh? That's the name? Very good, Chief Lei," Cilas said. "Looks like we're ahead of the lizards, so we're cleared to move. Nighthawks, get to the Thundercat and prepare for launch. Ray, put Chiron on surveillance; I want to know if even an asteroid makes it within jump distance of Maahes. I want Arae to find Arisani and stay within the vector of the planet and the moon, Argan-10. If anything moves, *Ursula* is to track it, and if the signature is Geralos, I want to know about it immediately."

"Aye aye, sir," Raileo said.

As if on cue, Helga brought up her starmap and synced the Thundercat to the radios of both the Arae and Chiron drones. She brought on the terminals that showed the feeds around the ship, then closed her eyes and whispered a prayer to the maker or anyone beyond that would be listening. She couldn't qualify her feelings but she was nervous, as if she anticipated something going wrong.

Helga tried to get past it using breathing exercises, blaming nerves and mission atrophy from the lengthy shore leave spent on Sanctuary station. For several long minutes she fidgeted with the controls as her eyes periodically shot up to the screens to see what the Nighthawks were doing. Once Cilas made it onboard, she counted three Nighthawks and one Jumper in the seats, so she updated Zan and pulled up the ramp to seal them in.

"Ready for launch," she announced, and got the confirmation quickly from the commander. Helga pulled on her helmet and surveyed the dock.

Her eyes found the railing where Dr. Cleia Rai'to was waving her farewell. Helga saluted the Traxian before starting the countdown as alarms began to blare out their warnings. Shields appeared around the perimeter, protecting the key areas of the dock from the incoming loss of atmosphere. When the timer reached zero, the deck below them slid open, and the *Ursula* ejected the dropship.

Helga let them stall for a time, watching the corvette drift away, then she grabbed the controls and applied enough thrust to start them moving towards the satellite. "Thundercat is clear, Zan, you are free to assume control," she said into her comms, and smiled when the *Ursula*'s android pilot confirmed. "Applying max thrust," Helga said into the intercom after glancing up to make sure that everyone was still seated.

With the connection to the drones being established, Helga got a full holographic view of the satellite. The Thundercat, though able to cloak, would not have the energy reserves to remain shielded. If the pirates became aware of their approach, they could fire a weapon into their unprotected hull. A manned rocket couldn't destroy them, but it could hit something vital, not to mention it would accelerate the timeline for the Geralos to collect their hostages.

Cilas slid into the seat next to her. "How're we looking? What's our ETA?" He wasn't wearing his helmet, and had busied himself with examining the hologram of the satellite.

"We're looking at an hour's worth of thrust to make the station," Helga said, her eyes fixated on the pulsing light of the satellite in the distance. "I figured that if I come in at this angle"—she demonstrated it with her finger—"I can dock on this level meant for maintenance crews and emergency vessels; then we can make our way down to the living area. We'll be cloaked so they should not see us on approach. What do you think?"

"With you in the cockpit? Getting in isn't my concern. What I do worry about though, Hel, is that coming in cloak will make it possible for the enemy to destroy us with a well-timed torpedo."

"They can try, but with what, really? A shoulder-mounted RPG, fired from behind the shield barrier of their dock? I have to say, Rend, the likelihood of that happening is pretty slim. Still, if that's how they want to play it, I am more than confident we can evade it. Aside from that, at the angle we're approaching, they won't be able to see us from any of the windows."

"What about radar?"

"It's an old abandoned satellite, stolen from the Arisanis, who used it for things not related to the war," Helga said. "There's no radar, just communication and starmaps. Unless the pirates brought something with them, they are extremely cutoff in there."

Cilas reached over and lifted her helmet off so that they could speak naturally, face-to-face. He had expressed in the past how much he distrusted comms, even though he knew deep down that it was senseless paranoia. "Helga, I'm struggling," he admitted. "I've never been in this position before, and I'm starting to see the issues that come with what we have."

"Which position?" Helga raised an eyebrow. "Being commander of your own ship, or do you mean something else?"

"Both, actually. It's so much easier when we're the ones being deployed, and the only worry is the mission. Now I have other concerns that I'm having to repress to be effective. *Ursula* has no captain right now, and even with the security and contingencies, a part of me fears that she will be boarded. Then there's you. If something were to—"

"Cilas," Helga whispered, "don't. We said we would figure it out, didn't we? Well, here is our test. Every mission I worry, and you can see it in my eyes, but when things start to happen, it goes away, replaced by confidence. Everything we've done, everything we've survived, it makes me know that we are better than anything the Alliance throws at us. We believe in you, and those aren't just words from someone who knows you better than most," she said, smiling. "You're Cilas Mec, and we're your Nighthawks. What's a bunch of pirates to an ESO?"

4

With the Thundercat cloaked and tethered to the unsuspecting satellite, the four Nighthawks and Sundown had to prepare themselves to spacewalk the distance to the maintenance access point.

In Powered Armored Suits (PAS), this would be simple enough, but Sundown—not having one of his own—would be forced to do it using an EVA suit. There were several on the *Ursula*, the one that he wore now being a less-bulky Alliance Marine issue, but he would need to rely on manual rockets to steer, which took countless hours of practice to master.

The tether was a tracker beam, which acted as an anchor, locking them in with the rotating satellite as if an invisible rod held them in place.

Helga made sure that everyone was masked and present on her helmet's HUD, which took a bit of finagling to get Sundown registered since he was the only one not wearing a PAS. He was dressed in EVA, but Cilas had given him a PAS helmet back on *Ursula*, so she could now see that he was pulling oxygen, and was waiting with the rest of the men.

She dropped the ramp and the four of them floated out into space, where they activated their rocket boots and flew in a line towards the satellite. Helga was nervous watching them go on the holo-feed; she just knew that from Sundown, this was asking a lot, and he was lagging behind the rest of the men, maneuvering himself clumsily but managing to keep up.

Once they were inside the enclosure that was meant for ships docking, Helga left the cockpit, manually activated the ramp, and jumped through the closing gap to fly towards the rest.

They made quick work of entering with the satellite not having a functioning security system. It was an abandoned relic of a former age, once a bustling space station for communication. Now, it wasn't even a refugee hub, which was typically what would happen to satellites in disrepair. For one reason or another, it had remained empty and powered down, but someone had managed to bring it back to life some time ago.

Hurrying down a corridor, weapons ready and comms only echoing Cilas's breathing, they emerged into a wide-open compartment that had the largest set of bay windows that Helga had ever seen. This was saying something, given the *Rendron* had pretty big ones on the luxurious Nero deck, but even Sundown seemed wowed by the size of these transparent portals.

At the moment, however, the outside view offered nothing in terms of scenery as they rotated away from Hiyt, which was the only celestial body in close proximity.

Helga took it in quickly at a seconds glance, too busy monitoring her radar and the shadowy corners of that space. In single file they hugged the bulkhead near the window, then up a ladder to a tall ledge that wrapped about the circular compartment.

Below, over the railing, Helga saw twelve bulb-shaped fusion generators powering the station and keeping it afloat. Until today she had only seen them in vids, and it surprised her that they were this accessible. If they had come to destroy the station, all it would take was a bomblet tossed into their midst.

"Move," Cilas shouted, and they were through a door and into a long dark passageway whose lights were flickering on and off. She heard the muted thumps of a pistol and raised her own, but a second later she was stepping over the dead man, since they were now moving so fast. It was one of the pirates, which was evidenced by his clothes. He wore a motley mix of stolen fabrics, armor, and a helmet that should not have been in the hands of a civilian.

They were in the passageway for the heads and caught him exiting to return to his fellows. No one was talking since they'd spilled first blood, and now it was all about speed to limit the chance of discovery. Cilas was in his element, leading Nighthawks on a run of stealth and death, so Helga felt confident that they would succeed.

What she wasn't ready for, however, was what they would find when they made it to the hostages. Just being on this satellite, knowing that there were incoming Geralos, put her senses on high alert.

The passageway ran into a cross-section that rotated before them, presenting different doors, labeled with names that meant nothing to any of them.

"Pulling up schematics for this place," Cilas said. "Cover me, and watch your aim. A hostage will have a chaperone, so if it's solo, drop it. We cannot afford to be made."

They all still wore their helmets despite the breathable atmosphere, so their speech was restricted to comms. Cilas put a hand to the side of his mask and squatted down, while the Nighthawks and Sundown aimed out at the carousel of changing doors.

"Tutt, take the left passage," Cilas said. "There's a ladder leading down to the main. Get down there and hold that exit. Ate, you take the right and do the same. Ray, backtrack and climb up to that hatch we passed on the wraparound that brought us here. It's tight, but there's a crawl space for maintenance that will take you to a vent that sits above the space where our people are being held. Wait for my signal. Sunny, you're with me. One of these doors leads to communications, which is a straight shot through to our target.

"When you have eyes on the hostages, let me know and hold your position. We want all the marks dead before they can endanger the civilians. To do this, we need coordinated shots, and no one is allowed to miss. We want zero civilian casualties, and remember, we need one of those *thypes* to talk. Ray, our capture is yours; hit him where it hurts but we don't want to kill him. Any questions?"

He waited for a response, then with a nod they dispersed to their separate assignments. Helga reached down and pulled a knife from a pocket on her rocket boots, and held it up with her pistol as she walked her end of the passageway. It curved in slightly as she went along, and with the poor light, it had her on edge. Though it shouldn't have taken long with her pulsing rockets, it felt like an eternity before she found a door.

Listening in, she heard noises, and the radar on her HUD showed activity ahead. Taking a breath, she eased the door open and peered inside to see the back of a crate. This new compartment was massive, built for storing ship parts and large equipment, but when the satellite was abandoned by its owners, refugees from Vestalia had turned it into a home.

It should have been filled with people living and striving to feed their families, but it was a ghost town, empty, save for a clutch of bodies seated in a circle in the center of the crate homes. Helga had to wonder if the five armed men she saw holding them hostage had murdered the original inhabitants. How would they have done it? Airlock? Sold off to become slaves on someone's junker casino rig?

This last thought made her angry. She had dealt with pirates not too long before this mission, and had seen how they forced captives into slavery through the use of debilitation implants. Helga saw these men as the same ones she and Cilas had cut down to free their Alliance brothers and sisters from bondage. They were the worst form of Vestalians, preying on their own for credits, territory, and power.

"This is Tutt. I'm in position, with my eyes set on a tall, white-haired dirt bag."

"Hold your position, Q," Cilas said.

Helga had to smile. Of course it would be Quentin in position before anyone else. It also meant that he was in the compartment ahead, and would need her in place in case he was discovered. Snapping into action, she slid behind the closest crate and surveyed the area to see if any were looking her way. The coast was clear, so she flew up to the top of a stack and knelt next to an electric generator where she picked out one of the men to be her victim.

"This is Hellgate, in position, and I have my eyes on a big guy in red. He should be easy to spot so don't go stealing my kill, Raileo."

"He's all yours, ma'am," Raileo said, and she could hear him smiling behind his words.

The thought of him happy lifted her spirits, but the ice was still in her veins. She shifted her position so she could lean against the generator, using it as leverage to assist her aim. The other Nighthawks got into position and gave Cilas their updates, and now they were all waiting for his command.

"Drop 'em," he said, as if he knew the power of his words, and rightfully so, for in that moment Cilas Mec was a war god ordering death. His Nighthawks responded with deadly accuracy, each killing their man, though Raileo Lei shot two, including Helga's out of spite.

It all happened in the space of a second, simultaneous fire, killing four men and wounding the fifth. One second they fired, and the next they were moving forward, walking amongst the people, informing them that they were there to help. It happened so smoothly, with no mishaps, and in an instant they had changed from assassins to guardians.

This can't be it, Helga thought, as she helped a frightened young woman to her feet. She looked around, expecting Arisanis, but every one of these captives were human.

"I thought that these were nobles taken from an Arisani pleasure boat," Helga said into her comms.

"These are Vestalian nobles who live on Arisani," Cilas said. "That group of pirates segregated them from the Arisani passengers and took them here. Why? This, I don't know. Tell you what though, we're going to find out from our new friend right there." He gestured towards the wounded pirate that Quentin was now holding up. "While we work on him, Ate, talk to a few of the people and find out what they know."

Cilas pulled off his helmet and Helga and the others did the same. As soon as she inhaled, Helga regretted it. The place smelled like a week-old refuse dump. That's when it hit her, the desperation of living in a place like this, in these conditions, with no hope, and no home planet to offer you help.

She had known about hubs her entire life, and people would say, "You don't want to end up there," but she had never thought about it, and now that she was here, it broke her heart to think that this was the reality for so many Vestalians. To live like this, hopeless, and then have pirates swoop in and capture you to sell to ...

"Geralos," she said suddenly, causing several people to gasp. "Did any of those *thypes* mention Geralos? Do any of you know why you were brought here?"

"One of them did say that," said a wide-eyed woman, who Helga thought looked regal in her dress of white and gold. The woman stepped forward with her chin held high and her smooth umber skin glistening beneath the lights. For a second Helga thought she was wearing a shawl but it was thin black braids about her shoulders. This hair—and there was much of it—was held in place by glowing threads that pulsed a shade of gold periodically, completing her ensemble.

It was fascinating to witness such a royal presence within a Vestalian. Helga couldn't imagine this woman kneeling in front of anyone, let alone a group of filthy pirate thugs.

"That one there," the woman said, pointing to one of the corpses. "He said something about selling his soul to the lizards." She then pointed to the man that Quentin and Cilas were dragging back to one of the crates. "When he said it, he was reprimanded by the one you kept alive."

"Commander, that one there's the leader," Helga informed Cilas Mec, who upon hearing this, gave a nod to Quentin Tutt.

"What happened here?" Helga asked the woman, gesturing to the abandoned crate homes. "Hubs like these are rarely empty, yet you and all these nobles are the only ones here."

"Are you inferring that we live in this *schtill*?" said a bearded man who had been eavesdropping on their conversation, and Helga made a sign for him to be quiet. "Alliance," he grumbled. "Aren't you all supposed to be patrolling space? Now we have pirates attacking our ships. As if the Geralos weren't enough."

"Thought they were tough? Say something else," Helga said, and the man mumbled an insult but quickly crept away. "Now madam, I see your clothes and know that you all were brought here from somewhere ... fancy, but there used to be people living here. Do you have any idea what happened to them?"

"They did a lot of talking, but not much else. Complained about the smell, the state of this place, and how they hated being put on guard duty. My thoughts were that they haven't had anyone here for a long time. May I ask you something, officer?" the woman said, leaning in closer, "What do you intend to do with us? They took our prince, and he is hurt. We must find him and get him some help."

"What's your name, madam?" Helga said, wondering at the woman's age—it was always hard to tell with nobles since they took such good care of their skin.

"My name is Inodal Mulsa-Aren Tonakit Dar, child. Lady Mulsa-Aren to the commoners, but Inodal to friends and members of the esteemed first caste."

Helga wanted to roll her eyes, but pushed her politics to the side, reminding herself that correcting isms was not her duty as an ESO.

"Inodal." She said her name loudly, not caring that she was one of the commoners who was to refer to the lady by her formal name. "We are with the Alliance Navy. You sent a distress call to the *A'wfa Terracydes*, and we're who they sent to rescue you. As to your prince and the other non-humans, we are still looking for them. They were taken on another ship."

"Are any of you hurt?" Raileo asked loudly, and several people groaned or raised their hands.

"Rescue is on its way," Helga said to them. "We have a physician who will get you all patched up while we take you back to your families."

"What about the prince?" several said, and Raileo Lei gave Helga a helpless glance.

"The Alliance has vessels out searching for the pirates," Helga said, addressing the group of nobles. "We know that they are somewhere above Genese. If they still have your prince, we will retrieve him and bring the rest of these traitors to justice. Now, you all need to worry about yourselves. Gather your things, and if you're wounded, give Chief Lei your name so that we can get you help as soon as we're back on board the ship."

"Bless you, child," Inodal said, bowing to Helga. "May Cyris forever smile on your line."

"Thanks for all your help," Helga said graciously, then left to look for Cilas and Quentin Tutt.

She waded through the crowd, moving quickly to get past the curious who reached out to touch her PAS suit. Once free, she observed the crates and how they were jammed together in rows, with some stacked like stairs going all the way up to the overhead. Everything was welded together with pipes, the top floors made accessible by ladders spanning the sides.

This was a true settlement, a satellite town, and though they were given the nickname "hubs" they were no different than small towns on a planet's surface. To see one so abandoned broke Helga's heart, because she knew that it would have been violent and frightening to eject everyone from their homes.

The blood-curdling wail of a man in pain revealed where Cilas and Quentin worked, so Helga found the crate and stepped inside, almost gasping at what she saw. Cilas had the man's arm outstretched on a table, while Quentin Tutt stood over him, slowly fileting the skin from his arm.

"Helga, you don't want to see this *schtill*," Cilas said, glancing at the doorway as if he expected someone else to come in.

"After what I just heard, I want to see it. A woman out there just informed me that these men did admit to holding them here for a Geralos pickup. Can you believe that, Nighthawks? Do you know what that means? To think that some of our own are actively hunting innocent people then selling them to the *thyping* enemy. They're communicating with lizards. Please tell me I am dreaming this *schtill* because—"

"Ate," Cilas said suddenly. "Focus. We have to get them out right now. Are we clear? I got word from the captain; we are to load them up and make for the *A'wfa Terracydes*. Bring the *Ursula* here. Take whoever you want, but we'll need to be quick. We've learned from our new friend that it's likely an assault ship full of lizards coming to make the pickup. There's either a base somewhere close where they have more people, or a starship of some sort, since whatever they have here is recurring, and there are no Alliance eyes on this region."

"They've got our attention now, that's for sure," Helga said, looking over at the man who was now telling Quentin something. "I will tell Zan to bring her in and dock the Thundercat, then I will need you and the others to get those people to the main exit hatch. Zan will have the jump primed for *A'wfa Terracydes*, and we can get them there in little to no time. The woman, Inodal, says there's a prince of some sort out there with them."

"Everyone proclaims themselves royalty on Arisani," Cilas said, dismissively. "Even if he's someone important, it really doesn't matter. We're not offering concierge services here. They're all civilians in need of rescue, nothing more and nothing less. We get them out, drop them off at their station, and then see if we can do more to stop this trade from happening in the future. Get us safe, Lieutenant," he said, giving her a playful wink.

"Aye aye, Commander," she said, feeling a bit let down by how he'd reacted. He was classic Cilas, straight to the solutions, and everything done without emotion, but could he not see the madness in what was happening? How could he not react to something like this? Even Quentin had looked up at her when she explained that the humans were to be traded to the lizards. Vestalians were selling Vestalians to the brain-biting Geralos. How could anyone be calm about that?

"Ray, you're my wingman, fall in," she said as she stepped out to catch him flirting with a freckled, redheaded woman. "*Ursula*'s waiting and we need to get the Thundercat back onboard before we jump. We have some time, and it's a bit of a walk, so fall in, will you? We have lizards incoming, so hop-to."

Helga contacted the *Ursula* and informed Zan of the change in plans. She also told Dr. Rai'to about the five injured Vestalians. She didn't like how exposed they were inside this satellite with multiple docking points, but rescue was the mission and Cilas had given her a direct order.

"Let's hope this doesn't take long," she mumbled, looking out of a window as if she could see the incoming Geralos.

Raileo Lei fell in next to her, and she shoved him playfully into a crate. "That's for the stunt earlier, you little *schtill*," she said, shooting him an icy glare.

"You know what I'm realizing?" he said, so comfortable with his rocket boots that he was turned around facing her, gliding backwards as he spoke. "I've killed ten times the humans and allied species than I have Geralos, the enemy that has our planet. Who would've thought?"

"Yeah, who would have thought that a boy who made it out of a place like this would be complaining about killing *thypes* preying on little boys, just like him," Helga said, surprised at herself for how serious she sounded. "You should be proud to be one of the few that has a chance at making a real dent, Ray. Even if that means killing greedy men who sell our people to the enemy for their consumption, or corrupt politicians who people like that little boy look to be somewhere fighting for them. It's much bigger than the lizards, Ray, and in time you'll be killing plenty. Now chin up, damn you. I chose you to come along 'cause you're my mate."

"Ate, I don't know whether to be offended, disappointed in myself, or motivated, but you made me feel something just now, and though it's confusing, I'm ready to kill something," he said, laughing.

5

Getting back to the maintenance hatch took a lot longer than Helga expected. It was bizarre; finding their way in and carrying out the rescue seemed to have happened so fast, yet the peaceful walk back was dragging on forever. When they finally reached the airlock, Helga looked back the way they came, caressing her pistol in case of anything. It was senseless paranoia, especially with Raileo Lei next to her, who was always ready for action.

"Is it me, or did this trip take a really long time?" she said, pulling on her helmet.

"Didn't notice the length," Raileo said, donning his helmet as well. "I've been thinking about those people and what you said about the war. We're but five operators, in a war that affects billions. How many other Vestalians are out there right now, being held inside hubs forgotten by the Alliance? Not to mention the people who were here. How many have been killed or taken by the lizards? On Meluvia, I was convinced that we made a dent; but now I'm beginning to wonder if we're just delaying the inevitable."

"Meluvia was a dent. We destroyed deadly ordnance that could have harmed thousands of people. Sure, we can't singlehandedly wipe out the lizards, but we can move up the timeline on intelligence, which I would argue that we have. The information we recovered led to action by the Meluvian military. We're talking armed forces from multiple continents, stomping out every cell of the MLF. You may have seen it as us running and gunning through that jungle, but the aftermath of our actions is still going on."

"I didn't know," he said. "That does make it count."

She touched her mask and made a ready signal and when he acknowledged she pulled open the airlock. They stepped into the space beyond and she sealed them in and floated over to the exit hatch. "How are you looking on power?" she said, since he had been using his rockets their entire walk.

"Still near full, I'm good to go," he said, and she nodded her approval.

Raileo turned and pulled the airlock shut, sealing them inside. Red lights began to flash, warning them that they were about to be exposed, and the emergency lock on the exit-hatch came off. Helga grabbed the handle and pushed the hatch open, floating out into space. She then bent her legs and straightened them quickly, triggering her rockets to come alive.

Together they made their way from the satellite, staying close to one another for extra security. Helga brought up her wrist-comms and took the Thundercat out of cloak, then together they flew below it, where she worked at the stubborn hatch until it accepted her identification.

On board, Helga took a quick survey of the space, wondering at the likelihood of them fitting twenty bodies on a ship meant for eight. It was against everything she had been taught, and would mean death for many if they were attacked.

"Looks like we'll be making two trips," she said, shaking her head at the prospect. "I don't like this."

"Me either. We're alone out here with no backup incoming, and all we have for eyes are my drones," Raileo said.

"Anything there?"

"Nothing," he said, expanding the holo image to appear above his wrist-comms. "What are your orders, Lieutenant?"

"Get strapped in. I'm going to dock and bring on the wounded and our pirate guest of honor. That's us at capacity, but I want to take three more. They can sit in the center at your feet, I'm thinking we can hold twelve. I'll jump us out, make the drop, and then you will remain behind to take the helm."

"Me?" Raileo said, suddenly surprised.

"The commander wants a Nighthawk in place just in case this goes to *schtill*, and I don't trust that pirate. I want him made into an ice cube until we're all safely aboard."

"And you think Zan wouldn't pull him apart if she saw him break out of his stasis cuffs?" Raileo said.

"Oh, she would want to, but what could she do? Cel-tocs can't hurt organics. It's part of their core programming, Ray, you know that."

She powered on thrusters and turned them about, making the adjustments needed to line them up with the satellites dock.

"Part of their core programming, yes, but someone else on crew, organic or otherwise, would certainly pull their weight. Even Cleia has training, and she's not too bad with a pistol," Raileo said, forgetting for a moment who it was that he was speaking to. When Helga stayed quiet, he looked away.

"Raileo Lei, you and the good doctor? 'Not too bad with a pistol,' he says. Well, I just can't see it, but I'll take your word for it, lover boy," she said, laughing out loud. "Earlier you made mention of wanting to shoot something. Was that a double entendre? And I recall that during our launch the two of you were nowhere to be found."

She kept on digging, waiting for him to crack and protest his innocence, but he didn't. She brought the dropship down to attach it to the exit tube, then locked in the brakes and took a breath.

"It's not going to be a problem, Ate. She's technically a civilian, and we're on the *Ursula* together. The worse we can do is miss each other when I'm off on missions."

Helga stopped him at the hatch, and turned him by his shoulders to face her.

"You know, all this time I was wondering why that cute new doctor looked so familiar," she whispered, her hands holding him steadily in front of her. "I put it out of my mind, thinking that maybe it's because I haven't known many Traxians, but the way you responded to my joke makes me think that, yeah, I know her. She's the woman you brought back to the Empyrean, and then lied to Quentin and me that she was a prostitute. Is she even a doctor, Ray? A real doctor?"

"Yes. The prostitute thing was a lie because I didn't want you all in my business. You would make a big deal about it, and I just wasn't in the mood. We were on Sanctuary, and I was happy, and even though it would be temporary, she represented something that was missing in my life."

"So you figured out a way to get her on our ship." Helga inhaled then dropped her hands. "I hate that I love this. It's so romantic. I never thought that men like you existed. *Thype*, Ray, you're so foolish, and to think that you admitted it to me. I'm still your CO." She punched his shoulder. "But you just knew I wouldn't tell, didn't you? Okay lover boy, but Cilas isn't dumb, and you all aren't hiding it too well. Play at some flirting, talk about her to the guys, ease them into it and pretend you just met. They'll eat it up and it won't be a problem. Now get your narrow butt out of my ship."

As was planned, the wounded came first, along with a handful of others. They traveled back to the *Ursula*, where they helped the doctor retrieve her patients, then quickly converted the dock into a temporary camp for their guests.

The dock was part hangar, with shelves for storage, and eighteen recessed compartments meant for cargo, but Quentin and Raileo had converted some of them. One was now a gym, and there was a range, a miniature barracks, and a makeshift changing room.

Nine of these, they assigned as temporary berthing, housing two refugees per compartment, with access to the head in the stern. The tenth was made into a cell, occupied with a stasis pod in which they shoved the prisoner and froze him. He already looked dead, but Helga had taken Quentin at his word that the man was unconscious. With him out of the way, they focused on their guests, and Raileo stocked their new berthing with crates and foam to serve as beds.

Helga left him and took the Thundercat back, feeling more alone than she had felt in ages. There was something about this space on the edge of the galaxy and knowing that no other Alliance ships would be in the vicinity. She wanted this over fast so that they could return to *Rendron,* or at the very least somewhere close.

Coming out of max thrust, she saw three vessels on her radar headed towards the satellite. These were ships whose signatures she couldn't recognize, so she immediately assumed them to be Geralos.

"Commander, we have three incoming," she said, ".3 light-seconds out. We need to hurry. This is going to be tight, and so everyone needs to get to that hatch. Do you copy, Nighthawks, we're going to have a hot evac?"

"We copy, Ate, bring her around, and we'll make sure everyone gets on immediately," Cilas said. "How long do we have for contact?"

"I'm hoping an hour, but if I'm seeing them then they are seeing me. They could ramp-up to supercruise speed, and I doubt we'll have time to outrun them," Helga said. "We may have a fight on our hands, and it won't be easy. It all depends on how fast we can do this."

"We're not to be discovered, so let's get this done," Cilas said, but Helga wasn't so sure it was up to them.

She docked the way she'd done before, unlocked the hatch, and waited until the tube was attached and sealed to the dropship. As soon as she was settled, the airlock came open, and Sundown was ushering several of the nobles through the tube. They floated in slowly, clumsily righting themselves from the gravity when they got aboard the ship. Bringing up the rear were Cilas and Quentin, and they did a headcount before giving her the approval to detach from the hub.

It was during the countdown for her jump to light speed that the first barrage of bullets found their shields. Alarms went off, and the people in the back began to panic and scream, but Helga couldn't hear them; she was too focused. She disengaged the computer-assisted navigation, turned on hardpoints, and gripped the controls. This wasn't a fighter, but she had fought with a dropship on multiple occasions, so she was used to its sluggish movement and limited arsenal.

"Sunny, up here, I need you on the guns," she said into the comms, and the darkly clad Jumper made his way up to the front.

"Are we positive they aren't ours?" Cilas said, which didn't surprise Helga, who had already confirmed it.

"That is a Geralos assault ship, with two cruisers in tow," she said. "Q, there's a manual energy cannon mounted above deck. Get up there and hit anything that comes across your sights."

"On it, Lieutenant," he said, and Helga brought the Thundercat around to the far side of the satellite, putting it between them and their attackers, staying tight to the hull in order to confuse the enemy's radar. The Geralos assault ship dared not come that close, but fired after them with little care for hitting the satellite.

For five long minutes this continued, her flying a tight circle while the Geralos followed, trying in vain to destroy them. Helga wanted to pull out and take her chances in open space, but the only way out now was for her to disable that assault ship.

"It's getting kind of hot up here, Tutt. What are you doing?" she shouted, pulling off her PAS helmet and clipping it to her chair. She could see that he was trying; there had been concentrated fire on the assault ship, but it wasn't doing anything. "If we aren't jumping in the next ten minutes, then those cruisers will be joining the fight," she said.

As if on cue, one of the Vestalians in the back began to sing at the top of his lungs. The rest picked it up, and it became a chorus, altos complemented by sopranos, with a bass chiming in once in a while. It was a song Helga knew, the anthem of a nation now lost due to the Geralos occupation. The words were for victory, and it hit her right

ANGEL OF THE ALLIANCE

where it counted, and she too began to sing, causing Sundown to stop his firing and look over at her to make sure he wasn't imagining it.

Helga took them away from the satellite, rolling to avoid as many of the shots as she could manage. She brought them about at a dangerous angle, nearly clipping one of the silos that extended from the satellite's core. The sudden change in direction took the assault ship by surprise, and while the Thundercat was considered slow, the enemy ship was much slower.

Quentin's energy cannon flashed deadly beams of light, draining its shields, and the assault ship changed its course in an attempt to come about.

"Brace for impact," Helga announced over comms.

"Why? Ate, what are you doing?" Cilas said.

"We're toast if we don't go on the offensive, Commander, and this lizard is stalling us until the cavalry arrives. Their shields are failing and ours are still at 60%, so I'm going to see how badly they want it."

Helga engaged light thrust to bear down on the assault ship as it came out of its rotation, then maxed it suddenly, turning the Thundercat into a projectile. As expected, her target rolled to avoid the collision, and the Thundercat shot past without incident, coming so close that the hull vibrated, shaking the passengers violently.

Helga applied brakes and swung them about, flying around the satellite to come out at an angle that would have been in the assault ship's blind spot. Now there was a small window of advantage, and she wanted to make it count.

"Charge a torpedo and lock on to that region above its thrusters," she said to Sundown.

Once the assault ship's pilot recognized the caliber of enemy he faced, he went from hunter to desperate prey, trying his best to survive. But Helga was now on his flank, depleting his shields and refusing to let up. In time his flight patterns became predictable, and Sundown was given the order to fire the torpedo.

He did as he was told, but a zip-ship, having launched from one of the cruisers, flew between them and took the impact, exploding dramatically and forcing her to veer off. The sudden bright light from the explosion blinded Helga temporarily, and it took everything within her not to panic. With the PAS helmet, the glass would have shielded her vision, but it was still hanging from her chair, and now she regretted having removed it.

"Sunny, prime a second one," she said, looking over to see how he had managed through the light. He too had his helmet off, but it didn't seem to faze him, and he nodded to show that he acknowledged. Scanning the radar as red and white spots danced about her vision, Helga analyzed how long they had before the cruisers would be in range.

"Twenty minutes." She mouthed the words. They needed to hit the assault ship and fast. This cat-and-mouse chase had been going on for fifteen minutes, but it felt more like three hours, and they were down to a single energy torpedo.

She slowed them down and took another trip around the satellite, allowing the assault ship to assume that the torpedo missing its mark had rendered the Thundercat toothless. As expected, the Geralos took the bait and turned on them with all its force, letting loose gun batteries and a torpedo that missed, striking the satellite instead.

In a sequence of expert maneuvering, coupled with instincts learned from numerous dogfights, Helga used the extensions of the satellite as a shield, slipping beneath the communication disks, staying tight to the hulls and breaking off only when the assault ship was turning.

The Geralos pilot, recognizing this game, pulled away from the satellite to wait for backup, and Helga, seeing an opening, powered on cloak and maxed thrust, taking them out of the assault ship's range. Cheers went up in the back as the civilians assumed that she was taking them to *Ursula*, but the Nighthawk wasn't running; she only needed the time to reposition.

"Ready with that torpedo, Sunny?" she said, looking over at the Jumper.

"Just say the word, Lieutenant," he said, giving her a mock salute.

She bit her lip and nodded at him knowingly. He had fought with her a handful of times, yet she trusted him implicitly.

Putting everything into thrust, she urged the dropship forward, flying towards the assault ship who could no longer see where she was. Coming out of cloak suddenly, she put most of the power into weapons, leaving just enough for the shields to survive the impact she anticipated.

"Sunny, now!" Helga shouted, as she held their position to increase the accuracy.

The torpedo flew out, a white line of wicked, shield-eating energy, and the assault ship became a tiny nova, forcing Helga to close her eyes. This time when the cheers returned she happily joined in, reveling in her victory. With her heart pounding and cold sweat trickling down her cheeks, Helga relished in the moment, happy to get the hostages out alive, and happy to have done it against the Geralos.

6

The thrill of battle is a unique sort of high, but it is brief and the aftermath typically involves the three R's of reflection, regret, and repulsion. Reflection was the softest, since there were highs as well as lows that came with the memory, and regret was inevitable, especially when it came to the loss of life.

Repulsion, however, was self-inflicted, and would send the strongest spacer to the bottom of a bottle. That was what Helga wanted as the *Ursula* made its way out to the station known as *A'wfa Terracydes*, but with eighteen new passengers on the ship, she had to play the part of a proper lieutenant.

Five people had been injured and were being tended to by the doctor, who looked beyond excited to have something to do. Zan had the helm, allowing Helga to get some much-needed rest, but with the noise from the dock—where the Vestalians talked loudly and extensively—she had given up on that prospect and retired to the mess, where she now sat nursing a hot cup of coffee.

Cilas was in his cabin speaking to the captain, a daily ritual for him, it seemed, since they had shoved off from Sanctuary. Sundown came in wearing a tight blue shirt with the Alliance logo embroidered above his left pectoral. He wore black and charcoal BDU pants, Marine-issued jackboots, and his las-sword hung loosely from his belt.

He looked more smuggler than pirate in that getup, which brought a smile to Helga's melancholy face. He gave her a crooked grin and sat across from her, running his dark hand through his hair.

"Is it just us?" he said, looking around, and Helga nodded and met his eyes, wondering what he wanted to say. "Have you sat back and thought about the reality of us actually getting our planet back?" When he spoke his Virulian accent was thick, which led her to believe that this was a recital and not something concocted from his own conscious thought. She sipped slowly on the hot, bitter liquid and stared at the open doorway.

"I feel like I'm back in the academy," she said, glancing at him, "And Commander Sunny's about to give me a lecture. Anyway, yeah, I've thought on it. Many times, actually, and I've come to the conclusion that in time, with our continued efforts, the Geralos will run out of resources. Since they're one planet against many, with no allies—not counting the traitorous *schtills* selling off our people of course," she scoffed. "Since they are alone in their efforts, we will eventually bend them to surrender."

Sundown laughed. "You never disappoint, Helga. Now that is the answer I expected from a soldier, born and bred to be a soldier, within a system that rewards the best soldiering. I wonder, however, what the person beneath that uniform really thinks, if we were to remove all of that Alliance programming. Would she admit that this war is futile, and that we're all part of an orchestrated dance put on by something beyond our control?"

"You mean the maker? Are we onto religion now, Sunny?"

"Maker of what?" He laughed again, "Life? Vestalians? Casanians?" He shrugged. "Here's a fact, Helga. Casanians have the largest brains out of all the species in our galaxy. Does your large Casanian brain really believe that there is a creator of all that we know as life? Do you believe this maker has a maker? And if so, wouldn't there need to be a maker of that maker, and so on? And who started that cycle? I could keep on asking who and why, unless our reality is set on a loop.

"Some think that we are a part of a universe that has always been, and will always be, continuously making and remaking itself. They say our futures have already been decided, and anything we 'choose' isn't really choice. Have you pondered on these things, Nighthawk?"

"No," Helga said matter-of-factly, "I have enough *schtill* hurting my head." She was confused as to where he was going with this conversation, and why he needed privacy to broach it. Was he attacking her intelligence, or setting her up for a lesson of some sort? She had decided to play along rather than blow him off like she was prone to do with smarty-pants spacers. It took her mind off the past, and so it was a welcome distraction, but she disliked feeling as foolish as he was having her feel now.

46

"Of course you haven't thought of these things," he continued. "Your Alliance doesn't want thinkers in the uniform, they want obedient spacers and officers. Trust your command, that's the only thought you need, right?" And he put his fist over his heart in a mock salute for emphasis.

"Thinking beyond the war itself makes you a bad spacer, so they wired you to accept, lest you second guess your orders. But you are a thinker, Helga Ate, and it is why your dreams have haunted you the way they have. You don't believe the things you say, no matter how many times you repeat them, and you know deep down that there is another truth now, don't you? Every other Seeker I've known—"

"Excuse me?" she said suddenly, staring at him with a look of horror and surprise.

"A Jumper knows the chosen when he meets one, Helga, and you don't hide it well when it comes to the action. The things you do inside a cockpit, and the way you shoot, it goes beyond natural talent and training. You have been touched. It's why I wanted to speak with you privately because it became clear that you've kept it to yourself."

"And what is the truth behind the maker, Sundown?" she said, her anxiety setting her heart back to racing.

"That we are all insignificant as far as life is concerned. There is no cause and effect for our future as a species, based on fantasies created by these people we elect to lead us. If there's a maker, she would be neutral, choosing neither Geralos nor Vestalian to come out ahead. But evidence points to her not being neutral, doesn't it? Vestalia now has allies and technology beyond anything they would have developed on their own. If that first Meluvian explorer hadn't decided to roam the galaxy and risked visiting Vestalia, there would have been no help when the Geralos came. Hard to see it as chance, and there are other things that only my order can know."

"Are you recruiting me, Sunny?" she said, inhaling deeply to calm her nerves.

"You may qualify, but there's more to becoming one of us than being born with heightened senses, I'm afraid. If you are noticed, and that would take much more than the observations of this outcast, then you will be summoned, and as you know, refusing is never an option."

Helga thought on this and it frightened her. Jumpers called themselves agents or spies, but in reality they were monks with their own religion. To be summoned meant that she would be reset and made to forget much of her past, and it would be akin to death and rebirth. "So we're supposed to win, regardless?" she said, bringing him back to his explanation of life.

"Who is to know, but in the end, all a mortal can do is guess at it. Look not to admirals and councilors to give you the secret of life, or to control you with wishes and dreams of a glorious Geralos genocide. There are worlds beyond this one, Helga, vast sprawling worlds with their own politics, dreams, and thoughts that they are significant. You alone can control the way you digest the fact that we're nothing, and if you can accept it and press on, then your gift will become that much greater."

He grew quiet after that last sentence, and she thought on it as she stared down into the blackness of her mug.

"I used to think that Anstractor was so big that no one would ever have the pleasure of appreciating all of its beauty," she said. "On every planet and moon that I have visited, the world seems so vast that yeah, it lets you know just how small and forgettable we are. But listening to your words, and the strange way they registered with me just now, has me feeling more frightened than I have ever felt. Without a maker, we chance oblivion, don't we? And if oblivion is our end, then it becomes especially sad the way we all waste our lives. *Thype*, Sunny, I don't need this sort of crap in my head right now. Why didn't you come talk to me on Sanctuary when I was fully relaxed and drunk out of my mind?"

"You're a hard woman to catch by herself, except for the times when we've been together stalking or dodging bullets and bomblets. Everyone is busy tending to their stations, and I knew that you would take time alone to come down from the excitement earlier."

"You too." She smiled at him. "I've noticed since the pit. You take long breaks after fighting, and there's a running joke that you are incapable of sleep. On that topic, since you're being so forthcoming all of a sudden, what's with you, Sunny? You're the only Jumper I know that chooses a pistol over their las-sword. I've seen you use your blade, and you're amazing with it, so I'm confused as to why you have that LS-R. Isn't it part of your code to only use your order's chosen weapon? I never saw Lamia use a pistol, though he did carry around that laser-rifle."

"Other than Lamia Brafa, how many Jumpers have you known?" Sundown said, relaxing his shoulders.

"None, but I have always heard—"

"Rumors, conjecture, romantic notions of who we are and what we are about. We have codes, Nighthawk, but none to do with the weapons we choose. A Jumper is trained to win at all costs when it comes to a duel, survival in times of war, and healing when our allies are wounded. Any tool that assists in seeing these things through are not only permitted but encouraged. My brother Lamia was gifted with the blade, but if I was to guess, he was likely a soldier before he was reborn. If you have a question of my order, you need only ask it, and I will clear the haze. We sacrifice everything to become what we are, Helga, so I don't see the logic in being tethered to a las-sword."

"That makes sense," Helga said, yawning since the time had flipped over into the third shift. "I guess a lot of the things that I heard were the inventions of spacers bored enough to make *schtill* up."

"People are fascinated with my order because of our talents, but what comes with membership is our own to know, so naturally they fill in the blanks. Helga, your gift, it doesn't grow naturally over time; it must be trained and developed through conscious thought. Everything I told you about the war, life, and your unimportance in the grand scheme of things, they can discourage the common soldier, and you're going to want to ignore it. That is your training, stick to the mission, but the mind of a Seeker is uncomfortable. It is tortured, tough to deal with. You must consider every outcome of every situation, especially when it is painful."

"So, to become a better Seeker, I will have to let in the very things that I have worked to remove from my mind over the years? Is that what you're telling me?" Helga said, putting down the coffee cup to rub at a sudden pain in her temple. "Sunny, when you met me I was being attacked, and you saved my life. That version of me, the same one sitting with you now, is the reformed Helga Ate who can eat and sleep like a regular person so she's effective in the field. Before Sanctuary, I did let those things in, and as much as I tried to avoid them as you assert, they stayed on my mind every waking hour, and I was malnourished, tired, and one bad mission away from stopping the pain permanently.

"It took long talks with Cilas and seeing a psych for me to be able to function and get back to being a proper officer. These Seeker gifts you mention; are they just intensely realistic nightmares with hints of realism, or will I be able to manifest something miraculous, like flying my ship using only my mind? If you say no, and that the nightmares are what I can look forward to, then I will happily stay ignorant and work at forgetting that I have this so-called gift."

"I have an idea," Sundown said, standing up and reaching for her hand. "Words will not work on one such as you, Helga Ate, so let me show you something of what awaits you through that pain."

They walked together towards the stern of the ship, where there was an empty compartment meant for storage or extra berthing. When they were inside he locked the door, and looked about for any cameras. "Just a moment," he said, and sat on the deck with his legs crossed and his large hands resting on his knees.

He sat that way for a long time, but Helga dared not disturb him, for wanting to see what it was that a trained Seeker could manifest.

The child inside her wanted to try and kick him and test the legendary reflexes of the Jumper agency, but the need to know about her gift killed the urge, having been aware of it now for over a year.

"Follow my lead," he said, and Helga sat in front of him, crossing her legs in the same fashion before closing her eyes and waiting.

"I am merely a warrior, with some sight based on the training of my order," he said. "But you are blessed with the gift, and need only focus for it to manifest itself."

"Focus on what?" she said, impatiently.

"Something or someone you care about dearly," Sundown said.

Helga focused on Brise Sol, the retired Nighthawk, who she feared was now living on a hub, poor and destitute, having fallen from the graces of the Alliance.

She remembered his laugh, and his bad jokes, but most of all his short red hair. It made her smile, and a warmth spread from her core to the tips of her limbs. She became lightheaded, and though she wanted to open her eyes and stop it, she forced herself to bear it, knowing that eventually she would lose consciousness.

"Very good," Sundown said, and she opened her eyes to find him leaning against the bulkhead.

"What? How long was I out?" she said, scrambling to her feet and glancing at her wrist-comms, confused at what just happened.

"Maybe ten minutes, but that's of no circumstance. What did you see?" he said.

"Nothing," she said. "But I feel *thyping* amazing. Stranger still is that the person I thought about no longer worries me. I somehow know that he's okay," she said.

"Outstanding," he said, smiling. "Now you know what it takes to calm your mind."

"So, this is what you do after missions?" Helga said.

"Something like that, but more intense, being that I am merely a person and not a Seeker, such as yourself."

"Sunny, I don't know how to thank you for trying to help me, but I haven't talked to the Nighthawks about what I am," she said.

"I understand, and you've done well to keep it a secret. No telling what would come of it if the Alliance had that information. In the old days, before the Geralos, Seekers were sought out for their prescience in revealing things that would never be known otherwise. Seekers held high stations in the government, for good and bad. They were used for predictions, judgment, whatever their governments wanted. You know my complications with the Alliance, having seen the ugly side of the upper tier of politics. I fear what they would attempt if they knew an ESO star had the gift of sight."

"I didn't even factor them into the equation," Helga muttered. "Now I really want to keep it close to the chest."

"The ability to see is but one branch of the vast tree that is our abilities. When a Seeker has manifested a certain level of mastery, then is the time when my order takes notice. You can withstand the pain, Helga, not because you're Casanian and Vestalian, but because unlike other people, your power craves it to open those locked doors inside of your cranium. You've shown immense potential just from the way you tap into it during a fight. Tell me, how do you do that? How do you dodge cannons and strike targets when anyone else at your level would fail?"

Helga sighed and dropped her guard a bit, leaning against the bulkhead as she regarded him.

"I get angry," she said, smiling morosely at the thought. "All of the pent-up rage that lives within my heart seems to bubble to the surface when the boys or I are being threatened. I hold it back during petty squabbles, but out there I let it go. It feels ... good. Does it feel good to you as well, Sunny? It's exhilarating getting so worked up and then everything around me just becomes manageable. That's the best way that I can describe it."

"You own that branch, and this is why. Open your mind and you will become that much greater," Sundown said. "What you need to focus on is the here and now, what you stand for, why you fight, and own up to the fact that it could be futile. Look past the Geralos at the galaxy, and the individual planets, and the worlds within each and every one of them. Follow orders, but question them internally to know what their source was. It goes against everything you were trained to do, but our minds demand a vast education."

Helga thought on his words and everything she had done leading up to Sanctuary. She had worked hard as a young cadet to show up the bullies and instructors that made her out to be a small half-alien girl whose future would be in communications or the bridge. Her blood spoke differently however, since she was an Ate, from a long line of Marines and Vestalian soldiers. She aced all her tests and practiced hours on end to shoot straight and defend herself in a fistfight. This gained her second-class, a prestige only awarded to the top 5% in the Alliance Navy.

She was invited to BLAST, and survived it, which got her a spot on the Nighthawks, essentially accomplishing more in her short years of life than most people could hope for in their career. Yet, in all of that struggle and focused excellence, she hadn't dared to look into herself, to question why she did what she did or the reasoning behind their missions.

Sundown was right; she had set up barriers in both her mind and in her life. Even with Cilas, she had denied her wants until it became too unbearable for her to go on without seeing where his heart was.

She had all but jumped him, only to find that he too had wanted her. The leap of faith had paid off, and even now the memory of that night made her smile. Thinking back on everything she'd survived despite the odds, her bravery only had limits when it came to her wayward thoughts.

"So, all I have to do is allow myself to question things that I was told not to question?" she said.

"I will be here when you need me," the Jumper said, getting to his feet and dusting himself off.

After his long speech she saw him in a whole new light, no longer the gruff mystery who they found on the streets of a hidden space station. Sundown was a former assassin, spy, and several other things he would never admit to, but he was also a Jumper, and a monk with knowledge that was privy only to those of his order.

They were guardians of the Seekers who monitored the war from the inside, only lending their service to those who deserved it. To have him here meant that they saw something in the Nighthawks, and for the first time Helga realized that that something was her.

7

When the Nighthawks learned that they were to liberate Vestalian hostages, Helga hadn't thought about the fact that they would be with them for several cycles. Now, as she donned her uniform and took the time to make sure that everything was in place, she realized just how complacent she had gotten since their time on Sanctuary.

Two Vestalian months they had spent there, waiting for a summons to return to Alliance space, and in that time, she had become very familiar with her team members. Cleia was new, and Zan was a Cel-toc, but they were both outsiders to the naval world she knew.

Duty, duty, and more duty was the mantra, and you were always to look your best doing it. On *Rendron*—her starship home—it was all automatic, like the lights and the doors. You didn't have to think about life and how to go about it. The shift would begin, and so would you.

Since gaining the *Ursula*, however, she had become so relaxed that she would violate protocol, and let slights pass. Cilas wasn't the best at correcting these things, though his stare of disappointment would be enough most times, and though on its surface her liberties were minuscule, she knew that the Alliance demanded better.

Having these passengers walking the decks and being privy to them at most hours of the cycle had forced her back into being a professional, and now in hindsight, she wanted to slap herself.

Wasn't sleeping with the commander enough? Or was it about toeing the line until he blew a gasket? Her decision-making had been flawed, and she could hear Quentin inside her head, playfully reminding her that she was young.

She picked up her hat and decided it was too formal, then threw it on its hook and grabbed her pins. *Has it been that long?* she thought.

I've been so loose with my dress that I no longer remember how to carry myself as an officer?

She sighed audibly, and teased up her hair, then stepped outside to make her way to the bridge. This feeling of discomfort and wanting to escape from people reminded Helga of a much darker time in the past. It was she, Cilas, and Brise Sol stuck inside of a rigged-up floater, waiting on a rescue that wasn't to happen for months.

Here, she disliked the banter of elites who knew nothing of the war and the people it affected, whereas back then it was the war of words between the two men. She had played mediator, which was exhausting, and she hadn't known either of them well enough to do more than plead for civility. Now, she was a lieutenant that had enough pull to do something to silence the chatter from their guests.

She thought about putting them to work, which would have been grand being that most hadn't broken a sweat in their privileged lives, or sealing off the dock to mute their voices from the bridge.

Normally they kept the lifts open to allow free movement back and forth between decks, and the only lock was to Cilas's cabin, where he would have his regular chats with the captain.

Helga hadn't mentioned her feelings to anyone, not even to Raileo Lei, because unlike her and Sundown, the Nighthawks didn't seem to mind their passengers. Inside that pod, with nothing but time, and her fellow Nighthawks at odds, Helga had passed the time outside, wearing an EVA suit with mag-boots.

It would be a welcome escape now if they weren't at supercruise making for *A'wfa Terracydes,* so she decided on the next best escape, the one she was wired to do as a cadet: focus on her duty. Dismissing Zan to go recharge, she took her seat at the helm, clipped on earbuds, and tapped her wrist-comms.

No one was on, which wasn't unusual for the second shift, so she flipped the interface over to entertainment, selected a score, and closed her eyes, enjoying the hard-hitting symphony. It put her in the mood for action, so she ran diagnostics on the ship.

"Helga, where are you?" Cilas spoke over comms, and she glanced at the time displayed on the console. It was the middle of the second shift when they were normally free to do whatever they wanted.

There had been no meetings planned, no training exercises, so his tone surprised her. Did she somehow forget an assignment? She hadn't been with him since their return to the *Ursula,* so she wondered if this was a casual call for something else more intimate.

"Hey Commander, I'm on the bridge," she said, erring on the side of professionalism. "Did you need to speak to me?"

"Yes. I've got something urgent to discuss with you and the team. Could you get everyone to my cabin immediately?" Cilas said, but clicked off before she could acknowledge. She hated when he did that; it was something that both he and the captain were prone to do.

There was nothing offensive per se, but it bothered her all the same. It was difficult not to be bothered that for all they shared, he would order her about and not allow any questioning.

Yes, she knew this was unrealistic, juvenile, and whatever else on the surface, but it did hurt her feelings, and she could never bring herself to talk to him about it.

Helga was on her feet in an instant, marching back towards the mess, looking in each one of the recessed stations just in case Sundown was in one of them. Ever since she'd asked him to man the torpedoes on the Thundercat, Sundown had taken an interest in the ship's defense systems.

She had shown him how to access the schematics, but he would do it privately in one of the empty stations. He wasn't on the bridge or in CIC, however, and when she found the mess, none of the men were inside.

"Tutt, Lei ... Sunny?" she said into her wrist-comms, hoping that they at least had their earpieces in. Nothing, dead silence; it was as if they weren't even on the ship. That's when she heard cheering and laughter in the distance and realized that it was coming from the medbay.

Wondering what she would walk in on inside the space, Helga took a breath and hurried on towards the aft. *Ursula* had three decks: the top had the commander's cabin, and the bottom held the hangar, berthing, and dock—where they housed the Vestalian guests.

The main deck, which she was now on, held everything operative regarding the ship. From bow to stern, it was a straight shot through with the only doors being for the mess, medbay, and storage.

Starting from the cockpit, a spacer could walk through the bridge and CIC to a set of recessed weapons control stations and the first of two lifts. Past this section was the mess, then the new briefing room, and several small empty compartments—which would likely become additional berthing or storage as time went on. At the back was the largest compartment on the deck, which was Dr. Rai'to's medbay.

With all the laughing, Helga hoped that she wasn't about to walk in on something intimate or blinding. There were wounded civilians in there, resting, but the cheers grew louder as she drew near.

Touching the access-panel, she took a breath, not knowing what to expect. She walked in on a performance, with Raileo Lei being the man of the hour. In attendance were all the Nighthawks except for Cilas, and Helga was surprised to see the five patients sitting up inside their beds.

The compartment was circular, and the crew was either seated on an unoccupied bed or standing next to one. In the center, Raileo was singing and dancing a rendition from one of the *Rendron's* plays. He was very good, and Helga watched him for a minute, waiting for him to end his routine before joining the applause and approaching him.

"We're wanted in the Captain's cabin, Nighthawk," she said. "Sounds like it is urgent."

"Does that include me?" Dr. Rai'to said, her skin becoming deep blue and her face a mask of concern.

"Not this time, doc. This one's for the Nighthawks," she said. "You too, Sunny. You're one of us now."

She led them out into the passageway and up the ladder to Cilas's cabin. The door was open, and they all entered to find Cilas seated at a round table, with nothing on top of it except the coffee he was drinking.

Three empty chairs were set up for them to use, but Helga seemed to be the only one to have noticed them. She pulled out the one next to him and waited for him to give his approval. This he did with a nod, and she sat, followed by Sundown, and Quentin Tutt.

Raileo was still at the door looking around as if he was in awe of the space. When he became aware that they were waiting for him, he walked over and stood between Helga and Sundown.

"Thanks for coming on such short notice," Cilas began. "But this couldn't wait, and we need to get on it."

"What's the situation, Commander?" Quentin said.

"I just got word from the Alliance that there has been some activity on the moon of Argan-10."

"Argan-10," Helga said. "Didn't I say that in our last briefing? It's the closest potential hiding spot for the lizards, since they dare not try it on Hiyt."

"You were right," Cilas said quickly. "Not to mention our satellite Maahes was once in its orbit when it was live. Missio-Tral has drones about that moon, and one picked up a signal on the surface. There's no holo-vid or photographs, but there is some sort of mass, which could be a camp. The captain wishes for us to investigate, since he believes that it coincides with our mission."

"Does he suspect that the assault ship we encountered hailed from there?" Helga said.

"Had to come from somewhere, and there was no starship," Cilas said. "They were on their way in to collect the prisoners, which also hints at a local base of some sort."

"*Thype*," Quentin cursed, looking around at each one of their faces. "The stones on these lizards. That moon belongs to Hiyt, which is under the protection of the Alliance."

"Stealth and espionage is what they're best at," Sundown reminded him. "Quentin, are you really surprised at them making a move like this?"

"Wait a minute, Nighthawks," Raileo said. "We have a ship full of civilians expecting to be reunited with their families. Are we really going to leave them here with Cleia, and Zan ... the Cel-toc?"

"Cleia, Ray?" Quentin said, raising an eyebrow. "Do you mean Dr. Rai'to?"

"Yeah, are we really about to leave them here, waiting, while we go off to investigate this moon?"

"No," Cilas said. "But we're not docking with *A'wfa Terracydes* either; the captain has asked them to send out a shuttle to collect their people from us. Ate, when we're finished with this meeting, I want you to turn us around and wait. We'll contact the shuttle, send them our location, and transfer the civilians before heading back to that moon. Tutt, you spent some time with the prisoner. What did he say about their base?"

"He didn't mention a base, brother," Quentin said. "Everything I know, you already know, and he hasn't told me anything since. As far as the moon, he didn't mention it, but he did say the lizards own Hiyt."

"The Hiytans own Hiyt, and they are neutral to all this *schtill*," Sundown said.

"I don't think that's what he meant, Sunny," Helga said. "The lizards own the space about the planet Hiyt, but they remain hidden doing evil like wiping out the refugees on that satellite. If there is even a chance that they have an operation running on that moon, then we should go look for ourselves, and do what needs to be done."

"Exactly," Cilas said, "and this time, we won't be going in alone. *Missio-Tral* has drones in orbit over Argan-10, so we'll have intel coming in to help us coordinate our efforts. I will be in contact with them while we're on the surface so that we know precisely when reinforcements are coming. Helga, you will take us in, plant us somewhere outside of their radius, and we will use PAS to move in. Sunny, get fitted for a powered-armor suit; the EVA rockets you used last time wasn't enough. You're a Nighthawk now, and while I understand your individual needs as a Jumper, for assaults we all need to be identical, or the lizards may mistake you for our leader.

"This brings me to another topic that I need to cover. We have all had experience with the lizards taking over minds, so I don't need to tell you just how important it is that we remain undetected. There are things we do to mitigate the chance of discovery, however, and with Sunny being new to the unit, I feel it necessary to go over these things again. First things first: anything that could potentially lead to the enemy assuming that one of us is in charge, stay away from it. I'm deadly serious here; if you salute or walk over to me continuously for orders, you put me at risk of getting my head invaded.

"Second, individuality is forbidden. I know that it's exciting to be part of an ESO unit with the attention that comes from the rates, but what makes us effective is our silence and teamwork. The lizards should see us as shadows bringing death, and if they want to snatch a mind, it will have to be random. After Lamia, I am committed to not seeing a Nighthawk lost in this manner, not again, so take my words to heart: the only thing unique with our appearance is our height. If I could mask that as well, I would, but for now, speed and silence is our best defense. Kill the lizards fast and conceal their corpses and keep the rest of the team aware of your situation."

Sundown raised a hand, and Cilas stopped talking to give him the floor. "Commander, are you saying that my use of the las-sword will be restricted on our missions?"

"No, we need you at your best, Sunny, but save it for close-quarters combat. With Lamia, we grew reckless, if I'm to be honest. Having a Jumper in our unit tips the scales so much that it's easy just to send you in and have the rest of us mop up the scraps. Your predecessor was often the first one in, and I believe that got him marked. I won't do that to you, not unless it's one of those situations where only you and your skills are able to execute an order. Use whatever weapons you like; there are enough Marines using las-swords not to make me ban them outright. Any other questions?"

"These reinforcements from *Missio-Tral*, are they ESO or Alliance Marine units?" Quentin said.

"These will be Marines, and they will be there just in case we walk into something major. That's the thing about this op; we're technically recon until it's determined what the lizards are up to down there. Once we know, I'll radio command and they will give us our next steps, which could either be to clear the compound or back out. This will be by the book, Nighthawks. We cannot afford for any part of this to go to *schtill*, but if it does, we have *Missio-Tral* waiting to send in a Marine unit. Ray, are you good? You seem like you have something to say to me."

"Oh no, I'm just excited," Raileo said. "Recon means that I may get to use my new pistol."

8

With the *Ursula* anchored above Arisani, Helga decided that it would be a good idea to run some checks on the R60 Thundercat. From what Cilas had told them, they would be breaking atmosphere on a moon and executing a landing. That required a dropship, and since returning from the satellite, she hadn't taken the time to run diagnostics.

It was good practice to check on a ship after it self-repaired and regenerated munitions. The system was advanced, and for the most part, time was all that was required to recharge weapons and shields, but sometimes there would be glitches, and the system would throw false positives, misleading the pilot.

With the drop coming up, Helga didn't want to chance any problems with the Thundercat. All they had was time, since the shuttle had reported back that it would be there in a little under a cycle.

She could see to the ship, run some additional tests on the *Ursula*, and still have time to herself. Bypassing the lift, she found a ladder and slowly climbed down to the lower deck.

The earlier laughter and chatter of the people had become more of a murmur, which Helga guessed had to do with the news that a shuttle was coming. After the drama with the pirates and imprisonment on the hub, their Vestalian passengers were understandably skeptical of boarding another strange ship.

The chatter quieted down when her foot touched the deck, and she turned to find several people staring at her with what appeared to be fear. "Everything alright down here?" she said, looking from face to face.

"Nothing is wrong, ma'am," an older man said. "But we were wondering, why not take us yourselves? This was the plan before, eh?

We wonder, what have we done to make you change your mind? Perhaps we can fix or change whatever it is."

Helga groaned. Raileo had been tasked with informing the passengers of the change of plans. He was to be clear but careful not to divulge their intent on visiting the moon of Argan-10. What she was seeing now was that Raileo had told them, but failed to come up with an excuse as to why the Nighthawks were leaving.

"We cannot take you because we are wanted elsewhere," she said. "The place where we're wanted is classified, but involves us saving more lovely people like you. We aren't a charter shuttle, we are Alliance warfighters, and after rescuing you our prime concern is seeing to your safe return. The shuttle coming is from *A'wfa Terracydes*. That was your intended destination, wasn't it?"

Several of the robed men and women mouthed the answer, yes. "Another rescue calls your attention, you say?" the man said. "Do you know if it is the same pirates? Are you on your way to rescue our prince?"

· "Look, sir," Helga said, wanting an end to the questions. "Even if your prince was our target, and this was connected to what happened to you, I wouldn't be at liberty to tell you. Missions are classified, period, and I would ask that you not pressure my men for details either, the way you just tried to pressure me. This is what you need to know: a shuttle is coming for you, and it will be here in less than a Vestalian day. It's likely to be luxury, so you will have all of the comforts you are accustomed to. We hope that you are reunited with your families soon, all of you, including your prince."

"Thank you, Lieutenant," he said, finally showing her respect. When Helga marched toward the Thundercat, she exhaled a painful bubble of relief. It was one thing to face down an enemy that you were allowed to shoot, but to be assaulted with questions on a classified mission, that was beyond tough. She took a moment to look in on their prisoner, who was still frozen in stasis. Helga didn't find him the least bit frightening, and was a bit disappointed in the reality of this so-called pirate.

As a cadet she had heard so many stories about those hardened men and women with their demonic tattoos and cybernetic body parts. What stood before her was just a man, no scarier than the average hub-dwelling vagrant. "I wonder what the captain wants with you?" she whispered, as if the man could hear, then tapped the glass gently with her fist before making her way over to the dropship.

There were people milling about, some exercising, others dancing, which Helga felt was absurd. The ship they originated on was a party cruiser, but to dance now when they were refugees on an ESO ship? It seemed rather ridiculous, but she envied the time that those people had to enjoy their young lives dancing, and the freedom to do whatever they wanted to do.

Helga entered the ship, started the checks, then sat in the pilot's chair and kicked her legs up, taking a moment to catch her breath. She became anxious, but there was no trigger that she could identify.

One minute she was enjoying the silence and the smell of the Thundercat's cockpit, then the next she wanted to run out and get into a wide-open space where she could extend her arms. Something about that would calm her down when she was feeling trapped or closed-in, and that was how she felt now, as if she would never be able to escape that cockpit.

She bravely fought through the discomfort until the checks were finished, then quickly made her way off the Thundercat. When she descended the ramp to gain the hangar and dock, Helga stopped, frozen in her tracks.

Despite the expensive clothing—which at one point was probably adorned with even more expensive jewelry—the belly of the *Ursula* had somehow transformed into a hub.

Helga hadn't noticed the similarity before when she had defeated her angst to walk amongst their guests, but now it hit her like a trace-laser broadside from a cloaked infiltrator.

She found it fascinating how different the once empty compartments and makeshift storage looked now that they were used as berthing. The satellite from which they were rescued had been the only hub Helga had visited, and though she hadn't taken the time to look inside many of the crate homes, she had seen enough photos and vids to know what to expect inside of them.

There were too few people here to consider it a proper "hub," or refugee camp, but the clothes hanging from the overheads and sloppy upkeep of the general area gave her flashes of that desperate reality.

It bothered her, this chaotic and sloppy transformation; it was further evidence that their guests were privileged snots with servants who did all of their cleaning up. She wondered if they would remember to shower and eat without a lowly Arisani or Cel-toc to tell them that it was time.

Helga turned her nose up in disgust, unaware that everyone in her vicinity could read it on her face. "We'll be out of your hair soon, daughter," said an older man to her right, and it was enough to snap her out of that momentary funk.

She was about to turn on him to tell him to clear the Thundercat when a familiar alarm blared, putting fire into feet that were once planted with authoritative disdain at the state of her dock.

Sprinting as if it was an obstacle course at BLAST, Helga found the ladder leading up to the bridge's deck and scaled it skillfully to make her way to the cockpit. Zan was at the console staring forward blankly, charging as she had been ordered to do when Helga wanted absolute control.

"Snap out of it, girl, we have a situation," she ordered, and Zan, recognizing Helga's voice and tone, powered on quickly and translated the warning.

With civilians on the ship, Cilas had asked that the intercom be relegated to emergencies only, and anything relative to the ship or a perceived threat to the crew be delivered directly from their resident Cel-toc whose CPU was linked to the ship. In doing this, *Ursula* became Zan, in as much as a ship could talk and walk about, and the Nighthawks became accustomed to treating her like crew.

"Lieutenant, seventeen minutes ago an unidentified vessel came out of light speed to track our location. It is currently headed toward our vector at supercruise speed," Zan announced. "Attempts to make contact have been rejected and based on my calculations, it will break our impact perimeter within 1.5 hours. Thrust has been raised to 80% and shields maximized to reduce the chance of impact. We await your orders, Lieutenant."

"*Thype!*" Helga shouted loudly, and glanced around angrily for someone, anyone, from the crew. "Where is everyone?" she said, fighting back the panic. The bridge was clear but for the Cel-toc, and she still wasn't used to the corvette's independence of a proper crew. A situation like this should not be left to the logic-based algorithms of a machine, no matter how "real" she came off with her soothing voice, adoption of Vestalian Navy slang, and as Raileo would put it, "her anatomically perfect female form."

It was especially odd that Cilas wasn't on the bridge at this early hour, and since she had just come from the dock—which he barely ever visited—she assumed that he was in his cabin, stuck in another brief with their captain. "Hey, commander." She spoke into her wrist-comms after activating the rarely used, emergencies-only feature.

It was nearly forbidden to disturb a commanding officer while he entertained a high-ranking member of the Alliance, but Zan's report had sent a chilly spike down her spine, and with civilians on board, she did not want to risk.

Only once before had she used the emergency feature, and that was due to too much drink, her having a free cycle, and the growing casualness between she and her commander.

Helga had thought it would be funny to wake him up with an emergency comms summons, just to alert him that she was outside his door.

Cilas was normally easy when it came to her "clowning tendencies," as he labeled it, but that stunt had apparently been the invisible line being crossed. He had responded with as much urgency as could be expected from a seasoned warrior professional, but upon learning that it was a ruse, her Cilas vanished almost instantly and was replaced by Commander Mec, leader of the Nighthawks.

Not only did she not spend the night, but he did not speak to her for nearly three cycles. This wasn't so devastating—having differences and arguments were all a part of what they had—what was tough, however, was knowing that she was wrong, yet being too prideful to apologize for it.

Now, they were on great terms, and she would spend two out of five late shifts in his arms, but they had never overtly conversed over what had happened that fateful cycle. It made using it now extremely complicated, because when he answered, she knew that he would wonder if she once again was playing a game.

It had been the biggest point of discussion between them, the wonder if their coupling would affect their military service. Hesitation was death, and she had hesitated before using that option. He would likely hesitate to answer it, not wanting another awkward set of cycles, and that twisted the knife inside of Helga's heart, the fact that her drunken impulses had managed to turn her love into a liability.

"Helga," Cilas's voice came on, unamused. "If you're outside of my door, or anything short of this being a crisis, I don't care what came before this very moment, I will have you doing first shift PT rotations for five cycles along with writing out records from our last two drops. Now, what is it?"

"Commander, we have an unidentified vessel bearing down on us and it is unresponsive to the *Ursula*'s request for identification," she said, too petrified to respond in her typical, lighthearted sarcasm. "I need permission to activate hardpoints and sound the alarm for battle stations."

"Do it, I'm en route. Put a trace across their bow to let them know we are serious. Punching in my approval to the system now. Keep me posted, I'll be down as soon as I can."

Helga was one of the youngest spacers at her current rank of lieutenant junior grade. It was a position that came with much scrutiny from her peers, particularly those who only knew of her by name. To the handful of people that had experienced the Nighthawk in action, however, there was no questioning her rank or ability to win.

She was special, and though she had been reminded of this multiple times, she still had those moments when she'd stop and wonder if she'd bitten off more than she could chew.

Even now as she ran to the bridge, shouting frantically into her comms, she wondered at her position, and why it was that she had been so lucky in surviving these last two years of hell.

Either she was the luckiest spacer on Anstractor, or she was some sort of maker-selected chosen one. Seeing enough death up close, however, made it impossible to believe it was either, and what she did believe was that it was only a matter of time before her number would be up.

This fear—if you could truly call it fear—kept her extra salty whenever it was time to act, taking charge when Cilas wasn't present and being decisive with their options. Helga, as a student to both Cilas and Captain Retzo Sho, knew only excellence under pressure, so when the walls were closing in, she was at her best.

"I'm just a little girl that likes space ships," used to be her answer to outsiders commending her on her success, but the truth was that she didn't know how she'd come this far. The only thing that was certain was that none of it would have been possible without the support of the ranks that believed in her.

Her cadet commander, Loray Qu, had helped her to survive the abuse of those first years as a spacer, then there was Captain Retzo Sho to approve her application for BLAST training.

Cilas Mec accepted her onto the team, despite her being too small, and to certain parties, too female for the role, and now she had operators like Tutt and Sundown to support her in becoming better at the job.

Helga could say that she had been lucky, but did luck push people to support you even when you weren't of their blood? She was hot-blooded and she held grudges, and tripped over just about every social hurdle presented to her.

Would she like herself if she was made to serve under her? That was what she couldn't answer because even as Helga Ate, she had never been comfortable in her own skin.

"Zan," she said as the Cel-toc walked over and took the seat next to her. "Engage hardpoints and place a trace warning across that incoming's nose."

"Hardpoints have been engaged, Lieutenant," the Cel-toc said. "Tracer deployment in three, two, and one." She wasn't moving but her actions were still faster than three pilots at the helm. Zan was synched with the *Ursula*'s system, so she in essence was the ship.

When Helga commanded her to engage hardpoints, it was a mere thought become action, just like the firing of the tracers. "Unidentified vessel has altered course, Lieutenant. I await your next command."

"So our friend values his life," Helga said under her breath, and wondered what should be their next step.

"Unidentified vessel has increased thrust," Zan reported mechanically. "Collision is imminent. I suggest that we take evasive maneuvers."

"Do it," Helga shouted, grabbing her wrist-comms. "Ray, get on a cannon and put some holes in her hull. Tutt, get our passengers inside their cages, and tell them to strap in. Everybody else, battle stations. I need as much firepower on that ship as we can manage."

Helga grabbed the controls, strapped in and placed her feet up on the deck, easing back as if she was in a fighter instead of a slow-moving, armored corvette. She increased their thrust, barely avoiding the incoming ship, which was much smaller than their own but was armed with torpedoes and energy cannons.

Raileo Lei was on one of the cannons, whittling down the enemy's shields as it put out a tracer, forcing Helga into evasive maneuvers. The result was a jolting escape from the vicinity of the laser, and Helga brought them about to the side where the tracer could never reach.

Broadside to broadside, they exchanged cannon fire, and the *Ursula*'s alarm began to blare, warning its occupants that the enemy was arming a torpedo.

Their shields were at 70% and dropping, but Helga knew that the enemy was worse off than they were. Zan was arming a torpedo, and when the shields fell they would break that suicidal ship's spine in half.

A chase like this, using a technique as insanely violent as a ram, had to be pirates, and Helga was confident that it was the same ones, coming to get their cargo.

"Willing to call my bluff and we don't even know each other," Helga said, as if the ship's captain could hear her.

"Tracers online, Ate?" Cilas said from his chair behind her, and she was stunned for half-a-second, wondering why he hadn't stepped in earlier.

Maybe he just got here, Helga thought, putting it out of her mind. "Trace laser is ready, Commander," she said, proudly, loving to see Cilas take charge as an actual warship captain.

"Gut the *thype*, then pull us out to prepare to nuke her from a safe distance," he said.

"Zan, tracers on the broadside, coupled with our cannons. When the shield fails, exhaust the trace, then jump us out to a safe distance for torpedo deployment."

"Yes, Lieutenant," the Cel-toc said, and for an instant Helga looked over, loving the ease of delegating. Whatever she said would happen, and there would be no botched clicks, overloading, or any of the other human mistakes.

She watched the ship try to pull away as the *Ursula's* accurate cannon fire put a strain on their shields. Helga let them pull off before bringing them to face their attacker, who had now become the runner.

"Zan, what are you waiting for, girl? Let fly my tracers and split them," she said.

From the *Ursula* came several long columns of laser light, tearing a gash wide enough to fly a transport through. The vessel veered away from the *Ursula*, who was now flying circles about her like a predator.

The desperate captain engaged thrusters, flying perpendicular to the *Ursula's* cycle, but Helga, anticipating them doing this, reduced thrust and locked on to where the thrusters and engine stood out.

"Put a torpedo on that region, Zan," she said, then looked back at Cilas for confirmation.

"Horrible waste of life if you ask me," he said. "You see what they force us to do, with threatening these people?"

He nodded his approval and sat back down inside his chair. The result was glorious, a flash of light, that left a cascade of color in its wake. They had struck the exposed crystal core, which in turn crippled the ship.

"Harpoon that floater, Ate, and anchor us here pending an investigation. I want to board that ship and see who they are to attack us, and then hopefully we can get back to ESO business," Cilas said.

9

Helga stared out through the large window above the *Ursula's* cockpit, watching the three dark figures making their way out to the disabled ship. It was a common exercise for the Nighthawks, spacewalking to invade an enemy vessel.

Normally they were all together, the four ESO's and now Sundown, but Cilas had commanded her to stay so that he could take the lead. It wasn't a decision that she could argue; there needed to be an officer to hold down the bridge.

The choice was made for the rest of the Nighthawks: Cilas, Quentin Tutt, and Raileo Lei. Helga and Sundown were left behind, so she busied herself getting prepared for any disaster that could possibly occur.

They had tethered the wreckage, so now they were sitting ducks, stalled out and vulnerable to any other attackers. She instructed Zan to keep the hardpoints on, and to charge a torpedo, ready to fire on her command.

Shields were undergoing repairs, though the energy for the weapons made it slow. After their brief, she had instructed Sundown to see to their passengers below deck. To Helga's surprise, Dr. Rai'to joined him as they went from cage to cage, checking to make sure that the Vestalians were doing fine.

Once they completed that simple job, the pair left together for medbay, which gave Helga pause as she began to wonder if she was wrong about the doctor being with Raileo Lei.

Had she mistaken innocence and kindness for love and affection for the young Nighthawk? Raileo did admit to manipulating Cilas to bring the doctor onboard, however, so she pushed aside her assumptions to focus on the men finally reaching the disabled ship.

What Cleia Rai'to did with her time was none of her business, anyway. So what if she had two Nighthawks vying for her attention? She was an extremely good-looking woman, and that sort of attention was the curse of being attractive.

What worried Helga, despite it not being her business, was the conflict that could result from having a love triangle on such a small ship. It had worried her when she thought that Raileo was somewhat interested in her, and selfishly she knew that any such conflict would bring a quick end to what she and Cilas had.

Even Helga had to admit that had it been her, she would find any excuse to be with Cilas. He was her man, but beyond the tenderness that they shared, he had the biggest bed that she had ever slept in.

Even now, she considered climbing the ladder and using his cabin to play at being captain. It was juvenile, she knew, but it was one of those mischievous goals she intended to act on one of these cycles.

Instinctively, she felt the need to check in on their passengers, just in case there was something that Sundown had neglected to report. Instead of pulling up the feed on the HUD, she walked back to CIC, then made her way towards the mess.

On her wrist-comms was a small link, showing the life signs of Cilas Mec, Raileo Lei, and Quentin Tutt, and though she could hear them in her ear, she kept glancing down at it, as if anticipating disaster.

Helga walked over to a terminal and stared out at the eighteen civilians in the dock. She no longer felt hostile towards them but still more than anything else wished that they were off the *Ursula*. Having them onboard complicated the Nighthawk's lives; not only socially but the strategic decisions made in combat as well.

An ESO knew death's gruesome visage better than most, but these wealthy humans from the mountains of Arisani were not to be harmed or put in the way of danger, which were Cilas's orders via the captain. Having them here limited options, and limited options were a liability where space combat was concerned.

Now instead of charging in to use shield and thrust manipulation to outwit the enemy, they would have to run and do what they could to stay out of the fight. She smelled the leather before she could detect Sundown's presence, and though she hated when he would sneak up like this she continued staring forward at the screen.

"Starting to think you have a little crush there, Jumper," she joked, finding it hard not to smile in anticipation of his response.

"I am afraid that your senses need a lot more honing, la'una. This Jumper's heart is on ice until he is again acknowledged by his brothers in the agency."

"And?" she said under her breath, expecting a snarky follow-up. Sundown could pick up on sarcasm and innuendo better than anyone she knew, and would answer with something wise and above her head, before adding his own sly comeback.

"And, I don't think your commander would approve of me attempting to dock within an occupied station."

It took all of the willpower Helga had to not turn on him angrily to inquire what exactly he was hinting at. He knew about her and Cilas, and though she had assumed it, this last quip was more than enough of a hint that he was in the know. She inhaled and held it until she started to feel her head float, then exhaled it steadily, no longer able to focus on the terminal.

"Hey Sunny, I know we're joking around, but can I ask you to make that topic classified, as in never bring it up again?" she said.

"I am a Jumper, and we don't know gossip, la'una. What we speak about, regardless of topic, stays between you and me," he said.

"Great," she said, now turning to square up with him, crossing her arms. "So, you've given me a new nickname and I haven't a clue what it means. If this is another half-alien slur, I'll give you a name that you will never live down, and all the Nighthawks will be ordered to use it on you. Now, what is a la'una?"

He smiled again, and she took notice of how much easier he was now that they had discussed her Seeker gift.

"Ahh, I get ahead of myself, Helga. La'una is a Virulian word, and I struggle to find a good Vestalian meaning. The closest I can come up with is, child that hasn't fully realized her potential, or maybe, a scholar that has only begun to truly study. It isn't meant to be offensive, especially the child portion, which I now see can be misinterpreted considering the differences in our age, but you can—"

"So it's a cute name for someone with my abilities that hasn't the faintest clue as to how to control them?" she said, watching his dark, bloodshot eyes.

"Yes and no, but in time perhaps I will find better words to explain it. For Virulians it is a word within the heart spectrum of our language. We do not call everyone with your potential 'la'una.' It is reserved for the top students, normally called that by their masters, or fathers with their sons, mothers with their daughters. Do you understand?"

"Yes," she said, feeling a bit embarrassed. "You're saying that you see something inside of me, and you care enough to give me a Virulian pet name. Are you trying to be my daddy, Sundown?"

"No, but as far as rituals are concerned, we have bonded whether we want to be or not. We have exchanged life debts, spilled blood, and shared knowledge of the dark education. For me as a Jumper to ignore this energy would take violating everything that makes me what I am."

"I like you too, Sunny, but right now all I'm concerned with is getting us away from that ship. We're ripe for an ambush if we're not careful lingering about, and I'm of the mind that our captive there is implanted with a tracker, sending our location back to those pirates."

"Have you told the commander?"

"He knows, but we can't do much about it," Helga said, turning back to the terminal. "You remember Wolf? Oh, wait, you weren't with us then, but yeah, the last hostage we had with us was back on Meluvia, and he came with a tracker node hidden beneath his skin. We already scanned our pirate friend, but unlike Wolf, we can't just cut him open to find the bug and disable it. So, here we stand, waiting to be ambushed inside of a recovering ship."

"Let them come," Sundown said, as if her concern was as menial as wanting more wine for their stores. "After this victory, and our sacking the station, if these men don't know they're outclassed, then they deserve everything coming to them if they continue to pursue our ship. No, Helga, I doubt there will be anymore coming. What is likely to happen is more pressure being levied to the Genesians to pay their ransom.

"That prince they have in captivity, he is worth more credits than you can imagine, and there will be important people who do not subscribe to the laws of our Alliance willing to give the outlaws whatever they want for that man to taste freedom again. We should be very careful moving forward, as I believe that our actions could set off a shockwave that comes at the price of numerous lives."

"We're only here for the transfer, but these Arisanis are taking their time." Helga sighed. "I want them gone, Sunny, like last cycle, because then we can return to the mission and get away from playing transport."

"On that we agree, young Ate. I too wish to see what the Geralos have hidden on that moon."

"You haven't had a chance to use your new las-sword either," she said, smiling. "You would never admit to wanting to use it, but I can't wait to see you in action with that thing."

There was a buzz inside her ears before Cilas's commanding voice came on. He sounded hushed and out of breath, as if he'd just finished running or fending the enemy off. "*Ursula* command, this is Rend. Do you copy? Hellgate, are you there?" he said, using callsigns and codenames the way they were taught. When communicating across an open comm-link, you never knew who or what could intercept your signal.

"This is Hellgate, with Sunny. What's the situation?" Helga replied.

"Thrust is on cruise, and we're looking good, but stay on standby just in case we need rescue. The enemy is disorganized and panicked, so barring complications, we should have control within the next hour."

"I'll hold you to that," she whispered, but he was already gone and she felt foolish for uttering those words. *That was too casual*, she thought, inwardly scolding herself for the faux pas. *I need to be careful.*

"Have you told him what you are yet?" Sundown said, causing her to look over at him wide-eyed, as if she'd just swallowed a ration bar whole. She didn't realize that he had heard her, and now her face was flush with embarrassment.

It was a legitimate question, being that it came from the one person who would understand her struggles, but this did nothing to belay the anxiety that came rushing into Helga's mind, causing her to feel suddenly fatigued.

Of course she wanted to tell Cilas that she was one of the gifted that the Geralos sought, but what would come from that? He would have to tell Captain Retzo Sho, and then she would be sidelined to avoid contact with the enemy, or worse, promoted to a position that guaranteed her stay, safely onboard the ship.

Helga was quiet for a long period of time, unaware that Sundown, seeing her struggling, now regretted asking.

But her paralysis soon broke for her to stutter out an answer. "Excuse me?" she tried, and when he gestured for her to ignore him, it only served to make it worse. "I'm, I mean that I do plan to, but haven't and … well, you know how it is, Sunny. Should I? Does it even matter if he knows?"

"In the case of children, you may want—"

"Sunny," she said, louder than she wanted, but it was out before she could compose herself, embarrassed that he would suggest something so absurd. "We are not having children. What in the worlds would make you ... *thype*, man, no, there won't be any children. If that's what you're concerned about, I will never falter where that is concerned. Think I want to give the Alliance another poor child to mold into one of us? You can forget that *schtill*, man, not going to happen. Moving on," she said loudly, as if to drive the point home that they were finished with that discussion. "Earlier on the dock, when you looked in on our passengers, how were they managing down there?"

"Restless, frightened, and demanding," Sundown said quietly. "Most of them have key positions in the government, and wanted me to ask the commander if they could use the communicator to send a message back home. I had to explain the difficulty in doing such a thing, and explain that there were limits to what we—the rescuers— will do for them." He sighed. "Of course, the correspondence they want isn't even dire, just political queries, and a bunch of minor quips that could really be handled within the ten cycles or so it will take to get them back to the planet. The doctor was a great help in keeping emotions in check, often translating my meaning when I came off too harsh."

"So, they listened to her," Helga said, pleasantly surprised to hear this about Cleia Rai'to.

"She's an impressive individual," Sundown said, and then there was enough of a pause to have Helga wondering whether or not he would say more. "As you know, I've lived on Sanctuary for over a Vestalian year, and in that time I have come across all manner of abusers in positions that gave them access to countless lives. Doctors and security officials are trusted to carry out the duty of their station without much oversight, and on Sanctuary more than anywhere else, the abuse I witnessed was extensive.

"Dr. Rai'to, and the humble way in which she carries herself, despite having one of the hardest degrees in her field ... well, that alone tells you, doesn't it? She's one of those rare breeds, doing a job not for credits or position, but because she really does care. Down there she took control, speaking to the Vestalians, and taking note of their ailments and provisions that they needed. They not only listened to her words, but one magistrate offered her a position. She refused it, Helga. We're talking about an Arisani clinical job, beyond the war, and with enough pay to have her living like a queen."

"*Thype* me for being the only spacer on this ship that the good doctor hasn't won over with her charm," Helga said, glancing over at him.

"I'm surprised," Sundown said. "She speaks highly of you on a consistent basis. One would argue that she admires you greatly, and wishes to be like you in many ways."

Well look at me playing the part of the insufferable jerk now, Helga thought, feeling terrible for questioning the doctor's motives.

"I don't deserve that level of adoration from someone as accomplished as you make her out to be. I'm just another unwanted, mixed-species brat that got left outside the front door of the Alliance's starport. Even now I second-guess myself, because life is moving fast and I have yet to figure out where it's taking me."

"You don't give yourself enough credit. From what I see, your career is on a collision course with command or a second seat to an Alliance figurehead," Sundown said.

"Nice of you to say those things, Sunny, but I wish that my career meant more than it actually does to me. I feel like I've been going through the motions, leaning on Cilas and Captain Sho to be my sole point of navigation. I keep thinking that one day a light will go off, and everything will make sense to me in this universe. Not meaning-of-life stuff, but clarity and purpose for why we are where we are, and what I want my piece to be. These last few years I've just been following orders and accepting what comes from that, but I have to tell you, Sunny, it isn't enough."

"Why don't I have any real individuality anymore? When I set out to be a Nighthawk, I had goals and aspirations just like everyone else. Now it's just a blank, and to be honest it's truly frightening."

"One day you are going to see something, or be somewhere that will reignite that want for something of your own, la'una," he said. "On these missions that take all of your focus to dodge and deliver death in the art of fighting, you don't get to be romantic or reflective until the smoke clears. You and I both know that in the aftermath, the pain of reflecting is much to bear, and from what you've told me, you are unwilling to face it, so it keeps you in a state of going nowhere."

"I knew that you would somehow work this back to me facing my fears and whatever other rhetoric is inside that Jumper code of yours," she said, smiling.

"Doesn't make it any less true, now does it?" he said, and though she wouldn't give him the pleasure of seeing her agree with him, inside her mind Helga decided that he was right.

10

Upon reaching the hull of the disabled cruiser, Cilas Mec and the Nighthawks worked their way into the hole created by the *Ursula's* torpedo, and Raileo went to work, hacking a door that had been sealed in order to protect what was left of the ship.

They were through it in minutes, resealing it behind them as they took to a wide, hexagonal passageway, but an alarm started to blare, warning the ship that there had been a loss of atmosphere.

"We're exposed," Cilas grunted into the comms of his PAS. "Stay sharp, they may have civilian captives. Fall in on me. Ray, cover our flanks; we're going straight for the bridge. Don't get distracted."

Jogging at half speed with his auto-rifle primed with soft kinetic rounds, Cilas was surprised to find the ship as empty as it was. Doors stood open, some malfunctioned from the electrical failure caused again by the torpedo to the ship's main generator.

There were a few corpses, and it soon became obvious that the crew had been ordered to abandon the deck.

"Ladder," Quentin announced, and Cilas reached for it and started up with the two Nighthawks close behind. After four steps he pushed down hard and jumped, pulsing his rocket boots to take him up several rungs until he emerged on another deck.

They were in a small space, with a solitary door that opened out into a passageway that looked more merchant ship than Navy. There were supplies and replacement gear hanging from the bulkhead, and the overhead too was laden with equipment.

As they crept down it quickly they came upon more effects from the *Ursula's* payload. Through a fallen door, with the atmosphere smoky and stinking of extinguisher cream, lay an open mess hall damaged beyond repair, the lights flickering and sparking from where wires had been shredded.

"We did a number on this beast, didn't we?" Raileo said, grinning, and Cilas fought back the urge to scold him about staying focused on the mission.

He didn't have to tell the Nighthawk. Raileo was always ready, despite his penchant for jokes at the most inconvenient times, and had saved their lives in several situations where his immaculate aim caught the enemy by surprise.

Cilas saw movement, so he slid down to a knee and stared into the scope of his auto-rifle. The reticle took on a deep-red glow, indicating organic life, so he waited to see if he could make out what it was before alerting his men to go in.

A blue, unshaved face poked out and glanced in his direction and Cilas squeezed the trigger and dropped it immediately. Quentin and Raileo, picking up on his cue, rushed into the compartment and took up positions behind tables, firing back at four other figures that had started shooting at them.

Cilas duck-walked past several fallen chairs, relying on the armor of his PAS to keep him alive. One of the men who was shooting saw him approach, but before he could pick off the exposed Nighthawk, Cilas put another round through his head.

The other three fell fast, two from Quentin, and one—a runner—cut down by Raileo's sidearm. "Press deeper, they're guarding something," Cilas said, and they cleared the mess before exiting back out into the passageway, running now as if something sinister was imminent, until they found another ladder leading up. Here it became interesting as they climbed into another cramped compartment.

"Judging by the size of this junker, this is the bridge deck, and we're going to have resistance," Cilas said.

He urged open the door, and stared upon row upon row of Vestalian spacers, tethered to the bulkhead like stashed cargo, every one of them in an EVA suit, and possibly in stasis for the journey.

Beyond them was a sealed door, which Cilas knew would take them to the bridge. "What are they doing here?" Cilas whispered, staring through the mask of one of the sleepers, trying in vain to determine whether they had been put here voluntarily or forced.

"Maybe we can get Cleia—I mean, Dr. Rai'to on the comms with a visual sync to find out?" Raileo offered, and Cilas looked at him skeptically, knowing the mask would hide his suspicions from the young Nighthawk.

Since the arrival of the doctor—who he would be the first to admit was a much needed and excellent addition to the team—he had seen a change in the sniper, who had gone from childish prankster to focused team member all of a sudden.

Still, his suggestion had merit, and having a medical professional on hand could get them the answer they needed quickly, rather than reaching out to *Rendron* the way they had before.

"Get her on comms quickly, to run her diagnostics or whatever," Cilas said. "Tutt, you cover that exit, and I'll watch this one. Ray, you have three minutes, and pray that this isn't a decoy or trap that we've willingly stepped into."

"Aye aye, Commander," Raileo said excitedly, and then his comms went silent as he reached out on a private line to the doctor. Cilas and Tutt exchanged knowing glances and the bigger man shook his head.

Unlike Cilas and Raileo, he wasn't creeping around with a crew member, and though Cilas knew that they knew—through body language and barely disguised innuendo in their off-the-record chats—he didn't like the fact that he had been tricked into bringing the Traxian onboard.

He could hear Helga's suppositions bouncing around in his head: "What if they split and hate each other, then Ray gets hurt and she's forced to treat him?" or, "How do we know she isn't some Alliance counselor's plant, playing at spy for our ESO business, all while pretending to be our doctor?"

He chose not to dwell on these thoughts because of the fact that he too had crossed the line with his young, feisty lieutenant. If he said anything, Raileo could volley back his concerns, and what could he say to that, outside of, "Yes, I'm a hypocrite, but Helga is different."

What a mess I've allowed myself to be in, he thought, watching the door as he knelt with his auto-rifle raised and ready. "Ray, how's it coming?"

"Patching her through now, Commander," he said, and then Cleia's melodious voice was on the comms, guiding Raileo on examining the equipment to see what had been done.

"Those people are in a peculiar state of cryogenic stasis. Frozen within their EVA suits," she said quietly. "Possible cause is lengthy travel with a shortage on supplies. Life signs are normal, however, though there are several species represented that won't do well once revived. It's unorthodox, but a good solution for preservation in a ship that lacks enough proper cryogenic equipment. The subject that you are observing, Raileo, is a 52-year-old, Arisani female. The one next to her is Vestalian, and looks to be in his twenties, which is comparable based on lifespans. Perhaps this is the replacement crew for the ones that are operating the ship, currently?"

"Perhaps, Dr. Rai'to," Cilas said, feeling a slight chill. "Though I disagree with your hypothesis on these being crew. Some have cuts and bruises on their face, so my guess is that they are cargo, stored to be bought and sold at a future station. That complicates this salvage. We can't very well just clear, strip, and reduce her to debris." He sighed audibly. "Ate, you there?" he said, connecting to her comms. "Go to my cabin and find the communicator. We need to alert the captain to what we just found, and request a rescue immediately from any Alliance ship in the sector."

"Aye aye, Rend, I am on my way," she said, though he could hear the hesitation in her voice, wanting to ask him why.

"Alright, we've lingered too long, let's get moving," he said. "With this important cargo occupying this space, there's bound to be something waiting on the other side of that door."

He checked the HUD for their readouts and saw that his were the only shields below 100%. Raileo's heart rate had increased. Was the ice-cold sniper suddenly afraid? Or did it have to do with whatever private discussion was now happening between him and the doctor?

I'm going to have to talk to that man, he thought, already dreading the exchange. What was he to say? "Stop this thing between you and the Traxian?" As if that wouldn't drive Raileo closer to her, or force him to call out the hypocrisy.

It made him miss the old crew, where all that mattered to them was the mission. Sure, some of the men disliked a brother or two, but that only came out during idle times, when they were impatiently waiting for an assignment.

This new crew, for all its talents, however, were more than Nighthawks, and it made his role difficult. They were friends, and lovers, with a new doctor that hailed from Sanctuary station, who had no Navy connection, outside of the young, rash, Raileo Lei.

"Are you good, brother?" Quentin said in his ear, and Cilas saw that they were waiting on his command.

"Yeah, I'm about to crack the lid on this bio-extraction unit," he said, amused at his own joke. "*Schtill* is bound to fly out, so sound off when you're ready."

Both Nighthawks confirmed, so he activated the locking mechanism that screeched an alarm before the circular door spun counterclockwise and hissed before collapsing into itself. Cilas's PAS shields were back to being fully charged, so he took up point and stepped out into another compartment.

The bio-extractor on a ship was a mechanism that collected the waste from the heads and broke it down into chemical properties. The reusable fluid and minerals were processed for a number of uses, none being consummation or contact with the organics in the crew, while the remaining, vile-smelling refuse was "extracted" out into space with the rest of the trash.

Cadet academy boomers often joked about the contents of a bio-extractor, so when Cilas pulled open the door, both Quentin and Raileo knew to expect a world of hurt. Expectations were met as a shot struck Cilas in the shoulder, spinning him out and away from the open portal.

Stunned, heart racing, and eyes moving about rapidly to assess his health, Nighthawks, and readouts, Cilas stood to the right of the doorway with his back against the bulkhead.

Shields were at 20%. Whatever had hit him had been enough to render his PAS nearly worthless. Quentin was on the other side of the door, and Raileo Lei was in the back, lying flat on his stomach, using a raised portion of the deck for cover.

They were both firing back through the door, and Cilas put the auto-rifle to his chest and tried a deep breath to calm his nerves.

"Arming a bomblet," Quentin announced, bringing Cilas out of his daze to gesture for him to stop.

"They're next to an exposed power supply," Cilas said. "That's why they chose that passageway, it connects to the engine room, and presents them with a natural dead man's switch. Blow them up and the ship follows along with us, and with it being tethered to the *Ursula*, it may do enough to cripple her. No, we need to play this smart with precision shots and suppression. Ray, you're quiet. What's your situation?"

"I'm looking at a case of sealant next to that power supply, Commander. If I can hit one of those cans, it will explode and take the rest out with it. I'm thinking that will cause the ruckus we need," the young man said.

"It could work, but if it doesn't, I want you to go fully auto so that Q and I can move in on these *thypes*," Cilas said. He looked over at

Quentin, who seemed perched on the edge of action as he leaned towards the open doorway, fidgeting with his pulse-rifle and looking back at Raileo.

"Taking the shot," Raileo announced, then fired a single round from the deck, where he was wedged behind a natural barrier and a fallen spacer in an EVA suit who had been clipped by one of the pirate's shots and killed.

There was a loud, popping noise, and the far compartment filled with a cloud of smoke and flames. Quentin whooped and moved in, followed closely by Cilas, who had his rifle back over his shoulder and his sidearm raised with the supporting hand gripping a knife in the ESO fashion.

They were on top of the coughing defenders, dealing death liberally like hungry wolves within a roost. Their PAS's suffered— these defenders could fight—and Cilas noticed that some wore old Alliance armor, which reflected their shots or absorbed them.

It was absolute chaos with flailing arms, blind fire, and angry screams and shouts inside that crowded passageway. Raileo Lei had come up to join his brothers against the five remaining defenders of the eight that had occupied the space.

One lay cut open and in a heap below the power supply that Cilas had warned them about, and the other two were dead from bullet wounds, one from Cilas's close-range pistol shot, and the other from Quentin.

They cleared the passageway before noticing that several men had retreated back onto the bridge. They sealed the door, and a frustrated Quentin punched the panel when it wouldn't respond to his commands.

"We can't have them in there stalling us while maker knows what is incoming," the big man shouted. Raileo shouldered his OKAGI "Widow Maker" and walked over to where he stood to try his hand at getting the door open.

While they worked on this, Cilas bent down to examine the men. Judging from their clothes, they were definitely pirates, dressed in a motley of armor and expensive fabric stolen from the Arisanis they had ravaged earlier. Their weapons were neither Alliance nor Geralos; they were kinetic pistols and rifles, meant for hunting animals or killing innocents that didn't wear armor.

Cilas found this to be confusing being that earlier he had been shot with something that would have killed him if not for his personal shield generator.

"There's a fusion cannon missing here, Nighthawks, be careful with that door. You saw what it did to me, and I was hoping that we got to the *schtill* who hit me. He's bound to be in there setting up another ambush, and as soon as we get in, he will hit us."

He looked around and his mask adjusted, clearing the smoke to give more detail to where they were. To the left of the door that Raileo was working on stood a large bay window out of which he saw the *Ursula* looming, its bow and cockpit visible.

They were running out of time, and with so many lives at stake, he found himself petrified at making the wrong decision. "Ray," he said, "how much longer will that take?"

"It's going to be a bit, sir, and I suspect that they're rigging it to explode as soon as it comes open. Our only advantage is our PAS, and the fact that we're shielded from exposure. I say thirty minutes and we can punch through, but we're bound to have a surprise waiting inside," he said.

"Any thoughts Q?" Cilas said, looking over at the big man who was pacing impatiently in front of the door.

"Is there a vent? Maybe one of us could get around by crawling through that," he suggested. "Or maybe going out to the hull, the way we did back on *Rendron* to shut down Aurora."

Cilas thought about what he was suggesting, then switched his comms to private and called up Helga. "Ate, are you listening in?" he whispered.

"We're here," she said, "and we can see movement through the windows of their bridge. Sunny has locked in surveillance to see if he can make out what is happening over there."

"Their shields are down, correct?" he said and she confirmed, making him stop and rub at the back of his neck, conflicted with his decision. "Tell you what, scan the bridge for any lifeforms that look trapped, bound, placed in stasis, or duress. I want to know if there's only bad guys on that bridge, and if there's any civilians present, I want you back on these comms immediately."

"Orders received loud and clear, Commander. Please stand by while I have Zan run some scans."

She clicked off and Cilas walked over to touch Raileo's shoulder.

"Leave that alone; we're leaving. I'm about to have Ate lase the bridge and suck them out. Once it's cleared we're going to enter it from the outside, access the console, and activate blast shields to plug up the exposure. We've done all we can to investigate, and we don't have time to salvage or *thype* around anymore."

"We're leaving her stranded?" Quentin said, gesturing about him to indicate the vessel.

"No choice now that they're likely calling in reinforcements. We'll spare the time to get the prisoners onto the *Ursula*; at least that should be easy since they're all in EVA suits. Then pull what we can from the console, star maps, correspondence records, whatever, and then we'll reduce this *schtill* to stardust and be out of the system, double time."

"What about the meet-up that's supposed to happen with the Arisanis to get their people?" Quentin said.

"It was a setup, Q," Cilas said quietly as he walked back to the compartment with the prisoners hanging unconsciously against the bulkhead. "I will speak to the captain, but as far as I am concerned, we were set up by someone on *A'wfa Terracydes*. That will be our next stop, to not only drop off our passengers but to get some answers on what happened here. The captain will understand my decision to pursue this perceived threat. And if we can find who did it, we can pull out more answers on this whole pirate situation."

"Rend, you there?" Helga said in his ear, and he confirmed with a grunt before stopping and waiting to hear what she'd found on the bridge. "I have three Vestalian traitors, armed, and one is performing surgery on that door panel, likely to be rigging it to do something nasty upon entry. They don't seem right, Cilas... they seem robotic, if that makes sense."

"Blow out the window," Cilas said, not bothering to concern himself with the behavior that Helga reported. "Time to move," he announced and started moving towards the far door, leading them away from the bridge. "Good work, Nighthawks. We cleared her properly, but you cannot predict the actions of desperate men. These *thypes* are selling our people to the enemy, and have made it a point to attack us to try and slow us down. Time to take the offensive, what do you say?"

"Let's go," Quentin shouted, drowning out Raileo's response, which came off like a grunt of exasperated readiness. An alarm blared as the ship shook from the *Ursula's* cannon fire, which on Cilas's command had shredded the reinforced pressure-glass on the bridge.

The Nighthawks were moving, switching to rockets to navigate the ladderwells and passageways to get out of the ship. No one spoke; they were all of a single mind to mount a speedy rescue before getting back onboard the *Ursula*.

As always, things did not end up the way they planned, but Cilas was sure he had made the right decision.

Still, something inside him made him wonder if this was true.

11

In the cycle that followed the Nighthawk's return to *Ursula*, it was all hands on deck for not only bringing onboard the surviving captives, but to reconfigure the dock to house some of the more stable Vestalians from medbay. There was only so much space, and the beds had been taken up by the wounded from the satellite rescue. Additional stations had to be made from crates, portable feeding tanks, and replacement chair cushions.

Helga was impressed by their guests, who she assumed would complain now that their space had become more crowded, but the Vestalians pitched in where they could to get the dock prepared, some even stopping to thank her for everything she'd done. The rescue effort was led by Dr. Rai'to, with assistance by Quentin and Helga, who was making an effort to be nicer to their new Traxian crewmember.

Cilas and Quentin took on the complicated part of the job, which was to gain access to the bridge and regain some atmosphere by sealing off the busted windows. Malfunctioning power made this difficult, and eventually the Nighthawks had to give up. Out of desperation, they grabbed the control box from the cockpit just in case the *Ursula*'s system could find a way to hack into it. If successful, they could learn the history of the ship and what purpose it served before the pirates.

Removing the box took the better part of three hours and had everyone on pins and needles, worried for their lives. With the generator ruptured from the earlier torpedo, the ship was showing signs of an unstable power core.

Helga couldn't build a jump drive or explain in detail how the technology worked, but she, like most pilots of her quality, knew that an unstable core was death, which was precisely why she'd ordered

Zan to strike at it. Her assisting Cleia Rai'to was a way to prevent herself from being on the comms pleading with Cilas to come back.

Taking the ship's control box would have taken an hour at most with an engineer or pilot that knew ships the way she did, but her command was on *Ursula*, and arguing with Cilas would have only delayed the effort further. When the time eclipsed the three-hour mark, she got on her comms and then clicked it off quickly after thinking better of it. That was when Raileo had come onto the bridge and urged her to oversee the efforts going on down on the dock.

"It could use a woman's touch," he had said, teasing her in that subtle way he would do whenever she was ready to explode with rage.

She had turned from the cockpit, ready to tear into him with a gibe of her own, but that big childish grin of his had been enough to melt the ice from her mood. Grasping his shoulder, she returned the smile, which caused him to blush and back down. His reaction made her laugh and together they went down to the dock, where she took the reins in coordinating the berths.

Thank you, Ray, she had thought to herself when Cilas reported that they had gotten what they needed, and were ready to come back onboard. Five hours later and they were untethered from the derelict and plotting a jump to Arisani space, just out of tracking distance from *A'wfa Terracydes* station. This was Cilas's direct order. They were to make the jump away from this system, and wait for his talk with Captain Retzo Sho.

His plan was to take Sundown to that station and shake down their people to learn who the pirate's mole was. If the captain didn't like this, they would coordinate a rescue, which would be instant, considering their proximity to *A'wfa Terracydes*, and limit the chances of another attempt at sabotage.

Zan confirmed the jump coordinates and turned in her seat to stare at Helga, awaiting her approval to initiate the countdown. *Ursula*'s sultry voice came over the intercom, warning all passengers to find a jump station and snap on their restraints, just in case of an emergency. It was a well-intentioned request but futile considering the number of passengers was well beyond the corvette's optimum capacity.

"This is Lieutenant Helga Ate," she said, cutting off the intercom. "Just a point of clarification for our Arisani guests on the dock. We don't have enough stations, as you can see, so I must ask that you go to your berths, lay down and strap yourselves in. Medbay crew, please make sure that all occupants are restrained and the atmosphere regulator is on blue. Tutt, Dr. Rai'to, awaiting your 'all clear' before activating this jump."

"This is Tutt, Ate, we're all good to go down here," came Quentin's voice after several long minutes of waiting.

"Lieutenant, the medbay is a go," Cleia Rai'to announced over comms, and Helga finally looked over at her synthetic pilot to give her the nod of approval. They immediately accelerated to supercruise speed, though the *Ursula*'s advanced atmosphere regulator kept the passengers clueless. Jumps could cause panic in people who didn't spend their lives on a vessel, so Helga activated blast shields as they moved out of range of the disabled junker.

They jumped to light speed after the appropriate warning, which Helga kept hidden from the crew to reduce the chance of panic. The window before her went from speckled to a distorted funnel of thin, laser-like lines, and then it darkened to blackness, as they slipped past the restrictions of time and space to emerge in another area of the galaxy at the predetermined vector outlined by the *Ursula*'s system.

As expected, the massive red form of the planet Arisani appeared when reality adjusted in front of her. Helga kept the system on mute and relied on Zan to relay to her the status of the ship.

"Commander, we have reached our destination," she announced to Cilas behind her, who thanked her before removing his restraints and retreating to his cabin to contact the captain. "Nighthawks, *Ursula* crew, and guests, we've come out of light speed," Helga said. "Feel free to move about the ship and resume your regular duties and activities."

She stood up and reached over to place a hand on Zan's shoulder, which was rewarded with a look of bashfulness, followed by a big warm smile. This caught Helga by surprise. She didn't know much about Cel-tocs to experience just how like people they were, and since this was the first time that she'd touched her, it was also surprising how real and organic she felt beneath the uniform.

Helga wanted to tell her just how proud she was for her actions during the assault of the pirate ship, but decided that the touch would be enough to convey her thoughts. Inside her chest was a heaviness, a presence of nerves, and she didn't know why. They had left the unstable vessel, and were now underway to dropping off their passengers, and the Nighthawks had returned without anyone being hurt or left behind.

Logically she knew these things to be true, and they should have been enough to put her mind at rest. But for some reason she felt as if they had forgotten something, or were about to make a dreadful mistake.

Oh, how she hated this feeling, this crawling discomfort that lay below the surface. She would much rather deal with a definitive enemy, slight, or upcoming threat than this mysterious fog that refused to come clear. She growled audibly and decided it was time for a walk. They would be at supercruise for half a cycle, and she didn't want to spend it staring out at the streaming stars.

Helga could hear Sundown's voice inside her head telling her to face the source of her worry rather than run away and look for a distraction. *Maybe now is the time for me to depress myself with that internal fight*, she thought, half-jogging to the stern of the ship, looking for a compartment—any compartment to isolate herself from the men.

She stopped in front of the briefing room, which they had used once for the satellite mission. It was perfect. No one outside of Cilas was likely to happen by, and he would be on a lengthy call with their captain. Closing the door, she grabbed one of the chairs and sat staring at the translucent planet rotating slowly above the central table.

Helga decided that she was lonely. Despite everyone being nice and respectful, she wasn't truly free to be herself. She could if she wanted to, Raileo would love it, and Quentin would ignore her immature jokes, but as their lieutenant there was that invisible wall of respect that would only become weak with her antics. Even Cilas, who had seen every bit of her 160 cm frame, was still too much of an authority for her to let her hair down fully.

She missed Joy Valance, and wished she had her here to chat. Despite their rivalries—which were as significant as they were superficial—Joy had become something of a family member to the Nighthawk. If she were here now, there would be laughter in the atmosphere, and no matter her anxiety, Helga would at the very least feel loved.

Thinking this made her realize that this was the ache inside her heart. It had been lonely without her sister, and she wasn't yet ready to let anyone else inside. While sharing the commander's bed provided warmth, she knew that they were merely using one another, and it would never go beyond physical gratification. That cold wall of duty prevented him from ever claiming her overtly, and it wasn't bringing them closer; quite the opposite.

Sitting forward, she grabbed her hair while resting her elbows on her knees, then closed her eyes and thought more on Joy and everything that came with her memory. There was angry Joy, screaming at her on the bridge of the *Inginus* to dress in her flight suit when coming to one of her briefs. Then loving Joy, hugging her closely by the fire on Meluvia as they looked up into the sky, wondering if *Rendron* would survive the night. Feisty Joy was a constant, and gentle Joy was reserved for Cilas.

Was it guilt she was feeling now as she reminisced about her friend? Guilt for taking her place in the commander's arms, yet delaying correspondence out of fear of having to tell her what they were doing. Tears fell to the deck as her chest began to ache, not over Joy, but this refusal to allow herself any happiness. She needed a drink.

"No," she whispered. "No more crutches. Nighthawks persevere."

It was enough to slow her tears, and she sat back suddenly and took a breath. High emotions like this weren't new, but digging into the source was the plan, and alcohol was merely a distraction. Several deep breaths followed by slow exhalations made her head swim with dizziness, but it served to calm her down.

"Lieutenant," came a voice in her ear, which she recognized as Zan's.

"Yes, Zan," she croaked before clearing her throat and repeating it in a stronger voice. "Yes, Zan, what is it?"

"Lieutenant, there's an urgent communication awaiting a response. It's from the station *A'wfa Terracydes*. Would you like me to patch it through?"

Helga sat up and took a breath before using her fingers to comb back her disheveled hair. It should really be Cilas to take the call, but she didn't want to disturb his communication with the captain.

"Please go ahead, Zan, I'll take it in here," she said, standing up to start pacing about the table.

"This is Angor Rian of the Anstractor Alliance. You have entered protected space and must identify yourself or we will be forced to disable your ship. Non-compliance with our directive will be considered an act of war. This is your last warning; you have five minutes to either leave this system or send us your identification."

"Oh, *schtill*," Helga whispered when Zan pushed the communication through to her wrist-comms. A holo-readout popped up, hovering just above her arm, identifying the vessel that was hailing them, and it was definitely an Alliance Marine assault ship. *Guess the Arisanis called in a favor to deal with the chance of any more pirates*, she theorized to herself. "Sergeant Rian, this is Lieutenant Helga Ate of the Nighthawks ESO, standing in for Commander Cilas Mec."

"Hold while we verify your claim, Lieutenant," Angor Rian said, and then she was on pins and needles for a grueling forty seconds while she waited. "*Rendron*?" he said when he came back, and Helga hesitated too long, questioning whether or not he said the name of their starship. "Are you from *Rendron*, Lieutenant Ate?" he repeated.

"Yes, *Rendron*," she said. "We're from the starship *Rendron* and you're with a Marine unit. How are you out here alone with no fighter presence, Sergeant Rian?"

"We're merely scouts assisting the local volunteer Corps, ma'am," he said, sounding exasperated. "There are a number of us sprinkled about to keep things safe for our allies, the Arisanis. Well, let me not keep you, Lieutenant, I know that you and your crew have a mission, though it's good to know that the *Rendron* is here to help."

"What other starships have units here?" Helga said, her curiosity too much not to ask.

"Just Helysian, but it is enough to vaporize any so-called pirate looking to come in and strong-arm vessels," he said proudly.

"Good chat, be safe Marine," Helga said.

"The same to you and yours, Lieutenant. Things must be really bad for them to request a Special Forces crew," the man said, taking on a more casual-than-usual tone.

"Let's just hope it's over soon, so that we can go back to killing lizards," she said, already out the door and heading towards the bridge to prep the crew.

She clicked off before he could say anything more, and sent a message to Cilas to update him of their status. Once he confirmed, she got on the intercom and openly announced that they were finally heading towards the station. Their passengers had been through a lot, and since the plan to pass them off to a shuttle had gone awry, she thought that right now they could use some good news.

There were no two stations alike, and *A'wfa Terracydes* was no exception; just one glance was enough to know that the rich and powerful paid for and lived within its belt. Shaped like a wine glass, with a belt about the stem and a shielded dome where the wine would normally be poured, it wasn't as massive as Sanctuary station, but what it lacked in size it made up for with style.

Docking was an automated process, and before Helga knew it, she and the Nighthawks were in their PAS suits, escorting the passengers onto the station. This they did through a docking tunnel, to the sound of music being played by a welcome party at the end of the gangway. It was so bizarre that not three times did Helga and Raileo exchange glances, and the people receiving them were so happy and jovial that it was as if there had been no pirate attack.

On the station, they were asked to give up their weapons, but Cilas pushed back aggressively, reminding the blue-uniformed officer that they were Alliance ESOs. There were some words exchanged which put Helga on edge, since a muscular Arisani was trying to remove the commander's sidearm. It was one of the passengers that defused the situation by saying something in their native tongue. The man's demeanor changed to one of deference, and Helga wondered what had been said.

"Looks like the senator there pulled rank for us," Quentin said laughing. "Arisani is a neutral planet in our war, and aside from taking in the Vestalians, they don't know what an ESO is to afford us the flexibility that other stations would. Our friend there just told them what we did on that other station. Did you see their eyes? I think they're frightened of us."

"Q, you speak Arisani?" Helga whispered, grabbing his arm to pull him close to where she waited by one of the guard rails. They were on a bridge of sorts, connecting the access tunnel to the dock, and while Cilas was handling business, she'd hung back to watch his flank.

"Some, from my past life as a planet buster, traipsing all about. There was a girl, Cagina Nova, she taught me much of the Imperial tongue—as they call it—and then I took some time to practice with our Vestalian guests on the *Ursula*. Some of them are important diplomats and ambassadors from Arisani nations, but most are actually retired. They were on that ship to celebrate with their prince," he said, settling in next to her with his elbows on the railing.

"This prince that they're all so concerned about. Is he their ruler, and are they all from his continent?" Helga said.

One of the younger men near them smiled and fanned the air in front of him—which was a Vestalian gesture with derogatory implications. Helga slatted her eyes and glared at him.

"You're a bit of a hard one, aren't you, Lieutenant?" he said, turning to face her now in his fancy robes. "The prince, Joras Kane, is son to our ruler, the honorable Joras Yog, but we are more than his subjects. He is my friend, which is why I was invited here. We weren't on *Lucia* to serve him, but to join him in celebration of a wonderful merger, which now might not happen unless the Alliance can stop those pirates."

"Thank you, Zelon," Quentin said. "That was a better explanation than the one I was cooking up, and I can assure you that our leaders will see to the prince's return and some righteous punishment to those traitors."

"Mr. Tutt, you were a breath of fresh air during our stay on the *Ursula*," Zelon said, walking up to clasp forearms with the giant Nighthawk. "This whole ordeal will have me in nightmares for the rest of my life, but if it had ended with the Nighthawks, and your lessons on self-defense, I would have considered it bittersweet, understand?"

Helga examined this Vestalian in his red and gold fineries that cost about as much as a small home on the planet. He was dark-skinned, bald, and reminded her of the late Cage Hem, but unlike the old master chief, this man was no warrior. While she didn't care for his confusing, sugary sweet semi-insults, she did feel bad for not having given him and the other passengers a chance. She disliked strangers since her past had given her plenty of reasons not to trust them, but on a ship so small with a handful of crew members, she could have been nicer, and his attitude revealed this.

"I'll leave you to it, good Quentin Tutt. If I see you at the bar later on, your drinks will be on my tab," he said with a wink. Before he took his leave he offered Helga a bow, then turned to leave before she could respond.

"Well, that one obviously likes you," she said when he was gone.

"Zelon is one of the good ones, Ate. He has a brother on Missio-Tral, but he's too young for me to know who he is. Much of my time on the dock these last few cycles have been with that one and the woman over there, a former Marine named Terra. She served on *Aqnaqak* until her 40th year, and then used her credits to take a one-way trip to Arisani, where she got involved in a revolution which resulted in them naming her a ruler over some territory. They all had crazy stories like that from their past, so it was quite an honor meeting and listening to them. Can you imagine retiring just to have something that major happen to you on a planet?" he said.

"It sounds too good to be true," Helga said, deciding to double-down on her disdain.

"Well, I believe them. The details were just too strange and specific to be smoke up the thrust, know what I mean?"

"I do, Nighthawk, I get it," she said as her eyes caught Cilas waving them over. "Looks like we're cleared to enter, thanks to your newfound friends in high places."

"It sure does," he said, laughing as he moved to catch up with the commander. Cilas was bordered by Cleia Rai'to, Raileo Lei, and the darkly clad Sundown.

"Race you to the bar," Raileo whispered as soon as she was within earshot, and though she knew that he was joking it was music to her ears.

12

The station of *A'wfa Terracydes* passageways were darker than a starship's and shaped like a subterranean tunnel. There were no windows looking out to remind you that you were in space, and condensation from an unknown source made the cylindrical walls sweat and the floor glisten wetly below the fluorescent lights.

Cilas, led by two armed security guards, was taken to the offices of ACLOP, the Arisani Crime and Loss Prevention services. ACLOP was the law enforcement arm of the station, and the team that coordinated the rescue of the hostages along with Captain Retzo Sho. They wore body armor similar to PAS suits, minus the rockets and HUD upgrades, and their loadout was reduced to stun batons, edged blades, and an occasional sidearm.

Seeing the five Nighthawks armed with pistols visibly still resting inside of holsters made for a number of reactions from the clueless security team. ACLOP headquarters had the same sterile, unfriendly atmosphere that Helga felt on the *Rendron's* medbay. The stark white walls and furniture reminded her that this was a place where fun was unwelcome, and the hard men and women in armor all about them drove that point home without having to say anything.

They were taken silently past several occupied desks, with what appeared to be detectives flipping through holo images and vids when they weren't taking notes or on a call. Helga expected to see a few prisoners inside of cells, but the station was big enough to lock away their undesirables on a completely different deck. This one, it turns out, was for receiving guests like themselves, and conducting interrogations.

"Nighthawks, welcome to *A'wfa Terracydes*," said a stately Arisani in a black-collared shirt, officer's pants and boots. He looked more diplomat than law enforcer, and ogled Helga curiously as he gestured for them to step inside his tiny office. "I am Trisk A'lance, and I am in charge of ACLOP's operations."

"Sergeant A'lance, I am Commander Cilas Mec," Cilas said, which gave Helga a warm feeling in her stomach when she heard him state his title and name. She still wasn't used to Cilas being a commander and captain of his own ship, even though she had been with him all throughout that ascent. "This is Lieutenant Helga Ate, my second in command, and this is Sergeant Quentin Tutt, Chief Raileo Lei, and agent Sun So-Jung of the Jumper Agency. Our ship's doctor Cleia Rai'to is also here on your station, but since this is a military affair, she has moved on to stock up on supplies."

"Welcome, welcome," Trisk A'lance said, and clasped forearms with Cilas before returning to his chair. "We have plenty to discuss about these pirate bastards, eh? So come in and take a seat, and let me see how we can help."

There were exactly five chairs facing the half-moon monstrosity he used as a desk, and above his throne—for it was a chair that was bigger than any Helga had ever seen—was a beautiful painting of what she could only assume was an Arisani goddess.

The figure was resplendent in a white robe, which blended in with her alabaster skin and hair. Large, gold-rimmed eyes glowed red, burning holes into the onlooker, and the ends of her robe were a tempest holding her aloft above a body of turbulent water.

Helga didn't know the painting's meaning, but the power it exuded made her want a copy for the *Ursula*. The goddess's looks made Helga wonder at the beauty standards of the Arisani people, since she hadn't had the privilege of meeting one until now.

From a human standpoint, they were a good-looking species, taller than the average Vestalian, with high cheekbones and slender, muscular limbs that seemed to come from genetics and not a rigid workout discipline. Their skin was stark white from what she could see, though some varied into shades of grey. Though their skin varied in shades, all flawless and smooth in texture, their long silver hair was an absolute constant, though some of the women chose to employ the usage of dyes.

She and the Nighthawks sat and waited as he and Cilas discussed the situation at hand with the pirates, and he relayed to the Arisani how there was a possible mole on the station, sending the pirates updates on their situation. There was universal agreement until Cilas suggested that it was someone high in their power structure, possibly one of his officers. This was met with push-back, as Trisk A'lance said that there was too much at stake for an officer to lose for one to be in league with pirates.

"I respectfully disagree," Cilas said at one point, standing up to approach his desk. "We cannot afford to think of pirates as faceless thugs and killers, randomly robbing ships of cargo and crew. There is a war going on out there, and many of my people are suffering without their planet home. Some choose to fight, like those of us you see here, while others were rescued by charitable planets like your own. But there are some who see opportunity, and use the fear and hate we all feel to further fuel their ability to grift. That's what we're up against, Sergeant, it's why even your officers could be true believers, despite the fallout if they get discovered."

Trisk A'lance raised a hand to indicate understanding, then stood up and walked around to the front of the desk. "Commander Mec, you make a great point, and eloquently stated at that. For I have known greed in the most disappointing places, so I'm no fool not to consider that it could happen among our ranks. How do you suggest we find who it is? Arisani law decrees no arrest be made without proof beyond a reasonable doubt."

"We will need to put our minds together, Sergeant," he said. "We brought along the box from a ship's computer. Whoever it is will have a contact code, one we could call from in here and trace its source back to our traitor. The problem is we haven't been able to crack it, not just yet, as we were forced to jump here in order to bring your people home."

Trisk A'lance bowed. "You are heroes to the Arisani people, Commander Mec, so know that I will do my best to help get you the answers that you seek. A box, you say? As in a control box from the console of a fighter?"

"That's the one," Helga said, surprising them both, but it wasn't as if Cilas was speaking to a superior officer, so she didn't understand the reverence and respect being shown by the other men. "Ship was a luxury cruiser; probably some rich diplomat's love boat that got taken and converted into a battering ram. If you have a cipher that can hack into modern-day equipment that should be sufficient to get us the logs on their communications."

"Very good, Lieutenant. That we can do," Trisk A'lance said before turning to give Cilas a smirk. "Not much happens on a station, as you can imagine, so I'm looking forward to cracking open this box to see what was happening before that ship ran into you. The traitor hunch, I can't qualify it, but what I look forward to finding is exactly where this ship was taken, and who was on the manifest prior to it being robbed."

"Bound to be hundreds of dead people, or worse, Geralos captives. Are you sure you want to go prying into that sad reality, Sergeant?" Cilas said.

"Plenty of people have been missing over the years," Trisk A'lance said, his voice barely a whisper as if the words caused him pain. "Had the people on the *Lucia* not fought the way they did, they too would have just vanished, and us none the wiser for it. That is why you are heroes. You brought back survivors that were there, people who fought to reveal these pirates, so we now have an answer to the disappearances. So to answer your question, Commander, yes. That sad reality will provide some closure to a lot of families here."

"I understand fully, Sergeant A'lance, and I hope you find it, but I look forward to reading those logs to see what communications were made on this station."

Cilas gave him the control box, and they exchanged more words and assurances before going their separate ways. It was now a matter of waiting for the sergeant's cipher to crack the box, so Cilas suggested they split up, just in case the sergeant was the traitor, or someone else in the station that could tip off their mark.

"Okay, this station is a ring," he said, "and on this map you can see that it's segmented into four distinct regions—A, B, C, and D. We're in A, the largest region, so that's where Ate and I will remain, but I want you, Sunny, in B, Ray in C, and Tutt in D. We're looking for anything suspicious, like someone trying to escape to gain the port. The sergeant's people will be scanning those logs heavily, and it is likely that our mole is someone on the inside. You see something funny, use your instincts, but keep me up to speed on comms. Got it?"

They all concurred and then they were off on their separate assignments. Helga smiled when she realized that he had chosen her as his partner, ignoring the fact that it looked extremely fishy, especially when he sent the others far away from them. She wanted to gloat and tease him about it, but thought better of it when they were in the passageway leading out.

There were lots of people—Arisanis, mostly—going about their business, but Cilas seemed dead focused on wading through them to gain the greater mainline. When they reached it he seemed to relax, and she jogged forward to fall in next to him. "Well, that went well, I think," she said, looking up at him, but he was still staring forward, pretending to not see her trying for eye contact.

"Let's hope he isn't the one we came for," he said, exhaling. "We can handle much when we're in PAS suits, but an entire station of armed guardians, armored at that? I don't say this often, but we would be *thyped*, though a part of me knows that we would get him somehow."

"Oh, he'd go down, Cilas, you know he would, either by your knife, Ray's quick-draw, or Sunny doing some magical Jumper thing," she said, laughing at her words. "It's the loss you don't want, and being that I was there with you on Dyn, I know the cost, and I don't want it either. I think he's honest, for whatever that counts. I was watching him when he spoke to you, and he really does seem to revere us as heroes. I say he's going to give us our mole, and then we can find the rest of them and do what ESOs do."

"I love your fire, Lieutenant," Cilas said, finally meeting her gaze. "Oh, how *thyped* those boys are going to be once we catch on to them. It will be a righteous culling."

"Will they sing of our conquest, sweet Cilas?" she teased, and surprisingly he laughed and shoved at her playfully as they walked. They became serious when they passed the dock again and entered the commerce block where the crowd was so dense that all they could manage to do was get through it. "And we're supposed to somehow monitor this zoo?" Helga said. "If you wanted to get me alone, there were much better ideas to get rid of them."

"This is 100% real, so stow the accusations and get salty," he said. "I didn't choose you to mess around; I chose you because you have a knack for finding things that don't fit. That, and you're the one that I trust more than anyone else on that ship. No disrespect to the men, they can fight, and they go above and beyond at their duty, but like you mentioned, it was you that was on Dyn. Helga, I can't express to you how grateful I am to you and all my Nighthawks who stood in that cave, fighting off maker knows what, all so that Varnes could perform surgery on my abdomen. Any other unit would have pushed on without me, especially with a capable team leader like Cage Hem. But you all stayed, and Wyatt nearly died for it. Yeah, I don't get along with Brise, but I appreciate him just like I appreciate you, because he was in that unit that stayed with me."

"You know, Cilas, a simple 'because I trust you, Helga' would have sufficed instead of bringing up memories of *schtill* I want to forget," she said, shaking her head. "Plus, it wasn't up to us. Cage loved you like a brother, and it was evident. He wouldn't hear any other options; we were going to patch you up and wait however long it took until you were mission-ready. Brise and I were rooks, evergreen, and it was just following orders, nothing more. But we have been through a lot, and you're damn right you trust me more. I was the crazy *cruta* running at guns to help save your stubborn bum down on Meluvia. Remember that?"

"Of course I do. You take every opportunity to remind me," he said, laughing.

"Seriously though, Cilas, I've been thinking. Why do we do this? Are we that messed up, me, you, Ray, Tutt, Sunny, Brise, and all of the other ESOs? Do we have some wiring missing up here, something in our psych examination that says 'a splendid candidate for the suicide corps'? Because what we do is nuts, Cilas, absolutely batty stuff. They send a handful of us at ships full of the enemy, onto planets that we don't know, to try and root out one of their own. Who does that? We do that, and why? Because we can? Because they put us through BLAST and turned us into professional killers and psychopaths? What are the positives to being a Nighthawk, outside of the bump in commission and the individual berths?"

"The positives?" Cilas said. "That's easy. We get to see more of the galaxy than most ambassadors and space explorers. As to the negatives, it depends on the person, but if I wasn't me I guess I'd say it's the constant game of chance with our lives. The life expectancy of an operator is a third of your average crewman. We live fast, awful lives, filled with pain, death, and nightmares, but none of us in this unit are what you would deem normal, now are we? I had a pretty dreadful upbringing, so the chance to get out beyond the starship was well worth the risk. Point me to an ESO that comes from privilege and I'll have a hundred credits ready to meet that lunatic."

Cilas stopped and touched her on the forearm, bringing her around to face him. "You really don't get just how good we have it, do you?" he said, giving her a sad and patronizing smile. "These security officers you see, standing at attention by every door. Haven't you wondered why they're using people instead of Cel-tocs? It's because the credits it costs to keep a Vestalian employed is significantly less than maintenance for an android."

"But this place is beautiful, and those guards all live here with their families," Helga said.

"The station is beautiful because it is owned and operated by the Arisani elite, but for an outsider to be given refuge," he whispered while widening his eyes and giving her a nod for emphasis, "they would need to commit to certain conditions, like—"

"Working for practically nothing," Helga cut in. "Great, so we brought back kidnapped Vestalians to their slavers. Tell me, Cy, are all stations *thyped* up, or am I just the unluckiest girl in the galaxy?"

Cilas didn't answer, just stood frozen as if in stasis; he wasn't even blinking. Helga had slipped in the name Cy, which she would call him when they were intimate. It was done on purpose to knock him off his throne, which she didn't like him using to school her as if she was a cadet. She couldn't count on him not exploding, but he knew her better than most, so she decided to roll the dice to try and change the subject.

"Helga, don't call me Cy when we're in uniform," he said. "Wait, I'll go further because I know what you'll say next. I meant uniform metaphorically, got it? Can we not go where this is going?"

Helga let out a laugh before using her hands to seal her mouth. "Alright, Cilas" she said. "I'm sorry, but I really, really like the name."

He touched her chin playfully and lifted it up, then caught himself and exhaled, before starting back down the path.

"You're awfully quiet," he said after a while, and Helga decided to take her time to answer.

"I was just thinking that with places like this, I am constantly being reminded that there is life beyond our war with the Geralos. Like Sanctuary, none of these people give a damn about us, yet on our ships all we hear is that the galaxy is doomed if we let the lizards win. Puts things in perspective really, now that I am finally getting the whole view. I am what I am, just like you are what you are, Cilas Mec, and I don't think either of us would be good with a life that would see us grow bored."

"Already thinking about retirement?" he said, smiling. "There have been plenty of spacers to find a station home once they've been discharged. I doubt you'd have to live like the Vestalians here, since your commission would be decent, and you could save enough to float you as an old woman."

"As if either of us will grow old," she mumbled, annoyed at his poor attempt at a joke. "No, I don't have any station aspirations, Cilas. You asked, and those were my thoughts."

They found themselves inside of a seedier area of the station. It was a hive of apartment homes, their windowed doors stacked closely in columns with their inhabitants crowding the passageways. They were dressed like hub-dwellers, in simple clothing that were a touch above rags, obvious hand-me-downs from the wealthier citizenry.

"Looks like we've finally reached the honest part of the station," Helga said, as she observed the fearful looks they received from just about everyone.

One glance inside a home whose door was malfunctioning showed a rack and bunk installed on a wall behind a metal table with chair, and a looming glass window, circular and decorative, which let in a cyan light. It had charm, and would have been a dream for a young cadet, Helga mused, but for the five Vestalians who lived there, it had to be crammed and uncomfortable to live in.

"No wonder they all sit out here in the passageway," she said. "Want to bet it's no coincidence that it took us walking thirty minutes to find it from the port entrance?"

"Careful, Helga, we're here to conduct an investigation, not judge the Arisani government on their treatment of refugees. Best to file this away inside your memory for the future as a reminder of how lucky we are to be a part of the Alliance," Cilas said.

"Are we lucky though, Cilas? Are we really?" she said. "We fight an endless war, while the rest of our people hole up in corners of the galaxy, living in *schtill* and squalor. Now you see why our passengers bothered me, living like kings while this happens right above their planet. I get it, they chose to come here and live in a storage cabinet, but everywhere we've gone, it's the same helpless situation for Vestalians."

Cilas chuckled, which annoyed Helga because she knew that she'd either said something stupid or juvenile and was about to get a lecture.

"A few more missions under your belt and I wonder how much your thoughts and comments will have changed when it comes to holes like this. I used to think the same thing, having come from a hub, where all I knew was survival, and distrust, especially of my fellow Vestalian unwanted. I was just a boy when I got sent to *Rendron*, but I can still remember the hunger that came with life on an abandoned station. At least here, they get healthcare, security, and rations. I have yet to see an emaciated child begging for food, or someone getting shanked, raped, or eaten. The way you speak tells me that you haven't seen the real Vestalian refugee situation, and until you do, I would suggest that you stow your opinions. This isn't bad, it really isn't, and we don't want to make trouble for these good people."

"Got it. I'm sorry I said anything," Helga said, checking her rage.

He was right, as he tended to be on subjects such as these where he was more than an authority, and though she disagreed that seeing worse conditions would somehow soften her stance, she didn't want another argument that ended with her feeling naïve and foolish.

13

As Helga explored the station with Cilas, looking for someone or something they did not know, she began to pick up on the culture and the little tells that revealed what was below the surface. Things weren't really as put together as they appeared. There was a stark difference in the statuses of the three species that called it home.

First you had the Arisanis, who dressed well and were generally pleasant people. They were the politicians, business owners, and anything they wanted to be. Then you had the Genesians who served them, who were the managers, law enforcement, and clerks inside the stores. Helga could tell them separately from the others since they wore their planet's flair. The last were the Vestalians, who had the biggest population of the three. This struck her as odd, since *A'wfa Terracydes* was an Arisani station. She also noticed the downcast eyes and general fear they exhibited.

"Are we sure these workers aren't slaves?" she said to Cilas.

"Slavery is outlawed throughout the galaxy, Helga. Do you think they are so brazen that they'd have it here?" he said.

"Maybe," she said. "You can't tell me that you haven't noticed all the signaling."

"I have, but I think what you're seeing is shame, and misreading it as fear. You aren't from a hub, so let me explain. When they see these PAS suits, they know we're Alliance, which they see as either crazy or lucky, depending on the hub and the people. Here, they feel ashamed around us, because we're fighting the Geralos. Arisani culture is big on strength, so the Vestalians can't escape feeling guilty about not being a part of the fight."

"So why not join the Alliance, if it's so shameful?" Helga said. "We could use the numbers, that's for sure."

"You already sound like a recruiter. I should tell the captain so he could send you back to Sanctuary," Cilas said.

"That's not funny, not from you, Commander. The fact that you can actually do it makes it the most terrible sort of joke."

It was hard not to notice the comfort that Cilas displayed with walking through the slums. Helga had decided that that was what this was. Unlike her, he didn't seem to mind the staring and touching that occurred. It was almost as if he was used to it, and after a time it became too much for her to ignore.

"So, you're actually good with this?" she tried, and he looked down at her, surprised.

"There are hubs everywhere," Cilas said. "It doesn't matter if it's on a planet like Meluvia with towering high-rises, or on a satellite like this. They call them different things, sure, and the reasons behind them vary depending on the situation, but everyone deserves a home, don't they?"

"Of course," she said. "I wasn't inferring that they shouldn't exist."

"I know," he said, "but my point is that hubs provide homes for those without, and the conditions are merely a circumstance of that, not the intent."

"Well now I feel like *schtill*, Cilas. Thanks for that," Helga said, reeling.

Cilas stopped suddenly and touched her elbow, making her turn to face him.

"Alright, Nighthawk, bring it in," he said. "If we're going to talk, you're going to have to let down some of those defenses. When I correct you, it's on things that I know. Piloting, now that's your area, and when it comes to that, I shut my mouth. Now, hubs, knife-fighting, leading ESOs, I'm the authority, despite how much you think you may know. The fact is you're young, Helga, and you don't like that feedback, but it's a fact. I have five years of experience on you, so stop taking everything so personal."

"I'm not being defensive," Helga said. "It's just you lecture me a lot, Cilas, even when I'm just talking *schtill* to pass the time, and, well, you know."

"Noted," he said, and then motioned for her to follow him through a set of double doors.

They emerged into a domed space with tiered decks staggered up to the ceiling, each holding a neat row of buildings. Surprisingly, the ceiling itself didn't show videos of a sky, and it didn't use holos to give that illusion. *A'wfa Terracydes* wasn't going to pretend that it wasn't a space station, which spoke to the directness of its people.

Helga found herself hesitant to continue the conversation. She had seen the change in his demeanor, and wondered if her honesty had somehow damaged their relationship. Cilas was not a talker, and could become rather cold to those who he felt was not worth his time.

"I'm sorry," she said. "It's just that sometimes I feel as if you see me as a child."

"There are no children on this team, Helga, only operators," Cilas said. "I trust each and every one of you with my life. I'll go easy on the preaching from now on, how's that? Now, as to hubs and the refugee situation, you will just have to deal with that in your own way. We Vestalians, we no longer have a home. We're a species of vagrants, and not everyone is going to be okay with that. Acknowledge this reality and you will be better for it, because this is what counts." He pointed to his heart, slamming his fist into it with a salute.

"We, the victims of the Geralos, no longer belong to just one planet. We belong to Anstractor, our galaxy, and we can be found everywhere, whether they like it or not. Our refusal to fade into irrelevance is why many won't understand us, or go out of their way to help. But you know what? That's alright. We have friends in the Alliance, and none of us are going to stop until we win this fight."

Where in the worlds did this passion come from? Helga thought, looking at him now in a different light.

Cheers went up around them, and both Cilas and Helga were surprised to see a small crowd of children converging.

"Are you an Alliance Marine?" a young teen said. He was dressed in coveralls smeared with grease, and was smiling up at Cilas.

"Something like that," Cilas said, waving to the others as they gathered around.

"We want to hear more," another young man said, this one shirtless and gnawing on a ration bar.

"Your words inspire hope," said a tall girl. She had a shock of thick grey hair despite her youthful features.

"How many people have you killed?" said another young girl, who looked to be no older than twelve.

"Think that one was directed at you, Hel," Cilas said, grinning.

"We kill Geralos, not people," Helga said quickly, hoping that would be enough to satisfy her.

The mention of the lizards made the children go silent, then more questions followed, this time with twice the animation.

"Do something cool," one cooed, and "I hear that you can fly," and, "Is she your girlfriend?" which made Helga's face turn red with embarrassment.

She looked over at Cilas for a strategy to escape, but the Nighthawk looked to be enjoying it.

"I want to be like you when I grow up," said a tiny waif with the biggest amber eyes that Helga had ever seen. The sight of them weakened her resolve and she reached down and lifted her into the air. "See, told you that girls can be Marines," she shouted at a boy, and stuck out her tongue in triumph.

"You can be whatever you want, little spark," Helga whispered into her ear, then put her back down and tousled her hair.

"Time to go, children," Cilas announced, still smiling despite their loud objections.

"Please don't go. You can stay a while. We want to hear stories about the war," one of the younger boys said.

It broke Helga's heart to feel so loved and adored by Vestalians not born on a ship. Without Cilas there she would have melted, falling victim to their whining, staying and relaying her stories and songs, playing big sister to them. She looked around for their parents, and saw groups of adults looking on, but they were too bashful to approach.

Cilas reached inside his pack and brought out a handful of chocolates, which he held over his head to the delight of all the children gathered around. These were *Arielle's*, an expensive brand of candy, whose manufacturer donated them to the ships. The rates often used them as a form of currency, and Helga recalled Quentin and Sunshine gambling for them. The children wouldn't know their worth, outside of them being a brand of candy whose packaging held the Alliance's stamp. Had they known, they could have traded them for bags of cheaper stuff that could keep them in sugar for a whole year.

Still, they jumped and screamed excitedly, as Cilas held them above him, egging them on until they were practically a mob. He passed them out eventually, one to every child, and it was the distraction they needed, allowing them to finally press on.

As they walked away, Helga chanced a glance back at the girl with the large amber eyes. She was standing apart from the rest, clutching at her shirt and staring after her with stars in her eyes.

Thype it, she thought, and jumped up into the air, pumping her legs to bring her rockets alive. She flew up to the ceiling and turned, waving down at her tiniest fan. The girl screamed and ran back to where her mother was patiently waiting. They hugged and the tyke pointed up at Helga, too excited to formulate words. She would never forget it, and Helga knew it, recalling similar times as a cadet.

"That poor mom won't hear the end of it until she's forced to ship that child off to the Alliance for training," Cilas said, shoving her playfully when she landed. "Helga, the recruiter. You're a natural!"

"Do you ever stop?" she said, exasperated. "I did it for the baby, to give her some happiness. She looked so miserable when we took off."

"I used to be one of them," he said, "running out to meet every uniformed stranger that showed up on our block. You don't want to give them false hope, Helga. I saw you with that little girl, and I just knew you were going to tell her that she can be anything she wanted to be. For adults, those are just words, and they do sound good to hear, but for a child coming out of here, it is a lie. Arisani has strict rules against their citizens leaving to join the Alliance. It is why you don't see any of them within the ranks.

"Leave, and you get a bounty on your head, and worst still, the Alliance won't take you in. Doing so would violate the agreement we have with this people, and could lead to them becoming our enemies, which is something we cannot afford. Our people have it good here, regardless of how it looks, and while it's admirable that they want to fight, they cannot."

"That really stinks, Cilas," Helga said. "But anything is possible if you have access to a ship and someone willing to help. That little tigress could stow away with any Marine that docks here, and the Arisani wouldn't even notice. She is Vestalian. Really, how would they know?"

"You're right, and I'm sure it has happened in the past, but I'm just informing you of how things are here. You're able to see past the smiles, and that is good, but there are deeper rules that enforce the status quo," Cilas said.

"What's the story on the Genesians? They're an odd bunch. Robes and sneers to go with their noses so far up the Arisani's rear. You

would think that they went to school for it. I've known a lot of
Genesians, and none that I've met have been anything like the ones
I'm seeing here," Helga said, throwing her hands up with disgust.

"Yeah, well these were born here, that is why they're odd," Cilas
said. "They look like us, and that became a problem when the
Vestalians were given refuge on the planet. Now, they go out of their
way to differentiate themselves, by toadying up to the Arisani to keep
a permanent seat at the table. It's infuriating, and I assure you that
the Alliance Genese are not proud of their behavior. These Genesians
you see here, they aren't built like Tutt and the honorable men and
women back on *Rendron*. These are descendants of engineers who
were sent to assist with the building of this station. By birthright, they
are highborn, very much like the Arisani they serve, but they owe no
allegiances to our cause. We are but a nuisance to them."

"Sounds like you've had some dealings with them," she said.

"Not exactly, but I know enough Marines, and those boys love to
talk. Genesians here are no different from the Louines. They see what
the lizards have done, yet do nothing to help us when they can."

"You would make a great politician, Cilas. I could see you holding
a seat on our council," Helga said.

"That's for bridge-hugging console jockeys, Helga. No disrespect,
but when I die, there'll be a weapon in my hand."

"Not if the captain can help it," Helga said. "He's practically
grooming you to replace him, and it makes sense.

"Makes sense how?" Cilas said, and the defiance was gone,
replaced by a tone of genuine curiosity.

"You're the same make and model. Marines that rose from poverty
to fight, thus earning a name for yourselves. Everyone knew Retzo
Sho, the ESO, just like they know Commander Cilas Mec. I will never
forget when we arrived on *Aqnaqak* and the mere mention of your
name was enough to get us easy passage. You have countless missions
under your belt, you've commanded craft, and are on a first-name
basis with our beloved captain. He will make admiral, you know, and
when he does, I just know that he'll formally recommend you for the
seat. Hopefully by then you will be ready to accept it."

Cilas was silent for a time as they walked through a darker
passageway illuminated by floating lights. The sound of loud music
could be heard from an open door, and when they walked past they
saw a crowd of Arisani dancing. It was a stark contrast to the domed

living area, but added to the exotic allure of *A'wfa Terracydes*. They came out into another open space, this one busy with vendors.

"You know me, Helga. You know that I am not a man of tremendous ambition," Cilas said. "I'm just a Marine that wishes to see the lizards off our planet."

"That's why you're the perfect man for the job, Commander," Helga said. "Other men say those things, but unlike them, you really believe it."

14

Although Cilas picking her to accompany him wasn't the romantic getaway that Helga hoped for, she did enjoy their time together, even if at times it bordered on contentious. Helga was young but self-aware, and much of her frustrations had to do with her second-guessing herself.

He had called them lucky for being in the Alliance's Navy, and though that bothered her—considering the constant gamble with their lives—she forced herself to see it from his side as a child of a hub. Her not having had that experience, she couldn't assume that he was wrong, but youthful stubbornness made silence difficult, and she would at least share her side.

To Cilas's credit, Helga's need to argue didn't seem to faze him the way it would with any other spacer of his rank and file. This drew her to him, and strengthened their bond, and she felt as comfortable with him now as she felt when they were the two surviving Nighthawks on the infiltrator, *Inginus*.

Back then, she liked him and was too frightened to act on it, but they became close as survivors, when he showed her how to improve her aim and helped her to learn more of Vestalia's history. Now they were lovers, but it frayed the little freedom she had with her words, since she was now forced to constantly monitor her speech.

They were still in the slums, but Trisk A'lance called Cilas to give him an update on where they were with the hack. Fifteen minutes of waiting and she was already nervously fidgeting with the grip on her sidearm. There were several characters giving her the eye, and being that she couldn't tell the predators from the prey, she wasn't taking any chances.

When Cilas finally returned from taking a walk—which he would do whenever he wanted privacy—he took her in his arms, lifted her up, and planted a wet kiss on her lips. It was so sudden and out of character that Helga stood there as if stunned, until he took her hand to pull her along, back the way they had come.

She wanted to ask him what had changed, especially with the kiss that had been seen by every curious citizen in the passageway, but she kept her mouth shut and jogged to keep up. If Trisk A'lance had asked them to return to the station, it meant that he had the logs, and they would need to scrape them to track down the communication.

"Turns out there was a message sent from this station," Cilas said when they were back on the crowded mainline, moving as fast as they could towards the offices of ACLOP services. "The other Nighthawks are on the way, but we need to be ready to help the security officers apprehend the mole. Once that's done, we can get back to business, and it will be Nighthawks and the *Ursula* crew, no more passengers."

"What about the pirate that we took hostage?" Helga said, glancing up to meet his eyes.

"I'm handing him over to the Arisanis; we got all that we needed from him back on the satellite. Doctor's suggestion made me decide on that, since his condition tanked once stasis was off. Filthy business, taking hostages, Helga. If there's any part of the job for you to avoid, that would be it. Tutt and I ... the things we had to do to get the words out of him inside that house ... you're tough, but you don't want to have to do it."

"I've seen your work," she said quietly and flashed him an ironic smile. "Pirate ship above Dyn, remember? When you needed answers from their so-called captain. You became a monster, but you had to, though it was difficult to wrap my head around you after seeing what you had done. Still, is it any different from razing a town or butchering civilian troublemakers? Let's be honest, we've all done some *thyped* up *schtill*. You've always told me not to worry about it, and so I don't. You should take your own advice. That killer deserved every bit of the pain you and Tutt served up to him."

"Well, Lady Hellgate, you sound like a Marine. If only Tutt were in attendance; you would move up several degrees on his impression meter," Cilas said, laughing.

"Tutt loves me, it's quite alright. Impressing him more won't gain me any additional points," Helga said. "Plus if he was here, he would have seen my commander hoisting me up for a kiss. Wonder what he would have said, had he seen that?"

"He would have said nothing, at least for now, but he would have a lot of jokes coming for me later on when it's just us," he said, dismissively. "They probably know and talk about us, but I haven't seen anything suggesting that it's causing any discomfort, jealousy, anger, or whatever *schtill* comes with a ship full of hard legs and two women."

"Tutt wouldn't want me. I'm not his type," Helga said. "And Raileo may have a slight crush, but now that we have a pretty Traxian on our decks, he has no eyes for me, only excuses. Sunny is a Jumper, so we know that he already knows and will never share, so that takes him out of consideration. And we have three women, Commander, not two. You forgot Zan. While she's a machine, and linked to the *Ursula*, she is modeled after an attractive Vestalian. Have you seen her legs? Yeah, and she's got a personality in there, a cute one. Anyone desperate could give her some attention and there would be an instant connection."

"You can be so dry, you know that?" Cilas said, as if what she suggested with the Cel-toc was the most ridiculous thing he'd ever heard.

"You've never known Marines to *thype* Cel-tocs?" she said, daring him with her eyes to deny it.

"I have, sure," Cilas said. "There's a whole section on Nero deck back on *Rendron*, where they have units dedicated to lonely spacers, but Zan is our pilot and important, I don't want to confuse that with Ray bringing her to his bunk."

"Cilas I am so joking. Zan isn't built for that, and even if she is, I doubt Ray would be the type of human she would go for."

"Who would get that honor?" Cilas said.

"Me and Sunny, you know, the only two crew members that speak to her on our regular rounds. Sunny has some sort of history with Cel-tocs, knows how they're wired and how to run maintenance, so he's always talking to Zan. Me, I've grown to like her. She may not be real, but if I was stuck on a ship with her as my mate, I really don't think it would be all that bad."

"I'll take your word for it, but I'm not going to consider her as the third female on the *Ursula*, Helga Ate," Cilas said. "We'll get more eventually; I can only imagine with our recruitment to fill our berths. Then no one will care enough to worry about us."

They got to the office and walked inside where they were escorted back to the sergeant's office by another Arisani officer. Raileo was waiting and rose to salute them when they entered, and Helga returned it before taking a chair on the far side of where he sat. The Nighthawk could be immature with his antics but she liked him, and he was her partner-in-crime when it came to these boring briefs and war scrums.

When Cilas had echoed her concerns that the other Nighthawks knew, she felt awkward sitting with him, and needed a break from her thoughts. After five minutes passed, Sundown appeared in the doorway, with Quentin Tutt behind him with his sidearm out. They greeted their comrades before taking their seats, and Quentin leaned over to casually place an elbow on his knee.

"Where is this man?" he growled. "I'm over this station. The sooner we're back in open space, the sooner I'll be able to *thyping* breathe."

"Someone's grouchy," Helga said, not bothering to look at him because she knew exactly how he would respond.

"I don't blame him. This station is only a step above a hub," Raileo said.

"It's surely not Sanctuary," Sundown added, and then the three of them began to laugh.

"Looks like I owe you an apology, Commander," Trisk A'lance announced, startling them as he came into the room, sweating, as if he had just been running laps. "We have quite a situation here, and I will speak to you in private about that. Our cipher is still making sense of the data, and will have a full report for me to share with you and your captain. The person involved makes for a complicated situation, and out of concern for your safety, we would suggest that you shove off before we share the results."

"How bad can it be? We're Nighthawks," Raileo whispered to Helga.

"Guess it could be bad," Helga said. "As in sabotage, like if someone important blows up a section of this station. You know how desperate rats can get when they want to keep their identity a secret. No PAS suits could protect us from a ruptured bulkhead blowing us out into the black, and that's precisely what could happen if we're here. I like the idea; they can take their time and catch the mole, while we will learn where next to jump to catch these pirates looking for ransom."

"Alright, Sergeant, let's chat," Cilas said, standing and turning to face the rest of the team. "Nighthawks, you have two hours, after which we're meeting at the port to make our egress. This is a station-world; take advantage of it and get some supplies for yourselves and the ship. Get something for your berth, mess, whatever. We don't know the next time we'll be afforded the privilege of a place like this."

"Don't have to tell me twice," Raileo whispered, showing his teeth. "I'm going to see what they have for loadouts. What do you plan to do, Ate?"

"Me? I don't know, maybe get something to sleep in? No, I should get some artwork for my cabin, or one of those holo-butlers that welcomes you home when you power on the lights," she said, giggling foolishly. "I'll figure it out, but tell you what, if you see a pistol I would like, I'll give you back the credits."

"I know that I will already, so I will keep that in mind when I buy it," he said, winking as he walked out behind Quentin and Sundown.

They all went their separate ways, and Helga picked up several items that would make downtime more enjoyable on the ship. She got some comfortable shoes that were easy to slide into for the times when she was bored and would traipse up and down the deck. Normally she would do this barefooted, which wasn't ideal since the metal was cold. She got an outfit for Zan, to give her some variety that she hoped would inspire the other Nighthawks to engage her more when she was present.

By the time she was finished the two hours were nearly up, so she made her way back to the dock with a bulky bag of knickknacks that she bought. An hour later and everyone was back aboard the *Ursula.* Cilas had been given the decoded files with a promise that the station security would go after the pirate mole. They shoved off not long after boarding, and Helga took them away from the station, jumping immediately to get out of the Alliance Marine's jurisdiction.

The station would remain safe under the watchful eye of the Alliance, and once Cilas was done poring over the logs, he would confer with Retzo Sho and they'd have a new mission. Would it be the moon of Argan-10? A part of her hoped not, given that it gave her chilly recollections of the Louine moon Dyn. *Last time we set foot on a moon, we lost five of our eight operators*, she thought. *Makes me wonder what chances we have, us five, to make it out alive.*

Her thoughts on death and the fear associated with it were more for her brothers than herself, since she was still numb to the prospect of being killed. When she would try to focus on it, there would be nothing, just a blank mental block where others would literally be shaking in their boots. Helga reasoned that this was either her conditioning as an ESO preventing those thoughts, or something more sinister like a mental wall put up due to the trauma she'd experienced.

Either way, she welcomed death. It was just another adventure to a great unknown, but what she feared more than anything was losing Cilas violently, and seeing him opened up from a las-sword the way she'd seen Cage Hem, Horne Wyatt, and Casein Varnes.

The image of those three men that she'd grown to like being massacred by that cruel blade sent chills down her spine. She could never forget it; this was a permanent vision that could only be hidden but never destroyed. For that to happen to Cilas, she would cry blood, and become something terrible. This was what she feared with going down to that moon, especially if it had Geralos Special Forces.

"Hello, Lieutenant," said a melodious voice that could only come from Cleia Rai'to, whose presence was felt before she spoke.

Helga leaned back in her comfy pilot's seat then turned to face the doctor slowly, forcing what she hoped to be received as a warm, welcoming smile.

"Hello Doc, how may I assist you?" she said, and the blue-skinned beauty volleyed back the smile. Traxians had pronounced eye-teeth that could make them look predatory even though they were plant-eating pacifists. The teeth were an evolution to help them tear at fish, which was their only source of meat, though being off Traxis made fishing impossible, so most stuck to ration bars that were manufactured out of algae.

"I am not here officially or anything," Cleia said, "just wanted to... how you say? Build on our relationship, if you will let me. May I sit with you as we navigate the stars?"

"You're really cute, do you know that?" Helga said, understanding now why Raileo was head-over-heels for the woman. "Sit, sit, you're more than welcome. How are things with your medbay going? Do you miss your patients now that they're all gone?"

Cleia inhaled as if to calm her nerves and closed her eyes, seemingly pleased with the texture of the cushions.

"This ship is very nice. I want to be here for as long as I can. In Sanctuary, all we had was the municipal hospital in the Freedom District, which was crowded with talented medical staff, so me and many others were on a waiting list. These last few days, or cycles as you all say"—this made her giggle—"I have felt very much a part of the crew, because you needed me to treat those people. They were all so gracious, and complimentary, to be honest I didn't want to see them go. But to know that we saved them, and they will remember us fondly now that we're gone. It does warm the heart. I am content, lieutenant—"

"You should call me Helga when we're casual, Cleia. Everyone else calls me Helga, and since you're not navy, it's not like I can force you to respect the rank. Most I could do is correct you, but I do prefer Helga over lieutenant."

"Helga," the doctor said, repeating it several times, as if she enjoyed the way it sounded. "Helga, I have a question, please. Since leaving Sanctuary, we have encountered several enemy ships, and I was wondering if it is easy to tell a pirate or Geralos from an Alliance or neutral vessel?"

Did I just hear that right? The doctor wants to learn about spaceships? Helga thought, ready to burst with excitement. Here was an opportunity to school someone new on the fine nuances of identifying ships, as well as the rules of engagement. She rubbed her hands unconsciously, her eyes widening with anticipation of wowing the doctor with her knowledge, but then she remembered times in the past when her overly-detailed explanations caused her listener to check out.

"There's a lot that goes with it, Cleia, I won't lie," Helga said. "But I will do my best to explain. Just stop me if you see that I am going too much into detail. Sound good?"

"Yes, I'm excited, please continue," Cleia said, her skin becoming a lighter shade of blue, which Helga noticed immediately as it brought out the freckles on her cheeks and above her nose.

"I see you have spots like I do," she joked, reaching up to brush back her hair so the doctor could see the Casanian spots near her ears. "Have you been to Traxis?"

"No, this is my first time leaving Sanctuary, but it is a life goal to swim the oceans of my mother-planet, though a rather far-fetched one until I can save up the credits necessary for such a trip. Tell me, Helga, will your Nighthawks missions take you to that region of space, or is our concentration on Meluvia? I've heard you mention that planet quite a few times—well, both you and Ray... I mean, Chief Lei."

"Cleia," Helga whispered, looking around for any eavesdroppers before leaning in close to the Traxian physician. "It's okay to call him Ray, just like it's okay to say Q, Sunny, and Helga. Now, the commander is the commander, unless he himself tells you differently as to how he should be addressed. This is his ship, so there are rules, Navy or not, but he's the only exception as an officer. Anyway, as to Traxis, our jurisdiction is the galaxy, every meter within it, as long as there are bad guys to be killed and good guys to be rescued. I can't tell you when we'll be there, but in all likelihood we will sooner than later, but I wouldn't rely on that. I would save my credits just in case another opportunity arises.

"Now, in terms of ships, how can I best explain this," she said, staring forward through the *Ursula*'s glass. "There are several classes and sizes of ships spanning three factions of Alliance, Geralos, and civilian, which we call, merchant, luxury, or pleasure. Fighters are smaller killing machines, like my Vestalian Classic you see parked on the dock. There are several classes of fighter, but that's too much information, anyway. In the Alliance and Geralos ranks these are the smallest and easiest to identify. So if the radar, which sees things about 12.8km out, picks up a fighter that isn't Alliance, we know immediately to prep for action. Understand?"

"I do," Cleia said, still smiling and nodding as she absorbed the information.

"Next up are cruisers. These are multipurpose ships that cause the most confusion. They vary in size; some can carry an entire company of Marines, while others are built for spatial warfare, so they are heavy on the armor and light on the berthing. Cruisers that have been disabled in war are often converted into merchant vessels then sold to corporations to use for trade and transport. The Geralos know we do this, so they commandeer cruisers and use them as decoys within their fleet. I can go farther, but it's too much for someone new, but when we see a cruiser, we normally prepare for the worst."

"That large ship that attacked us, was that a cruiser?"

"It was, and if you recall we didn't sit on our hands, I primed a torpedo and reached out on comms, practically begging them to identify themselves," Helga said. She then touched several areas of the console to produce a holographic image of the disabled vessel. "As far as Alliance standard, you next have infiltrators, which are built exclusively for combat and function as junior starships in a sense. Still with me? Yeah, those you cannot mistake for anything else." Helga touched a few more symbols and buttons, and the holograph transformed into the infiltrator, *Inginus*.

"They are all so beautifully designed, but what about the Geralos?" Cleia said.

"Almost there, Doc," Helga said, pleased at her enthusiasm for a topic most shunned in the cadet academy. "Starships, as you know, are the largest of the vessels. They hold thousands of spacers, and are equipped with ordnance meant to obliterate other ships. These vary in sizes as well, with the average of—wait, this is too much information—just know that most starships are classed as destroyers, but the bigger ones are known as battleships, like the one we hail from, *Rendron*. Now as to the Geralos—"

There was a chime and the holo-image vanished, replaced by the Alliance symbol. Zan's face appeared above the console, and behind her was the Cel-toc charging station.

"Sorry to disturb you, Lieutenant, but the commander would like you to gather the Nighthawks for a briefing inside of his cabin," the Cel-toc said.

"We'll pick this up later," Helga said, resting a friendly hand on Cleia's shoulder.

"I look forward to it," the Traxian said, and repeated the gesture, completing the Vestalian bonding ritual. "Now I know to hide whenever I see anything smaller than an infiltrator incoming."

Helga made to correct her, but when she thought of the logic in that statement, the doctor was actually right. They knew the signatures of all starships and infiltrators in the Alliance records, but the vessels with masses less than those could go either way. This included their corvette, which was part of a cluster of alien models that Helga had dreaded getting into because there were just too many for a non-pilot to absorb.

She hated that she was interrupted, since this was one of the most refreshing conversations she had experienced since Sanctuary. Helga had wanted to go into detail about the Geralos flotilla, but duty came first and they were being summoned, so she would have to table it for another time. Knowing that someone else had a love for ships brought a lightness to her heart that she couldn't explain, but now she looked forward to the rest of their conversation, and future late shifts where she would continue Cleia Rai'to's education.

15

When Cilas Mec was given the command of *Ursula*, something told him that it would mean more missions, more accountability, and more problems. Stepping away from the communication station that sat in the corner of his cabin, he collapsed into the closest chair and stared up through the transparent overhead at the distant stars.

Cilas was bone tired, mentally exhausted since leaving Sanctuary, which was exasperated by a four-hour conversation with both his captain, Retzo Sho, and his executive officer, Commander Jit Nam. The two men had been grilling him on the situation at *A'wfa Terracydes*, wanting every detail down to the minutiae.

He had told them everything, from the stealthy entrance made to avoid detection by the kidnappers, to the shootout and escape that led to the ambush when they were told to wait for a shuttle. Aside from divulging all the steps made to get the Vestalians back to their Arisani homes, he had Helga send the logs over to *Rendron*, as well as the footage recorded from his PAS helm.

The two men had expressed concern for his "state" as they had phrased it, since he wore his exhaustion on his face. Typically he could hide it, the same way that his captain could—being a master of wearing masks—but with the news that a high-ranking member of *A'wfa Terracydes* was instrumental in the pirate attack, it became impossible to relax for the young commander.

"We've done our part in securing the Vestalians, Cilas," Retzo Sho had said, exchanging looks with the ever-stoic Jit Nam. "*Missio-Tral* is near your location, and can send in their ESO Shrikes to look into things on the moon. You should return to *Rendron* and get in some time with the psych. Admiral Mor's outline on the events at Sanctuary has been both disappointing and disturbing, to say the least. The Nighthawks have performed admirably, but you're starting to show cracks and I don't like it. Both the *Inginus* and *SoulSpur* are out hunting Geralos, so you will have the time to fill those gaps within your ranks."

It was a tempting invitation, and Cilas wanted nothing more than to bring in more Nighthawks and crewmen to transform the *Ursula* into a formidable war machine, but it violated everything he believed in as team leader. How could he turn over the reins to another set of ESO when the Alliance had hand-selected his team to carry out the moon mission?

Selection was favor, and out of all the ESO units, his was in that rare category of being seen as, "deadly-effective." To stop now meant that the Shrikes could take their place, and they would be back to mediocrity, doing salvage runs and chaperoning elites—the type of missions that made him dislike his job. Hearing this "kindness" from his commanding officers made him wonder if they were having doubts with him in his current position.

Ursula wasn't an Infiltrator, but she was an expensive warship that he had been loaned. She hadn't been built and newly christened; she was a convert, a means to an end, and that end had been Sanctuary station for an emergency escort mission. Unfortunately, things had gone about as badly as they could, and Sanctuary became an ironic name, for yet another battlefield where he and the Nighthawks had to shoot and fly their way out.

Cilas had wrongly assumed that after all that excitement, his team would be eased back into mission rotations while he was able to send out feelers for recruits. This pirate situation, however, had occurred very close to their vector, so they were called in, and here they were again, scrambling to do the will of the Alliance.

The captain was right. No one would begrudge him for putting his team first, but the mission was to investigate the moon, and the Shrikes didn't have the intel that he and Tutt had gathered from the satellite. If they didn't do it, things could go wrong and more innocents would die, and that would be the type of guilt that no psych could ever cure.

"Thank you, Captain. I appreciate your concern, but we'll finish this mission and then head back to mother, where I can fully brief you in person. If *Missio-Tral* can provide support, that would be more than enough help for us, especially if they can intercept any dropships coming in once boots hit the ground," he had replied, hoping that they wouldn't push the issue, and to his surprise, Retzo Sho seemed relieved.

Now as he stared up at the stars, he wondered if that decision was a good one. He was the commander, but he hadn't spoken much to his crew to gauge morale, health, and true battle-readiness for something as delicate as investigating a possible Geralos hive. With only four Nighthawks, he should have done that, but his pride had made him answer quickly, committing them to the mission.

Lifting his wrist-comms to his mouth, he summoned everyone to his cabin, taking the time to appreciate the fact that he was able to do this. On *Rendron* his berthing was your average officer's wardroom, sizeable and comfortable, but only an eighth of the size of the one he had now. They all filed in separately, with Helga bringing up the rear, and they sat where they could about the compartment, which had ample seating for eight.

"Hey team, thanks for showing up on such short notice," Cilas said, "I need to catch you all up so that you have time to prepare for this mission. Currently 1.25 light years from the *Ursula*'s current location is the planet Hiyt. Helga, am I correct in that estimate?"

"That sounds about right," she said quietly, and he could tell that she too was seeing something off about him.

"Okay," he said. "Above Hiyt is a ship-building station named Espiera. It is the home of over 50,000 scientists, engineers, and academic elite. There's a security force of 1,200 Marines, as well, stationed there with the primary directive of protecting that community from outside invaders. They are well-trained warfighters, donated by the Alliance who, as we know, depend on those stations to build the generators that power our ships. Well, just two cycles ago, when we were on *A'wfa Terracydes* making our drop-off, a transmission was received from an encrypted source, issuing demands for a warship.

"Being that the pirate attack on the diplomats of Arisani had been communicated across the Alliance, this transmission was taken quite seriously. It included a vid-feed of civilians being held at gunpoint on the deck of a ship, recognized to be the *Lucia*. One of these civilians was Prince Jorus Kane of Arisani, an extremely important diplomat from everything I've been hearing. Not only is he loved by millions of people on the planet, but he's the key to an important resource that can aid in the development of future starship technology.

"I see it in your faces, and yes, this whole thing is a stinking soup with extra fecal matter added each and every cycle. Smarter people than me are connecting the dots to see if the prince was targeted or just happened to be unlucky. From what I was told, the pirates haven't mentioned him, which leads us to believe this was random. Either way, the white suits at the helms of starships can puzzle over it while we go hunting for some lizards. How does that sound, Nighthawks?"

There were shouts of confirmation, including the now familiar "Sambe!" that Quentin Tutt would use from his native Genesian tongue. It was slang, twisted from the phrase "asram beyt," which translated to "get angry" in the new universal tongue. Quentin, however said that the literal translation was off, and the phrase was closer in meaning to "get active," or "let's go."

"Lizards, Commander?" Sundown said, causing everyone to quiet down quickly. The Jumper was an enigma who only spoke when it was absolutely necessary, and it was as if everyone knew that so they quieted to hear his words. "Have we been given a new mission that actually involves the Geralos?"

"Yes and no. Sunny, this mission isn't new, but there's a chance it involves the Geralos camp where the Vestalians we rescued were to be transported to. The satellite was the drop-off, and we disrupted what we now know is part of a net that involves the trade of Vestalian brains to the lizards. This makes it our fight, Nighthawks, so we can no longer view this as us just 'lending a hand.' Since we've been given more than enough proof that the enemy is in league with the Geralos, our captain has asked us to investigate Argan-10 to win some leverage over these traitors.

"Normally, as you all know, anyone attempting to squeeze the Alliance would be reduced to debris in a manner of seconds. This time, however, things are a wee bit more complicated, since unlike most lifeforms ransomed for a prize, Prince Jorus Kane has been deemed too important to die. So, instead of responding with overwhelming force to send a message to future extortionists, our captain has asked to investigate a suspicious signal on the moon, Argan-10."

"Oh, so we're back on for our original mission then?" Helga perked up, a bit too excitedly, and Cilas gave her a wink before thinking better of it. He was immediately miffed with what he did but hid it well, though the surprise expression on her face made it worth it.

"Helga is right. We're back to where we started when we were waiting on a shuttle to take the Vestalian rescues off our hands," Cilas said. "We are to drop on Argan-10 and conduct an investigation into what the Alliance believes could be a Geralos feeding camp." He walked to the end of the cabin and touched an area of the bulkhead, causing a section of it to light up, becoming a terminal.

"If you look, here, you'll see the information Tutt and I pulled from the screaming maw of our captive. The pirates are definitely in league with the lizards, and the Vestalians they sell are for what we call a 'hive'. It's a cold storage for Vestalians placed in stasis to use as conduits for the lizard's *thyped*-up, brain-eating religious exercise. By disrupting that operation, the pirates could be forced from this system. The camp is likely connected to their network, and the ship they're demanding would strengthen their position with the Geralos.

"As of right now, the Genesians have promised them a state-of-the-art cruiser. It is a lie to placate them, but can be reality if we fail to find anything on that moon. This is to be as tight as we can muster, stealth and professionalism, the type of mission meant for ESOs. If we're discovered or killed, there's a chance the pirates will get desperate and kill more hostages, including the prince. For this reason, we're going in alone, but the XO is coordinating moves with several ESO teams. The Shrikes from *Missio-Tral* will be investigating a satellite above Argan-10, and can provide us support if we need. It is a Geralos satellite, one of several about the moon, and is monitored by the lizards, so that should keep the attention off us."

"As if we need it," Quentin said, grinning. "We have one of the best pilots in the Alliance."

"Sambe!" Raileo shouted, causing Helga's face to turn red.

"I'll tell Zan you said that, Q," Helga said, masterfully deflecting the praise. "Though I'll be the one taking us down on Argan-10. I'm no Cel-toc, but I'll do my best to make sure we touch down in one piece. How's that?"

"Good enough, Helga," Cilas said, loud enough to quiet down the low-rising banter that had taken on its own life. "The Alliance has enlisted the Jumper agency to rescue the prince and keep him hidden until we've cleared the base. As to the other hostages, this will be delicate, and our number one priority is to be quick, thorough, and undetected. This won't be Sanctuary with the enemy being badly-behaved civilians with junk weapons. There may be lizards, Crak-Ti even, so you need to be mentally ready to see some *schtill*."

"This sounds like Dyn all over again," Helga muttered. "Except this time we'll know exactly what to expect."

"Dyn will never happen again, not while I'm involved," Cilas said. "They asked us to make this drop because we've shown that we're effective, and the individuals inside this cabin are of the quality necessary to see it through. We showed them what we were made of firsthand on Sanctuary station, and now the Nighthawk name is revered by the top council members of our Alliance. That's not bragging, that's reality, so now we get another chance to show that they aren't wrong."

"I think I'm getting goose pimples," Raileo whispered, looking about excitedly before putting his fist into the raised hand of an equally excited Quentin Tutt.

←————————————————————

It felt good to be inside the cockpit of the R60 Thundercat once again. Although Helga much preferred a smaller fighter, she appreciated the flexibility that a dropship offered. After the brief they had prepared, strapping on armor, prepping their loadouts, and running even more diagnostics on their vessel to make sure that when things went awry—which they always did—they could rely on their ship.

To have equipment failure occur with no engineer was practically suicide, and having been there with Cilas on that first mission to Dyn, Helga was obsessive in her preparation.

"Everyone strapped in," she said into the comms. "The system has given us the all-clear to jump."

"How far are we from the Ursula, Lieutenant?" Raileo said, and before Cilas could silence him, Helga replied angrily, making sure to be as technical as she could.

"We're at a hot 685.9 meters per second, with thrust on nosebleed, four waves out from the Ursula. Once I slide the launch lever up, we'll enter supercruise, which is going to suck if you are not strapped in like I asked."

"Pilot-speak, beautiful, uh... got it Lieutenant—" Raileo tried, before Quentin cut him off to call him out on being ignorant of everything she told him. He wasn't wrong; she had done it on purpose, using a combination of pilot's slang and nonofficial measurement.

Only Cilas and to a certain degree, Sundown, would have known what she meant fully, so she cracked a smile and turned up the feed on her HUD to see for herself whether or not they all were ready.

They were joking around and having a good time, which was the typical mood before an exciting new mission. All helmets were on and the Nighthawks were restrained, so she placed a finger on the icon that would approve the system's query to begin the FTL jump countdown.

"Jumping now," she announced before looking at her wrist comms for the time. They had thirty seconds, and that should have been enough. Anyone still unrestrained after she'd given them multiple warnings would have to deal with the complications that came with the compression of space about the Thundercat.

Helga adjusted her helmet and inhaled a deep breath. Oh, how she hated FTL travel in smaller vessels like their dropship. It would be difficult to explain to Raileo, how even as a pilot she dreaded those readouts that flashed red and yellow to warn of the impending jump.

At twenty seconds in, the Thundercat bolted to supercruise speed, and Helga grabbed a hold of the sides of her seat. The blast shields slammed shut to protect them in case of a breach, and all around the cockpit were those familiar chirps of warning. In the silence of that moment, Helga studied her HUD, particularly the vital signs of her comrades. Everyone seemed calm, especially Sundown, which didn't surprise her, considering how she'd seen him perform in a shootout on Sanctuary.

As if on cue it happened: they passed from one area of space to another, and the queasy feeling that came from the sequence wasn't as bad as it could have been. Helga was relieved when no alarms went off, and the console lit up in white and blue lights. The system spoke, a cold robotic voice that was nothing like the Ursula's.

"Arriving at the specified coordinates, at approximately 36,000km from the moon of Argan-10. Crystal-core is on standby for 2.5 hours, now at supercruise and decelerating thrust to allow for manual control and operation."

When the blast shields cleared the windows, what appeared before them was a rust-colored expanse, broken up by white and gray splotches that Helga guessed were debris clouds in Argan-10's atmosphere. Whole wars had been waged above this moon, back when the Arisani and Traxians fought over control of trade. This was before the Geralos, and Vestalians being forced into space, but it was a popular topic for academics, so Helga knew about it from her schooling.

"Everyone good?" she said, her eyes moving rapidly over their readouts.

"Aside from regretting that MRE I choked down before coming aboard?" Raileo said.

"We're good, Helga," Cilas said, and the other two men grunted their agreement.

"We've got about an hour to break atmosphere if there aren't any contacts," Helga said. "Feel free to stretch out, but be ready to strap back in whenever I give you the warning."

Helga removed her helmet and unclipped her restraints, then threw a leg over the side of her chair and slouched into the cushions to try and put her mind at ease. This wasn't her first dance, but it was never easy, and after experiencing a crash-landing on a hostile moon, she had to actively work at not panicking.

Her mind went back to Joy Valance, and the masterful way she would find ways to calm her down. She wished she was here in the vacant co-pilot's seat, cracking jokes and questioning her love life, which was always a point of annoyance. Oh, how Helga wished she'd known back then how much she would miss those annoyances now.

"On your flank," someone said, and she turned around, hoping that it wasn't Sundown with another lesson. Quentin Tutt rapped a knuckle on the top of her helmet, then took a seat in the co-pilot's chair, grinning as if he was doing her a favor. Helga slatted her eyes as she surveyed him, and as expected, he was restless with adrenaline. The normally stoic giant was somewhat addicted to violent action, and before every mission, she had noticed that he would normally get like this.

"We're hunting lizards, Helga," he sung, and held up his hand for her to punch it.

Helga completed the greeting and her gloominess vanished, as if the older Marine had whisked it away with their contact. During their time together on Sanctuary station, when all they'd had was boredom and an open bar tab, the two Nighthawks had become quite close, her seeing him as something of an older brother.

Quentin was still a young man, not even thirty, but he had seen enough of the galaxy to make any spacer jealous. Not only this, but he had a photographic memory, and his stories would come to life whenever Helga could get him talking.

"Ever been to Arisani?" she said after they'd been talking for a while.

"That *thyping* desert? No way, the Alliance doesn't have jurisdiction there, so I haven't had the privilege. This moon will have to do for our galaxy map, eh, Ate?" he said, referencing a practice they had begun of checking off planets and moons they had visited.

"Last moon I was on, I was a literal popsicle hanging from a hook," she said sadly. "It would be something to beat the level of suck we faced when we landed on Dyn. Eight Nighthawks then, five of us now. You would think we get off on putting ourselves in the worst possible situations."

"Don't we though, Ate? Let's be honest. I am a Marine, and you're a pilot; we're both conditioned to chase the flames. We all signed up for a reason, didn't we? To make an impact on this war, and we get to look amazing in our PAS suits as we take on the things that no one else is qualified to try."

Helga had to laugh because it was true. Back on Sanctuary she had been pulling her hair out, desperate for something to do. At the time, Cilas had anticipated a week or two of shore leave before they would get another mission, but they were grounded for five and a half while their ship, the *Ursula,* was receiving an upgraded system.

"Time to get locked in, Nighthawks," she said, noticing for the first time that they were about to reach the moon. Quentin chose to stay in the co-pilot's chair and strapped in securely while Helga pulled on her helmet, then braced herself for entry.

The dropship shot down past the cloud of debris, and Helga lessened their thrust, adjusting for gravity taking its hold. Flashbacks of Dyn slammed fists into that closed chamber of her mind, and it came open for the first time in months, threatening to flood her thoughts with an ocean of trauma.

Tears poured down her face despite the entry being smooth and uneventful, and she was happy that her helmet hid it from Quentin's observant eyes. With these thoughts, Helga found herself frozen, staring at the surface of Argan-10 below. It was quite a sight to see, glorious canyons and plateaus, with a splash of vegetation here and there. Off to one side there was an expanse of ocean, with several rivers running away from it to slip between a set of looming mountains.

"Good job, Hel. You alright up there?" Cilas spoke through a private comms into her ear. It was what she needed, and him using that pet name forced a smile to break the ice on her face. She sat up and inhaled, cleared her throat, then pushed back against the darkness that shrouded her mind.

"All is well, Commander, thanks for asking," she said, then switched to the ship-wide comms. "Nighthawks, prepare for landing. Oh, and welcome to Argan-10."

16

"Hang on back there, I'm bottoming out on the clear," Helga announced. "Helmets on and be ready to move. This isn't our moon, and I'm not certain we weren't spotted. Clearing comms."

She triggered the cloaking sequence on the dropship to render it invisible to the naked eye, then put them down low to the grassy surface, limiting the chances of them being on radar. To be safe, they had come in approximately 451km from the structure they were to investigate, and chose what appeared to be a vast jungle to break atmosphere over.

For the twenty minutes it took to get underway to their destination, there hadn't been any signs that the enemy knew that they were there. Above Dyn, however, they had been hit immediately, which had not only injured Cilas, but killed Adan Cruse, their pilot.

In remembering all this, Helga had her nerves on edge and her heart pounding thunderously in her ears.

"Get ready," she spoke into the comms, and took the Thundercat down into a valley lush with vegetation and rivers bubbling and throwing up steam.

She took them through this scenic gap between the mountains, then across a vast stretch of wasteland, where they could make out tracks from something mammoth-sized and segmented. This too sparked memories Helga wished she could forget, like that of the Meluvian brovila, which had latched on to her arm, injecting her with venom and scars that were still visible to this day.

Helga didn't have the best relationship with worms, snakes, or anything that crawled on its belly. The thought of facing a giant one now made her wonder at what this disaster would be. Sundown whistled and clucked his tongue, then Helga saw what triggered that reaction.

There was a crashed ship of some size, far off in the distance, which the Thundercat's system identified as their destination before generating a holo-image above the console.

A number of vines and branches from the surrounding trees were growing around it, revealing that it had been there for quite some time. There also looked to be a perimeter fence of sorts, constructed of something that appeared to be rocks.

"That's no compound, that's an Arisani cruise-liner," Helga said to the Jumper. "What sort of surveillance was the Alliance doing out here for them to mistake an obvious civilian ship for a Geralos war camp?"

"It's likely that it is one and the same," Sundown said, leaning forward to get a closer look at the holographic ship. "From orbit, the disk-like shape and the purposeful clearing out of a perimeter would fool any captain that this is a structure, not a downed ship. Are we the first to actually investigate the situation?"

"We are," Helga said. "To be fair, there was no reason before, considering Arisani and Hiyt are neutral planets."

"Can we get a sit-rep back here, Helga?" Cilas said, and Helga realized for the first time that she hadn't made an update since clearing the clouds above the moon. The beauty of everything around her and this strange, saucer-shaped vessel had been enough of a distraction for her to zone out.

"Coming up on the LZ now, Commander, nothing appearing on radar, and we can see the, um, crash site of the ship that we've been led to believe is a Geralos compound. There's likely drones patrolling the immediate area of our op, so I'd like to take it down here and have us cover the rest on foot."

"The structure is a ship?" Cilas asked, and she could feel his frustration grow from the intel missing such a crucial bit of detail. "Well, structure, camp, or ship, whatever, our mission is the same: we're going to have a look at it. If the lizards are still blind to our arrival, we still control the element of surprise, so set us down as soon as possible, Helga. We'll travel the rest of the way using PAS."

Helga shifted the Thundercat's energy, giving full power to the shields. Even if someone was to find where they landed, she wanted the damage to be minimal if they attempt to destroy their ship.

There were several rock formations near where they flew, tall, stacked boulders, like giant, gravity-defying cairns. It was a forest of stones stretching out for kilometers in all directions, and Helga put them down inside a tiny, rubble-filled clearing, masterfully avoiding contact with the rocks.

She and the Nighthawks gathered in the dropship's hold, double-checking their PAS suits and loadouts. Helga grabbed her auto-rifle and slid it into its place behind the pack on her back.

Tucked under her arms were two hidden holsters, a Hooligan accessory, courtesy of one Raileo Lei. There she slid her favorite sidearm as well as a new addition that Quentin had gifted her back on the *Ursula*.

Every piece of gear that she now wore had sentimental value that brought her closer to her team. There was the PAS suit itself, the armored representation of an ESO, and the thing she had looked forward to wearing back before BLAST training and the long road to becoming a Nighthawk.

Her auto-rifle, a Vestalian element-loading ASR, was picked up in the war-battered streets of a town in Meluvia on her second mission with Cilas, and first mission with Quentin and Raileo Lei. One of her handguns was meant to be ceremonial, as it was engraved with her name and callsign, but it was such a beautiful pistol that she now used it as her primary service weapon.

The final and most sentimental piece was the black-steeled *Jang*, a marine-issued knife. This had come from Cilas, who made her promise to keep it close so that she would never be captured again. Like the others, she tucked the blade into its place on her rocket boots, where it would rest until close-quarters combat demanded it.

Once the Nighthawks were ready to go, they congregated at the ramp, and Cilas inspected their gear, something he normally didn't do before missions.

"This will only go to *schtill*, if we let it," he said calmly. "If Ate's right and we got the drop, then we control this battlefield, starting right now. Remember that. We are the ones in charge of how this plays out. Do you copy?"

"Loud and clear," Raileo said, a little too loudly.

"Once the ramp drops, we're flying low, using the rockets on our PAS. Don't disturb the stones. I don't know what this is, and I don't want to know. Let's get to that downed ship or whatever nice and quiet before Lizzy gets wise. Ate, you take us in. Nighthawks, we're live. There's bound to be hundreds of lizards, and if an alarm goes off, they'll swarm on us like a plague. Stay together, stay tight, and we're going to find out what they've got going on down here. If it's a prison camp like we believe, then the mission is simple: lock it down, and call for backup.

"Now, if it's something else, we gather intelligence and stay undetected. The plan is to sweep the entire place, eliminate all threats, and report our findings back to the captain. Ate will take us in, but comms stay clear unless you have something to report to me or the team. Once we breach, I'll take point, but the four of you will operate in pairs. Sunny and Tutt, Helga and Ray. Keep your maps up, just in case we get separated, and we'll switch to private comms if we're forced to split-up once we're in. Any questions?"

"When we're finished, do you think that we could explore this moon a bit?" Raileo said, and when the rest of the Nighthawks shot him a questioning look, he countered with a smile to show that he was joking.

"Will you be looking for a flower to brighten up a lovely Traxian's day?" Helga whispered to Raileo on a private channel. Even through his mask she could see his face go white, and it was all she could do to not fall over laughing, but this wasn't the time for games. No one else spoke, so Cilas started his countdown which ended with an alarm from the Thundercat's intercom.

The Nighthawks ran out onto the rocky surface before Helga sprinted and jumped to activate her rockets. Like birds of prey, they flew together in silence, Helga in the front, Cilas and Raileo staggered behind her, and Sundown bringing up the rear with Quentin Tutt.

Helga's focus was on the rocks and navigating through them, though they could have flown higher to avoid it all, and risk detection by radar or a reaper drone patrolling.

She would periodically glance up at her PAS suit's HUD to account for the other Nighthawks' location. Dyn seemed ages ago, but the scars from her experience there were still present. Nighthawks dropping at every juncture had become the norm, and a part of her expected the same thing here.

One positive thought that made her smile was seeing how comfortable Quentin was now, flying about in his powered armor suit. When he had become a Nighthawk, he had struggled with the nuanced, cerebral controls, but now he was an expert, slipping through the stones just as gracefully as he would if they were on the ground.

The forest of cairn-like structures ended with a drop-off into a scenic basin. So deep and wide was its beauty that for a moment Helga's anxiety was replaced with a sense of wonderment.

Nothing made you feel more insignificant than seeing the creativity of nature, unprovoked. The misty land below them would hold a number of vicious, territorial creatures, and somewhere ahead was a Geralos operation, but from where she flew, the only thing that mattered was the experience.

Helga had to admit that where Dyn was a dull grey rock, full of craters and shadows, Argan-10 was a lush, lovely splendor, and flying freeform above it all took her breath away.

It looked every bit the exotic escape that the wealthy elite would use for vacation homes, and in the distance above the clouds, like detached stalactites rebelling against gravity and inertia, drifted several floating islands with their own set of trees and stones.

Now she understood why Raileo wanted to explore the place before they left. Why was this the first time she'd heard of Argan-10? It was a mini-Vestalia, and would have been a great source of refuge for the displaced Vestalians living on hubs.

She made a mental note to ask Cilas and Quentin. Perhaps the moon was considered sacred, or there was something else below the surface that kept out all manner of spacer but the Geralos.

From the shots she had seen from the orbital drones, as well as the fly-by they had done after breaking atmosphere, the so-called compound that they were to investigate was a disc-shaped vessel that had crash-landed on the surface. This meant that it was accidental, and unlike Dyn, the moon wasn't being used as a refuge.

The atmosphere was toxic, there was that, and a person living here would never have the privilege of feeling the sun upon their skin. Terraforming was possible, but that would still be limiting, and every trip beyond the oxygen generator would require a 3B XO-suit.

One of the floating isles appeared below her through the mist, so she descended and landed on its surface, running between the trunks of its trees as she stared up through the canopy of leaves above them.

"This is surreal," she muttered to no one in particular, forgetting that she had been on a private chat with Raileo Lei.

"Surreal is an understatement. I want to live here," Raileo said. "Though this thing we're currently on is starting to move, and I don't like it."

Helga picked up her pace before leaping and taking flight up and off the island, twisting and diving expertly into the mist, as the other Nighthawks struggled to keep up with her. It began to rain, a light lush affair that threatened their visibility as the mist seemed to grow, and the wind picked up, threatening to toss them.

Knowing the danger in flying through a storm, Helga dove deeper into the basin, until they could see the tops of the trees. Argan-10 was untamed, and this was evidenced by the way everything grew, without the interference of civilization or industry.

She kept them low, flying through the dampness of the mist until they were a kilometer out from their destination. Landing again, she checked her fuel gauge, and was pleased to see that she had only consumed a quarter of her reserves. That meant that they had half a tank to toy with while they investigated the downed ship, and would be able to fly back out the way they'd come, easily.

Helga was always impressed with the PAS's handling of energy consumption, and wished that whoever had built them would use those talents on outfitting spaceships. She had never been stranded in her PAS suit, but twice in her life, she'd been stuck inside of a cockpit recharging her crystal reactor core while counting down the seconds before a Geralos spotted her.

Even the memory of those two unfortunate moments served to give her goose flesh below her armor's protective shell. The PAS was attractive, form fitting, and malleable, not to mention it had a tool or function for every situation. It was what had made her want to become an ESO, and now that she was one, she still felt privileged to own and operate it.

"On your lead, Commander," she said over the general comms. "We're about one klik out so we should avoid the air. As you can see by those bent trees and the unnatural fissure cutting through them, this is where that ship touched down and wrecked everything in its wake before slowing to a halt up ahead. We can follow its tracks, so to speak, and make our way to it, silently. Anyway, I'll shut up now."

"Good flying, Ate," Cilas said, walking up to place a hand on her shoulder. "I was a bit worried when you started flipping around, but you got us here so fast I didn't have time to be frightened. Now, let's get moving and keep your eyes open. Don't let the beauty of these trees lull you to sleep because it's very likely that we're walking into an ambush."

"Commander," Sundown said, causing Helga to look in his direction. The Jumper never spoke, and she worried that his superior senses had picked up on something they missed. He pointed to a thicket of trees on the left side of the wide, jagged depression that they were in.

Helga saw a myriad of lights, obscured by the mist and darkness from the tree's thick leaves, blocking the sun from above. The lights seemed to wink and dart about, and she wondered if they were in fact fireflies.

"*Thype* me," Cilas exclaimed. "Good eye, man, we need to move." He was already sprinting alongside Sundown, who had his las-sword free and out to the side where it had less of a chance to nick any of them. Helga reached back for her auto-rifle and grabbed a clip full of cryogenic rounds.

Whatever Sundown had seen would be near the flora, and she didn't want to be responsible for burning down a whole forest just to ward off a predator. Then she went down, hard, her face planted into the sand, as something with some weight bore her down.

All manner of shouts were in her ear, and she could hear the chattering of Cilas's auto-rifle and the hum of Sunny's las-sword. Chaos ensued, and she found herself unable to move her limbs, not because of injury, but because whatever it was that had mounted her had both her arms and legs pinned down.

For five minutes of hell, she stared at rocks and listened to terror, and though she could answer the queries that came in amidst the screaming, she was helplessly stuck, listening to it.

Eventually the pressure was gone, and she scrambled up, surprised that the glass on her helmet was intact. All about her was what could be best described as splattered, crablike monstrosities with their blood and guts still wet on the stones.

Cilas yanked her up and pointed behind her, where one of those creatures was missing a head. It had twelve segmented legs, like a Vestalian crustacean, though its shell wasn't strong enough to withstand kinetic bullets. Her attacker had fallen to Sundown's blade, but was so heavy that it had kept her out of the fight.

Helga got her bearings and looked about, praying that none of them had been seriously wounded. Everyone was breathing heavily, and she could see their heart rates spiking on the readouts of her HUD, but they all seemed to be unscathed as they paced about the area with their weapons out.

"Guess this answers my question as to why no one has exploited this paradise moon," she joked, her voice cracking from the adrenaline.

"Yeah, and something tells me these were mere annoyances compared to what awaits us within those trees," Quentin said. "We need to move, double-time, especially now, since it's likely the lizards could hear our weapons."

Cilas cursed to show his agreement, then walked around to give her armor a quick examination. "Their legs have spikes, as you can see, and that one there was trying to pull you from out of your shell. It damaged the surface, but the weaving held, thank the maker. Are you alright? How do you feel?"

"We should move like Quentin said, Rend. I am good. Nothing is hurt, thanks to your swiftness stopping it short." She caught a lump in her throat and stopped to collect her bearings before the emotion of her narrow escape could break her down.

She took the time to close her eyes and inhale deeply before exhaling steadily between her teeth. "Good looking out, Nighthawks, thank you," she managed before starting ahead of them down the path. *And thank you, Sunny,* she thought, remembering how he'd sounded the alarm.

The auto-rifle was a powerful, reliable weapon, but when they had been jumped she couldn't hoist it fast enough to react. Remembering this angered her, along with the prospect of having to be rescued. She was irritable, angry, and annoyed, and since the weapon was part of her failure—as far as she was concerned—she replaced it with her trusty handgun.

As they marched, she brought it up to examine the craftsmanship that had made it special enough to be a commemorative weapon. Engraved was her callsign "Hellgate," which in this instance gave her a clarity that she needed.

"Are you sure you're alright?" she heard Cilas say over private comms.

"Golden, unless a bruised ego counts as an injury," she joked. "Let's just get to that ship and find what we came here for so that we can get back to *Ursula*."

17

"Movement," Cilas announced, and Helga checked where he was pointing and raised her pistol, ready for action.

The ground in front of them exploded, showering them with rocks, and Helga dove to the side, tucking and rolling, ending up on one knee. It was reflex, borne from drills practiced hours on end, and as she regained her senses from what she assumed had been an attack, she spun around to check on the Nighthawks. They too were recovering from their reactions, but none of them seemed to be injured or down.

In the area of the explosion, however, was one of the creatures that had attacked them before. This one was a juggernaut, easily dwarfing the others, at four times their size. The explosion hadn't come from a landmine or bomblet, it had come from the crustacean escaping the tunnel it burrowed below.

It was perched above Quentin, who was seated with one hand shielding his face and the other gripping his knife. The creature had two of its appendages raised, poised to punch a hole in his PAS.

Cilas was up, firing into the creature, who slammed down its legs, causing Helga to scream in horror. Stones flew up with a loud thud, where its legs barely missed the Nighthawk. Quentin had timed the strike and rolled, leaving a deep gash in its abdomen.

Helga was already firing from both of her handguns, but the creature had nimbly tucked back into its hole. Now they were all up and running, knowing that at any time it would burst out from below them. Helga took the initiative and launched herself into the air, activating rockets.

"Nighthawks, fly. You need to be off the ground," she screamed into the comms as she stopped her ascent to hover several meters above the rocks. She realized immediately that the warning was unnecessary, since they had followed her lead to hover just below the tree line.

The creature emerged once again, rocketing upward from the dirt, but Sundown powered off his rockets to fall on top of it, driving the las-sword down into its skull. A horrid scream came from its gaping maw, sending chills down Helga's spine.

"What are those things?" Raileo said, barely catching his breath.

"I think they're called szilocs." Sundown said, using a bit of fabric to wipe his sword. "They pick up on vibrations on the ground, like the kind we make when we walk."

"It's settled then, we're staying afloat," Cilas said. "Planets, what gives? Tell me, of all the ways to go ... impaled by a lobster is not how I want to be remembered."

"How many of those things do you think are below us, waiting for a thump right now?" Raileo said.

"I don't care to know. Kill the chatter," Cilas said. "Let's get to that *thyping* ship; we've been delayed enough."

"Not to be the bearer of bad news, but we're not out of the *schtill* just yet," Helga said. "We're all pulsing our rockets to stay off the ground, which doesn't take a lot of energy consumption as you know. But over time it will drain our reserves, and if you recall we just spent an hour crossing a misty basin of maker knows what."

"What are you saying, Ate?" Cilas said, flying over to hover in front of where she drifted.

"We need a contingency, Rend. What we have in reserve is our only means of getting back to the ship once this is finished."

Cilas cursed then looked around, wracking his brain for another means to avoid the bloodthirsty szilocs.

"Commander, if you'll let me?" Sundown said, and Cilas almost seemed relieved that the Jumper had saved him.

"What do you think, Sunny?" he said, flexing his legs to keep his altitude when his rockets began to idle.

To the horror of Helga and the other Nighthawks, Sundown cut his rockets and touched down. He bent over and placed his hands on the ground, and stood like that waiting for a time.

"Please don't be alarmed," Sundown said into comms after a minute had passed with him crouched and frozen, "I have experience with similar subterranean hunters that operate on sound or smell. Now, these szilocs live beneath us in a very deep and complex hive, similar to ants. Sounds from the surface attracts their hunters, but they use the same tunnels to travel, only punching holes in the surface to grab their prey. As you can see there are no holes about, even though we were attacked by so many. What that means is that they reseal their holes, so that future victims will remain unaware."

"So what's the plan then?" Quentin said, sounding every bit as impatient as he looked.

"Vibrations are everywhere, but particularly concentrated below the wreckage. I think that ship crash-landed in a most inconvenient place, directly above the heart of the hive. They burrowed a path below the one that we're on, so they've been picking up on our footsteps instantly. We have two options from what I'm seeing here, Commander. We can take our trek through the jungle, and come around to either side of the crash site, or, we can collapse their tunnel, blinding them, and they would in time be forced to burrow another path. That would buy us at most a Vestalian day, and we can be gone before they pick back up the hunt. On your lead."

"Let's cut around," Cilas said, quickly. "I don't want to frig up this moon any more than these *thypes* we're after have done. Knives out, and switch to cryo rounds. We want to suppress our action now that we're within range of the lizard's operation."

"Should I drop a bumper?" Raileo said, referring to a device he carried that would pulse and make noise for several hours. Typically bumpers were thrown to distract the enemy in the field, but due to its patterned pulse, which would be thunderous to the senses of the szilocs, it would keep the hive occupied and distracted.

Cilas approved and they went to work, planting the bumper and plotting an alternate course to make it to the wreckage. Once they were set, he led them off the path and through several meters of trees before touching down on top of another strange stone pileup.

The trees all about them were tall, twisted, and speckled with glowing droplets of sap, and every branch was covered in a thick, drooping blanket of mossy growth. A multitude of roots, like rebellious tentacles, climbed up from the dirt to serve as obstacles for any foolish invader daring to walk.

The soil itself was a slurry of mud, making it practically impossible to move, so the Nighthawks were forced to once again rely on the rockets of their PAS.

Helga felt annoyed by Cilas's decision. While she understood his respect of the natural life on the moon, the mission would be impeded if one of them suddenly found themselves fresh out of fuel.

Without everyone's rockets powered enough to get them back to the Thundercat, they would be forced to navigate the misty basin and whatever apex predator ruled its domain. Whether that meant more burrowers didn't matter, since none of them knew this moon enough to get ahead of potential threats.

Argan-10 was indeed beautiful, in much the same way an unknown alien flower could be considered beautiful, until you take a sniff only to find out too late that its scent is actually toxic and leads to death. That was what they were dealing with, a vicious terrain masked by its splendor and remoteness.

Preserving native lifeforms was noble; it was what they were taught as Alliance soldiers. But at the risk of conserving fuel? Oh, how she wanted to say something to him.

"The way is clearer further this way," Quentin said, utilizing the tracker's instinct he'd mastered as a Marine planet-buster. He was always comfortable in the bush, and Helga recalled how on Meluvia, he'd vanish for hours only to return having scouted kilometers ahead, dispatching any would-be ambushers.

Helga wished she had even a sprinkling of Quentin's skills when it came to surface fighting. The man could vanish into the trees, and before the enemy knew it, he would be on them, employing the use of his wicked knife.

She noticed that unlike her, he seemed relaxed, happy to be out of the range of the szilocs. Maybe it was his excitement of being in the jungle, she considered. Either way, the pensive Quentin Tutt from before was gone, replaced by the tracker, eagerly taking point to guide them along.

There was so much vegetation, much of it too alien for Helga to know a local vine from a serpent. Bugs of a million varieties took to her armor, some trying in vain to burrow through the metal, and some sort of animal was following them from the branches, but it was too dark for her to see what it was.

It felt like mere minutes had passed since the first sziloc attacked Helga and pinned her to the ground, but it had been two hours since they exited the Thundercat, and the skies were getting darker by the minute.

Helga pulled up a map on her HUD, but since Argan-10 was not in their system, all she could make out was the terrain in their immediate vicinity. It was Meluvia all over again, even down to the damp vegetarian making it difficult to proceed. But Quentin had picked up the pace, and she trusted him more than her helmet's computer, which was throwing out educated guesses as to what was coming up.

When she was at her limit with their creeping stalker, she growled and raised up her auto-rifle, peering through its superior laser sights to get an idea of who or what was the shadow.

Sundown used a hand to slowly bring her weapon down, before stepping in close and pointing towards Quentin. Helga followed his finger to where the big man was stepping out into another clearing.

"I'm using the scope's night vision, Sunny. I wasn't going to shoot it. Do you think me that dumb?" she said, turning on him now, annoyed at him questioning her actions.

It was an odd interruption to what she and the other navy personnel would have known to be a routine check of her surroundings. Sundown being a Jumper, however, hadn't been with them long enough to pick up on this, and she could see from his slightly wounded expression that he regretted having touched her gun.

"Look there," Raileo said, suddenly. "What in the twelve planets are those?"

The rest of the Nighthawks turned to see what he was pointing at, and that was when they saw where the ship was wedged in among the trees. All around it in a neat circle were the corpses of szilocs. It looked as if someone was using them to create a wall, but on closer inspection they saw that the creatures were not dead, just sluggish.

"Sound off, Nighthawks, what am I looking at?" Cilas said.

"They have a stasis field generator on the top of the ship," Raileo said, pointing to the large, disc-shaped vessel wedged in amongst a set of bent and broken trees. It had been there long enough for nature to make it a part of the moon, and the vegetation that now grew on it made it appear as a mossy outcropping of stone. The only telltale sign of it being alien to Argan-10 was the pulsing red light of the generator that Raileo was showing them. "See, it's the same kind we use for camping, though they've tweaked it to weaken anything that makes contact instead of rejecting them outright like ours."

"This seems unnecessarily cruel," Sundown said, and Helga had to agree as she watched the szilocs twitch with about as much effort as they could manage.

"Sounds like Geralos," Quentin said.

"Or our pirate psychopaths," Helga muttered. "Nothing about this comes off as Geralos to me. I was in one of their camps; they don't waste time on concocting random *schtill* like this. No, this comes from people stuck down here bored, with a deep hatred for these crab things. Maybe this ship was stolen and shot down above this moon. Pirates don't have the Alliance to call for help when they get into trouble, and out here where they've been preying on merchant ships, their allies would be few. They would be *thyped*."

"Pirates? Is that what's inside that ship?" Quentin said, not even trying to hide his disappointment.

"Now, hold on, we're just speculating," Cilas said. "The mission is to get inside there, to learn who or what has been using that thing. Our leaders suspect Geralos, and they seem pretty confident that the lizards are operating down here. For all we know, the pirates were the ones to set this up, but the lizards could have come later and taken it over, turning it into one of their feeding camps."

"And how do we get in?" Helga said, replacing her pistols and reaching back once again for her cryo-loaded auto-rifle.

"Drop in from the top, ma'am. The field is only generated by those four poles," Raileo said, using his wrist-comms to quickly draw a diagram that he then pushed to the rest of their HUDs.

"Ah, so it is like the barriers we use for camping," Helga said. "Can you power it down? It would be one heck of a distraction if they suddenly had a storm of crabs trying to cut into their hull."

"Szilocs," Sundown corrected her, but she ignored him and looked at Cilas for confirmation.

"Shut it down, Ray," Cilas said. "We need this area open in case we need to escort any survivors out or call reinforcements in to help us."

Raileo Lei retraced their steps, then took another route to gain the back of the downed ship, pulsing his rockets to speed up his pace, then flying up and over the tree line to land inside of the perimeter near the generator. The rest of the Nighthawks watched him with their weapons primed, halfway expecting something to go off the rails and risking the young chief's life.

It took fifteen minutes for him to crack open the stasis generator to reveal the vulnerable controls. Upon Cilas's command, he rejoined them near the depression that had been made when the ship crash-landed. After a brief countdown as they hovered, Raileo fired a bullet into the generator's controls, causing it to spark and power down.

Almost immediately the ground exploded with szilocs, freed and raving mad at anything within their vicinity. Not even their own number was spared the deadly lashing out of limbs, and several went down screaming from their wounds. Once they were recovered, however, they moved like a well-coordinated cavalry on the ship.

Szilocs scrambled up its sides, slamming forelegs into the hull, screaming out in a cacophony of earsplitting shrills, as they attacked what they perceived to have been the cause of their stasis prison. Helga was stunned by the sheer number of creatures. There were hundreds that had been at the perimeter, but now more were climbing up out of the ground, joining their fellows.

"We would never have survived without PAS," she muttered to no one in particular.

"Can you imagine?" Cilas said.

"I really don't want to," Helga said, looking disgusted.

"Alright, we need to move. Let's get on that thing and find a hatch that will allow us to gain the interior," Cilas said. "If there's anyone alive inside, they should be losing their *schtill* right now over the sudden attack from those creatures. We need that chaos to keep them sleeping, and the longer we wait, the higher the chances that some smart lizard commander will get wise to the distraction."

"There's a hatch near the top there, Commander," Raileo said, pointing to an off-colored block on the far side of the saucer, which was the taller side of the tilt, well above the tree line.

Cilas didn't answer; he just took off towards it, showcasing his mastery of the PAS. Helga was up and after him as fast as she could, and as a unit the Nighthawks soared, leaving the szilocs and the rocks to land on the more familiar surface of a hull. The hatch was standard for a Genesian-built ship, so Cilas and Quentin were able to start working on the controls.

Helga scanned the skies about them for drones or any other sort of surveillance that would alert the Geralos of their approach. Sundown walked the length of the hull to where the szilocs were scrambling over one another to get over to where they were, and powered on his las-sword before holding it out to one side.

He drew an invisible line in front of him and when the first sziloc crossed, he began to twirl one way and then the other, lopping off the legs of the first eager violators. Fifteen of them went down by the time Cilas got the hatch open, and the creatures' intelligence showed when the others grew wise and tried to make their way around him.

Cilas and Quentin entered the hatch, finding a pair of ladders leading down into the blackness of the hold. They went down it together, followed by Helga, while Raileo started shooting cryo rounds into the climbers. Sundown barely made it in, and Raileo secured the hatch above them. Helga had to wonder if Cilas had a plan for them to get out once they were done.

Inside the crashed ship was just as wonderfully alien as the moon. Where Helga had expected a layout of tight passageways and compartments filled with equipment, what they found was the interior shell of a spacecraft.

If there was ever metal on the bulkhead it was now gone, stripped clean to the hull, and the deck was overtaken with soil that sprouted nocturnal plants and wildlife. Helga descended from the ladder onto a strategically placed mountain of rocks.

It reminded her of a cave, it was so open and different from what she had expected to find. Whoever had crashed here had spent years stripping all the metal from the bulkhead. But why? That was the question that was driving her insane, unless they had salvaged the metal to take it off the moon. But she hadn't seen any piles of metal outside.

Helga decided that the answer would reveal itself to them eventually, and put it out of her mind as she made her way over to the men. They were standing around a hole at the center of the space, but it wasn't just a hole; it was a shaft, outlined in metal. It was wide enough to accommodate ten bodies, and like the hatch leading in there were two ladders, allowing for multiple entry.

"I'm guessing we have to go down there," Helga muttered, to which Cilas grunted in agreement.

"Rend, look here," Quentin said, and they all turned to find him pointing to a wall of brown crust that was growing on the bulkhead. "Recognize this stuff?"

"Of course. That's the confirmation I needed that this is indeed a lizard op. Damn it. Listen up, men, you have to be ready. What we're about to see down there may be enough to have you lose your rations inside your mask, or stay sleepless for many cycles. Steel yourselves, and be strong. This is what you struggled through BLAST and the Jumper agency to prepare for. Helga and I were victims of one of these places, and it's bound to bring up *schtill* we hoped to forget, eh, Hel?"

"Yeah, sure," she said, nodding, wondering if she had only imagined him calling her "Hel" in front of the other men.

"If you feel weak, just remember," Cilas said, putting a finger in the air to indicate the space above them. "This is what they're doing to Vestalians all over the galaxy. Before you get sick, get *thyping* angry, and keep your eyes open for any Vestalian prisoners. They need to learn that we aren't to be trifled with. That we have our own, Craqtii, and we're out to uproot every one of these stations."

"Let's *thyping* do it, then. My fingers are itchy," Quentin said, positioning himself over one of the ladders.

Helga expected Raileo to add something clever, but the Nighthawk was uncharacteristically silent.

Cilas took the other ladder and started descending it, with Quentin across from him on the other side, followed by Raileo Lei and Sundown, while Helga perched on the lip above them, aiming down.

Once in a while, she would look up and observe the space around her. It was a massive vessel, almost as big as the *Ursula*, and through the night vision of her PAS's HUD, she could see where the Geralos spores had covered every inch of the bulkhead.

The spores grew from a substance that was manufactured by the Geralos. It was a convenient way for them to take over Alliance vessels since it converted oxygen into something akin to what they breathed on their planet. Helga had inhaled it once and almost lost consciousness immediately. She remembered its scent to be incredibly foul.

Even now, the memory of it made her want to gag, and she almost lost it when she saw something wriggle from a hole to fall to the deck where it buried itself into the soil.

"Come on down," Cilas said, and Helga complied, gripping the handles and sliding down quickly, using her rockets to slow her descent. She landed in a small room covered in spores, where three of the walls held doors that had once belonged to the disabled ship above them.

"Hold," Cilas said, and then he placed his forefinger near the mask of his helmet. It was something he would do whenever he was stressed or in deep thought, and Helga found it curious that he was doing it in full armor. "It's denser down here than on the surface. PAS isn't able to use sensor waves to map out whatever this place is."

"Denser than a ship's hull?" Helga said, ready to argue logic against the absurdity that she was hearing.

"Maybe dense isn't the word I'm looking for. Can any of you make out anything beyond this room?" Cilas said.

"Negative," Quentin said. "This place is a void. My map's interface is showing static, like something's bugging out."

"That's likely what's happening here," Helga said, her eyes locked onto a door, nearly willing it to open so that something, anything, would happen. These breaks in the action were always the worst, knowing that at any time they could be jumped and someone could lose their life.

"Going in blind is annoying, but far from enough to prevent us from doing our job," Cilas said. "Our locations are synced, so until we find the jammer, we can keep track of our path as we explore it. Spores mean lizards, and we know it's likely the szilocs can burrow into here. Stay half-cocked, but smart. We are all professionals, so let's *thyping* act like it."

"Should we split up, Commander?" Raileo said, and Cilas seemed to consider it before shaking his head.

"We're blind, and it's likely to be a maze in here, but together we run the risk of being trapped," he said, undecided. He made the motion of running his hand through his hair—another tell from him thinking deeply—sliding his gauntleted palm across his helmet. "Tell you what, Nighthawks, let's see what we're dealing with here. Line up for the breach, and Ray, pick a door and fry it so that we can take a look inside."

Since the doors of the room came from the ship and used proximity sensors, any fool willing to play with the locking panels could end up exposed when it suddenly opened. Raileo, having proven himself an expert at breaking into locks, could override the automation, tricking the system into thinking that the ship was out of power.

"Ready, Commander," he said, and placed his palm against the door, glancing over his shoulder to where the rest of the Nighthawks were crouched.

Cilas stepped up into the center of them, leaning into his pulse-rifle as if it were a form of support. Once that door came open, anyone vaguely humanoid would be the first to drop from his deadly, accurate fire. Helga had never been on the receiving end of a breach, but the surprise and death that came with it made survival seem unlikely, so she was glad to once again be on the other end.

"Pop it," Cilas commanded, and Raileo Lei pulled the heavy door open just a crack. Cilas stepped forward and hopped back, giving his

PAS time to record what was inside. Raileo slid it back shut, then backed away with his weapon raised.

"It's a tunnel, and it's tight. We would be foolish to take it together at this point," Cilas said. "Three doors underground, and with no maps to assist. It looks like we're splitting up.

18

The tunnels of the subterranean compound reminded Helga of the ant farms that a handful of spacers kept inside of their berths. It was a privilege to own pets or any sort of life inside of an overpopulated ship of war, but officers had the credits and approval to do it, since it helped to boost morale. A shaken Marine may not care to fight through a unit to get back to his duties on the ship, but if his fish, plants, or ants needed feeding, he would manifest greatness on the battlefield.

Helga had never felt the need to purchase a nest or bring home a plant, but she did find them alluring, and now she wondered if this was how it felt to be one of those imprisoned insects. What she thought was dirt caked up on the bulkhead turned out to be a strange blend of spores and carapace chunks.

Why is this being used to coat the walls and ceiling? Helga wondered. She knew the spores were for the lizards to breathe, but it didn't explain the strategically placed sziloc chunks. After stepping through their assigned door, she and Raileo had found themselves inside of what felt like an endless tunnel.

Lights were mounted on the ceiling—more borrowed assets from the wreckage above—and lumber, which hinted that time had been spent to cut down trees to support whatever this was. It was a sturdy, well-built shaft that stretched on into blackness, despite the lights, and Helga became increasingly worried at what they would discover at the end of it all.

"Hey, Helga, how are you and Ray looking over there?" Cilas said over the comms, causing Helga to pull up short and flag down Raileo to tell him to stand guard.

They had been through two rooms already, connected by tunnels lined with more metal from the ship. At odd places Helga noticed there were roots pushing through the walls. She wondered if they were in the szilocs' old hive, now co-opted by the Geralos.

"We're good, Rend, but nothing so far. I'm starting to think we missed this party and whatever was here's long gone."

"Stay sharp, you never know. Remember, make some noise if you see anything."

"Contact," came Quentin's shout over open comms, and as Helga prepared herself mentally for whatever it was that was coming, she and Raileo exchanged looks of concern.

"Target neutralized," came another voice, this time from Sundown, who spoke as evenly as if he was informing them about a change in temperature.

One day I'll attain that level of calm, Helga thought, frustrated with the anxiety she felt, waiting to be overrun inside of this tunnel. *What was Cilas thinking splitting us up? Does he really have this much confidence in our abilities, or does he know something else that he hasn't divulged?*

"Good kill," said Quentin. "But what in the worlds is it?"

"Were you discovered?" Cilas said, cutting him off, though Quentin's question made Helga wonder if the target Sundown killed was something other than a Geralos.

"We're still dark, Commander, though I think we need to discuss what we're up against now," Quentin said. "Hold for visual," and the comms went silent as he worked at sharing his helmet's feed so that the rest of the Nighthawks could see the corpse.

When the image came through on Helga's HUD, she gasped in horror at what she saw. On the ground, bleeding out, was a being that at first glance appeared to be human. But when Quentin knelt close to show them more, she saw that the dead man did not have a nose or lips, and its small, open mouth revealed long teeth, pointed and jagged just like the Geralos.

"I'm sorry, Q, but what are we looking at here?" Cilas said. "Is that what happens when we breed with lizards?"

It was the question Helga had been asking herself as she surveyed the footage coming from Quentin's helmet. Being the product of an interspecies coupling herself, Helga had always wondered if it was possible.

The very thought of it shook her to the core, with both repulsion and rage. It was supposed to be impossible, considering the differences in physiology and genetic makeup.

Greg Dragon

Genesians, Meluvians, and Virulians were branches on the same human tree that birthed Vestalians, so it was natural for those species to mix. Casanians, Traxians, and possibly the Louine were humanoid, and shared many of the same genetics. Louine genes were the exception; they were practically supreme, and so a mixed-species child would be born with no trace of the non-Louine parent.

Helga's existence was not only proof that Casanians and humans were compatible, but that the offspring could inherit the seeker-gene, which many still believed was exclusive to Vestalian women.

Geralos, out of all of Anstractor's races, was a unique species with no evidence of having shared an ancestry. They were deemed monsters, and the ultimate parasite, coming from a smaller planet with the sole goal of conquering and eating everyone else. At least that's what spacers like Helga had been raised to believe, and seeing this abomination lifeless on the floor made her wonder again at their history.

The sight of it sickened her, but not enough to look away. Was it a product of love? Could a Vestalian be so far removed from her pride to lay down with something as dangerous and vile as a Geralos lizard? And what were those veins, which spoke of pain, and something else cruel?

"I believe that what we're seeing is a fusion of sorts," Sundown said. He was kneeling over the corpse now, going through its pockets for anything informational, while stripping its body to reveal more of its features to the Nighthawks. When it was completely naked, it was even more horrific. The genitals were that of a human male, grossly malformed, assuring more nightmares in the future for the young lieutenant.

All about its abdomen were raised lines, like badly healed incisions, and when they began to writhe, Helga was pushed past her limit and broke.

"Maker's sake, *thype* this, Cilas. We are not equipped or trained to deal with bio-engineered monsters full of parasites. I am literally shaking right now, and... and..." She closed her eyes and breathed, hoping that Raileo hadn't noticed her reaction. She had muted her comms when she spoke her truth, though no one would have heard her, she had to say it.

What are we doing here? she thought again, staring up at the roof of the tunnel. *We were excited to come kill Geralos, the true enemy of the Alliance, and now we have this.*

159

"Everything good, ma'am?" Raileo said, causing her to flinch.

"Yeah, I was just checking above us to be sure that we hadn't missed anything," she lied, but it didn't help that her voice had cracked. "Alright, look, Ray, that thing they killed. This is all new and I am really just trying to process this *schtill*. I don't need help or concern, I just need time to think. We need to prepare ourselves for more surprises inside of this pit."

"Will we ever prepared though?" Raileo said. "Seems to me that this is exactly why they sent us in. We're reconnaissance, the eyes of the Alliance. An Alliance that is just learning that our own Vestalians have been selling out our people for the lizards to create weapons like him. Can you imagine the response on *Rendron* if they learned about this hybrid?"

"Oh, I can imagine. I'm half-Casanian, and though both my parents came from allied planets, the xenophobia and distrust was already a problem. Something like this gets out there to the ignorant spacers on our starships, and the Geralos won't have to do anything; the crew would implode and wipe itself out."

"I don't believe that for a second," Raileo said, turning to face her. "Most spacers I grew up with were like me, Tutt, and the commander. It's us, as in the entire galaxy, against them, the Geralos lizards. That exclusive human rhetoric comes from the bored, deck-scrubbing losers, grounded forever on our ships. I am confident that most of us want the same thing: Vestalia returned to the Vestalians, and Geral reduced to the galaxy's biggest asteroid field."

"Look at you, all grown up, Laser Ray," Helga said before reaching forward to place a hand on his shoulder. "We should get going. If either of the other teams gets discovered, this narrow tunnel of doom is not where I want to be."

"Maker," Cilas suddenly whispered, bringing their attention back to the comms.

"You good, Commander?" Raileo said.

"Still kicking, Chief, but I'm about as far as I dare go. Nighthawks, I found something. The door that I took led me to a short passageway, lifted from the ship. There's now a reinforced door, with a tiny glass window like the ones that lead into the *Ursula*'s mess. I'm about to share my visual. Helga, you will recognize what this is immediately," Cilas said.

A small prompt appeared at the corner of Helga's vision, and when she accepted the uplink, it expanded until she was seeing everything that Cilas was seeing at that moment. In front of her was some dirty, cloudy glass, but beyond it she could see a line of human bodies, standing with their backs to the wall and their hands above their heads.

Helga knew what it was immediately. She and Cilas once hung from hooks in a Geralos prison just like this. Inside that room, the temperature would be freezing, and there would be a chemical in the air that would instantly put them to sleep if they inhaled it.

She saw now that aside from the mutant Geralos that Sundown had killed, this underground facility was a Vestalian processing camp, very much like the one they had escaped two years before on Dyn.

Cilas was still talking them through it, but Helga didn't need to listen. She had been here, and knew what was to come for the poor souls trapped inside that room. She began to count them, guessing that the room would be a square, and with every centimeter holding a captive, there would be more than 120 prisoners.

"Looks like we're going to need to call in help to get these people out," she said.

"That shouldn't be a problem once we clear this whole place of the *thypes* that did this," Raileo added, bitterly.

"I'm going back to the first room to wait," Cilas said. "It's going to take all of our manpower, if we're to get them out. Finish mapping out your areas and stay up on comms. Evaluate the situation before charging any rooms, and above all else, Nighthawks, remain in the shadows. If you hit a wall or dead-end, head back and join me, and together we can rescue the civilians. Helga, how are you and Ray looking?"

"Cruising, with no sign of the enemy, so far," Helga said. "Though to be honest, Rend, we're still making our way. This has to be the longest tunnel in the known galaxy. I could swear we've been on it forever."

"Stay sharp, you never know. Look out for hidden doors, decoys, and emergency escape holes above you. I don't know how they're keeping the szilocs from burrowing into here, but if it was that field generator we blew, it is only a matter of time. Remember, alert us if you run into anything. Don't play at hero; this is an order."

"You have my word," Helga said, embarrassed by what sounded like a little too much concern for her well-being. She felt good hearing it, but if she didn't know him it would come off as patronizing.

"This facility and everything about it puts my nerves on edge," Sundown whispered.

"It should," Cilas said. "This is what they took our planet for. To set up all sorts of evil like this. They have the gall to have one here, in what is supposed to be neutral space. Listen to me, Nighthawks, we absolutely cannot afford to be taken hostage down here. It is crucial to this mission—no, this war—that we get our footage of this facility back to Alliance HQ. We fail and this continues for maker knows how many more years."

"What are they doing to them inside that room?" Raileo asked Helga on direct comms.

"They are either dead or frozen in a kind of stasis that shuts down their local consciousness. You just fall asleep and have lengthy dreams. It's like you take a trip to another dimension, knowing that it isn't real but incapable of getting out, no matter how hard you try."

"How did you get out?" Raileo said.

"That's a question for Cilas," Helga replied. "He rescued another Nighthawk and me. As to how he managed to do that? Your guess is about as good as mine."

Once they could see the end of the tunnel, she and Raileo quickened their pace. Knowing that Cilas was waiting on them lit a fire beneath them that was necessary; not because they feared his reprimand, but because of the danger to his life.

They came upon another door at the end of the tunnel, and when Raileo glanced back at her, Helga gave him the go-ahead to pull it open. There was movement, and in the span of a second, she saw two suited figures turn towards them.

Helga's auto-rifle was already chattering, perforating the vulnerable breastplate of one of these men, turning his internal fluids into ice. Raileo slid down to a knee, angling backward to evade the retaliation. One shot from his pistol was all it took, and the second figure toppled over, dead before he could react.

The two Nighthawks quickly secured the room, peering under the two rows of benches, and in the corners behind a line of hanging EVA suits.

They were inside of what appeared to be a changing room, judging by the discarded bits of gear. The light was low, but bright compared to the tunnel, and when Helga finally surveyed the corpses, she was relieved to find that they were Geralos.

"Think we're clear," Raileo said, sounding out of breath, then walked over to the far door and stood guard as Helga made the call to update Cilas.

"Commander, Ray and I found some sort of changing room occupied by two lizards—now neutralized—and too messy to cover up. They looked to have been making their way out."

"They must have seen or heard the szilocs somehow," Cilas said, whispering a curse. "*Thype* it, I didn't expect things to stay quiet this long anyway. Search that room and press on, Helga. See if you can find anything that would give us an idea of the layout of this place. Ray, there's bound to be more contacts, so be on your game. Let Helga worry about the discovery."

"Got it, commander," Raileo said, and he crossed the room to the far door, where he stood with his rifle raised, ready to give the next intruder a cold surprise.

"Copy that, Rend, we'll see what we can find. How are Tutt and Sunny doing?" Helga said.

"They've been quiet since that last call to show us the mutant. Switching off comms now. Just keep me posted on any surprises, alright?"

"I'll be diligent, Commander," Helga said, then marched over to the wall and began searching the suits and other equipment that were stored inside. She was surprised to find that many of these were Alliance-issued, which hinted at spacers being nabbed and traded to the Geralos by the pirates.

The longer she looked, the more it angered her, and by the time she was finished she had vowed that every pirate she met after this day would meet the *Ursula*'s airlock or her sidearm.

"Nothing here but old junk," she said. "I'm starting to think that this isn't a changing room, after all. This appears to be where the lizards discard the suits of the Vestalians they bring in here."

"That doesn't make sense, Lieutenant," Raileo said. "The numbers don't match; there had to be a hundred people in there."

"Let's keep moving, the answer will come," Helga said. She had to admit that Raileo was right. Perhaps there would be another storage like this one on the far side, where Quentin and Sundown were stalking.

Helga got on one side of the door and Raileo the other, with one hand on the panel, ready to trigger the release. In his other hand was a hand cannon that she hadn't noticed him holding before.

It was a spectacular weapon, intimidating and alien. It had to have come from *A'wfa Terracydes*, black and bulky, with the fattest barrel wrapped in aqua lights.

She raised her auto-rifle up to her shoulder and took a breath to prepare for any surprises.

"Punch that *schtill*, Ray," she commanded, and he slammed his fist into the panel. The door slid open with a hiss, and Helga depressed the trigger, just a hair, as she chanced a glance.

Inside was a much bigger room, with troughs lined up in rows, each holding a variety of vegetation. Unlike the dark tunnel they had come through, or the low light of the one they were in, this underground garden was as bright as day. The ceiling glowed with blindingly bright light, coming from tubes crisscrossed above it all.

"Is that a bench?" Helga said.

"The lizards built a park down here?" Raileo said, and he pointed to where there was a table, chairs, and what looked to be an algae-conversion unit. "Wait, Ate, my PAS is saying that there's oxygen in here, and I don't see any trace of the surface's poison. If we wanted to, we could remove our masks."

"Which means that they built this space for humans!"

19

For several long minutes Helga and Raileo patrolled the length of the underground garden, looking for clues to explain its function. The plants were plentiful but they were all the same, and with trough-shaped planters built into the floor, they looked to have been strategically placed.

Helga's initial thought was that it had been a sort of peaceful refuge for the human captives, but the more she observed, the more it looked as though it served a different purpose. What evaded her, however, was the lack of spores on the walls. The room's size was significant, roughly the size of an assault cruiser. Did the plants require oxygen? That would make sense, but why then have fountains and benches? It was all so bizarre. Helga just knew that at any moment, the vines would start moving and they would learn that the plants were all parts of one monster.

"Have you ever been to an algae farm, Ray?" Helga said, pausing to get a closer look at one of the leaves.

"On *Rendron*, sure, but there wasn't much to look at," Raileo said. "What makes you ask?"

"This layout, the way they're planted. Doesn't it strike you as more of a farm than a garden or park?"

"It's crossed my mind, yeah. Do the lizards have vegetables in their diet?"

Raileo whistled and when Helga looked over to see what he wanted, she saw that he was scrolling through some information on his wrist-comms.

"Find something good?" she said, not expecting much since their wrist-comms were limited in terms of data.

"Untamed moon and over a hundred humans to feed to preserve their lives," he said. "These plants were flown in. I knew I recognized them. They are *pigmy war crests*, from the wetlands of Traxis. It's what we use for our ration bars; these plants are essential to the survival of those captives. If you look at the ceiling above those lights, you will see a sprinkler system that I bet is on a timer. Near the benches there, those grooves at the edges is where the water gets drained and recycled."

"I see," Helga said, stunned. It was so easy to forget that Raileo had more to him than his pistol aim. "This is quite something, isn't it? The lizards built this all to keep those people preserved for them to bite."

"Commander, I think we've found their communications room," Quentin said over comms, nearly causing Helga to jump. "There's equipment in here from the cockpit of a ship, and it all seems to be functional. It even has a starmap and a torpedo guidance system."

"What's displayed on the map, Q?" Cilas said.

"The station, *A'wfa Terracydes*, and I see three—wait, make that four drones relaying back this signal."

"What in the worlds do the lizards want with the Arisanis?" Cilas muttered.

"Commander, if you will allow me," Sundown said. "I think this has more to do with our pirates than the Geralos."

"How so, Jumper?" Cilas said, sounding past his limit.

"Well, I have been observing the rooms within this structure, and they are strategically set up to house both the Geralos and their captives. There are vents above us, pumping oxygen through converters, purifying the moon's toxic atmosphere. In the area where you are located, the spores were plentiful, but none are in here. This tells me that the lizards built a shared space down here, and there is bound to be another way out, which they use to transport prisoners from the surface."

"Want to bet that other entrance is near the greenhouse that we're in?" Helga said to Raileo Lei.

"None of this makes any sense to me," Quentin said. "What in the worlds are they doing down here?"

"That's not for us to figure out," Cilas said. "Smarter minds in the Alliance can solve the puzzle once we're done. We've managed to find the room with the captives, a communications room, and proof that the pirates are trading with the lizards. Now what's left is for us to finish clearing these rooms, and then we can call in aid for these people. Helga, grab a recording of those plants, and anything else odd that you find. If that communication room is truly functional, we can upload what we find to the Ursula."

"Now I regret not grabbing footage of all those szilocs swarming," Raileo said. "You know those thrust heads back on mother won't believe us unless there's—"

He held up a hand and quickly crouched, which prompted Helga to do the same. She still held her auto-rifle, despite them having walked the entire length and breadth of the room because it held two more doors besides the one that they had come through.

One led to the room with the Vestalians hanging from the walls, and the other was a mystery, though she was sure it pressed on deeper, towards the same communication room that Quentin had just discovered.

Helga peered through the leaves that obscured the last door, and when she saw movement, her heart rate skyrocketed. She reached over and grabbed Raileo's arm, dragging him back towards another planter. "Contact," she said through clenched jaws, and then she saw four Cel-tocs tending to the plants.

"They'll reveal us to the lizards," Raileo said, reaching into his pack to bring out a gun that Helga hadn't seen him use before.

"Going up," Helga announced, then jumped and rocketed towards the ceiling, spraying the line of androids liberally with cryo-rounds. Her shots did more harm to the plants than the Cel-tocs, though one got hit in the arm, and it did nothing to stop or slow him.

Raileo was running and firing, dropping one and wounding another. There was something different about his gunfire, though, and Helga immediately noticed it. The Cel-toc that had been wounded was only shot in the arm yet it too went down, twitching as if malfunctioning.

"What are you firing at, Nighthawks?" Cilas was shouting over the comms, and it took several long seconds for it to register to Helga, who had come back to the ground to switch her ammo from cryo to kinetic.

"We have Cel-tocs, and they know we're in here," Helga said, barely able to talk. "They're tough, not a model that I'm familiar with—"

"Commander," shouted Quentin Tutt, suddenly, his booming voice cutting through the comms, "I see four dropship signatures above the moon, and they don't appear to be Alliance. Are we expecting anyone?"

"Those aren't friendly, they're likely stolen," Cilas shouted. "*Thype* me, did we walk into a trap? Nighthawks, new mission. Kill everything and find that other exit, fast. We have to leave these hostages. Right now the focus is on uploading our intel and surviving long enough for rescue or escape. Q, Sunny, lock down that communications room. I'm on my over, now."

On cue, Raileo started pressing on the Cel-tocs, who seemed confused and incapable of defending themselves. Still, "kill everything" had been the command, and Raileo Lei wasn't the type to pass up showing off his skills on mechanical targets.

Helga rushed to join him now that her ammo had been loaded and charged, but the Cel-tocs were already down, lying in the alleys of the planters, with blue smoke rising from their wounds.

"What are you shooting with, Ray?" Helga said. "I know those aren't kinetic rounds."

"Rupture rounds," he replied, and she couldn't tell from his tone if he was joking.

"Rupture rounds. Are you making *schtill* up?" she said, scanning the area in front of them for movement.

"No, they're fusions, sort of like our explosives," Raileo said excitedly. It was obvious that he had been waiting to talk about them. "I don't know what they use to make them, but you can't question the results."

"Did you get those from *A'wfa Terracydes* as well?" Helga said, though she knew the answer would be yes. "Maker, you must have spent a year's rate there. You're positively reckless."

"Says the Nighthawk," he laughed, causing her to reflect on the irony.

"We shouldn't joke about our mortality. Not now at least, when we have our people hanging like meat inside of that room."

"We'll get them, Ate," Raileo said confidently. "You heard the commander. Nothing inside here is going to make it out alive. Do you want a cartridge? I have a spare, and its energy-charged; you would only need the one."

"Thanks, but I'm good with my kinetics, Ray. I can't bring myself to trust those black market rounds. Anyway, let's cut the chatter and press on into the next room. Those dropships will need to find a clear space outside to land, and you saw it yourself that there is nowhere around here that can accommodate one, let alone four. This means that we missed something. There's a landing platform, a camouflaged base, or something else beyond this crashed ship."

"Only one way to find out," he said, and walked over to the door that the Cel-tocs had come through.

Helga got to one side, and Raileo fried the panel and pulled it open. Inside was a room full of all manner of equipment. There was a generator, which Helga assumed powered the underground facility, and lines from it running to several computers that were unlike any she had ever seen before.

On the walls near the door where they entered stood several rows of Cel-tocs charging at their stations. In the back were shelves, stacked with supplies for the plants, and samples pickled inside of jars that glowed in the low light.

"If the plants are food, then these are cooks, I'm guessing," Raileo said, and then raised his gun and started shooting each one of the androids in the head.

It seemed excessive and unnecessary, but Cilas had ordered them to kill everything that wasn't a Vestalian survivor. Helga joined in on the executions, and in a minute all eleven Cel-tocs were fried beyond repair. She reported their findings and checked the map to make sure that the additional room was added, and then went through the supplies to see if anything there could give them information on the Geralos.

"Looks like this is a dead-end," she said, frustrated. "Tutt finds the communication room, and we get a glorified greenhouse."

"We should make the best of it and snag a few seeds to bring back to the *Ursula*," Raileo said, flashing her a smile.

"Terrible idea. We don't know what the lizards have done to anything down here. We could take that home and cook it up, and the whole lot of us transform into mutants, all because you want to play at farmer," Helga said.

She led him out of the room and onto the next, which was opposite the equipment room that they had originally come from. "If this is another storage facility, I am going to laugh," Raileo said, kneeling down to hack into the panel and fry the circuits to trigger yet another manual override. Again, this breach didn't yield a room full of the enemy or an alarm from the system, so the two Nighthawks didn't hesitate to slip inside.

There was another tunnel, this one wide and well built. Its walls were made of stone, and it was wide enough to fit a transport through.

It was also well-lit, with lights so high in the ceiling, Helga wondered if they were merely holes coming from the surface. The effect they had gave off that illusion; someone had put time into building it to withstand the test of time.

"This is starting to feel like a bunker," Helga said. "And this tunnel that we're in feels military."

"I'd imagine that if this is a base, they would deck it out in the same manner that we deck out our spaceships. We've found the food supply—let's call it the mess—communications, brig, and an equipment room. We have yet to find their berthing, some sort of head, though I don't even know if the lizards drop waste like we do," Raileo said. "So, berth, head, entertainment? If they're down here for as long as it takes to build rooms and cut stone and metal, they would need some release, so I expect to find a brothel, theater—"

"Did you say brothel?" Helga said.

"Yes, a pleasure hole. Maybe a bar, and oh—where was I? Oh, a barracks, right? Maybe a training facility with ranges to keep the lizard Marines on their *schtill*."

"I think you got it all, Nighthawk," Helga said, laughing, "Good job. I personally think that this place is a sort of lab, but the rooms that you're describing aren't far-fetched. Let's keep moving. I don't want to be this open if something comes out of that door."

With that they pulsed their rockets and shot forward 40 meters to the end of the tunnel. By this time, they had been through so many doors that the communication was automatic. Raileo got it open, and Helga rushed in with her weapon raised and ready for action. This time the room was a cave, as long as it was wide, and they were above it on a mezzanine installation, with steps leading down into darkness.

Helga's night-vision cut through the blackness of the space to reveal a warehouse loaded up with giant tanks wedged in between its support columns. It seemed to be void of life, another massive room whose purpose was solely to support the Geralos facility. Raileo grabbed her arm and pulled her down to the floor, where he gestured for her to follow him as he crawled forward to peer over the edge.

Directly below them was a Geralos commando, armored and bigger than any Helga had ever seen. He was pacing about the floor below them with a laser-sighted auto-rifle in his hands. The two Nighthawks didn't dare move a muscle as they waited, watching him and scanning the room for more guards. Nothing moved, and the HUD radar was still not giving them any information.

"We don't have time for this," Helga complained, as she placed the barrel of her auto-rifle on the railing to employ the use of its scope. With slow, focused breathing, assisted by her innate senses, she scanned the darkness for more enemies, possibly hidden in the deeper corners of the room. Her eyes found one they had somehow missed, sleeping with his back up against a tank.

"I have eyes on a lizard in the back," she whispered. "I'll take him out if you can neutralize that monster."

"Taking the shot," Raileo said, and he got up to a knee and aimed down at the giant Geralos. He fired, and so did Helga, though where Raileo's kill was clean, hers grazed the scalp of the lizard in the distance. Her shot, however, struck the tank behind him, and it started to leak a thick yellow liquid onto the floor. She fired again, striking him in the forehead, killing him instantly, and he toppled backward into the gunk.

A reaction occurred upon the Geralos's fall, as the liquid not only melted him but started to grow, eating through both metal and stone. When it touched another vat, the supports were ruptured, causing it to collapse and break open, adding more liquid to the mix. This sped up the process, and the Nighthawks watched in awe as the room began to collapse onto itself.

"We should go," Raileo whispered, helping her back up to her feet.

"Damn my aim, Ray. What if it keeps growing?" she said, frightened. "This could bring the whole *thyping* place down!"

A loud screech came from behind them, and Helga turned to face the open doorway as a section of the tunnel broke out. A sziloc stepped out and upon seeing them, screeched again and started towards them, followed by several more. Without saying a word, the Nighthawks began firing, Raileo's rupture rounds putting holes in thoraxes and blowing apart a number of legs. More poured through, and in less than a minute the tunnel became packed with the creatures scrambling along its walls.

"Commander, we have szilocs swarming beyond the plant room," Helga reported above the loud chattering of her auto-rifle. "Ray, we need to cross that room," she said. "There is another door and we have our PAS. Let's take our chances there before we get pinned back and fall into the sludge coming from those vats!"

She ran and jumped over the railing, triggering her rockets to take her over the hole and the smoking chemicals that were rapidly eroding the floor and walls of the room. Worried for Raileo, she glanced back to find him on her flank, rolling masterfully to avoid a vat that collapsed after she passed it, nearly showering them with its contents.

The room was large, and they covered it in no time, but Helga could see that the szilocs were beyond persistent at chasing them down. The first few that followed had crawled out into the liquid, and it melted their limbs as they stubbornly pushed forward. More crawled on top of them, and more on top of those, forming a bridge while the others took to the walls to keep pace with the Nighthawks.

It was absolutely nightmarish, but Helga was well beyond fear, and as they gained the door and pressed on inside, her thoughts grew quiet, replaced with action, borne of training and instinct.

"Ray, seal the door," Helga shouted before pulsing her rockets to zip past the tables to reach an open doorway in the back. Unlike the numerous doors that had been breached to get here, this one seemed unfinished. The frame was installed, but there was no door, and beyond it she saw another shaft leading up, this one having a set of concrete steps to allow easy access up and down it.

Her comms came alive to Quentin Tutt, and the distraction caused her to glance at her map. She was surprised to see Sundown's signature directly above her location.

"Ate, is that Ray's rifle I hear down there?" Sundown said.

"Yes," she started, wondering why it was that Raileo was still fighting when she had just told him to seal the door. Glancing quickly behind her, she saw the cause of his hesitation. Several szilocs had bypassed the door and torn through the concrete to gain the room, only to be met with rupture rounds from Raileo's double pistols.

She switched chat to general comms. "Commander, we're being swarmed by szilocs," she shouted. "They're coming through the walls, and we're about to be overrun. Sunny, Q, if you can make it over here, we could use some help. *Thype* me, they can break through solid stone, and there's an endless number of these things."

"Okay, what happened over there, and why am I just learning of this now?" Cilas said, angrily. "How is it that they got in all of a sudden when these tunnels have gone unprovoked for years? I need answers fast. We have civilians imprisoned down here, and if we cannot stop the szilocs, they will break into that room and shred every single one of them to pieces."

"Commander, it was me," Raileo said, before Helga could utter a word. "There was a room full of tanks and I accidentally hit one of them when we coordinated shots on a pair of lizards."

Helga wanted to strangle him. Why was he lying to Cilas when they both knew she had taken that shot and was now at fault for whatever would come from the szilocs?

"Commander, I will explain everything once we get out, but right now, we're in the middle of a fight," Helga said. "Our guns are hot, and we're pinned down. Either lend us some help, or we are going to die."

"Sunny, get over there," Cilas said. "Q, stay with me, in case they manage to break in before I get this message out. Upload of the feed is near completion, but if we leave now then all this was for naught. Dead or alive, the Alliance needs to know what we've learned down here. Helga, they're giant bugs, and we're in PAS. If it gets to be too much, the three of you should make for the surface, and we will join you once the upload is done."

"We found an exit near where you're fighting, Ate," Quentin said. "You should see it on your radar now, though much of the detail is still obscured. Sunny knows the way, and can lead you to it. The room with the exit hatch has metal walls, so the szilocs shouldn't be able to pursue you once you've made your way out."

Helga cursed when the heat warning on her auto-rifle went off, as she peppered the head of a new invader that had managed to slip past the door. Raileo Lei was in the zone, but she knew that his guns were just about done.

The OKAGI "Widow Maker," which was his weapon of choice, was already cooling in its place on his pack. He always carried several weapons, but to see him down to pistols revealed the reality of their crisis, and Helga wondered just how much longer they had before the creatures would overpower their guns.

"How are you doing Ray?" she shouted above the gunfire.

"Guns getting hot, and they're still pressing like mad," he said.

What a way to die, she thought, *down here below a moon that the Alliance barely knows about, on a mission that we shouldn't have accepted, to creatures that no Rendron spacer has ever encountered before.*

She glanced down at her auto-rifle and the ammo gauge was flashing red. It was too late; the gun was now frozen, locking the trigger so that it could no longer be depressed as it started the lengthy sequence of cooling off.

"*Schtill!*" she screamed, and Raileo, aware of what just happened, took one arm and shoved her back into the room with the stairs.

In a beautiful display of gunplay, he alternated shots, each having devastating effect. This was Raileo Lei at his finest, a matchless gunslinger with his back to the wall. With his hands a blur and his face a mask of somber focus, Helga pulled out her own pistols and ran up to assist in defending the room.

"Ate, go. You're our pilot, and if you die then we all die. Leave me your pistols and catch up with Sunny. I can hold them off while you get the dropship."

What he said made sense, but for his voice, which had a finality that Helga didn't like. She loved Raileo, the same way she loved Joy, Cilas and Tutt, and to imagine life without them was just too difficult. Adan Cruser had died in the atmosphere of the moon of Dyn, and she still had nightmares of seeing him with that gaping hole where his mask one stood.

"No," she whispered, and grabbed him by his pack, activating her rockets to pull him up and out of the room. *Thype this mission, and this underground hell,* she thought. *No more Nighthawks are going to die on my watch.*

20

Cilas Mec was on pins and needles as he surveyed his HUD, watching his three Nighthawks slowly making their way out of the facility. He wanted to ask for a visual, but didn't want to distract them as they fought through the swarm of szilocs thirsty for their blood.

As he paced the room impatiently, he studied the linear map generated by the PAS helm's AI. The layout of the facility had been a mystery when they first entered, but their powered suits were built to adapt to these situations. Separating his team had given their synced interface the reach that it needed to create a rough sketch of the underground.

Now that they had managed to explore the majority of the rooms, he could not only see their locations, but the path he would take to reach them. What concerned him, however were the dropships that had appeared above the moon. They were no longer present on the starmap, and he knew that meant they had broken atmosphere, and in a manner of hours, would be landing.

Pirates were an easy fight for the highly trained group under his command. Geralos, if they brought along Craqtii, would be tough despite his confidence. What he hadn't counted on was the szilocs, who had slowed their progress to a crawl. Had they remained silent, as was intended by command, they would have had time to formulate a method to help some of the captives get off the moon.

"Never goes as planned, does it?" Quentin said, grinning. "Even when the plan is for it all to go to *schtill*."

"Next time a cadet asks me what it's like to be an ESO," Cilas said, "I am going to grab him by his legs and march him to the fourth deck of Aurora, and when he starts screaming at the top of his lungs, I'll say, you feel that, buddy? That's how it feels to be one of us."

He was about to say more when a chime on his comms alerted him to the satellite completing its uplink. The message with the maps, footage, and discoveries from the Nighthawk's findings had been received.

Upon receipt and after some brief discussion, the Alliance council would send in their Marines. They would be better prepared for a full-on battle with the Geralos, and could eventually take the base with an infiltrator in orbit to shut out any reinforcements.

It was what Cilas hoped would happen, but with the dropships incoming, they needed to find a way out, fast.

"Nighthawks, get to the surface. We're done here," Cilas announced. "How are we looking, Helga?"

There was no immediate answer, and he and Quentin exchanged glances. Expanding the map on his helmet's display, he scanned for their location and saw a blank space where before he could at least see their life signs. If the three Nighthawks were in the middle of a fight, Helga would have a difficult time answering her comms. Still, it was unlike her to not make the effort, so he knew they were at their limit.

"Ray?" he tried.

There was some static, but no voice. He could hear something akin to the humming of Sundown's hot-edged las-sword, and then there was nothing, only static. What was happening, and why weren't they answering?

Ice-cold fear found its way into veins too seasoned to allow for panic. But his Nighthawks were in trouble, and they were much deeper into the facility than he remembered. If they didn't act, he could lose three members of his team, and there was still the question of the dropships Quentin had seen landing on the moon.

"I see them in the room leading out to the other exit," Quentin said, and when Cilas glanced at his map, he saw their three dots blinking in and out in an area of the map that had yet to be defined.

"Something in there is interfering with their comms, and it looks as if our sync has been severed, as well. Let's move, Q. We need to catch up with them, or none of us will make it out alive."

Another tone in his ear, and Cilas looked up at one of the terminals to see that the computers were now reporting a new arrival to the facility. An image appeared above them, projected from cameras tucked away in the corner of the room. It was a three-dimensional grid of blue lines, which rotated to become a holographic map of the underground facility.

It showed the room they were in, with two blue blobs representing Cilas and Quentin. From there it contracted, showing more blue blobs scattered about inside what appeared to be a three-layered underground bunker. It was as Cilas feared; they had only scratched the surface.

In the three seconds of visuals revealed by the system's display of the map, he saw more rooms below them, and hundreds more blue blobs swarming the room which led out to the exit.

Cilas felt foolish. In his mad dash to upload the information to the Alliance, he hadn't thought to dig into the computer to look for information or a map. One-dimensional actions were suicide, and he had let the chaos of those szilocs shift his focus to the mission instead of his team.

Splitting them up had seemed the right thing to do, but in hindsight he wished that he had just led them to this communications room. Raileo was their resident hacker, and could have done wonders with this whole setup, yet he chose Quentin as his partner, and left the young Nighthawk with Helga to fend for themselves.

Suddenly he was angry, not only with himself, but for whatever they were in, because now he knew there would be many more captives trapped inside the rooms below them.

"Let's go get our people," he said to Quentin, and the big man, who had been waiting, slid open the door a crack before quickly motioning for Cilas to get back.

"Two lizards on approach," Quentin whispered, pulling out his knife as Cilas raised his pulse-rifle and stepped behind the starmap.

When the door came fully open, a Geralos rushed in, and Quentin cut him off, spinning low and gutting him with the razor-sharp blade. He wasn't armored, so his oily entrails spilled out onto the floor, along with the rifle from his lifeless hands. Hours of training at this exact maneuver had Quentin complete the dervish with another stab, this time through the glass of the dead Geralos's mask.

Cilas had seen it all happen in the blink of an eye, but he too operated on instinct, and dashed past Quentin to kill the second Geralos that had been too slow on retaliating. There was no thought in either of their actions. They were both seasoned fighters who had performed these same maneuvers many times before.

When Quentin joined the Nighthawks, the two men had quickly bonded, having shared so many similarities, but it was on Meluvia when they fought together that they learned how efficient they were as a team. Helga was his heart, and Raileo was an unmatched sniper with the brains to match his aim, but when it came to fighting, he and Quentin operated of a singular mind. They moved out in silence with guns raised, ready for any and all Geralos surprises.

"Lizards jammed our comms, you think?" Quentin said, sounding out of breath.

"Of course they did, and it explains the szilocs invasion as well. They've gotten desperate and are willing to sacrifice this level to us to preserve whatever is happening below," Cilas said.

He touched the area of his helmet that opened the comms to everyone.

"Nighthawks, this is Cilas. If you can hear this, the lizards know we're here. Contact with mother has been made, so help is on the way," he said. "That's the good news. Bad news is that we have more lizards incoming. There are plenty more rooms below, with signatures moving on our location, and dropships have landed, bringing in more. It's going to get hot, so find an exit and wait for us if you can."

"Rend, this is Ate," came a voice that forced Cilas to stop in his tracks. "We can hear you, but for some reason, you don't seem to be hearing us."

"Helga, do you copy?" Quentin tried.

"I copy, you big bastard. Are you alright?" she said, laughing nervously. "Finally, *thype*. Q, are you with the commander? Me, Ray, and Sunny are in this ... what did you say it was, Ray?"

"A lizard lobby," Raileo said, and Cilas didn't know whether to laugh or be annoyed at their humor at a time like this.

"We're in the lizard lobby, and there is a big ramp leading out to the surface," Helga said. "The szilocs took off running. Can you believe that, Cilas? As soon as Sunny showed up with his blade, it's as if they recognized him from before and decided they would rather keep their lives."

"Q and I are coming," Cilas managed, overcome with emotion from hearing her voice. Losing her to the szilocs would have crushed him permanently, especially after coming to terms with his poor decision-making. "Did you catch what I said about the lizards?"

"Yeah, they let us roam around blind while they brought in reinforcements," Helga said, still sounding too happy for someone on the brink of losing her life. "I'm not worried. After what we just went through, I am convinced the maker is on our side."

"They've lost their *thyping* minds over there," Quentin muttered over private comms, and though Cilas wanted to agree, he was just happy to hear they were alive.

"It's been hit after hit since we came down that shaft, Marine," Cilas said. "But did you hear Helga, about the szilocs? If they recognized Sunny and chose not to fight, then it means that they're intelligent, which is downright frightening."

"Let's not assume them to be geniuses for having fear," Quentin said. "Most animals have the ability to learn, but it doesn't make them strategists."

Cilas sighed. "Q, those are not the same szilocs from outside. The *thyping* things are communicating somehow, which is bad. Their silence could very well be due to a greater strategy to strike at us when we least expect it."

"But the lizards found a way to keep them out of here," Quentin argued. "How do we know that they didn't simply turn on the repellant once they got us away from the captives? We know that there's more coming in from the dropships, and I bet they know exactly where we're located. They see that they have jammed us towards the back, with only one accessible exit, and there's maker knows what waiting out there for us, as soon as we make our break."

"So, you're thinking it was a coincidence."

"I do. Sunny engaged them, and the lizards decided to push them back into their holes," Quentin said.

"That's a pretty big coincidence, Q, but I guess we'll see if we encounter any on the surface. If they are communicating, then they will likely stay away, knowing that we're with the Jumper. But if it's like you say and this is the lizards' doing, then we'll be up to our elbows in szilocs once we leave. Either way, we're *thyped* if we don't speed up our egress, so let's save this for later and get out of here."

They pushed through the rooms that showed evidence of them having been there before. Either there were dead Geralos on the ground, or the telltale burn marks of Quentin's rockets as he pulsed along across the floor. They were making good progress until they reached a new room, which was large and cavernous, with steel supports mounted in the center attached to grates on the ceiling.

There weren't many lights inside this space, and Cilas thought it looked unfinished, which made him wonder if they'd gone off course.

"Do you know where we are?" he said to Quentin, and though the big man confirmed, Cilas noticed that he was moving slowly and checking the shadows, the same way he did when they needed to clear a room.

When they were near the center, something moved in Cilas's peripheral vision, but when he raised his rifle, it was nothing but blackness and a discarded storage bin wedged into the dirt.

Now I'm seeing ghosts, he thought, annoyed, but redoubled his efforts to get to the end of the room, just in case it was in fact something. At the end, they made a left into another tunnel and made contact with another Geralos, who looked to have been waiting on them.

As soon as they spotted him, Quentin put a round in his knee, then climbed on top of his hunched-over form to put another in the top of his head. The wall shifted and a hidden door was revealed as another Geralos peeked out to check in on his friend. Cilas shot him in the face, then in the chest on his way to the ground. The door slid back shut, but there was no time to investigate, so they sprinted past it to another open door.

"Q, are you sure this is the way?" Cilas asked him again, ready to rip into him if he lied.

"Two rooms back was as far as I made it before abandoning Sundown," Quentin said, and for a brief moment Cilas considered punching him in the chest.

"We've gone down a level, somehow, and I doubt we're anywhere near the Nighthawks," Cilas said. "Maps are jammed and comms are iffy, so we need to get back on course or we're dead. Come on, Q, you're the scout. What do you suggest?" he said to Quentin.

"You won't like it, Cilas, but here goes. I say we retrace our steps, and use those shafts to go back up through the crashed ship and deal with the szilocs blocking that hatch. We take our chances with them, since they don't have guns, and we rendezvous with the others in the forest."

Cilas stared into his mask to see if there was even a hint of humor on the big Marine's face, but what he saw was determination, so he gave his suggestion some thought.

"Alright, Nighthawks, we're jammed in," Cilas started, and Helga tried to cut in but he quickly muted her comms. "Listen to me. Get out now, and find a place far away from here. Tutt and I are going to work our way back and will coordinate a rendezvous when we're out."

"I'll set up a beacon, trackable by your PAS, Commander," Raileo said, and Cilas unmuted his lieutenant's comms to finally hear what she had to say.

"Cilas," Quentin said, pointing in front of them, where through the open door was a ramp leading up and out into daylight. Helga was pleading for them to reconsider, and not to risk going back where she was sure the szilocs were waiting.

"Helga, we're looking at a third exit, it seems," Cilas said. "Get out now and we'll catch you on the surface. Got that?"

"Loud and clear," she said cheerfully, and Cilas quickly got off comms.

They took the ramp at a sprint, but as they got near the crest, Cilas saw a Geralos silhouetted against the sunlight. It was hard to make out his features, but all that mattered was that he wasn't aware. Cilas fired three shots in succession, hitting him in his abdomen, throat, and faceplate. He died silently, but before he could fall, the Nighthawks were already past him with rockets at full blast.

Fourteen transports sat parked in two long rows leading from the edge of the ramp, all the way back to the end of the clearing. Their mirror-like sleekness reflected the sun, and Cilas had to wonder if this area belonged to something other than the Geralos.

It was a parking garage of luxury transports, hidden within the forest. There was nothing else there, just a rocky clearing in the middle of nowhere. Above them the sun was starting to descend, and the clouds were gathering menacingly.

Whatever this place was, it was meant to remain a secret but for a path paved with small stones, built for the coming and going of the transports.

"I wonder where that leads," Quentin said.

"Probably to some lizard atrocity that I don't want to know about," Cilas said.

"Commander," Quentin shouted, but Cilas was already seeing the threat.

Before them, past the last of the transports, stood a line of Geralos armed to the teeth. They leveled their guns at the Nighthawks and started firing at them. The projectiles ricocheted off the transports, making it difficult to avoid getting hit. Several shots ripped up the rocks around their feet, and Quentin dove out of the way.

Three of the shots struck Cilas's legs, but his shields held up, despite them being of a heavy caliber. If not for their PAS this would have been the end of the two Nighthawks, but they were able to use the cover of the vehicles to fire back at their attackers. Now it was the Geralos that were scrambling, since their armor wasn't made to withstand penetrative kinetic-rounds.

A stand-off ensued, with the Nighthawks steadily pressing towards the gunfire. They were trading shots, but timing them to keep the Geralos on the defensive, all while they took turns jumping from behind one transport to the next.

Times like this, Cilas missed his old friend, Cage Hem, who was an expert with a stargun, a weapon used for suppressing bunched units like the ones they faced. They were still too exposed, but for now, they pressed on, trading shots and recharging their shields from the damage.

Cilas saw movement from above him and dove out of the way, only to see that it was Helga, employing her rocket boots to rain bullets down on the enemy. Raileo and Sundown joined in, materializing like phantoms from behind the transports. One of the Geralos flew back screaming as Sundown's incendiary rounds punctured his suit.

The Geralos scattered for better cover but Cilas pressed forward, seizing the advantage. The Nighthawks were all firing as they ran now, cutting down the Geralos before the ground gave out as several szilocs emerged to join the fight. Cilas caught a glimpse of one as it impaled a Geralos, tossing him up just to catch him inside its maw.

A rocket came in from out of nowhere, striking a transport, which exploded on impact. Cilas was thrown backwards, colliding with Quentin Tutt, and the two men went down in a heap. More transports exploded as a hovering dropship appeared above the tree line. Cilas's shields were depleted, and his helmet screamed warnings into his ears.

"Nighthawks, run," he managed to shout. "Cut into the trees and preserve your fuel. It's our best chance of surviving this and making it back to the Thundercat."

21

Into the trees the Nighthawks ran, dodging energy blasts and a hail of bullets. Helga didn't know where their destination lay, or even if there was a destination for now. All she knew was that she needed to put distance between herself and the Geralos attackers that had been waiting for them outside the facility.

She was beyond tired and sore, having been in the PAS for hours fighting for her life. It was BLAST all over, the rigorous test they had all undertaken to become Nighthawks. Days of running, climbing, and fighting for your life was rewarded with more running, until you hit a wall, and even then you still had to fight.

Upon graduation she had foolishly believed that BLAST was the toughest test she'd ever have to face. Yet, here she was, running for her life on limbs ready to give out, powered by a heart that was in overdrive.

The team had run in separate directions, with the confidence that over comms they could coordinate a rally point once the Geralos had given up the chase. By then, hopefully, the Marines would arrive, and their pursuers would be forced to rush back to their base. The shooting slowed down and finally ceased, giving Helga the break she needed to check and see if the radar was back online.

On her mask's HUD, she saw the simulated forest and nodes representing her Nighthawk brothers. Touching her wrist, she switched the visuals, bringing up the readouts on everyone's health. Heart rates were spiking, but for Sundown's, but that was no surprise.

Her confidence returned with their suits online; they were more formidable than before. She could call up to Zan on the *Ursula* if she wanted, or Cleia Rai'to, who was probably bored out of her mind.

The thought of the doctor made Helga smile. She was such an innocent-seeming person, and it felt good to know someone like that in a universe filled with treachery. Thunder boomed off in the distance, and the sky turned dark, streaked by lingering forks of lightning.

It was one of those strange sights to a space-locked boomer that was both beautiful and frightening. Helga had never seen anything like it outside of vids and photo archives, and now that she saw it in person, she filed it away inside her mind.

The trees grew denser, some trunks fusing together, it seemed, causing Helga to have to veer off track to keep on moving in the direction she was running. Suddenly the ground became an incline, and she found herself running downhill.

She cared not for the brush, branches, and vines that threatened to snatch her up and throw her off her feet because she was encased in the armor of her PAS.

"Whoa," she exclaimed over her comms. "Any of you men on this incline?" But no one answered, and for the first time she became worried. "Not the jamming thing again," she muttered, then tried them each on private comms, yielding nothing each time.

Helga thought of what to do next, trying her best not to speculate on what was happening. She pulled up her HUD and checked their life signs. Everyone was healthy, though their fuel gauges looked dangerously low.

Maybe it's just me, she thought. *They all seem to be alright, and maybe that concussion blast knocked out my comms.*

Taking to the air, she slipped up past the top of the trees, then flew down the hill past where it dropped off into the basin. Seeing the cliff face gave her a sinking feeling. She had known that it was coming from memory, since she'd flown over it when they made their approach. The exit near the transports would've made it difficult for the others to remember, however, and it was possible that one of them could have taken a fall.

The PAS had rockets, but they were difficult to master, and for someone that wasn't trained to fly spaceships, it could feel as if the suit had a mind of its own. Quentin was still clumsy in his, and Helga worried that if any had fallen, it was bound to be him. She dipped low, into the mist, hoping to see his signature, or anything really, to put her wandering mind to rest.

The winds picked up, pushing the trees sideways, and Helga found herself suddenly unable to maintain control. She pulled her legs up to her knees and performed a front-flip while powering her rockets off.

She came out of it into a glide, angling down past numerous branches before grabbing onto one of them. The momentum caused her to wince but she held on. It felt as if her arms would come out of their sockets as she hung there, swaying like ripened fruit.

Helga didn't remember who had said that Argan-10 was determined to take lives, but she was now in full agreement. Looking about, she heard noises as an animal growled within the bushes, so she jumped and re-activated her rockets, flying up and out of the misty basin.

May as well find my way back to the dropship, she thought. If everyone was lost, then naturally that would be the best option for a rallying point. That was if the Geralos hadn't discovered it hidden among the rock formations. Visibility was now low from the clouds and the falling rain, so Helga was forced to fly higher in order to avoid running into anything. It was a calculated risk, considering that a high altitude could put her on a tracker for the Geralos.

Helga leveled off, using the rocket in her pack, giving the pair within her boots a rest while she fumbled around on her wrist-comms. She activated a beacon on the R60 Thundercat, and its icon appeared on her HUD.

If the Nighthawks weren't heading there, they'd know to do so now, since it projected a virtual pin somewhere off in the distance, and all they would need to do was follow it to make it back to the ramp. Any Geralos close by in a transport would pick it up on their map, as well, but Helga was prepared for a fight. As long as she was able to board the dropship, she would happily scrap it out with any of them.

She found the rock formation with no incident, but still there was no one answering on comms. It was nighttime now, and she boarded the ship with her pistols out, checking every nook and cranny before feeling safe enough to enter the cockpit. On the comms there she tried again, and that was when she finally reached Cilas.

"Where have you been?" he said, sounding annoyed. "Was that you with the beacon? Are you off your *schtill?*"

"Fly up out of the trees and I can grab you," Helga said. "The ramp is down, so all you'd have to do is burn a bit of fuel to gain the altitude."

"Alright, we're in that basin, the one with the mist. It's been providing good cover. Ate—Helga, stay alert. They have a thopter patrolling, trying to find us," he said.

"I'll bring it down, but as soon as I do they'll be on me like flies, so you men are going to really have to move," Helga said.

She powered up the crystal core and tested the thrusters, bringing the Thundercat up off the ground a meter and letting it hover while she consulted a holographic simulation of the rocks about her. She had done a similar trick when she flew into the field to try and conceal the ship. Now, she didn't want to disturb them or knock them over with the wings, so she slowly maneuvered the Thundercat up and out of there.

Five minutes later, and she was zipping back the way she had come but with an armored and shielded war machine. She rolled and dipped it into the mist, skimming the treetops as she probed the radar looking for a sign. She saw nothing despite the dropship's window adjusting to allow for night vision. On the radar, however, she saw the four bright white dots of the Nighthawks escaping.

Do I risk telling them to make the flight up to me now? she wondered. *Is that thopter somewhere else lurking? Waiting for us to let our guard down?* Helga had a terrible vision that flashed across her mind. It was Cilas, flying up to the ramp, only to be hit by a torpedo. *Call them up before securing the skies, and that is one scenario that is likely to happen,* she thought.

Helga flew a wide arc around the basin, bringing the dropship higher and higher until she saw where the thopter was making its rounds. After activating hardpoints, the ship did something she hadn't anticipated happening.

To allow for shielding and the preservation of the internal atmosphere, the ramp retracted, making it impossible for her to collect the Nighthawks. She would need to dispatch of all enemies before risking opening the hatch again.

"This is going to be hairy, but stay down there until I give you the word," she said over general comms.

She rolled the Thundercat and opened up her guns, tearing off the thopter's leftmost wing. This went flying into the trees, cutting through branches like a hot knife through butter. The vessel, unable to maintain its altitude, buckled and tumbled down the cliff face. Helga didn't stop to examine her work, however, screaming into the comms for the Nighthawks to fly.

Tilting the nose of the dropship to the heavens, she disabled hardpoints, and opened the rear hatch for the ramp to descend. Almost instantly, she saw the signatures of the Nighthawks climbing towards the dropship, but the radar was showing incoming, and she knew she had gambled wrong.

Dipping lower to the treetops, she tried not to speculate on anything negative. This was easier said than done, however, as her eyes danced back and forth to track the Nighthawk's progress, along with the Geralos.

Sundown was the last to board, and Helga closed the hatch while simultaneously putting all the power towards the thrust. The boosters belched in protest as the ship shook violently before rocketing up and out of the mist. The Geralos matched their speed, however, and Helga saw that it wasn't possible for them to escape without a fight.

"Strap in tight and hold on," she growled, before re-activating hardpoints and powering up the shields and the four energy cannons.

"Need me on the guns, Lieutenant?" Raileo said, and while she was tempted to tell him yes, it wasn't worth him trying to gain the cockpit while she rolled around avoiding the Geralos attacks.

"Stay put for now, Ray. I got this," she said, and performed a series of maneuvers that took them through a narrow gulch and then back around, as if she wanted to return to the disabled ship.

The Geralos dropship had gained on her now, and his guns were depleting her shields. All she could do was run and try maneuvers to throw him until he made a mistake. Helga regretted turning them around now, since she'd lost the advantage of having natural obstacles like the mountains.

This would be ace against ace, but Helga was confident and ready to return to the *Ursula*. They had made it this far, past the vicious szilocs and the Geralos ambush. Now all that stood between them and escape was a Geral-engineered dropship armed with kinetic cannons and energy torpedoes.

Helga rolled to the left, forcing their pursuer to turn in that direction. As soon as he followed, she rocked them back hard to the right, rolling twice before moving left again, causing all of his bullets to go wide.

She was hoping to frustrate him into giving up on the chase, and instead try to distance himself in order to launch a torpedo. They kept this going for a long time until they returned to the fantastic scenery of the floating islands. Here, Helga took advantage of this splendor by wrapping about one of these landmasses, hugging it so tightly that the Geralos was forced to break off.

They weaved figure-eights between multiple islands, and a wayward torpedo barely missed the Thundercat. The comms were silent, and you could cut the tension with a knife, but Helga was in her element. The only thing she felt was anticipation for catching the Geralos slipping.

She flew towards a large island, rising slowly with the wind, and the Geralos launched another torpedo. It flew high above the Thundercat, striking the base of a floating isle. Rocks and dirt exploded into a cloud of debris, draining the shields and blinding Helga instantly. She pulled up and her pursuer accelerated, hoping to cut her off, but it was a ruse. Helga cut power to the thrusts and rocked the control stick hard to one side.

The Thundercat stalled and started to fall before Helga maxed thrusts again and they shot out from beneath the islands. By now the Geralos was trying to adjust, but Helga was already flying towards him. Shots were exchanged as they barreled towards one another recklessly, cutting off at the last moment in a deadly game of chicken. Missing one another, both ships came about and jousted again. In and out they weaved, coming close to crashing each time.

If the pilot wasn't Geralos, Helga would have wanted to recruit him, because his skills were extraordinary, and he was making her work to survive.

"You got this, Hellgate, bring him down," Cilas said, and it served to strengthen her resolve.

When the two ships came around to fly at one another yet again, Helga decided she wasn't going to avoid him. She shunted all power to shields, weakening her guns to the point where they would barely penetrate a hull, let alone kill the pilot. They came at one another, and the Geralos banked, but not before the nose of the Thundercat clipped his tail and caused him to lose control for a time.

With the shields powered, everyone onboard felt the impact of the crash, but the vessel wasn't damaged, and Helga still maintained control. She brought them about to gain the flank of the spiraling dropship and locked in on its thruster, pumping enough shots into the hull to tear a whole chunk of it off. Crashing into several branches, the enemy ship was barely able to stay afloat, but Helga was relentless and started charging an energy torpedo.

"Come on," Cilas shouted. "If you take any longer, there will be three more on us, just like it. Either let him go and jump us back to the *Ursula* or send that *thype* to the maker."

Helga ignored him and stayed on the Geralos, using her radar for guidance. They flew for a time, and the basin was expansive until they neared the face of a cliff, which Helga hadn't seen coming up until the very last moment. She activated airbrakes and pulled them up into a loop-de-loop as the Geralos ship banked late, thinking that she was still in pursuit.

As soon as he made this move, Helga fired the torpedo at the rocks above him. She knew his shields had been depleted, and his thrusters were struggling from her earlier shots. The cliff didn't just explode; it practically melted, showering the dropship with rocks and trees. Down it all went, causing the ground to shake, and the Geralos ship was no more but for a mushroom cloud that stood out above the mist.

"Yeah!" Helga screamed in victory, her eyes wet with excitement as the blood returned to her face.

"Hell of a job, Ate," Cilas said, which brought a smile to her face.

"Does this mean we can finally leave this nightmare?" Raileo said, not feeling the same excitement as everyone else.

"Why? Are you missing something sexy and blue?" Helga teased, causing the young chief to pause. "We're on private comms, Relax, Ray," she said, still laughing at the thought of him blushing behind his mask.

"Why is it that when you're happy, the rest of us have to suffer?" he said.

"Am I wrong?" she pressed. "Lighten up. We're about to head back, and you have something to celebrate with your doc."

22

Cleia Rai'to sat staring at the image of the dead, mutated Geralos for fifteen minutes. Helga, who had shared it with her on a whim, sat up on one of the vacant beds, playing at her wrist-comms while she awaited the doctor's opinion.

"On Sanctuary," Cleia said without turning away from the vid screen, "there's a brilliant professor by the name of Rhoan Aghesh. He taught at Noble University in the Freedom District, which was my district for most of my life. Dr. Aghesh rose to prominence with his theory that the Geralos are not a natural species to Anstractor.

"He theorized that their pattern of behavior was akin to predators developed inside of a lab. No one took him seriously, but his work has been gaining popularity over the last few years. This Geralos is no mutant or Vestalian hybrid, which is impossible, at least through natural conception. A human woman giving birth to a Geralos child would likely die from the pain."

"What about the other way around?" Helga said. "A lizard giving birth to a human child?"

"I've studied all of Anstractor's species, Helga," Cleia said. "Let me show you why science makes either scenario an impossibility."

With that she waved her hand in front of the large vid screen, and the mutant's image was replaced with a diagram of interlinking circles, each of them labeled with the name of a species. Helga's eyes naturally searched for Casanians and saw connecting lines going out to Vestalians, Genesians, Meluvians, and Louines.

"What do the dotted lines mean?" Helga said. "Like the one between Virulians and Genesians."

"Virulians may be humanoid, just like Vestalians and Genesians, but their physiology is different due to the conditions on their planet." Cleia said. "We believe that most of the planets share a common ancestry, and that Anstractor may have been the destination of travelers seeking refuge. This is unproven but likely, considering the genetic link between so many despite us all being so far apart."

"So, Virulians evolved too far out from their ancestors, to the point where a good horizontal docking doesn't guarantee pregnancy. Is that where you're navigating towards, Doc?" Helga said.

She knew that the crass slang she used for sex would rustle the tentacles on the overly-professional doctor, and when the woman's blue skin flushed indigo, she knew that her words had been received and understood.

"Yes, exactly," Cleia said. "Though in the medical field we say coitus, or ... never mind, I can see your smile through the terminal's reflection. Are you truly curious about this creature, Lieutenant, or is this merely an exercise to try and rattle me?"

Before Helga could reply and plead her case, the doctor walked over and got in her face. She was so close that their noses were practically touching, and she had to restrain herself from pushing the woman off.

"I may be kind and socially awkward, but I am neither stupid nor unaware of how I am perceived aboard this ship," Cleia said, her tiny voice rising up an octave. "You, however, have remained a mystery to me, because you shift back and forth from playing at friend to being somewhat of a bully, and I demand an explanation."

Oops, Helga thought, as she felt the tension rising inside the space. "Cleia—"

"Doctor. Until you can explain yourself to me, I no longer want to pretend that we are friends, Lieutenant Ate."

"Cleia," Helga said, hopping off the bed and placing both hands on the woman's shoulders. "I like you. Do you understand? I'm saying it clearly, so the language doesn't get in the way. As to my gibes, calm down, it's just my way. I don't mean anything by it. You're totally about to square off with me, knowing that you'll lose."

"Are you so sure about that?" Cleia said, baring her teeth, which would have been frightening if not for her small face and nasally voice.

Helga began to laugh. "Doc, I don't mean any disrespect, but look at you. You'd actually try me? It's surprising, really ... in a good way, and here I thought you were all needles and salves. There's a fighter inside you, and that makes me like you even more. So calm down, and forgive me, will you? Plus, why would I be here if all I wanted to do was annoy you? I'm here because I value your opinion as a scientist."

The doctor's shoulders dropped slightly, and she exhaled audibly, her skin returning to that beautiful shade of powdery blue. It was as if a weight had fallen off them, and she closed her eyes for a few seconds before opening them to give Helga a measuring look.

"You are certainly incorrigible," she finally said, then reached up and squeezed the Nighthawk's earlobe. "I get it. You're one of those that picks at the people you care about and ignores the ones you don't. It will take some getting used to, and I want to believe that you're worth it. Alright then, back to our Geralos. As I've explained, most of our species are linked, so there's a chance of reproduction regardless of the pair."

Helga found this fascinating, especially the thought of Raileo having a child with this woman. She had yet to see a human and Traxian hybrid, which struck her as odd, since on the diagram there was a dotted line linking the two as compatible. She dared not ask, however, not after their recent exchange.

Cleia walked over to the screen and pointed at the circle that represented the Geralos.

"See here," she said. "They have no lines. The Geralos cannot conceive with anyone else outside of their own. This uniqueness hints at two separate theories, the first being that they are the natural residents of Anstractor. The rest of us having come here from another galaxy, where we took to different planets and evolved."

Helga made to say something, but the doctor looked around and gestured for her to remain quiet.

"That first theory is controversial," Cleia whispered. "I am not sure you're aware. In certain sectors it is considered criminal to even suggest such a thing. The second theory, which was the one that Dr. Aghesh explored, was that in a time past, thousands of years before FTL was shared with the lesser evolved planets, a team of scientists set out to create the ultimate biological weapon, and terraformed Geral—then an uninhabited planet—to become the home of what we now call the Geralos."

"I haven't heard any of these theories in all my time on the *Rendron*," Helga said. "I don't know which one to believe, but I'm leaning on them being someone's experiment gone wrong. Their behavior ... they're like a virus, taking over and corrupting everything they touch. They bite into our brains in an attempt to suck out the gift of prescience from our Seekers. And why? To see into the future or some other ridiculous belief.

"If their goal was to eat us, and their attack on Vestalia was due to a food or resource shortage, that would make sense from an actual species. We could understand why they hunt us, and there could even be a chance of some negotiations. But they capture us to bite into our brains, killing us from the infection, then discarding our bodies like half-eaten ration bars. They don't care that this pursuit of the sight has led to genocide, or that literally everyone else in this galaxy has taken up arms to stop them."

"Right," Cleia said. "That single-sighted focus and their isolation is why Dr. Aghesh has suggested that they were made. This mutant you all found looks to be a clone or lab-born entity that hadn't been fully formed. If I was to guess at what was below the facility where you found, it would be that there is a lab where a new type of Geralos is being worked on."

"*Thype* me, but that's heavy," Helga whispered.

"I have a favor to ask you," Cleia said, powering down her computer, which caused the image of the Geralos to transform into one of the planet Traxis. "I am no Dr. Rhoan Aghesh, but my talents will be wasted here if all I'm doing is running checkups and patching up the occasional rescue. I am a scientist, and what you've shared has me wanting to learn more to help you and the commander."

"What do you need?" Helga said, glancing at the door, somewhat surprised that no one had disturbed their private talk.

"Samples. Had I known you were going to a lab, I would have asked you to collect some from the flora and fauna of that moon. Not only that, but this Geralos ... with a bit of his flesh, I could answer your question, and give some idea as to their intent. Right now, with only this image, we're still speculating, and to be honest I am frightened."

"I'm not sure Cilas would be big on us bringing potential bio-hazards back onto his ship," Helga said.

"I can talk to the commander and explain my intent, which benefits the war," Cleia said. "I have kits, along with instructions for using them, and they are small enough to fit inside your packs. They can even be worn on a belt, which is where we carried them back when I was a student doing my observations. Thank you for sharing with me, Helga. I see now that my earlier accusations were not only unfounded but premature."

"Don't apologize, girl, you're new here." Helga laughed. "We'll have you acting like a boomer in no time. Then it may be me apologizing to Raileo for corrupting you."

Helga expected a retort, but the doctor gave her the warmest of smiles and walked her to the door, where she placed a hand on the Nighthawk's shoulder. "He told me about your talk, and I'm glad," Cleia said. "Our ... relationship isn't so much of a secret as it is private, if you can understand my meaning. I am aware that everyone knows, or suspects. There isn't much hiding on a ship this small with six crew members."

"We all have our secrets," Helga admitted, and Cleia opened the door for her to leave the compartment. "Talk to you later?"

"I look forward to it," the doctor said, practically beaming as she stood in the doorway watching her go.

Leaving the doctor's office, Helga immediately went to Cilas's cabin to speak with him about everything she had learned, but he wasn't there. After several more detours to the mess, and then the bridge, she went down to the dock where she found him seated on the wing of the Thundercat.

"What are you doing up there?" she said, looking around, surprised to find the place so empty.

"Ray's in his berth, laying up for a bit, and Q's with Sunny at the stern somewhere, having a talk about something," he said, waving it off dismissively. "Me, I'm waiting to hear back from the captain, to see whether or not we're going back to the *Rendron*. We can keep our current trajectory, as long as we're out of radar contact from those moon-dwelling lizards. What brings you down here? Looking to practice some shooting?"

"Looking for you, actually. Do you have a moment?" Helga said, staring up at him from the deck.

"For you, always," he said, then nimbly hopped down to the deck. He sat down and beckoned her over before leaning forward to rest his elbows on his knees. Helga followed his lead and sat in front of him below the wing, crossing her legs in a full lotus, showing off her incredible flexibility.

"What's on your mind, Hel?"

"I spoke to the doc, and shared our theory that the lizards are experimenting with reproduction," she said.

"And what did she say about our theory?"

"That it doesn't make sense," Helga said. "Which is why I wanted to talk to you. But it's not going to be easy to digest."

"Well, considering I'm sitting here helpless, waiting for the council to decide our next move, I could use the distraction because the voices in my head are beginning to shout," Cilas said.

"Okay, here goes," Helga said, and she relayed to him the two different theories behind the Geralos, and the likelihood that what they had found was a processing plant to produce a better version of them.

Cilas listened with interest, and offered up a few theories of his own.

"If someone made them, then they are just as guilty as the lizards," he said. "I want to blame the Louines, but it will come off speciesist, so I will bite my tongue, but you know how I feel about them. War's been raging a millennia, and where have they been? Sitting comfortably out of it while half the galaxy suffers. Vestalians are being captured and processed while Meluvia tears itself apart from the inside. Virulia's resources are *thyped*, and we're not exactly winning this war. All it would take is one of their starships, as advanced and deadly as they are, and the lizards would be broken, but they don't help, do they, Helga? Why not? Maybe because they know that they're the reason why all of reality is falling apart."

"I don't disagree, but I don't see what the benefit to them creating the Geralos would have been," Helga said, reaching forward to take his hand. She knew that at any minute now one of the Nighthawks could come down one of the lifts, or scramble down the ladderwell, to catch her being intimate with the commander. He didn't pull away, however, but instead reached up and caressed her cheek.

"I know that it's not the Louines, Hel; it's likely something that is no longer here. But the reality is that we have to deal with them now, and you're telling me they're trying to evolve. If that's what's happening down there then the council needs to know, because just the risk of that happening will goad them into sending twenty hard cases down to that moon."

"How many do you think there are around the galaxy?" she said. "Labs, bases, processing plants; I can't keep up. Then there's the Alliance. We're already spread thin, fighting their dreadnoughts, destroyers, and battleships. We're not equipped for what we found down there, Cilas. This is ESO business, and there's just not enough of us to handle it."

The two of them sat in silence for a time, staring at the deck as they processed the information. Helga didn't want to view the work they did as futile, and she hated how her words had come off so defeatist.

"That isn't to say that I don't believe we'll beat the lizards back to Geral," she said cheerfully.

Cilas squeezed her hands, massaging them with his thumbs before bringing one of them up to press it gently against his lips.

"Sometimes it's just easiest to ignore the galaxy and worry about what's in your crosshairs and immediate vicinity," he said. "Talking about you, my Casanian, 2IC. I have been so distracted with everything that I haven't taken the time to tell you how proud you've made me. The Captain asks about you by name. Do you know that?"

"I don't, actually," she said, blushing. It was impossible not to grin. "What does he say?"

"How's Helga?" Cilas mocked in an attempt at Retzo Sho's voice and accent.

"That's really good," she said, laughing, and snatching back a hand to cover her mouth so no one above deck could hear it. "I appreciate you saying that, Cilas, but you only have yourself to thank for my success. You've been my mentor, icon, and now, something more unspoken. I was an empty shell before Meluvia, and then you scolded me and showed me just how much you really cared."

"Was it that bad?" he said, his face a mask of concern as he released her other hand.

"I stayed functionally drunk, but you knew that and I'm not exactly proud of it," she said. "When we were back on *Rendron*, after the psych, I got better, but I was still an empty shell fighting not to remember the *schtill* on Dyn. You and Joy became my drug, then Quentin and his CQC classes helped reignite the spark that had gone missing. Then we got to *Ursula*, and I forced you to take me to your cabin, and now, you know, I'm good with whatever. As long as you and the Nighthawks are with me."

"What about Joy?" he said.

"What about her? You mean us?" Helga said. "I no longer care what she thinks. I'm well past worrying about how she's going to take it. Cilas, you don't know it but when you were with her, she kept suggesting that I join you two in bed."

"I'm sorry, what?" he said, looking as if he'd swallowed something painful.

"Stop playing the innocent; you know her as well as I do. It's about something deeper than sex with her. She won't care about what we're doing," Helga said.

"What if I tell her that I'm crazy about you?" he said, smiling, and Helga bopped him on the thigh with a closed fist.

"She would see right through it, jerk, just like I do. You love being with me, I get it, but you're still head over heels for that *cruta*."

"Helga, I—"

"Stow it, Cilas, you cannot hurt me. Like I said, I know what this is. What would hurt Joy is if she believes she's been replaced in that deeper area of your heart. I'm her sister, and even if I claimed you, officially, I'd like to think that in time she'd forgive me. Hell, half our relationship is fighting. That woman is as stubborn as anyone I've known, but that is why she is who she is."

"You know, I was really worried about how she'd take this, until you said what you said just now," Cilas said. "Let me know when you contact her. It's too late for me to do it. I've waited too long, knowing she'd be livid, and that woman has a way of making me feel like a wad of *schtill*. You're very observant, and good at the psychoanalysis, but I haven't loved Joy since we returned from Meluvia."

"Don't say anymore, Cilas, please," Helga pleaded, knowing where he was about to take the conversation. "I know your heart, and I know that you're a man of principle. You may actually believe that you feel something for me, but I need it to be real before you say it."

"I know," he said. "But know that where Joy is concerned, you should only worry about your relationship with her. She and I were done a long time before our split, but I was too much of a coward to put a stop to it back then."

"Commander Cilas Mec, a coward. Now that's rich," Helga quipped, laughing at the absurdity. She was about to say more but then his wrist-comms came to life, and he scrambled to his feet, pulling her up effortlessly with one hand.

"That's my cue," he said. "I have to go. Let's see where our next stop will be. Will I see you tonight?"

"Maybe," she said, turning to leave, but he pulled her back and brought her in, pressing a kiss to her lips.

23

Back on *Rendron* after Dyn, Helga had a recurring nightmare that haunted her for countless cycles. She was on a ship of some sort, running from an assassin that had her contract. She was slower and weaker than she was in life, too frightened to move at times when he would attack her, and she would be left to bleed out on the deck, helplessly paralyzed.

In one of these recurrences, he had even taken her sight before putting her into stasis, where she could neither see nor move about. That had been the worst one yet, until this cycle when she fell asleep waiting on a call from Cilas. She started out running in her nightmare, feeling the assassin's presence close behind. She knew that she would be shot. If it was the same as it was on *Rendron*, the bullet would penetrate her spine and leave her helpless.

Time seemed to move along slowly as a calm settled in, removing the fear. This was new; she was normally panicking at this point, and she couldn't feel the crippling weakness like before. She jumped up and twisted acrobatically, firing a shot at her pursuer. A searing hot bullet from his rifle struck her shoulder but she couldn't feel it.

Helga landed from her flip and spun to continue firing, but her assassin was down on the deck, dead from a bullet wound in the center of his forehead. Her eyes widened in disbelief at the accuracy of that shot. Even Raileo would be loath to hit his target after pulling off that stunt. It felt amazing; she had never moved so fast outside of a cockpit, and her hand clutched at her chest as she sucked in gulps of air.

Helga's eyes came open to lights so bright they hurt, which caused her to slam them shut, hoping to return to her dream. The assassin was dead for the first time, and she wanted to explore more of that ship.

Wait, she thought, recalling seeing Cleia Rai'to when she had opened her eyes before. The Traxian had been seated next to her, seemingly watching her sleep. Helga forced herself up, gripping the arms of her chair. She opened her eyes slowly, giving them time to adjust to the light.

Turning her head, she looked over at the doctor, who was busy fiddling around with her tablet. *Maybe I imagined her being creepy,* she thought, raising her wrist-comms to check on the time. There remained twenty minutes before the start of the first shift. It was time for her to get up, though it didn't feel as if she'd slept six hours.

"Doc, it's early. What are you doing up here?" Helga said, watching the Traxian's fingers dance on the device.

Cleia leaned forward and touched an area of the console. A holographic image appeared. It was a man, possibly Vestalian, and he rotated slowly in front of them.

"Good morning, Helga," Cleia said with a bow. "I had a hard time sleeping after our chat, so I've been going through my records looking for an answer to the creature you discovered."

"You've become obsessed with the mutant," Helga said.

"It's not a mutant; please don't use that word. It's misleading when you call it that. For now, it's unknown—by the way, do you always sleep up here? It's not good for your back, you know? Though I must admit, these chairs are nice! I guess it makes sense for them to be comfortable considering the amount of time you spend in them."

Helga's tired glare caused the doctor to quickly shut her mouth, then she gestured at her tablet and the holo-image shimmered before splitting into two. Now it was a human standing next to a Geralos.

"What is this?" Helga said, her interest piqued.

"My theory on the Geralos you found," Cleia said. "There's too much to explain, so I'll get to the point. I believe that the corpse belonged to a mind invader."

"Really?" someone said from behind them, and the women both looked back to see the commander, toting a coffee mug. "I'm intrigued. Do tell, Dr. Rai'to. I don't think any of us have seen a mind invader in the flesh. Is that what they look like? Near-human and disgusting, with worms crawling beneath their flesh?"

"Commander," the Traxian said, getting to her feet and bowing, touching the knuckles of her right hand to her chin.

"Good morning, Dr. Rai'to," he said, cheerfully. "I forget my manners. Please do continue your explanation."

"Gladly, Commander," she said. "As to your question, no, this isn't normal by any means. His appearance is indeed unique, but I believe that this is due to..." She shut her mouth abruptly. "This may sound foolish for someone of my background to assert, Commander, but I want to remind you that this is a theory based on nothing scientific, just a ... how you say? A hunch?"

Helga reached out and touched her hand in support, since it was obvious that she was petrified of Cilas and his position. It was one thing for her to openly speculate during a friendly chat within her office, but with the commander she was worried that it could reflect on her status as a professional.

Cilas seemed to understand what was going on, and he gave Helga a wink before taking a sip.

"This is completely off the record, Dr. Rai'to," he said. "I know what you're presenting is merely a theory, and how can it not be helpful? All we have are guesses at this point, and the Alliance is still trying to figure it out themselves. Do continue, won't you? I am still unsettled by that thing. It will be a great help to hear your thoughts."

"Well, when you put it that way," Cleia said, flushing a multitude of colors ranging from blue to green. "The Geralos mind invaders, as you know, give up their lives in order to usurp the brain of their victim. They remove the person, effectively killing them, but they too die when their original body is abandoned. This makes it a tremendous sacrifice for the Geralos whenever they choose to invade a mind. Now, what if they could find a way instead to alter their physiology to mimic the host without losing their lives?"

"Are you saying they've found a way to look and talk like us?" Helga said.

"Yes, I believe so, Helga. The Geralos that you killed was in mid-transition, turning itself into a Vestalian. From the footage, which I've watched more times than I'd like to admit, those parasites in its abdomen weren't really parasites. That was the transformation working, though I'm not sure they have it mastered just yet," Cleia said.

"What are the chances that they do have it mastered and are posing as pirates, attacking civilians?" Helga said.

"It would explain a lot, that's for sure," Cilas said. "Though the implications are downright frightening."

"That is my theory, Commander," Cleia said. "They're using the Vestalians as avatars to alter their appearance. The facility you found is where they're mastering this, though there's likely to be many others, galaxy-wide."

"Thanks for sharing, Doc," Cilas said. "But I must ask you to never repeat what you told us here. News like this gets out and the morale will suffer within our ranks."

"I will not repeat it, Commander. This was just a theory that I wanted to share with a friend." She grinned at Helga, who returned the smile. "Now, if you will excuse me, I must return to medbay. Please alert me to anything if I am needed."

Helga watched her go and then turned on Cilas, ready to rip him to shreds.

"I was on with the council," he explained before she could get the words out of her mouth, and he showed her the coffee for emphasis. "I'm sorry."

"Well, that's an excuse I can't argue against." She got up from the chair to stretch. "Heavy *schtill*, huh? Lizards impersonating us through transformation. Here we thought all we had to worry about was them jumping into one of our minds. Now we'll have to wonder if a random Marine or officer is really one of them in disguise."

"I don't see how that's different, hence my lack of care," Cilas said. "Robbing a mind, taking the place of a spacer; it's the same thing for the rest of us that are ambushed by that thing. All this does now is give the lizard a chance to return to its hole once it's finished with its treachery. I told the doc to stay silent but I'm going to tell the Nighthawks in my own time."

Helga caught a glimpse of her reflection on one of the terminals, and her heart skipped when she saw how disheveled she looked. If any of the Nighthawks were to pop up on the bridge, they would see her speaking casually to the commander. It was one thing for them to speculate, but this could easily become a joke that would undermine her position. Despite Cilas's belief that it was already known, Helga wanted to maintain plausible deniability of their affair.

"I need to go, Cilas. It's half past the turn to first shift, and we both look as if we didn't get any sleep," she said.

Cilas laughed, though she didn't see the humor in it. She saluted, which he returned, before racing to the lift to make her way down to her berth. Raileo would have already been in the mess, sharing coffee with Cleia as they chatted, and Quentin would be inside the gym, working on his knife techniques. Sundown would be below the Thundercat, meditating in the way he always did.

Helga thought about joining him once she'd showered and dressed. Just imagining closing her eyes to rest lifted her spirits out of the grog that had her dragging her feet while hanging her head.

"Rough night, Ate?" someone said, and she looked up to see Quentin approaching the lift. It had just touched down to the dock, and she hadn't expected anyone to be there, so the surprise jolted her awake, and she stood staring at him in shock. "Are you alright?" he said, stepping forward, but she couldn't tell if the inflection in his tone was one of sarcasm.

"I'm alright," she said dismissively.

"Fell asleep on the bridge again?" he said, grinning, and it was hard not to read into it but Helga forced herself to play along.

"Yeah, and then Dr. Rai'to woke me twenty minutes before first shift to chat," she said, rolling her eyes for emphasis.

"Ah, now that explains the smoke coming from your ears," Quentin said, laughing. "Don't let me hold you up any longer. Sounds like you've already had quite the start. I'll be in the mess with a stiff cup of coffee waiting for when you come back up. How's that sound?"

"It sounds like you're my favorite Nighthawk right now," Helga said, smiling, as she walked past him to turn into the passageway, which held the three compartments they used for their personal berths.

Thirty minutes later, Helga was dressed in uniform and heading to the cockpit with coffee in hand. She hadn't bothered to stay and chat inside the mess, but Quentin didn't seem to mind, since he and Sundown were in the middle of a game.

Someone had left a ration bar on the arm of her chair, and Helga assumed it was Cleia, since the doctor had expressed some concern with her weight. Genetics and sporadic eating had kept her on the smaller side since becoming an ESO. Now stress, and the cycles where she would go the full rotation without eating, had contributed once again to her weight loss.

Cilas had even said something, and Raileo snuck in jokes, but Cleia had her popping meal tablets and meeting her daily in medbay for vitamin shots. At first, Helga resisted but then she started feeling the results—which were amazing— so now she ate and popped her tablets without having to be told.

"Hello, Zan," she said without turning around. She could always tell it was the Cel-toc by the pattern of her footsteps on the deck.

"Good morning, Lieutenant, how may I assist?" the android said, as she came up and took a seat next to Helga.

She was wearing one of the *Rendron's* flight suits with an Alliance insignia over the heart. It had belonged to Helga—a gift from Joy in a failed attempt to entice her to join the Revenant squadron. Now it was the Cel-toc's to wear, along with several other items Helga had gifted before Argan-10.

"Give me a status update on the *Ursula*, and are there any new ships showing in the system?" Helga said.

"Hold on that command, Zan," Cilas said, stepping onto the deck, causing Helga to shoot up to her feet and saluting as she had been conditioned to do as a cadet. "At ease, Ate. What are you doing?" he scolded.

"Force of habit, Commander. Don't you stand whenever a captain takes the deck?" she said.

"Yeah, but it's still strange for me, you know that. Anyway, could you summon the Nighthawks here for a quick update?"

Helga nodded and got on the *Ursula's* PA system, commanding the Nighthawks to get to the bridge. She noticed that Cilas was tenser than when they had spoken not two hours earlier. He was in a new uniform, which made him look important. He wore a grey and white coat over black pants with several medals denoting rank. His knee-high boots were polished to the point of perfection, and his face was clean-shaven where before he had started to grow a beard.

He waited for them to gather, Helga, Raileo, Quentin, and Sundown, who wore nothing but a 3B XO suit and tactical soft-soles. Cleia Rai'to brought up the rear, walking gingerly past the commander to slip in next to where Helga was standing. Even Zan stood up to lean against her chair, giving Cilas her full attention.

"Just heard from the captain," Cilas said, "We've got the location of those *schtill* traitors holding the Arisanis hostage. They are not over Genese as we were led to believe. Want to guess where they are?"

"Above Arisani?" Quentin said.

"Extra rations for the big man. Yes, they have remained here, cloaked and sending orders to their decoy ship in Genesian space. Thanks to our friends at the Jumper agency," Cilas said, giving Sundown a nod of respect. "We have taken control of said decoy, and are in communication with the pirates, who still believe that we're blind."

"How did they manage to do that?" Raileo said.

"Oh, I'm sure the original crew on that ship are happily in compliance," Helga said, smiling. "Hard to be loyal when you have a las-sword at your throat and several shadows threatening your family."

"We aren't that ruthless," Sundown corrected her, but she twisted her lips and gave him a side-eye.

"*Missio-Tral* Shrikes have been given the mission to board that vessel and rescue the prince," Cilas said. "Before you ask why them, I will remind you that we were on Argan-10 when the Jumpers were tracking that signal above Genese. Shrikes have been waiting to do their part, so naturally they got it, but that isn't to say we get to sit on our hands. Captain Sho has asked us to provide a distraction, forcing the pirates to fight while the Shrikes are on-site."

"Wait, you mean the *Ursula*?" Helga said, trying to imagine a fight where she wasn't allowed to destroy the enemy's ship. "They want us to waltz around sparring with that thing, while the rescue operation is left to the Shrikes?"

"They are ESO just like you and me, Helga. You sound as if I just told you it was the planetary defense force," Cilas said.

"It's just ... I don't know these men and their abilities, Commander," Helga said.

"That's the mission, Nighthawk. You don't have to like it," Cilas said. "A squadron from *Missio-Tral* is on their way to back us up, just in case the pirates get wise and call for help from their lizard benefactors. This is all for naught if we cannot get that Arisani prince out."

"How are we going to manage that?" Quentin said. "As soon as they see a ship, they'll cut and run."

"Not to mention, murder the prince and the other hostages out of spite," Raileo said.

"Finished?" Cilas said, and looked about the space, studying each of their faces. When he was convinced there would be no more interruptions, he walked over to the bulkhead and touched it, and it transformed into a screen. Appearing on its surface was Arisani space, where he manipulated several vessels to outline the plan.

"They won't see the Shrikes," he said, jabbing a finger at a tiny ship he'd drawn next to the pirate's vessel. "They'll come in quietly cloaked, and once they're onboard they'll move to secure him, and I will know their status the whole time," Cilas said. "Ate, the pirates are in an old dreadnought. Second-generation Arisani build. We need to cripple it immediately, and then provide cover for the Shrikes. Once they have the ship that's the mission. Shrikes will take the prince, and we'll return to the *Rendron*."

"*Rendron*? So we're going back already?" Helga said, dreading the thought of losing the freedom that came with being on *Ursula*.

"Just for a time. We need to recruit more Nighthawks, pick up some supplies, and the captain wants a meeting, face-to-face. Plus, Sundown and Dr. Rai'to need to be formally welcomed into our crew. Captain Sho would like to do that personally, and there may be commendations for our actions on Sanctuary. Genevieve will have uploaded the *Rendron's* location for you to plot that jump when we're done with this op. Any questions?"

"Yes," Raileo said. "It's about Argan-10. Did you hear anything about the effort to go down to the surface and rescue the civilians?"

Cilas winced as if he was in pain.

"One and the same," he said. "Our leaders decided that an assault on the moon would risk the lives of the Arisanis still held in space. They still intend to liberate them, but it will likely be sometime in the future when the Geralos aren't expecting us."

"Makes me wonder why they hadn't just done this in the first place," Raileo said, disgusted.

"Done what?" Helga said. She too was feeling irritable and angry at the Alliance council's choices.

"Send in the Jumpers, that's what. Get the prince out of their hands before sending in the Marines to wreck the traitors. They let us go through all we did, and now this with the Shrikes. All for what? To rescue some diplomat? Where's the concern for the Vestalians, and the things we found on that moon?"

"I know it stinks," Helga said softly. "But it's not for us to question, Ray. We're merely operators. We go where we're sent."

"What if we were still stuck on the surface?" he said. "Would they have helped, or would they have still sent those assault ships to assist the Shrikes?"

Helga studied Raileo's face and saw the rage reflected there. He was a boomer, born and raised on a hub, then rescued by his parents who sent him to *Rendron* to become a spacer. For someone from such humble beginnings, he had always seen the Alliance as the ultimate force of good.

Since becoming a Nighthawk, however, he had quickly learned that most of their enemies were not the Geralos but their own. With each discovery of treachery, a bit of the light would die in his eyes. Now she worried that he would give up hope and become an ice-cold executioner, going through the motions of his service.

Imagining "Laser Ray" not being a fun-loving teammate was a frightening thought, considering how good he was at his job. There were enough hollowed-out killers on the *Rendron* for her to know just how that looked.

She observed Cleia Rai'to standing next to him, smiling as she pretended to be in the present. Her eyes revealed the truth, however, as they stared off into the distance, piercing bulkhead, space, and everything beyond. Those same eyes that kept the light within Raileo, and were probably the only reason he held on.

"It's disappointing, you're right," Cilas said. "How do you think this makes me feel?"

"Why don't we go back and get them out?" Cleia said, causing Raileo to regard her with surprise.

"Because we will die?" Quentin said, knitting his brow before looking over at Helga helplessly.

"I would go back if we had some help," Helga said.

"No one's going back," Cilas said. "Dr. Rai'to, it's a noble suggestion, but we'd only be adding to the lizards' captives. We barely got out of there when we did. Those lizards were protective of something below where we were, enough to send in four whole dropships before we made our escape. I doubt they'll do anything to the captives, not after building all that infrastructure to preserve them."

"Another *schtill* mission that leaves me feeling dirty," Raileo said.

"Ray, why don't you go below deck and blow off some steam?" Cilas said.

The space grew quiet as Raileo saluted his commander, then marched off the bridge without looking back. Helga could tell that he was about to explode. She chanced a glance at Cleia, whose expression had changed to one of concern, and then they heard the sound of something being thrown against the bulkhead.

"I should go check on him," Cleia whispered, before bowing to Cilas and making her way off the bridge.

Helga looked around the space. "Can someone tell me what just happened there?"

"The pain of maturing, I guess," Quentin said, his lips having twisted into a scowl. "Anyway, continue your thoughts, Commander. The Alliance is delaying help, and you were saying?"

"Yes," Cilas said, "I was speculating on why they made this decision. We have limited resources, and this pirate *schtill* is a chance for us to earn favor with the Arisanis. The prince can get us aid for the war effort, not to mention more ships and spacers. Is the sacrifice not worth it? We all say no, but tell that to our leaders that are responsible for twelve other planets that dwarf this moon."

"It's *thyped*, but that's the reality of our war," Sundown said.

"What you say makes sense, but it's hard to qualify after what we saw down there," Quentin said.

"Anyway, you are all dismissed. Go about your duties but stay prepared. We need to be ready to answer that call," Cilas said.

24

With the Nighthawks having been briefed on what was to come, it was all hands on deck for the rest of the working cycle. Cilas predicted that they would have four cycles before the Shrikes would contact them, so the team went to work immediately after the brief to prepare for the upcoming fight.

Helga tasked Zan with not only testing the *Ursula*'s hardpoints, but optimizing the way they could be used during combat. She didn't want to take any chances in case they bit off more than they could chew and ended up having to fight a vessel with the mass to outgun them. Helga herself worked on the controls, making sure that *Ursula* was responsive to her commands, and correcting any delays due to language or protocol.

Much of this had to do with Cilas, as the ship's captain. *Ursula* recognized Helga as the pilot and second-in-command, but weapons systems required a captain's approval, and the delay in getting those could become a problem. Cilas knew ships but this was his first command of one, and he wasn't interested in navigating or micro-managing dogfights.

This was the biggest difference between him and Captain Retzo Sho. The latter loved the action, and took the reins on every aspect of strategy from the *Rendron's* bridge. Cilas, however, was big on delegating according to position and strength, and he trusted Helga's abilities and decision-making during a fight. He even seemed happy when she requested full access to the *Ursula*'s controls. After all, if she faltered, he was still the captain and could override her decisions with one command.

Helga tested her new power, ordering *Ursula* to arm and disarm various weapons. She took them through evasive maneuvers, fading their thrust in and out, jerking the brakes and testing response times, learning the corvette's response times and memorizing them, just like she would a fighter.

Until now, the biggest ship that she had used in a fight was the R60 Thundercat, which took some time to get used to. The mass made it slower on certain maneuvers, and more vulnerable to attacks. To make up for this, she had to always be one step ahead of their opponents, with contingencies loaded just in case she assumed wrong.

Ursula, a corvette over ten times the mass of the Thundercat, required eyes seeing combat from three dimensions, and lightning-fast decisions based on the status of the enemy and loadout. Unlike a fighter or a dropship, she wouldn't be able to do much of this herself. Piloting was her primary duty, and while Zan could be sufficient, an AI's answer to combat would become predictable, and the Geralos knew Cel-tocs better than anyone else.

It was why living aces were still valuable to the Alliance, since no two pilots were alike behind the cockpit. Joy and Helga were similarly wired in being fiery daredevils during a skirmish, but where Joy had a line, Helga had none. It was something the two women would argue about constantly, but illustrated how pilots were unpredictable. So she worked on becoming more commander than flight jock when the *Ursula* was her vessel, and that meant leaving the weapons system to her android co-pilot.

Tracers had been firing for hours as Zan taught herself the art of cycling through them seamlessly. She had gotten the timing down and programmed a new sequence into the *Ursula*'s system. It was a macro command for activating one tracer after another, each firing off a stream then charging while the remaining cannon took turns going through the rotations.

When Cilas received the corvette, they had upgraded the broadside cannons to these miniature tracers, and though they were superior, the time it took to charge when you fired them had made them only ideal against other mid-sized vessels. Going up against a squadron, dipping and diving as they whittled down your shields, would be difficult to defend using tracers. The engineers had thought about this, as well, and included several camouflaged turrets above the bridge.

These were manned by the remaining Nighthawks, using the recessed battle-stations that comprised the bulkhead about CIC. Helga ordered everyone in them to practice, even Cleia Rai'to, who she thought should learn something of the ship's defense systems. They were given virtual targets generated by Zan, but only on their HUDs. For hours they practiced, getting scores from the Cel-toc, who reported back to Helga, and she began to see the standouts were Sundown and Raileo Lei.

Other than weapons, they had their standard emergency drills, cranked up to a new level to simulate things falling apart during combat. Cilas cut off the gravity at one point while everyone was going about their business, but this was a weekly drill that they knew, so everyone reacted well and adjusted. They simulated a loss of atmosphere and oxygen, forcing everyone to scramble for their masks, but this had to be stopped prematurely since Cleia wasn't ready, and panicked.

Drill after drill they went through, preparing for a war, and while it was stressful and nerve-wracking, spirits remained high and everyone tried to do their best. By the time these exercises were over, they were sore, over-stimulated and ready for a break. The following cycle was quieter, since it dealt with general preparation, and everyone worked with a single focus of preparing the *Ursula* for anything.

Cilas wanted to be sure that if the Shrikes failed, the Nighthawks would be ready to step in. This meant preparing the cages within the dock for visitors, and stacking them with MRE, vitamin supplements, and water. The Shrikes were from *Missio-Tral* but they were still their ESO family, and in the event they needed rescuing, the commander wanted comfortable berthing for them. Even Cleia had twelve beds prepared inside medbay just in case, and she and Raileo developed a process for getting the injured transported in quickly.

In the cycle before contact, the team was instructed to sleep, or at the very least relax and unwind. In less than eight hours they would be escorting the Shrikes, and the commander wanted them sharp and decisive during that time. Helga found herself restless, so she went looking for Cleia to see if the doctor wanted to finish learning about spacecraft.

On her way aft, she stopped by the mess, where Sundown was alone, sipping tea as he scrolled through a tablet. He wore only a tank-top, which gave Helga pause, since she had never seen so much of his skin. Tattooed glyphs spilled out from his shoulders, trickling down to around his wrists. These "tattoos" seemed to be glowing, and Helga wondered if it was the ink and the contrast with his dark skin. She cleared her throat, and he looked up, smiling, then reached back for his jacket to cover himself.

"Are you doing that because of me?" she said, feeling guilty for disturbing his peace.

"Sorry, but I assumed that everyone was getting some shut-eye," he said.

"You're Virulian, right?" she said, walking over to take the seat across from him.

"Virulian, yes," he said.

"Is that why those lines on your arm glowed the way they did just now?" she said.

Sundown studied her face, then removed the jacket, and up close she could see that they were a patchwork of symbols that she couldn't recognize.

"The ink that they use for these markings is called Misen Mesh, and it comes from the crystal caves of Plesk, on the continent of Moru, Virulia. The extraction takes a very long time, but once it's been refined, the colors continue to change no matter the substrate. When you become a person in my order, you must choose one of three different paths. There is the path of the hunter, like Lamia Brafa, which focuses primarily on stealth, then there is the path of the scholar, reserved for those who are gifted with the texts. Me, I chose the last path, that of the warrior, which comes with the ink so that our enemies will know who we are."

"It sounds like something from an action vid, Sunny. They force you to get a tattoo so that you're never able to hide? Where is the win?" Helga said.

"I could ask you the same, Nighthawk. Where is the win?" he said, smiling. "I have been with the team for a short time, yet I have seen more action than the two years prior when I was a fugitive on a space station that wanted me dead. Are we so different? We serve masters with little consideration for our lives, and the more we kill and the longer we survive, the more we're utilized. Now, what's keeping you up, Lieutenant? You look tired, if you don't mind me saying."

"Nerves, I guess," Helga said, studying the intricacies of his braids, which were pulled back into a bun and tied with a bit of black cloth bearing the same glyphs as his tattoos. "I should be grateful." She rubbed at her neck. "This is leagues better than tussling in The Pit with criminals like your lady, Domina Ryse."

"The Pit was the result of power mongers overplaying their hand," Sundown said, reaching back to adjust his hair. "Your Alliance—"

"Our Alliance, Sundown. Our Alliance," Helga corrected him.

"Our Alliance," he said with a cursory nod, then took another sip from his mug. "Our Alliance elected the representatives on Sanctuary, who in turn used untrained thugs as their police force. Before you all came to the station, there was already trouble brewing. Satellite security was extorting businesses and many of the citizens were starting to take notice. People were vanishing, particularly those who were vocally challenging those of the untouchable elite class. When enough of these 'accidents' started to happen, the citizens looked to us outlaws to deliver their justice.

"Deliver we did, expeditiously, dear Helga, and the Alliance council began to question the lack of trust in their security squad. What they couldn't see from up high in their cozy little bubbles was that money and privilege will always trump the rights and needs of the people. To them we were criminals, dangerous vigilantes who they couldn't control. So they hunted us down and poisoned our name, calling us gangsters, killers, and all sorts of labels. It drove us deeper into the shadows, and what shadow's blacker than The Pit?"

"Sad that you think that way about the Alliance," Helga said, "Though I saw enough on Sanctuary to know that you're not completely wrong. Were you in love with Domina?"

"A Jumper is not allowed to fall in love," he said. "Not unless the subject of that love is a person."

"But, you were no longer a Jumper when you were on Sanctuary," Helga spoke carefully. "You were exiled, and worked as a gun-for-hire, or what did you call it? An outlaw? I doubt that hunting marks for credits vibed with your order, so I'm going to ask again. I saw the way you looked at her Sunny, before we turned her over to the council."

"Domina Ryse was not always a gangster. We found each other in The Pit, when we were both professionals trying to earn enough credits to go topside. We ... were close, but she changed. Something happened and, well, you saw it, the jewelry and the robes."

"So you did love Domina once, and acted on it back when your order turned against you," Helga said. "Now that they've reinstated you, and you're with us, you can no longer love her unless she somehow made it into the Jumpers. *Thype* me, no wonder you've been so spiky lately, Sunny. You do realize that everything we do is for the Alliance, right? Should I be worried?"

"No, that's ridiculous," he said. "I've already made my peace with the Alliance. I'm sworn to the commander, La'una, and as a Jumper, that bond is eternal, unless I'm asked to perform an act that brings shame upon my order. I'm sworn to you, as well, but it is different."

"What do you mean?" she said. "How are you sworn to me now?"

"Our bond is a traditional one, more ritualistic," he whispered, and she glanced about the compartment skeptically, wondering where he was taking this conversation. "I saved your life on Sanctuary, remember? Then you saved mine by vouching for me, and helping to convince the commander that I was worth a second chance. My life was forfeit in The Pit, and I was living on borrowed time. Our actions have completed the circle of trust that forms a seal between you and me."

"We're not getting matching tattoos if that's what you're suggesting," Helga said, and surprisingly he gave her a smile.

"Try some of the tea. It will make you sleep but not for long, la'una," he said. "Domina Ryse is likely to be dead now that she's been tried and found guilty of her crimes. I will always toast her, we had a lot of good times, and she was a light inside a place where I couldn't even see myself. All that to say, I hate the elite in charge of this galaxy and the war, but I know my role as a person within my order."

"Order-shmorder. You're a Nighthawk, Sunny, just accept it. You may not be Navy, but you're with the team, so as far as I'm concerned, you're one of us. Lamia Brafa was a Jumper with no ties to the Navy, but to us he was a brother, and he'll always be remembered as a Nighthawk."

Helga ran her fingers through her hair, trying to remember why she'd asked about Domina Ryse. She didn't know the woman well, but had always been curious about she and Sundown's past. He did save her life from an assassin who had been ordered to eliminate the Nighthawks. Ever since then they had developed a relationship, which started out bitter but evolved into something nearly paternal.

"I get it with the outlaw situation on Sanctuary," she said. "Those same thugs tried to kill me, and without you, maker knows if I'd be alive to be sitting here sipping tea. Sunny, the Alliance is our master, and it will fray our morale if we begin to question what we do. It's kind of the job as an operator. This whole service thing. We cannot allow ourselves to falter."

"I know. I too 'served' before the Jumper Agency claimed me from my unit. I'm not supposed to discuss it with outsiders, but many of us got recruited out of the Alliance Navy. That is all I can say; you're one of the chosen, so if you repeat any of this I'll say that you learned it from a vision," he said, winking at her devilishly. "You're like a psych. Anyone ever tell you that? I've never divulged this much information to anyone outside of Domina. Here, I barely know you, yet I've told you more than anyone, even the commander. Can I trust you to keep it to yourself?"

Helga tapped her forehead with her knuckles. "While this box of secrets is full, I'm sure that I can find a spot for the things I heard today." She glanced at the doorway to make sure that they were alone. "I do want to go back to a question you asked me during our last chat. The one about me telling Cilas what I am."

"Yes." He leaned back in his chair as he drained the last of his tea. "Have you told him?"

"No," she said, quickly. "I've decided against it. Do you find that disappointing?"

"It has nothing to do with me, la'una, but this burden that you carry, others knowing can help to lighten the load. Take our talks, for instance. Have they not eased your mind somewhat?" he said.

"They have, actually, if I'm being honest," Helga said. "No-one likes to be the only freak, and you understand that better than anyone else. Cilas is understanding, but it's still difficult because of his position and his relationship with the captain. He could ground me if he feels that I'm too valuable an asset for the lizards, and if he blabs to Retzo Sho, then he'll ship me back to Sanctuary for them to dissect me or something similarly *thyped* up."

Sundown laughed, a rasp that betrayed a former life of smoking. Its intention wasn't to ridicule, though Helga couldn't help but feel foolish.

"He would do no such thing," Sundown said. "The commander values you most on this team, and if he doesn't already know, I would be surprised. You were captured by the lizards and quarantined because they dared not bite into your head. A Casanian, whose blood is toxic to their palate, and a seeker that possesses the very gift they want. What you are is something wonderful; you have the positive traits of both your species. The ultimate weapon against the Geralos. In the old age, you would have wanted for nothing. Seekers had the ears of monarchs, many being seen as messengers from the maker."

"So, like I said, shipped off to be dissected in Sanctuary," Helga said. "Or your Jumpers will come knocking, forcing me to become a member."

"You have no interest in the Jumpers?" he said evenly.

"None whatsoever. It sounds positively awful," Helga said. "From what you told me, Jumpers lack freedom of choice, even more than the Alliance Navy. Then there was that bit about Domina and how you can't love her because she isn't a Jumper person. Before Lamia died, we used to have similar talks, and I believe it's because he saw something within me, as well. He told me that when you're chosen you aren't allowed to refuse them. Is that correct?"

"Yes," Sundown said, frowning. "When you're called, you belong to them."

"I hope that I'm never chosen, ever," she whispered. "I love being a Nighthawk, even with the Alliance's hypocrisy. It's the best job in the universe, really."

"You have nothing to worry about, la'una," he said, standing up to deposit his empty mug inside the replenisher. "It wouldn't make sense to recruit the very chosen that we're sworn to protect."

25

"Blackbird, this is Weasel, we're on approach," the Shrike commander said. "How do you copy?"

"Clear as glass, Weasel," Helga said. "Radar's pulsing and we've got eyes. Over."

"Excellent, Blackbird. Stand-by. Over and out," he said before clicking off.

Helga looked back at Cilas, who was in CIC going over his plans.

"Ready, Commander?" she said, and when he gave her the nod, she activated the *Ursula*'s cloak.

The exterior hull cooled, its black surface becoming opaque and rendering it invisible to radar, ship-guiding systems, and the naked eye. This was another upgrade from Sanctuary, to go along with their Louine-engineered system. Now, unlike the Shrike's dropship—which employed a Genesian methodology to become invisible—*Ursula* could avoid detection from even the most advanced Geralos warships.

The Shrike's ship was a V35 Vixen, sleek and top-of-the-line. It too was cloaked but remained on the *Ursula*'s tracker, due to a link they had shared during the prep. Helga had experience with the Vixen from a former mission on Meluvia, and knew its strengths and weaknesses where combat was concerned. It was outfitted with laser cannons and an energy torpedo launcher, which would be enough to put a hurting on anything equal or lesser to its mass.

If the clueless pirates had known that such a machine was en route with a belly full of deadly operators, they would have probably reconsidered their position. Through the windows, Helga saw a nebula of colorful gases that decorated the black with splashes of blues, greens and reds. It was a beautiful backdrop to what was likely to become an ugly operation, because somewhere in there waited the pirate's dreadnought, cloaked and clueless to their fate.

They were expecting a ship in exchange for the prince, but what was coming were the Shrikes, who planned to get onboard and exact revenge with extreme prejudice. While this happened, the *Ursula* was to disable their FTL capability, giving the Shrikes time to secure the prince. A full cycle had gone into the study of that model of dreadnought, and both Helga and Zan now knew where to place the trace lasers when the time was right.

They would cripple the ship, sending the pirates into a frenzy, but the Shrikes would have already breached if everything went according to plan. It would be quick and dirty but doable, since these were professional operators going up against a ragtag group of thugs. The worst they expected was for the pirate leader to get desperate and shoot the prince, but even that was unlikely, since he was their only leverage.

"How are we looking, Ray?" Helga said, turning around in her seat to spy the Nighthawk seated at one of the weapons control stations.

"Locked and loaded, Lieutenant. You?" he said, sounding a touch nervous.

"Bored out of my mind, shooter, what do you think?" she said, then turned to face her Cel-toc co-pilot. "Zan, I want you to prime two torpedoes and wait for my command. Controls are on me. Are you finally synced with the network about Arisani space?"

"Link has been approved and now established, Lieutenant," Zan said.

"Starmap's updated, Hel, I can see the whole system," Cilas said from behind them.

"Good" Helga said. "Zan, if any new vessels appear, whether from a jump or launch from the planet or station, I want to know about it. Do you hear?"

"Acknowledged, Lieutenant," the Cel-toc said. "Cloaked derelict cruiser on local radar. At current speed it will take 108 minutes to be within range of an energy torpedo. Displaying timer on the control console, and captain's personal terminal. Warning, dropship escort has just increased thrust. Adjusting trajectory to maintain distance and spacing."

"Here we go," Helga muttered, her fingers twitching on the controls. "Hold our current velocity, Zan. They're going to need time to get onboard, and we don't want to risk their cover by crowding them."

Cilas got up from his seat to pace the area of CIC about the starmap. He looked like a junior version of Captain Retzo Sho, sharp in his dress, a knit in his brow, and a closed fist resting on the small of his back.

"Let's talk contingencies if this goes off the rails," he said. "You're one of the best pilots I've seen, Helga, but too much of this rests on you, should say a Geralos destroyer uncloaks and turns its tracers on our shields."

Helga stood up and walked back to the raised area that constituted CIC, where she leaned against the railing and regarded her Commander.

"Worse comes to worst, you have two pilots, and I have the Vestalian Classic and Thundercat ready to deploy," she said. "If a destroyer jumps in, *Missio-Tral* will know and should come to our rescue within an hour at most. We could buy time, which Zan can handle, outrunning the zip-ships it deploys while I pick them off one by one. Ray is no slouch, he'll be gunning, and Q is familiar with the guns, not to mention Sundown. It's not ideal, but we have options, sir."

"It's a plan, but I still don't like it," Cilas said.

"Respectfully, Commander, that's because it's left to the *Ursula* and not to the strength of our ESO capabilities," Helga said, smiling. "Instead of stealth strikes and PAS, we would be in open engagement with a Geralos warship. I don't like it, either. We are no match for anything stronger than a dreadnought, and even then if accompanied by zips, we'd literally be fighting for our lives."

"We come here a lot, don't we?" he said ruefully, stopping to stare out the window at the stars.

"To quote a man I respect above all others, it's the job," Helga said.

"He sounds like a thrust head," Cilas said, and the two of them shared a friendly smile.

"If there's a maker, we're in her favor, Rend," Helga said. "Since coming on, I'm convinced that there is no stopping the Nighthawks."

"The lieutenant is more than capable, Commander," Quentin said, stepping up behind her to rest a hand on her shoulder. "I know what you're asking, though, and we can more than handle it. If the Shrikes go down and we're able to disable that ship, the three of us can get onboard and mop up the rest of those stains."

Cilas smiled at the sergeant's confidence.

"*Missio-Tral* is still sending in a squadron, right?" Helga said.

"As far as I know, yes," Cilas said. "An infiltrator is on its way here to Arisani space, and will deploy phantoms to back us up."

"The infamous Blood Wraiths," Quentin said proudly. "If we get jumped, I like our chances knowing they're who we have."

"And where's *Rendron*?" Helga said, annoyed.

"Mother's over Meluvia, keeping the lizards at bay, and *Inginus* is near Louine, running tandem patrols with the *Quasax* from Helysian," Cilas said. "No word on *Soulspur*, but I know for a fact that it isn't in this system. *Missio-Tral* is what we have, and this is hardly the time to be critical of their help. I like what I hear. Everyone is prepared in case anything goes off the rails. Remember your training, and the fact that we are leagues better than these traitors. You can return to your stations. I am going to get on comms and make certain that we're getting that help."

"Zan, what's our ETA?" Helga said.

"Fifty-five minutes left, Lieutenant," the Cel-toc said.

Time enough for some tea and some mental preparation, Helga thought, and she saluted Cilas crisply before heading towards the mess.

Ten minutes later, she was alone, sitting at a table with a mug in her hands, nose inhaling the musty fumes of the rowcut tea leaves. Time ticked by slowly as she sipped, draining her anxiety and replacing it with thoughts of family and friends. Reflecting on her brief career, Helga wondered just how different things would have been had her parents lived to see her become an adult. Would she have joined the Navy? Probably not, she concluded, since her mother would have pushed her towards the arts. Her brother, Rolph, would have likely served. Every generation of Ate had at least one member wearing the uniform.

Life outside of service ... Helga couldn't imagine it. The entire concept was so foreign that all she had was what she remembered seeing on Meluvia and *A'wfa Terracydes*. Still, they didn't compare to what she would have experienced as a civilian. When her parents were alive, the family lived in a cottage outside of a remote village on Casan. There was no imagining a lifestyle that she couldn't glean through a spacer's lens, and it hurt her head to even attempt a try.

"I am right where I belong," she concluded. "Born to fight. That's me."

"Lieutenant Ate, you're needed on the bridge," Zan announced over the comms.

Draining her mug so fast she nearly choked, Helga rushed back to the bridge, where she noticed that everyone was seated inside of their control stations.

Thype me, how long was I gone? she thought as she chanced a glance at Cilas, who was back inside his captain's seat manipulating the star map.

"It's a call from the Shrikes, Lieutenant," the Cel-toc whispered, and Helga, realizing that she'd lost track of time, whispered a thank you before taking up the controls.

"Blackbird, this is Weasel, copy?" said the Shrike commander.

"This is Blackbird, what's your situation?" Helga said, hoping to hear him say that they were onboard.

"We're dropping in on the LZ now. Going dark, but look for a sign," he said, switching off comms.

"Do you know what he meant by that, Commander?" Helga said, looking back at Cilas.

"It will be some sort of signal," Cilas said. "So keep chatter to a minimum, and pay close attention to that radar."

Helga looked up at the time and saw that they were now fifteen minutes out from the Vixen. She could see where they had stopped, but couldn't make out the pirate dreadnought on the radar. Everyone was on pins and needles, and you could cut the tension with a knife.

"Did you see that?" Cilas said suddenly, and Helga looked up to see the ship now visible through the glass.

"Enemy dreadnought is preparing to jump to light speed," Zan said, and Helga pulled them out of cloak to devote all power to their thrusters.

"Nighthawks, look alive," she announced, and urged the *Ursula* forward at max thrust.

"Enemy shields are online," Zan said.

"*Schtill!*" Helga said. "Doesn't look like they're panicking, they're getting the hell out."

"Target within range," Zan said.

"Commander, I am going to have to use a torpedo," Helga said. "It's risky, but if their shields are at full charge, it will knock them out while simultaneously crippling their ship."

"And if their shields aren't charged?" Cilas said.

"Then we risk harming the Shrikes, and the hostages as well," Helga said. "If we wait then they will jump, and the Shrikes will be left on their own in maker knows where."

Cilas hesitated, a thing that Helga was not used to seeing him do during a crisis.

"Hit 'em," he said evenly. "Launch a torpedo. You have my clearance."

"Launching torpedoes," Zan announced, and Helga whispered a prayer as she saw the lines of light leave from below them to strike the dreadnought. The shields flashed white, then dissipated, but as expected, the hull remained intact.

"Bring tracers online and give it all we've got," Helga shouted. "You Nighthawks on guns, aim for the thrusters. If you use your HUD, you will see the region where I marked our target."

Flying a wide arc around the dreadnought at a range of less than 250 meters, Helga regulated thrust to feed more power into the *Ursula*'s weapons. Since the dreadnought's only defense seemed to be a mounted turret pumping out kinetic rounds, she sacrificed shields and speed to give the gunners time to work.

"Enemy vessel's engine is offline," Zan announced to cheers, but then Helga saw several new blips appear on their radar.

"Lieutenant." Zan spoke to her directly. "A Geralos fleet has just arrived to Arisani space. I detect one destroyer class starship, three dreadnoughts, and five assault ships. Two assault ships are at supercruise, moving to intercept our vector. Estimated time for collision is less than three minutes. I await your command."

"Strap in, we have a lot of company," Helga announced, and pulled them away from the dreadnought where the shields could charge to 100%. "Commander," she said. "The Shrikes need time, and there are too many on approach for *Ursula* to manage. Zan can pilot if I can go below and launch the Thundercat or Classic."

"Out of the question," Cilas said, with such a finality that Helga didn't bother arguing.

"I need every crew member on a gun right now," Helga said into comms. "That includes you, Cleia. Get up here. There are five manual cannons. Find and man one. When I mark a target, I need focused fire on it, so pay attention to your HUDs and don't let anything pull you off. Zan, keep all torpedoes primed and ready for my command. Do you copy?"

"Yes, Lieutenant," the Cel-toc said. "Enemy assault ships are now within torpedo firing range. Displaying local combat map. On your command."

An area of the console displayed a three-dimensional combat grid with the *Ursula* in the center and the pirate vessel nearby, with the Vixen flying circles around it. Two ships appeared on the edges and the computer predicted their path, marking a dotted line across the *Ursula*'s bow. Helga saw that the Vixen was working at distracting the pirates from jumping, but its shots were doing nothing against the dreadnought's recharged shields. She brought them closer to assist, and stayed near the aft so that Raileo and team could work on the vulnerable thrusters.

In her hurry to help the Shrikes, however, Helga missed Zan's warning and a missile struck the *Ursula*, nearly disabling the shields. The bridge temporarily lost gravity as the Cel-toc reacted, diverting power from whatever it could to save them. Anyone not restrained was thrown, including Cilas, who bumped his head on the overhead.

Two more hits threatened to disable them, as the shields hovered a touch below 30%. Helga, in a fantastic display of flying, dodged the rest of the salvo by placing the dreadnought between them and their attackers. The Geralos assault ships were forced to cease fire to protect the pirates, and decided instead to try and give chase. Helga focused fire on the dreadnought, however, as she worked at keeping the newcomers blind to a clear shot.

"This is getting hairy, Commander. Where are our aces?" she said.

"Anytime now, Ate, just hang on," he said quickly, but the way he sounded made Helga somewhat doubtful.

The dreadnought's shields finally gave out, and the *Ursula*'s gunners delivered a finishing blow to the engines. They were now disabled, and it was only a matter of time before the Shrikes would take the bridge. There were two new complications, however, and several larger problems incoming, which included a whole flotilla of Geralos warships.

The assault ships needed to be destroyed quickly, and Helga wasn't keen on waiting for a squadron that was running late. She knew that the *Ursula* was better than any mid-sized fighter, and here was an opportunity to test if that theory was correct.

"More missiles incoming," Zan announced, and Helga did a series of maneuvers to keep the projectiles away from their hull. These were stalkers, however, and couldn't be shaken without a counterstrike, but Zan and the Nighthawks were unable to shoot them down.

Desperate, Helga pulled up the maintenance menu on her console. Locating the trash-compactor, she set it to eject everything they had. Five blocks were thrown out, attracting the missiles to strike them instead. It was an old trick Helga had been taught by Adan Cruser. You could only do it once, and it relied heavily on the trash having enough metal inside to distract the warheads.

An explosion occurred, and when the *Ursula* came about, Helga watched in horror as a missile struck the side of the Vixen. One assault ship moved in for the kill, liberally peppering the dropship with cannon fire. Surprisingly, the other flew away from the action, in what Helga assumed was a poor attempt to pull her off.

"Put a torpedo on that assault ship attacking the Vixen, Zan," she ordered, and the ordnance was out, depleting its shields as soon as she said her name.

"Nighthawks, I've marked a new target," she shouted into comms. "Put everything you can into the hull of that vessel. If we don't bring her down, the Shrikes will not survive. Now is the time to prove our excellence. Let's go!"

Spiraling like a corkscrew towards the Geralos assault ship, the *Ursula* let fly all her arsenal into its now exposed hull. All twelve tracers locked on to the engines, forcing the pilot to attempt to run. But *Ursula* pursued her mercilessly, and her shields stayed dead due to Zan's practiced rotation of the tracers.

A cursory look at the combat map showed the other assault ship behind them, but Helga was surfing on adrenaline and confidently in control of the situation. She wished she could stay in this state of calm instead of having it find her whenever her life was threatened.

"Are the remaining torpedoes primed Zan?" she said.

"All four are online, Lieutenant," the android said.

"What's the status on that dropship? Is anyone still alive?" Helga said.

"I'm on comms with their commander," Cilas said. "He says the ship's in really bad shape, but nothing that can't be repaired if the shields are allowed to replenish."

"Sixteen Geralos zip-ships incoming," Zan announced suddenly. "Twenty-two missiles have been launched. Taking defensive maneuvers now. Brace for impact."

"We're not bracing for *schtill*. Bring them down," Helga demanded, and the Cel-toc directed all weapons towards the ordnance.

"Tracers have successfully eliminated seventeen targets," Zan said. "Contact is imminent. Brace for impact. Estimated damage, less than a 20% drop in our shielding."

As predicted, the missiles struck with minimal effect, and the *Ursula*'s tracers went back on the offensive, mangling the assault ship they originally pursued. Now it too was disabled, with the engine showing signs that it would explode. Helga put everything into thrust and took their pursuer back towards the dreadnought. It tried to keep up, but the *Ursula* was too fast, and Helga again used the disabled ship as an obstacle to hide from her opponent. It gave her the crucial seconds needed to cloak and come around, stealthily winning the assault ship's flank.

"Launch all torpedoes," she commanded, and Zan complied, knocking out the shields and a section of the hull.

The zip-ships arrived just then, however, like a swarm of mosquitos, stinging at the *Ursula*'s shields. Helga again had to do some fancy flying to protect the *Ursula* from the relentless barrage. She was growing tired and distracted, sweating now as she sought for an answer to this new threat.

"Blackbird, this is Weasel, how are you faring?" said the Shrike commander over comms.

"Not good, what's your situation, Weasel?" Helga said.

"Home free with the package. Thanks to you and your team, this junker's finally ours," he said.

"*Ursula* command," came another voice over the comms. "This is Commander Aven Horne, Blood Wraith flight leader, *Missio-Tral* Squadron. Looks like you could use a hand with a few bugs."

Took you long enough, cruta, Helga thought, then cleared her throat and replied, "Some assistance would be phenomenal right now, Commander. Looking forward to seeing you and your squadron in action."

They came through like a rain of arrows, cutting through the zip-ships effortlessly, leaving destruction in their wake. In a blink of an eye it was over, and the only thing remaining of the Geralos was a memory. The *Missio-Tral* squadron reverted to patrolling as the Shrikes worked at transporting the hostages onto the Vixen. As for the Nighthawks, they were now long gone, making the trip back to the *Rendron*. It had been a successful mission, but not without its lows, and when Helga looked over at Zan, the Cel-toc gave her the widest of smiles.

"The cockpit is yours, Zan," she said. "We did it. Good job. Commander, if I have your leave, I'll be below deck, clearing my head."

26

While Helga and the Nighthawks were engaged with the Geralos, there was an assembly being held on *A'wfa Terracydes* by the top delegates of the planet. In a grand open space they sat in high-backed chairs, tiered and wrapped about a floating disc-shaped stage. The man of the hour was the chairman of industry, Sebi Lata'anda, an Arisani noble draped in black robes and wearing a thin metal necklace that denoted his name and rank.

It was an odd gathering for that time of year, borne of desperation, due to dire circumstances. Delegates that couldn't attend had Cel-toc representatives in attendance, some going so far as to have the androids made in their likeness. Attendees stuck in space and unable to be there physically listened in and commented via holographic projections. The room was packed, the best turnout they ever had, at a meeting that would only occur when there were decisions to be made that affected the entire planet.

The chairman stepped forward, his soft-soled, curly-toed boots making no noise on the smooth alabaster stage. He regarded the room, turning a full 360 degrees, with a practiced sequence of waves.

"Delegates of the empires, and representatives of the eight continents. First of all, thank you for allowing this most unfortunate interruption to your lives. Thanks for being here at this hour, in this space, physical and holo, at this, our most difficult time. As you might have heard, Prince Jorus Kane of the nation of Moss-Ekanoe was attacked and taken hostage. Prince Joras Kane is a close friend, business partner, and family man. Certainly not someone I could ever imagine who would have his life threatened by parasites."

"I am both angry and ashamed, as I am certain most of you are. *A'wfa Terracydes* was built for ... was built to be a bridge, for industry and outreach, as a means to establish trades with our sister planets.

We had the greatest intentions, but to be frank, we were naïve in thinking that we would be left alone to compete. That oversight has brought us to this awful place, my fellow delegates, and for that you have my sincerest apologies. If there is anyone to blame for this, it is I. Now, I see a number of hands, so maybe this is a good time to stop my blabbering," he said with a nervous laugh. "I'll answer your questions now. Lady Jerula, please, what are your thoughts?"

"Master Chairman, thank you," the hat-wearing Arisani noblewoman said. "My question is on security. There have been rumors of a connection between a citizen of *A'wfa Terracydes* and the attack on the *Lucia*, which led to the capture of our prince. Is there any truth to this, and what is being done about it?"

"Yes," Sebi Lata'anda said. "There was internal involvement—"

Before he could say anything more the room exploded into a raucous tornado of disapproval, as members of the board let him know how they felt. A sharp noise drowned them out, as Sebi depressed a tiny panic button hidden beneath his robes. The noise continued until they quieted, and then he spread his arms in a gesture meant to express unity and understanding.

"I would love to give you reassurances that punishing the accused will be the end of piracy and the attacks on our fleet," he said. "Unfortunately, to do so would be dishonest. Piracy is a galaxy-wide plague, and the only thing that can be done is for us to come together and agree on measures that will make it hard for them to try. On that topic, it may be best for you to hear from the man in charge of our Crime and Loss Prevention services. The good sergeant, Trisk A'lance."

The sergeant stood up from his seat near the edge of the stage, and ascended the stairs. He walked up to Sebi Lata'anda, who reached out and took his hand and shook it. The chairman then retreated to the floor, leaving the somber-looking sergeant alone on the stage. He raised one hand, and a holo-display appeared above him, showing a prison cell with two inhabitants.

"Thank you, Mr. Chairman," he said, clearing his throat. He forced a smile on his long, chalky-white face. "Good people of Arisani and beyond, it is my pleasure and privilege to be with you today. My hope is to restore some of your confidence in ACLOP, your security force. Now, above me on the display are the two men who coordinated the attack on Prince Joras Kane. The man on the left is one, Reiro Askier, a Vestalian smuggler who got hired on by the Lartrillo Company to help maintain our docks."

Several gasps went up from the crowd, mainly from Vestalian aristocrats who were embarrassed to see one of their own be involved with the crime. Others were shocked at the Lartrillo Company's lapse in judgment, and the thought that the same docks where their ships were now parked had been open to a co-conspirator of the pirates. Trisk A'lance seemed to have expected this reaction, since he stopped and waited patiently for the noise to die down.

"The other individual is a mystery. No credentials, and no ties to this station or our planet, yet he lived here in our social development housing with a family he was holding hostage. I am not telling you these things to frighten you, good people of Arisani, but to paint a backdrop to the reality of why pirates thrive in our system. There's a lot to cover, but I will try my best to be brief. We have been at a disadvantage against these raiders because of our isolation as a planet. What I am about to say is a difficult thing to accept, but piracy starts when desperate people make this choice as a means to survive. We see them as villains, rich, and plotting these schemes from the comforts of plush, stolen ships. But this assumption aids their cause because it blinds you to the reality that anyone can and will do it.

"Reiro Askier, our resident smuggler, has lived in squalor his whole life. Being poor around all this wealth, he had a choice: continue to push 50 kilo crates around for meager credits, or assist a group of robbers with some intelligence for intercepting the prince's ship. In his head it was a no-brainer. The prince is wealthy beyond measure, and they likely promised he wouldn't be hurt, just a bit of delay. We all know now that he got in with a pack of murderers, willing to take the lives of numerous innocents for a ship.

"What am I saying? We need to think bigger than arresting the Reiro Askiers when we find them. What we have here is a war, good people of Arisani, a war against a collective of desperate and ruthless people. They may be small, but they are organized, and have established a wide-reaching network, which unfortunately includes our station. And how do we root out the enemy when he looks like us? He's our neighbor, our employee, an officer in charge of our ships.

"The first step is acceptance. Eh? Not pretending we're above these attacks until it happens to someone as lofty as the prince. Arisani must recognize that these gangsters are a legitimate threat. We must be stalwart. We must become intentional. First, with the security of *A'wfa Terracydes* and the space about her, and second, with empowering our people to report things when they see them. Piracy is alive and thriving because most attacks go unreported. Ransoms get paid because merchant ship owners treat it as a hiccup that slows their business.

"With that being the pattern, why wouldn't they attack the *Lucia*? It's obvious that their system works. Right? We've allowed it. Being intentional means that we must alert one another, report all incidents, and accept assistance." He waited as if he expected applause, and when there wasn't any he put a hand over his heart and nodded at Sebi Lata'anda. "Mr. Chairman," he said, graciously, smiling despite the hostile air, and the older man took his hand once more and shook it, trading places with him on the stage.

"Ah, any more questions, please?" he said, dabbing a bit of sweat from his abnormally long forehead. "Yes, the gentleman in the back. Oh, Premier Codan, greetings, my fellow Knaak."

"We have been ask to communicate better, and that's fair, but aside from tips on reporting incidences, what is being done to assure us of our safety?" the portly man said, his hands becoming animated as he spoke. "For years we've heard from your office that these pirates are a minor threat. Now your head of security is telling us that it's on the level of a war. What, Mr. Chairman, are we paying you for? To sit on your hands and lie while a crisis reaches critical mass?"

The crowd erupted with loud agreement and Sebi Lata'anda looked ill as he stared at his countryman, who had hung him out to dry. He fumbled with the button, hesitating to press it. Why would they obey his noise now to give him the floor, when what he would be silencing was them questioning his job and position?

"Perhaps I can best explain," someone said, and the room quickly quieted as a Cel-toc, built to favor a thin, well-dressed Arisani, got to his feet and approached the stage. While his form was forgettable, the people inside the room recognized the voice. It was Joras Kane, the prince, who had secretly attended the assembly, utilizing the mechanical avatar of the representative from his district. The Cel-toc took the stage, and the holo-screens above him changed to show the face of the real prince.

"You all have a right to be angry, but no one here is as disappointed as me. To see my friends massacred, and all for what? Credits and a warship. That's what they wanted, a vessel, and to those with the means, it's nothing in exchange for someone of my station.

Right? No, wrong. Which is what the sergeant was saying. In a manner of hours, they segregated my friends and the crew of the *Lucia*, then took the poor Vestalians to a prison camp on a remote station. The rest of us, the Arisani and the Genese, we were locked inside a cargo hold without food and water.

"We sang songs and clung to one another for hope while our kidnappers issued threats to the galactic Alliance. Their demands? A warship in exchange for my life, and the longer it took for them to agree to this deal, the more of my friends they would shoot. This continued until my family reached out to the Alliance for assistance. I would be dead now, or worse, tortured within a centimeter of my life, if the Alliance had chosen to refuse them, and left me there to die. They could have done that, but they didn't. They showed me how committed they were to our trade, by rescuing me.

"So, what are we doing? We're joining the Alliance, not militarily but with resources, food, and supplies. This decision did not come lightly, since my initial intention was to establish a trade. But things tend to become clear when your life is threatened, and you see those you love taken away. Some of you will disagree, and I don't blame you. None of us want to be dragged into a war. I am not asking any of you here to do anything, but you're all here because something has to be done."

"Are you saying that you are seceding from the External Conflict Writ?" shouted Premier Codan, bypassing all protocol to object.

"That is what I'm saying. My trade with the Alliance will no longer be business. We have a formal agreement that until the end of the galactic war, Moss-Ekanoe will supply the Alliance with the resources needed for building their ships. In exchange, we will have presence above Arisani, a dedicated destroyer with drones, fighters, and well-armed Marines, keeping our merchant vessels safe."

"This will bring in the Geralos, who will be angry with us," Premier Codan said. "How could you be this selfish, Prince Kane? You've endangered all of our lives, and for what? To stop a handful of pirates? What you've done is take a blowtorch to a house in an attempt to stop a fly."

"You go forward with this, and there will be war," someone shouted, and more opinions followed along the same vein.

"I forgot to mention, members of the assembly, that before making my decision, I spoke with the leaders of the nations that border my lands. As of this moment, we have the signatures of Pacho

Moran, Mantup Rial-Mar, Junlop Moon, and Lady Talulah Harre. Five nations, including my own, which gives me quorum to move forward with my aid. There are high emotions in here, and rightfully so, because the Geralos are vicious, frightening creatures. But I spoke to a man named Retzo Sho, a war captain in the Alliance, who they tell me sent in his Marines to handle part of my rescue.

"He informed me that our pirates were dealing with Geralos. In fact, they are selling our Vestalian citizens off to them, which is why they segregated us. Now, do you mean to tell me that you are okay with this crime? That the Vestalian citizens that live in Fortnar and Knaak are not considered worthy to defend? Are we cowards? Is neutrality so wonderful that a handful of hoodlums can lock a station down? If so, then speak up and convince me. Tell me why I should allow the Geralos to commit crimes in our space, unchecked?"

The room grew eerily quiet but for a few nervous people clearing their throats. No one had expected the Geralos to have a part in the prince's kidnapping, and even if they disagreed with assisting the Alliance, they didn't want to get singled out. The Cel-toc began to pace the stage, his hands on his hips as he stared down the audience.

"People of Arisani, representatives of the three remaining nations, know that you're well within your rights to prevent our actions through war. You remain silent, but there are a few of you who will try that, and I must warn you of what that means. Aside from the five nations allied to assist us, we now have the naval support of the Alliance. So, think before you act. I would rather talk amicably than entertain any more threats.

"The downside is yes, we may have Geralos interference, but they will be met by our Alliance friends, while life as we know it will continue ... just not as quietly. The upside, however, is that business will increase. Supplies will be safer. The Alliance will be providing escorts to any merchant vessel that requires it, and so we'll have less losses to theft. Here on *A'wfa Terracydes* we've always loved our Alliance visitors. They spend their credits and make us feel safe, and aside from their boisterous ways and some cultural quirks, they've always been a boon to our merchants. As allies now, their number will increase, considering that the ships providing us protection will need to resupply."

"Ships need fuel, Jenna Harken," he said, waving to a small Genesian woman, who seemed to relish his attention. "Vandon, your algae supply will triple from you having to process soft and hard rations for your stores, and the planet as a whole will benefit, all for turning against the Geralos, who turned on us. Where is the bad in this? Where am I out of line?"

A low murmur in the crowd rose to a crescendo of discussion as representatives turned to their neighbors and excitedly began sharing their thoughts.

From a hospital bed within the medbay on the starship *Missio-Tral*, Prince Joras Kane made a sigh of relief, and reached out to a Meluvian doctor, who took it and shook his hand. Behind the doctor was a large vid-screen with live feed of Captain Retzo Sho. Standing next to him was his executive officer, a man by the name of Jit Nam, and the two of them were smiling as if they had just heard the most amazing thing.

"They said you were good, but that was just masterful," Retzo Sho said, laughing. "What do you think of his speech, Jit? Are you not impressed?"

"Impressed? We should be giving you your own starship, Prince Kane. Give a speech like that to the Geralos, and they might give us back Vestalia and quit."

"All jokes aside, Prince Kane," Retzo said, "it has been an unfortunate series of events that led us to this decision, and I don't want to make light of your tremendous sacrifice. The Alliance council has asked me to inform you that in one Vestalian year, you will have two dedicated destroyers outfitted with infiltrators, cruisers, and a fleet dedicated to the defense of Arisani. Meluvia, Casan, and Genese will be sending gifts to formally welcome you in to our fight. Your speech wowed me, and I am happy to have you as a friend. Welcome to the Alliance."

"Thank you, my friends," Joras Kane said. "I am happy we could do this, but my work has just begun. I look forward to further discussions on our trade."

27

For a war-tested, hardened graduate of BLAST, it would be a stretch to say that Helga Ate needed someone in order to feel "safe." Still, as she opened her eyes to the dusky atmosphere of Cilas's cabin, she felt safer than she'd felt in what seemed like years.

She could hear his shallow breathing and felt the rising of his chest as he went through whatever nightmare mission that he was assigned in the land of dreams. Her left leg was across his, resting in the gap between his legs, and her head was on his chest, where he held her to him with one powerful arm.

What they had was complicated and forbidden, which they had both acknowledged and chose to ignore. Helga knew the boundaries they were supposed to keep, just like she understood chain of command, but her young mind still struggled at the futile need for secrecy. It should have been simple: they would keep this private or face the consequences of separation if Commander Jit Nam or the captain were to find out.

Alliance command knew that operatives too long in the field were bound to develop relationships, but in this case it would be a high-ranking commander sharing his berth with a younger subordinate. The age thing burned Helga up more than the difference in rank because everyone expected her to behave irrationally, like a child. They didn't acknowledge her time in the field, and being raised in the sort of conditions that forced a young woman to grow up fast.

It was offensive to think that the same Alliance who trusted her with ships that cost millions of credits would think that mixing desire and professionalism was somehow beyond her. Cilas was neither her boyfriend nor a lovesick old man looking to add her to a list of conquests, but the Navy and its rules didn't seem to care about the details. It was all about optics, and she hated that.

In Helga's mind, both she and Cilas were supposed to die on the moon of Dyn. The Geralos had massacred their team and placed the two of them in stasis for future consumption. Escape led to isolation inside a pod for several long months together, followed by more missions, and more near-misses with death, until they were forced to surrender to the feelings they had for each other.

For their captain, Retzo Sho, not to have seen the connection between them, he would have had to be thick and blind, unlikely traits for a former ESO. Yet, despite what he assumed or knew in his heart was happening with his two lead Nighthawks, it still came down to appearances, so they still had to keep it a secret.

Helga wiggled out of his arms and laid on her back, enjoying the cool air from the vents on her warm, clammy body. *Shouldn't happiness be enough?* she thought. *And really, what do I want, a formal announcement?* She couldn't honestly answer that question, so she did what she'd normally do when confronted, and focused on the here and now.

She reached over and touched Cilas' nose, rousing him from sleep.

"Hey, are you awake?" she said, knowing that he wasn't.

"No," he whispered, opening his bloodshot eyes. "What's going on, Hel? Is everything okay?"

"What about Ina?" she said, playing with the stubble on his chin. Cilas groaned and tried to turn away from her but couldn't since she had him pinned beneath one of her legs.

"What?" he said, reaching up to rub his eyes.

"Ina Reysor, the pilot. Remember her? The red-haired Meluvian we rescued from that junker back before we docked with the *Inginus*."

"Yeah, I remember her. Why now? What about her warrants rousing me out of the little sleep I get?" he whined.

"I would like to recommend her for *Ursula*," Helga said. "Zan is good, but she's a Cel-toc, and we need an Alliance pilot for our ship."

"Is that it? You got it, alright. *Thype*. I will add her name to the list. She was amazing during that firefight, and after the capture as well. Hey, what time is it anyway?"

"Half an hour before first shift. Sorry to wake you up so early, but I wanted to talk to you before the cycle started."

"Thirty minutes of sleep awaits then," he mumbled, turning his head and closing his eyes. "Contacting Ina may be a challenge, though, Hel. The ship she left *Inginus* for was an old salvaged junker, and she was on really bad terms with Commander Lang."

"Who cares? That old *thype* was a traitor who you had to relieve of his command," Helga said, confused at him invoking the late commander's name.

"He was still Alliance when he would have given the report to her old starship, *Aqnaqak*, so it does matter," Cilas said. "When we ask to bring crew aboard, they go through intensive records checks. Cleia Rai'to went through it, and they even sent a message of inquiry all the way back to Sanctuary. If Lang questioned Ina's abilities, she will be all but forbidden from touching another console on an Alliance vessel."

"How could he question her abilities?" Helga said. "All he knew of her was that she was a captured spacer from *Aqnaqak* that he was forced to house until she decided that she'd had enough of Navy life."

"Even if he didn't knock her, I doubt that she would have left a contact code for us to reach her," Cilas said.

"Well," Helga said, sitting up, "if we can somehow reach her, are you open to the idea of bringing her back into the fold?"

"Helga, time is ticking. Get to the point or I am going to close my eyes and fall asleep on this conversation. Plus, I believe that I've more than shown that I am interested," Cilas said without turning to face her.

"I've been wracking my brain on how to reach her," Helga said, "and all that I can come up with is reaching out to Brise Sol."

"Brise Sol again? Why?" Cilas said, turning now to face her.

"After Dyn, when we were to be awarded with our medals, Commander Qu reached out to Brise to see if he wanted to attend as my guest. That means she knows how to reach him, and I never got a chance to see her for Brise's code. If we can reach out to her, we can call Brise, and I am sure that he's still in contact with Ina, since he couldn't take his eyes off her back when we were on *Inginus*."

"That is quite the reach, Helga, but I won't stand in your way, since it's Ina. I agree on her worth, and we need experienced spacers on our ship. Speak with Loray Qu, and if you have any luck finding Ina, I will speak to the captain about bringing her in."

"You're amazing," Helga said excitedly, planting a kiss on his cheek, and then made to get up off the bed.

"Wait," he said. "What about Misa Veil? Do you remember her?"

"I do," Helga said, remembering the spritely pilot from the starship *Aqnaqak*. Misa piloted the dropship that took them down to Meluvia on a mission to reclaim some stolen weapons. She was a veteran and an ace, so she was more than qualified for the job. Helga had gotten to know her a bit on the rough exit from that planet, but hadn't thought about her until now.

"Misa would be a solid addition," she admitted. "But what about Captain Tara Cor? I can't see her surrendering one of her top pilots to us."

"Do you doubt the influence of our captain, Helga Ate?"

"Where Captain Tara Cor is concerned, that's a hell no," Helga relented, laughing, surprised to hear Cilas hinting at something between the two ranks.

"That's up to her, just like the rest of our candidates," Cilas said. "It's an opportunity, that's all. She can always tell us no."

"Which do you prefer?" Helga said. "It's your ship, Commander, so you decide on who's a better fit for your crew."

"You don't stop, do you?" He pulled himself up to a sitting position. "Look, Ina went through *schtill*, just like we did. One could argue that she put up with more, and when the time came to act, she never hesitated. But I don't know much about her background, beyond her credentials as an ace that served on an *Aqnaqak* infiltrator. Misa is Captain Cor's personal pilot. There's no action in that job beyond being a glorified bodyguard, but to get the role, you have to stand out, and for a woman like Captain Cor to pick her for the job, it goes without saying, now doesn't it?"

"Still didn't answer my question, Cilas. Who do you prefer?" Helga said. "Both hail from the same ship, and have fought with us on missions, so I hold no personal bias towards either of them."

"You're so full of *schtill*, it's oozing out of your ears," he said, shaking his head in disbelief. "You and Ina Reysor were thick as thieves. You even snuck her a weapon after I warned you not to. She's who you want. I'll put out a probe, and if she's off the grid, then I'll reach out to Misa to see what she thinks. Helga, I have to remind you how Ina felt when we found her on that ship. She wasn't too thrilled with the Alliance. She felt that they had abandoned her and opted to discontinue her service."

"We aren't the Alliance, in so much as we are in the Alliance," Helga tried, her hands becoming animated as she puzzled over how to sell it. "Ina would be working for you, her savior, and she'll be flying with me, and as you said, we shared a bond of sorts from the beginning. We Nighthawks operate under a different set of codes than say, the Marines, and I think she will like that."

"I disagree, but I will try," Cilas said. "Don't get your hopes up, though. She seemed pretty set on her decisions. What's with you, anyway? You seem really set on us drafting anyone that you remember from the past. We have two runners, one having been discharged, and a captain's personal pilot. Who else?"

"I know it seems ridiculous to you, Cilas. You, who has always recruited from pools of the best, and had the genius to mesh them into a team that works well. To some of us, it isn't so easy to make new friends. These are to be our brothers and sisters. Men and women we rely on to put their lives on the line for us, and hold this team above everything else. I don't have your charisma and reputation, and I can't have another Horne Wyatt questioning my being here every chance he gets. You see what I'm able to do inside that cockpit, Cy, and Zan makes me that much better. This role isn't for a formal Nighthawk; it's for another pilot that is skilled and can take commands."

"Fair enough," Cilas said. "I too would prefer familiar faces to get the seats on the bridge, but this is about our missions, and staying successful. I'll entertain this role, for you, but as far as the rest ... No Brise Sol to be reinstated as our engineer, and no *Rendron* classmates looking to use my ship as a means of escape."

Helga stood up and stretched, unaware of how alluring she looked silhouetted beneath the low light. Cilas was about to reach for her but she danced away, picking up her clothes and flashing him a devilish grin.

"Speaking of familiar faces," she said. "I better go, lest I get caught exiting my commander's cabin."

"When we make dock with *Rendron*, I should get a hatch installed with access to your berthing. Your cabins are right below the mess hall, which is right over there beneath the communications station. Then there wouldn't be any hiding anymore. You can come up, or I can come down to visit," he said, grinning.

"Time to get up for you anyway, Commander," she said. "You're being hailed."

Where he had indicated that a hatch could be installed, there was now a flashing light with a holographic symbol of the Alliance hovering above it, spinning to get his attention.

Without waiting for him to confirm, she was out the door and tip-toeing down the ladderwell to the *Ursula*'s central passageway. Helga always loved the view whenever she would descend from his cabin. From the deck at the base of the ladder, she could see the bridge past the mess hall, lift stations and CIC. If someone was up and about, she would know it, and with so small a crew, it was rare to find anyone roaming about this early.

There was something different in this shift, however. From the open doorway of the mess, she could hear laughter and as she grew closer she recognized Quentin and Raileo's voices. Helga checked her wrist-comms for the time, and saw that it was 0:372, exactly twelve minutes into the first shift. *Thype*, she thought, trying to think of a way to get to the lift without being noticed by the men. Normally at this time she would be dressed in either her uniform, flight suit, or 3B XO-suit, with a singular focus of getting her coffee to start the cycle. Now here she was, stuck in shorts and undershirt, with her newly purchased slippers on her feet. Even if she were to walk in and pretend that she didn't care, one of them would notice, and then there would be questions.

She inched closer to the door, hoping to see that none of the Nighthawks were watching the doorway as they chatted. A tap on her shoulder froze her, and for the universe's longest second she waited for her heart to dislodge from her throat. Closing her eyes to calm herself, Helga turned to see Cleia motioning for her to follow.

The Traxian took her back to medbay, where she poured both of them some tea with a drop of brown liquid from a tiny vial. Helga took it and sniffed at it and almost dropped it due to the smell, but Cleia was already drinking hers and watching her.

"Oh, it does smell bad, doesn't it?" she said, making a face. "It tastes good though; you should try it. Removes the bland taste from the tea, which tends to linger, and can be disgusting. Everything on the ship is processed from algae and made to look and taste like other things that we're familiar with from our respective planets. Coffee is the exception, but I don't like it. As a Traxian, I am a tea-drinker, through and through."

"Disgusting?" Helga said, raising an eyebrow. She had always thought that the meal dispenser was one of the greatest inventions to come out of the Alliance. "You must have a really sensitive palate. Too bad your nose doesn't seem to work, because the smell alone makes me want to throw up."

"Humor me, Helga. Please," the tiny Traxian cooed, and Helga studied her face intently before holding her breath and taking a sip.

It was delicious, like hot chocolate, and as it warmed her stomach, she felt suddenly euphoric. All the concern for getting to the shower and dressing for the cycle dissolved, and a pleasant numbness found her limbs, with tiny pinpricks becoming a massage. Helga looked down into the mug, surprised, then back up at the doctor who gave her a wink.

"Now I know why you're always smiling, you little sneak," she said. "What's inside that vial? Liquid rowcut, or something else more potent?"

Cleia laughed, "I'm not a sneak. It's an energy supplement that I picked up from the station, crushed up and blended with a cocktail of my own. Which I cannot reveal until it's patented. Like it?"

"Love it, but you really ought to work on the smell. I feel like I just gulped down liquid *schtill*."

"That is absolutely disgusting, Helga, but noted. I forget that Vestalians can be overly sensitive to smells."

Helga sat down on one of the beds, and this time when she sipped, she did not hold her breath. Cleia watched her do it, then crossed the deck and brought out a small disk from a pocket on the side of her coat. Placing it in the center of her palm where it stuck, she used it to scan several areas of the Nighthawk's body.

"What are you doing?" Helga said, placing the mug down on a table.

"Well, Lieutenant Helga Ate, I am scanning you for injuries. You Nighthawks think that you're invincible inside your powered suits, but I have news for you, you're not. See here, there is bruising, and you have a hairline fracture in your right humerus. Have you had much trouble sleeping lately?" she said, then stopped to look Helga in the eyes.

"Since Argan-10 it's been a challenge, for all of us I think," Helga said. "My arm is fractured?"

"Not fractured; even you're not so tough as to walk around like that," Cleia said, smiling. "It's a hairline break on your bone, in the region right below your bicep. Don't you worry, though, my friend. We will get you patched up before you return to your duties today. There's an extra set of coveralls inside the bin for you to wear when you leave me, as well. You might want to consider keeping a change of clothes within the commander's closet."

Helga cleared her throat loudly. She still wasn't comfortable with discussing what she and Cilas had with anyone from the team.

"So, you saw me just now then, trying to get past the mess?" Helga said.

"You needed an excuse for coming from this side so early in the cycle," Cleia said, "and I needed to get you in here, and not just for your nutrition. You need a physical. Now, legs up, and let's get those slippers off. There, now let's have a look at you."

28

Eyes closed, legs crossed, and the cold steel of the Thundercat's port wing beneath her rear, Helga sat for a long time trying to get her mind to stop. It didn't seem possible. How could she do it?

How do you stare into the void and let it cushion you when you just sent over thirty Geralos to their graves? No matter what she did, she kept seeing the same scene. The tracers tearing a seam into the side of that hull, and the bodies falling out of it, clawing at space, frozen before they knew it, gone from the world. It wasn't regret or some deep wisdom she felt for being their executioner inside the cockpit, but something she couldn't quantify, since it wasn't an emotion she knew.

After leaving the bridge she had taken the lift down to the docks, then went to her room and got in front of the mirror, staring at herself for a while. She had wanted to speak to that girl whose reflection stared back with defiance, to tell her that she was beyond the line, burning out thrust as the g-force climbed. No time during that entire situation did she concern herself for the men and women on the dreadnought.

They had excelled and won, and the bad guys had been routed, their leader now in the capable hands of the Shrikes. But did she care for the future and what would happen to them? Did the Alliance really matter to her, the same way it did to Cilas? All that fire he exhibited when explaining his pride as a Vestalian, and Raileo too, with his anger at leaving those hostages behind, where was her burning fire? Did it not exist?

Staring into those weary brown eyes revealed a mystery about herself. Helga had come a long way in her recovery from Dyn, but deep in her soul there was still this loneliness. She gave up on quieting her mind, it just wasn't possible, and chose instead to focus on one of her toughest subjects. Normally the word family was but a word that she applied liberally to her closest friends, but when it came to blood and relations she drew a blank.

Her parents were dead, one from the war, the other from suicide over the first, and her twin brother Rolph, who had been separated from her, was somewhere else unknown. Her memories of him were vivid. He was very Casanian in his features, despite them being born the same time, and he was the apple of her mother's eye, just like she was to her father. There was love, lots of love, so much in fact that she didn't have to remember; it was fused into her DNA.

It was no wonder her mother chose to follow her father to the afterlife; she and her brother just couldn't fill the massive vacuum left inside her heart. Helga hated her mother for a long time, blaming her for the harsh life she was dealt when she came onboard the *Rendron*. The bullying, the trauma, the locked doors in her mind that protected her from their memory, Helga put it on her mother for being selfish, and choosing to leave her to a universe where she'd never fit in.

Over time her stance did soften, however, and when she first experienced love, she understood. Her hate morphed into acceptance, but she didn't realize that she'd shifted it to herself. Now the memories were faded, and all that remained was a blurry image of her mother on a field of grass, watching Rolph fly a kite. She didn't have a photo of her family, just murky images inside her mind. Her father was a Marine from the *Rendron*, and was known by the captain, but she had never thought to ask him for an image or token of his memory for her berth.

For the first time in over 92 cycles, they were back in the same system as the *Rendron*, her known home. Some of the crew were excited, some were numb, and some like Cleia Rai'to didn't know what to expect. She had asked Helga no less than five times how she felt about living on the starship, but the Nighthawk would never give her details, only riddles before quickly changing the subject.

Helga hadn't felt any positive emotions about the return, but she did have a knot in her stomach. The last time she was on *Rendron*, a Geralos had robbed a child of her mind, and both Quentin and Cilas had been in healing tanks from wounds sustained in action. She had been given a bigger role, mostly due to Cilas's absence, which gained her a promotion to lieutenant junior grade and all the perks that came with it.

She should have been happy to return, but all she felt was sadness for their adventures coming to an end. There would be more, but there'd be more crew members, and Nighthawk recruits, whose personalities she would have to learn. This alone stressed her out, though when she'd met Quentin and Raileo, it had been as easy as meeting long-lost cousins. Cilas had assured her that she would have a say in who came aboard, but this still didn't serve to calm her nerves.

Rendron was home, but it hadn't felt that way since BLAST, where the hardships of that trial forced her to look inward and accept who she was. Helga had been a half-alien cadet in an academy made up of mostly Vestalian children. They had prodded and teased her, pulling her into fights, but that wasn't the problem. The questioning of her lineage was what hurt.

When Helga recalled those days, she would feel proud of herself for being a natural fighter, never backing down despite the odds. She was small, but she was a spitfire, vicious with both her fists and her tongue, and if it got truly violent, she had the foresight to arm herself during her rounds. From spikes to knives, she was rarely without something sharp tucked away inside her socks. In time, she'd even stolen a gun and kept it secured inside her berth.

Being an orphan with barely a memory of her parents, Helga would often question whether or not the things she recalled about them were even real. Toss in insults from the other cadets insinuating that her father was a war criminal and she the product of something awful, and her world had shrunk to the size of a cockpit. The first time she'd heard it, she denied it easily, but after twenty times it had managed to sink in. Helga had never truly believed it, but the teasing created a lingering doubt. *Rendron* brought back those memories, and the feeling that she didn't belong, and not even Cilas's reassurances could do much to remove that doubt.

She recalled something that Joy had said to her before one of their biggest fights.

"You need to be careful, Helga," she had said. "Girls like us have a void that needs filling, and no spacer or Nighthawk will be enough. Though I don't expect you to listen, the way you carry on with the boys, it's a wonder you haven't gotten yourself into trouble yet. There will never be a man perfect enough to replace that image in your head, girl. Not the captain, certainly not Cilas, and not that big lug of a Marine, either."

Helga had heard her but disliked her words since they made her feel juvenile and foolish. Not to mention they were offensive. Though Joy was an orphan like most other spacers, she disliked her talking about her father as if she knew anything of him or her memories. For ten cycles she didn't speak to her after that conversation, until Joy being Joy, forced her to forgive her on the spot when she showed up at her cabin door drunk, refusing to budge until Helga let her in.

The memory of that cycle brought a smile to her face. Oh, how she missed her friend and their constant spats. Joy was her big sister in every way except blood, but they fought, argued and loved one another as if they shared parents and a childhood.

"There she is," she heard Raileo say, and she opened her eyes, uncrossed her legs, and inhaled patience to help exhale the negativity she had been focused on.

"Laser Ray," she said, as she walked to the edge of the Thundercat. She looked down to find him shirtless but for his cross-holster, with his dual pistols hidden in the small of his back.

He reached up to help her, but she fanned him off. "I got this, Nighthawk, but you're sweet for the attempt," she said, then rolled forward, sliding off the wing and landing skillfully on the deck. "What's on your mind, killer?"

"Not a whole lot, really. Killer?" He laughed. "Can you slow down on the nicknames? I think I have enough to last me for the rest of my career. I was about to go expend some old rounds when I looked up and saw the top of your bushy little head."

"Bushy, you say? I'm willing to bet I have more up here than all of you Nighthawks combined," she said. "Are you allergic to shirts now, Chief? I'm seeing a little pattern when you're down here, and I'm starting to wonder if this has anything to do with—"

Raileo laughed. "You made it, what? Two minutes before you gave me *schtill* about Cleia?"

"Who mentioned Cleia? I know that I didn't mention Cleia," Helga said. "Before you stuck your face into it, cutting me off, I was going to ask if this had to do with your little scene inside CIC."

He stopped and placed his hands on his hips and guffawed as if he wanted the entire ship to hear. "You are so full of it. Nice dig at my embarrassing outburst, by the way. Nothing gets past you, but we both know that you were referring to Cleia, who does like my muscles. But no, I don't dress like this to impress her. She doesn't come down here."

"So I've noticed," Helga said. "Can you tell me why?"

They were in front of a cell that had been converted into a range, and Raileo handed her a pistol, then stepped inside to access the computer. Helga thought that he didn't hear her, but waited patiently for him to get the space set up. After a minute of this he shrugged, and she could see that his delay was due to him puzzling over the answer.

"This stays between us, Ate, but she gets nervous around Tutt. It's nothing he did to her or anything like that; it's just that she's so tiny," Raileo said. He started gesturing wildly as if the right words wouldn't come out.

"Uh-huh," Helga said, crossing her arms. "So, our little Traxian is a speciesist?"

"No," he almost shouted. "It's not about him being a Genesian. It's about him being a huge Marine that can crush her tiny frame with barely a thought. Cleia has a past, just like all of us, full of tremendous *thypes* that deserved the open end of a barrel, and Tutt reminds her of someone from her past, so she limits her time on the dock."

"Poor thing," Helga whispered, rubbing at her chin. "But Ray, she's our ship's physician, and we're bound to get several more Tutts joining our little crew. What is she going to do then? Stay holed up inside medbay? I have my own issues the same way, but we rely on her, so this cannot go on. Plus, it's not fair to Q, and I simply won't have her hesitating if he gets sick, hurt, or worse. I like Cleia, I really do; in fact, I consider her now to be a friend. Between the two of us, we now have a mission, to get her pretty blue posterior in to see a psych. I'm being serious, Ray. If Cilas learns about this, he will switch her out as soon as we dock. Do you hear what I'm saying to you?"

"Solid copy. I agree. If it makes you feel better, though, she's made great strides. You remember the passengers from that satellite op? The two of them worked together on setting things up, and that did a lot for her. I think it was brave," Raileo said.

"Yeah, well I think you're in love," Helga said, rolling her eyes. "With the galaxy working overtime to pull itself apart, the last thing we need right now is a physician dodging a Nighthawk. I won't say anything, Ray, you have my word, but get her straightened out before I do."

"How much do you like this woman, Ray?" Helga said after he had fired off thirty consecutive shots at virtual targets that had no chance against his immaculate aim.

"I like her a lot, Ate," he said, and motioned for her to take her turn.

"Like her enough to quit the team if she asked you to?" Helga said.

"She wouldn't ask that," he said, and she stopped firing to square up with him, knitting her brows.

"She's a doctor, of course she will. Think the next time you return from a drop busted up and barely sucking air that she'll just be okay with patching you up? Come on Ray, think with this head," she said, jabbing two fingers at her skull. "Do you like her that much?"

"No. Hell no, not enough to go soft and let everyone down. We're into each other, alright, and I know what you all think of me, that I'm some *chiern*-chasing playboy, alright, but Cleia's different and I'm not some fool. If she asks me to do that, I will tell her no. Ate, I'm from a *schtill* hole where we shared bathwater recycled from a drain, and plenty of people lost a lot just to get me out of there. This isn't some job to me. This is life, and for every lousy lizard I kill, I know my father is out there, smiling at me, proud. Cleia will just have to understand. If not, then that's life, isn't it? Either you ride or you get left, and I don't intend to stop."

Helga aimed down the sights of her sidearm, and dropped fifteen Geralos holograms out of seventeen.

"You're getting ahead of yourself, and that's why you missed them," Raileo said. "But you've come a long way, Ate. I have to say, you're built for this."

"That's what I keep hearing. Though it's not the kind of feedback that makes me feel better about all this *schtill*," Helga said, switching places with him. "You excited about *Rendron*?"

"Oh, hell yeah. I get to sleep in my berth on Aurora deck again, possibly with a bit of company. Man, and the meal dispenser on Nero with the snacks. I'm going to totally empty that thing. Look at me, I'm getting goosebumps," he said, grinning. "What about you, Ate? You excited?"

Helga shrugged. "That's the thing Ray, and it worries me. It doesn't feel like home. Isn't that strange?"

Raileo stared at her for a long time, then reached for her weapon and checked it. "Wanna know why I'm so good at shooting?" he said, though it was a rhetorical question and he turned away from her to give his attention to the targets.

"Before *Rendron* and the Alliance, I was a runner for a gang. They were spice suppliers on the hub, keeping the people numb and damn

Greg Dragon

near enslaved with all the favors they ended up owing for a thirty-minute high. I always knew it was wrong, even as a boy, but they had rescued me from ... from some *thyped* up *schtill* back home. The boss, Kaszis Han, he brought me in and showed me how to fight. Man was an ace with any weapon; he had to be a former ESO or something.

"Anyway, he took me under his wing and became like a father to me, showing me how to fight. Got in a lot of situations with that gang, and each situation was kill or be killed. So, I learned how to shoot straight, along with a lot of other skills on that chart called survival. It made me different, and I didn't realize that until I became a cadet. Kaszis said I had the skills of an assassin, but that my heart was too good for me to realize my potential. It was him that paid for me to get on the big ship. Sent me off with a one-way ticket and a bear hug. I remember that he called me son."

He stopped and collected himself, clearing his throat loudly.

"*Thype*, but that's heavy isn't it?" he said. "My own parents were such trash, yet this cold-blooded gangster showed me nothing but love. If I was to quit this team I would *schtill* on everything that he sacrificed for me to make it. You have nothing to worry about. I'm a Nighthawk for life."

"Where's Kaszis Han now?" Helga said.

"Dead. He vanished off the grid and I couldn't get in contact, even when I had the means to get it done. Old friend from the hub, serves on *Helysian* now, well he reached out to me. Told me Kaszis died in a heist gone wrong," Raileo said, coughing out a laugh. "Damned fool. Get this: he smuggled on board a cruiser full of Marines delivering supplies and aid. You know the drill. Well, he chose the wrong compartment to hide in. The cruiser came under attack and they lost atmosphere in that particular area of the ship. Said he suffocated from the loss of oxygen. What a way to go. Guess the old man wanted to see more than those crates before he punched it."

"He was right, y'know," Helga said, handing him her pistol. "About your heart. You have compassion, and that makes you better than many of the spacers who would dare to judge you for anything."

"I always enjoy our talks, but this one was awful," he said, smiling at her ruefully.

"We'll have better ones later, over a drink or two, eh?" Helga said. "All we have is time left until we dock with that big beautiful starship. Thank you, Ray."

"For what?"

249

"I don't know, for always being honest with me, even when I'm giving you *schtill*. Cleia won't compromise who you are, if she knows what's good for her."

"Now you have me worried," he said, laughing.

29

Helga Ate stood, staring at her reflection for a long time, scrutinizing how she looked in her freshly pressed dress whites. The fun was over, that brief bit of existence under a commander as easy going as Cilas Mec, and they were back to the reality of salutes and chain-of-command.

She teased up her hair, once a defiant Mohawk but now a bald undercut, or bush, as Raileo had called it. Everything was tight and in order, and she looked every bit the officer, though no amount of dressing up could mask the look of disappointment plastered across her face. She forced a smile, using her fingers to drag up the corners of her mouth, which caused her to laugh.

"Suck it up, *cruta*, it's the job," she whispered, reaching for a bit of cloth to dab at her sweat.

There was a chime at her door, and she closed her eyes to summon patience, exhaled slowly, then collected her hat and crossed the compartment to open it.

"Ready?" Raileo said. He was standing in the passageway with Quentin, both of them clean-shaven and dressed to the nines.

"About as ready as I'll ever be. Lead the way, you great big thrusters," she said. "Where's the commander?"

"Still in his cabin," Quentin said. "But we're about to head up there to approach the gangway, so I came to get you. Figured it would look good to have us exit as a united front. The commander, then you, followed by Ray and me, then Sunny, followed by the doc. It will make for quite the feed for the reporters. We're tight, but this makes us look professional and together."

"Love it, but I docked us into the captain's private hangar. What reporters?" Helga said, and Quentin exchanged glances with Raileo Lei.

"There's um, a crowd of cadets and news reporters with flobots waiting for us to deplane," Raileo said. "I heard from Cleia just now, and she says that you can see them from the bridge. Looks like we're heroes for the day. News got out that we helped rescue that prince."

"News got out? How? We're ESO operators," Helga said. "What am I missing?"

"Word from *A'wfa Terracydes*, Alliance-wide, praising the aid of our forces," Quentin said. "I saw some of the feed. They mentioned *Rendron* by name, so naturally, the crew did the math. What surprised me is the captain allowing them on this deck. Guess the lines must have loosened up in our absence."

"Great," Helga said sarcastically. "Can't wait for the, 'how does it feel to be the only female Nighthawk?' questions, or the 'what do you have to say to all the Casanian children watching this feed?'"

"Heavy is the crown, eh Lieutenant?" Raileo said, and Helga laughed despite herself.

They walked to the lift and rode it up, and Helga took a moment to take in the bridge. She wouldn't be back inside that seat for quite some time while the *Ursula* was serviced, and a wave of sentimentality nearly crippled her.

"You alright, Ate?" Quentin said.

"Yeah, I'll be alright. Just going to miss the old girl, that's all. Funny how it feels so long since we first came onboard."

"All that action on Sanctuary then getting grounded for as long as we did," Quentin said. "I think we all feel like it's been a lifetime since we first set foot here."

"You know, there's been something bothering me ever since we got off Argan-10," Helga said as she walked past them, leading the way towards the stern of the ship.

"The hostages?" Raileo tried.

"No, not them. But now that you mention it, how can I not? It's too bad we couldn't rescue any of them, but my concern is for the Geralos that Q and Sunny found," she said.

"Oh," Quentin said. "The doctor's theory about them working to look like us?"

"Yeah. My thoughts are on that last push, and the extraction of the prince. The Shrikes aren't privy to Cleia's theory, so all they know is that the pirates are working with the lizards. That was us before Argan-10, ignorant to the fact that this goes so deep we'll likely never know. It's just that if Cleia is right, and they can mimic us through physical transformation, how do we know that the prince is the same person that got captured?

"*A'wfa Terracydes* is considered neutral, but Marines routinely visit the space to resupply. Some have families there, and the station has open contact with the Alliance council. The prince is powerful, so he ranks just about everyone stationed there, and could use his power to affect decisions that could ultimately aid the lizards. We cracked that box on the dreadnought that came for us, and that prompted an investigation into the station heads. If it were the prince, there would have been no investigation, now would there? And if the prince is now a lizard, everything we've done in the past week was for nothing."

"It's a valid concern, Ate, except for one problem," Raileo said. "The prince is Arisani, not Vestalian. The doctor's theory dealt with them mimicking us exclusively, but let's say they could dupe other species, then we're *thyped*."

"The Geralos have been robbing our minds for many lifetimes. This is a new turn in their methods, but not much different from what they've always done," Quentin said. "The Alliance will send dropships to Argan-10, loaded with a whole company of planet-busters looking to claim Geralos skulls—"

"And las-swords," Helga said, stopping and spinning to mimic the flourishes of Sundown.

"Yes, and las-swords," Quentin agreed. "They will break open that bunker and tear it apart. Once they're finished, we won't need any theories. We'll know what they've been up to on that moon. As to the hostages, we all feel bad about how it went, but our job was discovery, and in that, we were successful. Not only did we learn that the lizards were on the moon, but we killed one of their new mutants. Without us doing that, we would still be in the dark about what they're doing."

"All that tells me is they have a lot more experiments on other moons that we aren't privy to," Helga said.

They found the exit hatch, where Cleia, Zan, and Sundown were seated, waiting for the commander. Cleia looked practically regal in an eggshell-colored cloak draped over a black 3B XO-suit. Zan wore her blue *Rendron* coveralls, and Sundown was in a sharp, gentleman's business suit. His slicked-back hair was immaculate, a single grey streak down the middle, like the galaxy's dandiest skunk.

"Oh, Helga, you look so important," Cleia said, grinning.

"Is that a compliment, Doc, because I don't know how to take it," Helga said, winking. "You're looking official. I love it, and Zan, you

ANGEL OF THE ALLIANCE

look lovely too. Sunny, you look like a well-dressed, murderous pimp."

They all laughed and began trading barbs with one another to the astonishment of Cleia and Zan, who both stood back smiling, watching them act like children. When the commander emerged from his cabin, however, they all straightened up and got into their roles.

"I guess you all are ready to get off this beast?" he said, straightening his jacket and securing his hat. He was in his dress whites with medals and looked every part the captain of their ship. Even his walk had the confident air of a man who had control of his life. "*Ursula*, open the hatch and lower the ramp so that we can deplane," he announced, and the corvette quickly complied.

The hatch came open to cheers from a crowd of spacers waiting at the foot of the ramp. Halfway up it was Captain Retzo Sho, followed by Commander Jit Nam, immaculate in their all-black uniforms. Cilas stepped out and nodded at the crowd, and his eyes momentarily tilted to catch the flobot above him, filming video for the live feed. He closed with the captain and greeted him with the clasping of forearms, followed by a bear hug. He did the same with Jit Nam, and then together they walked to the end of the ramp.

They waited for Helga to descend, then Quentin and Raileo, followed by Sundown, and Cleia Rai'to. Unlike the rest who got claps, cheers, and sometimes shouts, the doctor evoked a chorus of wide-ranging responses. Traxians were not as well-traveled as their planetary neighbors, so most spacers had never met one before. Helga worried for her friend and what she considered to be a rude welcome, but the doctor was so happy she seemed to be floating.

Zan emerged last and looked so human that even she got a round of applause. One after another, they greeted the captain, then the XO, before retreating to stand at attention with their backs to the ramp. Captain Retzo Sho walked out into the center of the small hangar, and the crowd backed up to form a circle about him so that he could make his address.

"Welcome home, Nighthawks," he said to loud cheers and whistles. "And welcome to our new friends, who signed on to support them and Commander Cilas Mec. Welcome, you mighty crew of the *Ursula*, welcome, and congratulations on a mission well done. As you see, we have gathered today a large gathering of our *Rendron* family, but none of them are here by chance. Every one of them has ties to something that you've done. These cadets have families on hubs you

254

have liberated, brothers and sisters rescued from the clutches of the Geralos.

"Service is a hard thing to fathom for those who haven't yet been made to fight for something greater than life. And what is life without freedom? Peace without choice? We lay down our lives for the Alliance, because to the chosen, there is no other choice. But in this commitment, we get so focused on the enemy that it is hard to see the results from our strides. Like the fact that the Vestalians of Arisani are back home with their families, safe, thanks to the effort of multiple ESO teams.

"At times, it can seem like the hardest jobs yield the most meager of rewards if you're lucky. No one knows that you just saved millions of lives, and you can't discuss it, not even a hint. The congratulations are left up to us, your superiors, the captains, admirals, and council that order you to place your lives on the line. So allow me to thank you, Nighthawks, for your continued diligence and success in the most extreme circumstances. For being my hidden blade when I need you, slicing through bonds and the throats of our wicked lizard oppressors."

"Sambe!" Quentin shouted suddenly, which caused Helga to look over at Raileo, who could barely conceal a smile.

"Commander Mec, my commendations to you, our finest son. What you have accomplished with so small a team is a testament to your leadership. Now that you're home, it is time to become whole again, and when next you leave, I expect it will be with a full complement."

His speech went on for a long ten minutes, laced with the bravado and patriotic flair that the spacers loved to hear. Retzo Sho was a brilliant orator, so despite the length and their weary bodies, everyone was tuned into his every word, as he shifted praise from the Nighthawks to the unsung heroes on the hubs and warships. Helga didn't know why this return was so important for the captain to turn it into such a spectacle, but she felt honored nonetheless, seeing the awe reflected in the cadets' eyes.

It felt odd being on *Rendron* without the presence of Joy Valance, and once the speech was over and the crowd thinned, Helga found herself feeling incredibly alone. She looked for Cilas, but he was gone, tethered to the captain, who would want to hear every detail of their adventures. Raileo and Cleia had vanished, and Quentin was being interviewed by a reporter. The only ones left were Sundown and Zan, who was busy transporting their luggage to a lift.

Suddenly the reality of how much she disliked the starship washed over her like a black wave of doom. It brought with it depression, bad memories, and the need to run. But where could one truly escape on a floating city, packed with spacers wanting to worship you? To your berth, but for how long? And would that truly be escaping when at any time your comms would buzz, summoning you to a meeting that barely had anything to do with you?

When the Nighthawks first learned that the *Ursula* was theirs, Helga had all but done a backflip with excitement. It was to be her ship as much as it was Cilas's, but the joy came from the fact that they would finally be allowed to leave.

From her days as a cadet, Helga had set her eyes on Special Forces. Her instructors tried to talk her out of it because they saw it as a waste of her potential. How could they have known that she wanted to escape? She ignored their advice and signed up for BLAST, which resulted in her becoming an ESO.

Her first mission was a disaster, and the many that followed were just as bad. Still, they allowed her to see Dyn, Meluvia, Sanctuary, *A'wfa Terracydes,* and Argan-10, not to mention the starship *Aqnaqak.*

Helga was a blink away from her 19th year of life, and she had already seen and fought enough to make the most seasoned of Marines jealous. Quentin Tutt had said as much, and he had a resume that was a breath short of legendary. Yet here she was, back home, and feeling every bit the young outcast that she had been before she became a Nighthawk.

"Feels strange, doesn't it?" Sundown said, walking up to stand next to her, his black gloves resting in the small of his back.

"Do you have any Seeker tricks to make time go by rapidly?" she said. "I could use one right now to blank this place."

"You seem tortured here, la'una. Surprising, since I expected you to relish returning to your mothership."

"Oh, don't go feeling too sorry for me, Sun So-Jung," she said, rubbing at her neck. "You're lucky, you're Virulian, with nothing to physically other you from a Vestalian man. Me and these spots of mine make me a walking target for every soon-to-be sociopath on this ship, and even now when I look at them, I can't help but feel the rage deep inside my soul. Don't bother with the Jumper philosophy on this,

Sunny. I like my head right where it is, and nothing you say will change it."

"Didn't plan to talk you down from your hate precipice, because I know that emotion all too well. When people hurt you, there are two paths the mind can take: either the path of acceptance, oftentimes believing that the pain was deserved, or the path of the warrior, which you are now exhibiting," Sundown said.

"Odd hearing that from you, Sunny, but I've seen you fight, so I know that below all that blackness is bright red laser fire," Helga said, smiling. "Still, some would argue that there's a third path. The path of peace, in which you accept that the bullies were little *schtills* and that everyone matures and gets better and more accepting."

"And how is that fair to the victims?" Sundown said, and Helga looked up at him with some surprise.

"Oh, you're dark," she said, smiling. "Are you suggesting I walk in there, letting loose with my guns?

"I don't agree with either path taken to the extreme," Sundown said, "but a bit of both is what you need to choose. Consider the wheel of pain and its philosophy. One child hurts another, who grows up to rightfully seek revenge. The other child, the aggressor, grows up remembering all the bad that he's done. Either he regrets it and seeks absolution, or accepts it and relishes in the memory of it all. However, if he knows his victim is resentful and seeking revenge, he will train and prepare, if anything, to preserve his life."

"Then it becomes a circle," Helga muttered, understanding now where he was going with his explanation.

"Yes, la'una, a vicious circle of revenge that can poison your bloodlines, leading to years of pain, all because you gave your oppressors the signs they needed to prepare. Keep walking around here with that scowl on your face, and your enemies will avoid you, knowing you hold on to the past. Now, if you are calm and appear open, being the star ESO that you are—"

"They won't see me coming when I choose to attack?" Helga said, studying his face to make sure that this was what he meant. "I bet you were the most lethal assassin on Sanctuary, Sunny. That's some *thyped*-up advice, do you not see that? You're not only telling me you agree to me harming these men and women, but telling me to be sneaky so that I'm guaranteed to do it. I think that I love you."

"Everything's a joke to you, isn't it, Helga?" he said, his face reflecting his frustration.

"Come on, Sunny, don't be upset. Joking is my way to clear the air, and you have to admit, that moment we had was positively evil just now," she said.

"Maybe a wee bit," he admitted and started laughing. "I was sort of making it up as I went."

"Oh, I know, and you even spiced it up with the 'la'una' here and there. When you called me Helga, I knew that I had broken you, but regardless of you being full of *schtill*, Sunny, thanks for listening. Your terrible advice makes me want to play this game, and for every bastard from the academy I see, there will be a deceptive little smile."

"That's just how you get them," he said, leading her through the door to the passageway beyond. "You smile, pretend you don't remember, and when they think that all is forgotten—"

"Boom, I turn off the lights ... but not before I remind them of all they have done," Helga said, still smiling.

"You look like you need some alone time, la'una. I'll tell the others that you went to see an old friend," Sundown said, touching her shoulder then turning to walk away. After five steps, he stopped and looked back at her. "Remember what I told you about facing your pain?"

Before she could reply, he vanished into the crowd, and Helga checked her wrist-comms for the time.

"Four hours until we get to dine with Captain Sho," she whispered. "Let's see if anything changed on this ship."

30

After the speeches, debriefs, reunions, and awkward meetings were over, Helga bypassed going back to her berth and chose instead to explore one of the *Rendron*'s less popular decks. She had started walking the passageways with no goal in mind, just one foot in front of the other, eyes forward, thinking back on the events of their mission to Argan-10. As a cadet, she had dreamed of touching planets, moons, and remote satellites, but now that she had done it, she wanted to laugh at her youthful ignorance.

For a boomer growing up with decks, bulkheads, and uniforms for fashion, the allure of worlds endless in both beauty and culture made you feel trapped and displaced inside of a ship. No one had warned her about the dredges, brovilas, and szilocs, who owned their respective lands and were loath to share it with human outsiders. All they had were vids, simulations, and stories from well-traveled Marines.

Did she regret becoming a Nighthawk? If someone were to ask, she would inform them that they were asking the wrong question. What did she regret? Surely not her choice to become an Extraplanetary Spatial Operator. And what was regret? A word reserved for the tongues of more privileged spacers, who were given the choice of a life outside of the Alliance Navy. What choice did she have? She, the orphaned child of a Vestalian Marine and a Casanian artist? A child whose earliest memories were on the decks of this starship, being honed into a warrior for the Alliance?

What she regretted was how she'd gone about it all. Letting her rage dictate her choices rather than keeping a cool head. When asked why she had become an ESO, she had always replied with a story about seeing the PAS armor and wanting to have the training and prestige of an elite Special Forces operator. Even she had started to believe it, this lie she told, but in truth it was her anger that had driven her to BLAST.

Tough teenage years had stoked the fires of a troubled childhood into something akin to a thruster. She had worn a brave face, impressing the ranks into believing that she was one of the *Rendron's* brightest stars. Below it all she had been on the verge of eruption, and it made her aspire to be strong, stronger than all the cadets that had ridiculed her for being small, half-alien, and a girl who dared to compete with the boys.

Helga stopped at a mysterious black door. It was polished to the point of brilliance, reflecting her distorted image, with a shiny gold border around the edge, and in the center, the words, "Hall of Honor." She hadn't been paying attention to where she was, and had gone up and down several ladders before she wound up here. Now she looked behind her expectantly, but there was no one in the passageway. Just the bright lights of the overhead, and the sounds of spacers chatting from beyond.

She considered turning around to continue exploring the ship, but there was something about the door that drew her in. Hesitantly, she reached forward and placed her hand over the access-panel. The door came open with a hiss, revealing the biggest compartment Helga had ever seen.

Row upon row of thin black walls ran the length of the room, their shiny black surfaces covered with the names of those who had served and lost their lives. The foremost walls were the heroes, those honored as the *Rendron's* finest. The second set of rows was for the officers and rates that had commanded men. The last set took up the most room, in a space that to Helga seemed endless.

These were spacers who had received the Alliance's Medal of Service, which was a posthumous award for outstanding service. Every one of those names were dead, and they were the standouts, the one percent. It was such a humbling reminder of how much had been given to fight back against the Geralos that Helga felt foolish for her earlier thoughts.

"All of these people died to get us the footing we now have in this age, to stand toe to toe with the lizards and win," she whispered, as she ran her hand across one of the hero's names. The letters shimmered and projected out towards her, and a menu unfolded as the image became opaque. "Oh," Helga said, surprised. "I can go through their records?" She selected an icon that displayed his face, and the menu promptly shifted and became a life-sized hologram of the man.

"Well met, Lieutenant. My name is Jharo Mar, and I was a *Rendron* Marine," the hologram said.

It was a manifestation of the long-dead sergeant, with an AI imitating his voice to speak to Helga as if it were a ghost. She was so intrigued that she reached out to touch him, but her hand went through the projection, and she giggled like an excited schoolgirl. As a cadet, they were forbidden from coming to this deck, and it used to stay locked, since she had tried several times to see it. There had been a field trip that she missed due to being detained to her berth for fighting.

Helga had forgotten about this place, just like many other splendors that were forbidden to them. She realized then that the door had opened because of her rank and status as a lieutenant. This was holy ground to the captain, and aside from simulations, only at ceremonies were regular crew allowed to come here. Her eyes looked past the wall to the back row, where the names of the honored rates glowed ominously in the low light.

She thought about her father, Algo Ate, and something the captain had told her when she graduated from the academy.

"Algo gave up a lot to fight for the Alliance," he had said. "He was impressive. I'm surprised he didn't try for BLAST. The things they did on Meluvia, Traxis, and Casan. Men and women of his generation were made from different stuff."

To impress a man as important as Captain Retzo Sho was a feat that wasn't easy for anyone not named Cilas Mec. Was her father's name in this hall? Was there an Ate immortalized inside of this beautiful display of excellence? Helga walked to the back on legs that seemed to weaken with every step, and found the wall that corresponded with his years and rank, then started going down the list of A-names in the list.

"Algo 'Hounder' Ate," she read, a lump growing in her throat as she stood there shaking.

She touched his name, and the menu appeared, giving options for his biography, list of accolades, years of service, and details on his death. Helga touched his face and nearly fell backward when it shifted and his image appeared. His voice sent shivers down her spine, and his salute put the hairs on her arms on end. It was her father, as she remembered him, complete in his dress blues, a *Rendron* Marine through and through.

"D-dad?" she whispered in disbelief, unable to hold back her emotions.

"Hello, Lieutenant. My name is Sergeant Algo Ate, and I was a *Rendron* Marine," he said.

Helga spoke with him for a long time, learning as much as she could about his numerous accomplishments. She then looked for the dead Nighthawks: Adan Cruse, Casein Varnes, Horne Wyatt and Cage Hem. All three men were present, and surprisingly, Lamia Brafa as well. She was pleased to see that their likeness was as close to the real thing as a hologram could get. This warmed her heart more for having seen her father, and knowing now that there was an image to replace the fuzzy memory in her head.

The last time she had seen Algo, she was so small that he could pick her up in one hand. Then the war had taken him, and she and her twin brother, Rolph, were left with their mother, Peraplis. None of them had taken his passing well, her mother especially, and a few years later, the void in her heart had driven her to suicide. For so long, Helga had lived the same memory over and over, with her father coming to see them on shore leave, his face a mask of unspoken horrors as he feigned happiness playing with them.

Now as a lieutenant, she got to see him in his prime, handsome, strong, and unshaken. It gave her hope to one day join him inside this place, as well as in the afterlife, where they would become a family again. These lost Nighthawks lifted her spirits. She remembered their banter, and how as a rookie they had allowed her to gamble cards with them. She won a game or two, to the annoyance of Horne Wyatt, who had been her biggest critic until he saved her life, showing her that he cared.

They were her brothers, especially Cruse, who had taken her under his wing as a pilot. She had thought them lost, but here they were, for any time in the future when she needed them.

"Family," she whispered. "Your girl has come home, and you wouldn't believe the stories I have to tell."

Made in the USA
Las Vegas, NV
04 March 2023

68536046R00156